The Seaside Homecoming

Books by Julie Klassen

FROM BETHANY HOUSE PUBLISHERS

Lady of Milkweed Manor
The Apothecary's Daughter
The Silent Governess
The Girl in the Gatehouse
The Maid of Fairbourne Hall
The Tutor's Daughter
The Dancing Master
The Secret of Pembrooke Park
The Painter's Daughter
The Bridge to Belle Island
A Castaway in Cornwall
Shadows of Swanford Abbey

TALES FROM IVY HILL

The Innkeeper of Ivy Hill
The Ladies of Ivy Cottage
The Bride of Ivy Green
An Ivy Hill Christmas: A TALES FROM IVY HILL *Novella*

ON DEVONSHIRE SHORES

The Sisters of Sea View
A Winter by the Sea
The Seaside Homecoming

The Seaside Homecoming

JULIE KLASSEN

a division of Baker Publishing Group
Minneapolis, Minnesota

Published by Bethany House Publishers
Minneapolis, Minnesota
BethanyHouse.com

Bethany House Publishers is a division of
Baker Publishing Group, Grand Rapids, Michigan

Printed in the United States of America

Library of Congress Cataloging-in-Publication Data
Names: Klassen, Julie, author.
Title: The seaside homecoming / Julie Klassen.
Description: Minneapolis, Minnesota : Bethany House, a division of Baker Publishing Group, 2024. | Series: On Devonshire Shores ; 3
Identifiers: LCCN 2024025022 | ISBN 9780764241017 (paperback) | ISBN 9780764244018 (cloth) | ISBN 9780764244025 | ISBN 9781493448111 (ebook)
Subjects: LCGFT: Christian fiction. | Romance fiction. | Novels.
Classification: LCC PS3611.L37 S42 2024 | DDC 813/.6—dc23/eng/20240610
LC record available at https://lccn.loc.gov/2024025022

Unless otherwise indicated, Scripture quotations are from the King James Version of the Bible.

This is a work of historical reconstruction; the appearances of certain historical figures are therefore inevitable. All other characters, however, are products of the author's imagination, and any resemblance to actual persons, living or dead, is coincidental.

The Sidmouth Guide quote from chapter 26 is adapted from *The Sidmouth Guide* (John Marsh: Sidmouth, 1824), 22.

Map illustration by Bek Cruddace Cartography & Illustration
Cover design by Jennifer Parker
Cover image of woman by Abigail Miles, Arcangel
Cover image of historic Sidmouth by Print Collector, Getty Images

Published in association with Books & Such Literary Management,
52 Mission Circle, Suite 122,
PMB 170, Santa Rosa, CA 95409-5370
www.booksandsuch.com

Baker Publishing Group publications use paper produced from sustainable forestry practices and postconsumer waste whenever possible.

24 25 26 27 28 29 30 7 6 5 4 3 2 1

To Sara Ring,
with gratitude for our decades of friendship,
shared travels, and shared memories.

N
W
E
S
Peak Hill
3
2
Glen Lane
4
To Otterton
1
6
20
5
21
19

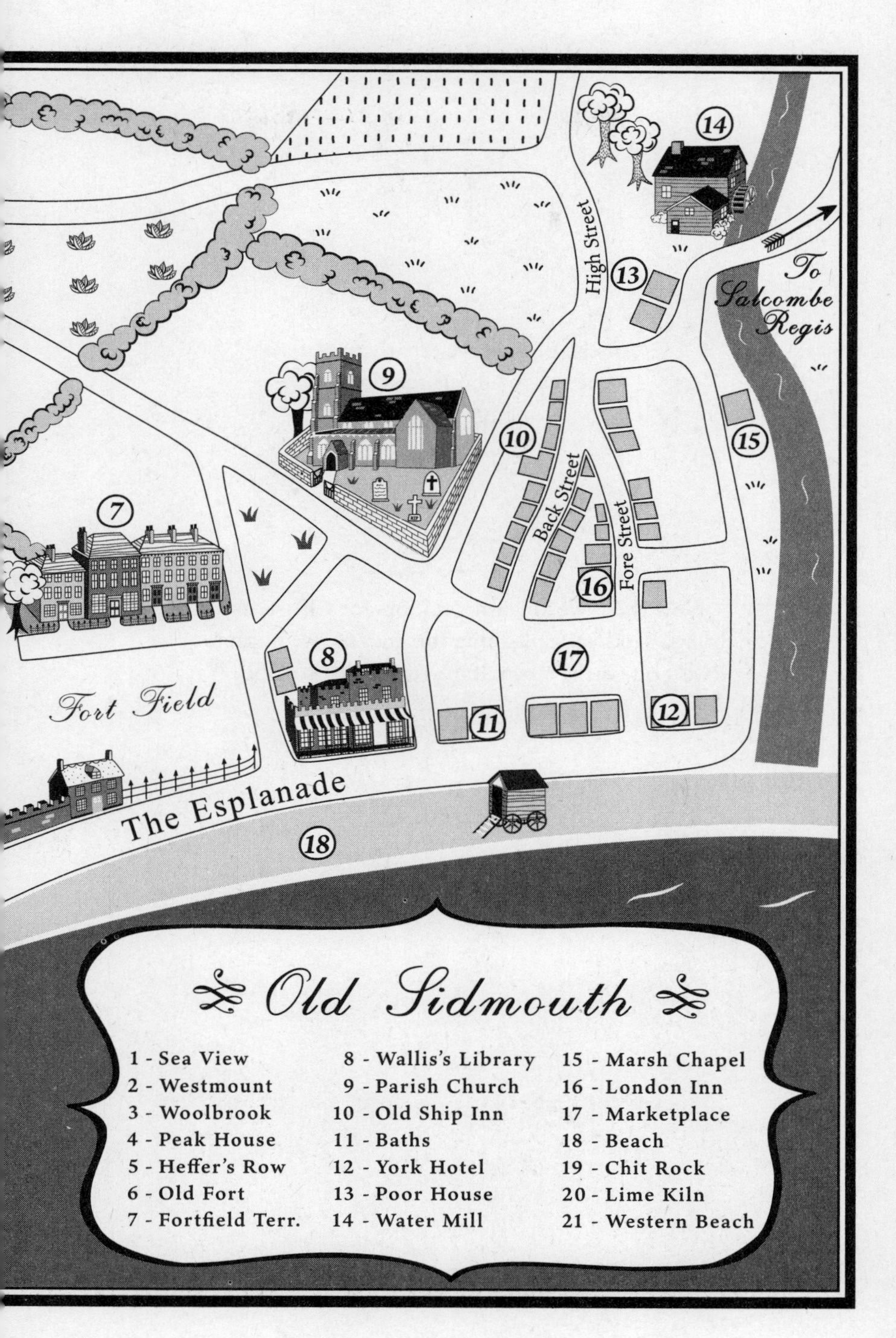

High Street
To Salcombe Regis
Back Street
Fore Street
Fort Field
The Esplanade
Old Sidmouth
1 - Sea View
2 - Westmount
3 - Woolbrook
4 - Peak House
5 - Heffer's Row
6 - Old Fort
7 - Fortfield Terr.
8 - Wallis's Library
9 - Parish Church
10 - Old Ship Inn
11 - Baths
12 - York Hotel
13 - Poor House
14 - Water Mill
15 - Marsh Chapel
16 - London Inn
17 - Marketplace
18 - Beach
19 - Chit Rock
20 - Lime Kiln
21 - Western Beach

For the present we greatly prefer
the sea to all our relations.
—Jane Austen

Now then, we are ambassadors for Christ, as
though God were pleading through us: we implore
you on Christ's behalf, be reconciled to God.
—2 Corinthians 5:20 NKJV

1

The rain depresses . . . My lady has been bored
to death. And in the clutch of Giant Despair.
—Charles Dickens, *Bleak House*

May 1820

Bleak. The weather, her mood, her life.

Miss Claire Summers pulled back the dusty velvet curtain and looked out onto another dreary Edinburgh day. Rain pelted the cobbled street two floors down, where a few merchant carts and hackney carriages passed with a clip-clop of hooves, their drivers' hats pulled low, and even the horses' heads bowed against the rain. The wet pavement was devoid of pedestrians, except for a butcher's lad who jogged past with a bundled delivery.

Then a coach stopped in front of the house. A man emerged, placing a beaver hat over fair hair as he alighted and strode quickly toward the door, disappearing beneath the protruding porch roof.

"Close the curtain!" her great-aunt demanded. "I've told you the light hurts my eyes."

What light? Claire thought. She bit her tongue, let the

curtain fall, and turned toward the shrunken figure in the canopied bed.

The door knocker sounded in the distance.

Head and shoulders bolstered by pillows, the old woman frowned. “Who is that? Dr. McClain has already been.”

“I don’t know.” Callers were rare except for regular visits by the doctor and the apothecary’s assistant.

“Humph. Probably that young man from the apothecary’s again. Seems to deliver some useless new tincture every other day. Remind him to use the tradesmen’s entrance and not the front door.”

“It is not him. I did not recognize the man.”

The old woman flicked a weak hand toward the side table. “Water.”

Claire walked over to fill a glass, but a soft tap interrupted them.

Agnes Mercer turned her head toward the bedchamber door. “Come.”

The ancient butler entered, calling card on a silver salver.

Her aunt huffed. “What is it now?”

“A gentleman has come to call. A Mr. Callum Henshall.”

“Henshall? I know no one by that name.”

“He asks to see Miss Summers.”

Surprise ran through Claire, followed by foreboding.

Sure enough, the old woman narrowed her eyes, a suspicious scowl carved into her brow. “What have you been up to, besides gawking at men from the window? Sneaking out to meet them as well?”

“Absolutely not. I know no one by that name either.”

Claire knew very few people in all of Scotland, having lived in relative isolation for nearly two years now. The one exception had been regular attendance at church services, until her aunt’s declining health had rendered her bedridden.

Another lift of gnarled knuckles. "Send him away, Campbell."

"Aye, ma'am."

Claire blurted, "Did he say what he wanted? May we not ask his business first?"

"No," Aunt Mercer snapped. "I said send him away."

The elderly retainer retreated. Claire helped the woman lift her head enough to sip water. Despite the care she took, liquid dribbled from the corner of her aunt's thin, wrinkled lips.

"Clumsy girl. I did not ask for a bath," she grumbled, although her tone lacked bite.

Claire quickly retrieved a linen napkin and wiped the water away.

The butler returned a few minutes later, a folded note now occupying the silver tray. "If Miss Summers will not receive him, he asks that she do him the honor of reading this."

Another scowl crossed her aunt's lined face. "Give that to me." Her hand flashed forward with surprising speed.

It was not the first time Aunt Mercer had insisted upon reading a letter addressed to Claire. In this case, Claire felt more curious than resentful, since she truly had no idea what message the stranger might wish to impart.

Aunt Mercer unfolded it and read silently, the line between her sparse brows deepening.

"What is it?" Claire asked. "What does he say?"

"Nothing to speak of. It seems this Scotsman met your sisters in Sidmouth and wished to pass along their greetings. As we have made it abundantly clear they are not to contact you . . ." She shook her head in disgust and began refolding the note.

A greeting from her sisters? Emily's doing, she guessed. Claire's stomach rumbled, hungry for news of her family. Loneliness gnawed at her, body and soul.

"Might I read it for myself?" Claire asked. "Or at least thank the man for taking the trouble of delivering it?"

"No, you may not." Agnes Mercer extended the letter toward the hovering butler. "Dispose of this."

He hesitated. "Shall I put it in the drawer with the others?"

Others? The word jangled in Claire's mind. She knew of only one. Had there been more?

"This one's not worth saving. Burn it."

Aunt Mercer had allowed her to read and respond to one letter, and she'd dictated every word of Claire's reply to discourage Emily from writing. Had her sister written again anyway?

With a regretful glance in Claire's direction, the butler dutifully took the message from his mistress, crossed the room, and tossed it into the fireplace. The flames leapt up to consume it.

Claire sank into a nearby chair and watched the paper blacken and wither. Gone in a moment, like her former life and hope for the future.

Sarah Summers stepped onto Sea View's veranda to shake out her broom, then paused to breathe in the fresh air of a beautiful Devonshire morning. She glanced toward the grey-blue sea to the south, and then to the west, where a sea of yellow daffodils was beginning to fade on the hillside, soon to be replaced by red poppies, orange lilies, and perhaps even purple-crowned thistles, which grew wild there.

Thistles were the symbol of Scotland, and Sarah could never think of them without remembering Callum Henshall. The handsome Scottish widower and his adolescent stepdaughter had been their first guests last spring. She still could hardly believe she had been bold enough to write to him. She had never done something so forward before.

It had been Emily's idea, of course. A fortnight ago the three of them—Emily, Viola, and a reluctant Sarah—had gathered for a private meeting while Georgiana was at the charity school visiting Cora, her favorite of the children there. The topic of the meeting? What to do about Claire. They had not included Georgiana because she had never been told the real reason their eldest sister had gone to Scotland. And they had not included Mamma, because she was still determined to obey her husband's edict. Papa had disowned Claire and forbidden Mamma from harboring her or even speaking her name. And she had chosen to honor that request even after his death.

"We must do something," Viola asserted.

"Why now," Sarah asked, "after all this time?"

"Because we have tried to contact her several times and have received no reply save the one I showed you last year. Remember?" Emily asked. "The brief reply to the first letter I sent, basically telling me to respect Papa's wishes and not to write again?"

Sarah did recall the only letter they'd received from Claire in the nearly two years she had been absent. When Sarah had read it for herself, she'd had to agree with Emily that it did not sound as though Claire had written the cold, impersonal letter. Yet Sarah had recognized her handwriting.

"And she signed it *Clarice*," Emily reminded them. "I used to call her that sometimes, sarcastically, when she ordered us around like a parent rather than a sister. 'Yes, Clarice. Right away, Clarice.'"

Viola said, "I remember that."

"I think it's a hidden message," Emily went on. "I think Aunt Mercer told her what to write and Claire was letting us know in a subtle way. Agnes Mercer is Papa's aunt, after all, and she is apparently determined to enforce his final edict, just like Mamma."

Sarah nodded thoughtfully as she considered that possibility.

"I wrote to her again anyway," Emily added, "to invite her to my wedding. No reply."

"I have written as well," Viola said, "to let her know the major and I are planning to travel to Scotland and would like to visit her. I received no response either. Why would she not reply?"

Sarah sketched a shrug. "To honor our father's wishes, as the letter said."

"Or," Emily theorized, "perhaps Aunt Mercer never let her read our letters. I might even be tempted to think Claire no longer lives there, if not for this one reply in her hand."

Viola said, "Jack and I are determined to visit her during our trip—whether Aunt Mercer likes it or not. But we plan to stop at several places along the way to break up the long journey and see the sights. It is our wedding trip after all, overdue though it is. It will take us two or three weeks to reach Edinburgh."

Emily tapped her chin and sent Sarah a knowing look. "In the meantime . . . If only we knew someone who lives near Edinburgh. Someone who could call on Claire on our behalf until Viola can?"

"Mr. Henshall, you mean." Sarah's mind began turning like a watermill, revolving through memories of their brief acquaintance during his stay at Sea View. Would it be presumptuous to write to him when she had turned down his overtures, even his request that he might write to her directly?

Sarah offered, "I suppose I could write and ask him to call *if* he is going into Edinburgh anyway. I would not feel comfortable asking him to make a special trip."

"Oh, I am sure he won't mind," Emily said with a mischievous grin. "Not for you."

So Sarah had set aside her misgivings and written to the man who was never far from her thoughts.

Dear Mr. Henshall,

I am writing on behalf of myself and my sisters Emily and Viola to request a favor. I hope it is not too presumptuous to ask after our relatively brief acquaintance.

You may remember my mentioning a great-aunt in Edinburgh. Our sister Claire has been living there as her companion. We have not heard news of her in some time, and recent letters to her have gone unanswered.

We are probably worrying for nothing, but it would greatly ease our minds if someone might call and make sure Claire is well and in good health. I remember you mentioning you sometimes visit Edinburgh, and if that is still the case, would it be possible for you to pay a call on our behalf? Of course, we do not expect you to make a special trip. In the event you are able to visit, I will close with our aunt's direction.

Either way, I hope all is well with you and Effie. We all send our warmest greetings to you both.

Sincerely,
Miss Sarah Summers

Sarah and her sisters were even now awaiting his reply.

The next day, Emily ran into the office, waving a letter in one hand and pulling Viola along behind her with the other. "It's here! It's here!" She thrust it toward Sarah. "For you. Postmarked Edinburgh."

Sarah accepted it and for a moment stared down at her name in his handwriting. A slight tremor in her fingers matched the quiver in her stomach.

"What are you waiting for?"

"Yes, yes. Give me a moment."

She sat down in one of the armchairs. Emily plopped beside her while Viola paced. Aloud, Sarah read,

"Dear Miss Summers,

I was surprised and pleased to receive your letter, although I am sorry for the concerns that prompted you to write. Thank you for entrusting me with the request. It is an honor and a privilege to be of service to you and your good family, of whom I have fond memories and the deepest regard.

Unfortunately, I am unable to provide a satisfactory report.

After receiving your letter, I traveled into Edinburgh as soon as I could and went to the address you provided—a house in the New Town. I introduced myself to a manservant, handed him my card, and asked to call on your sister. A few minutes later, I was turned away.

Having foreseen that possibility—I am a stranger to them, after all—I had taken the liberty of composing a brief note, introducing myself as someone who had met her family in Sidmouth and wished to pass along their greetings and ask after her well-being. The manservant accepted the note and promptly shut the door in my face. I hope he gave it to your sister but cannot guarantee it.

I am sorry I was not more successful and wish I could send you fulsome reassurances about your sister's health and happiness. If she or your aunt contact me (I provided my direction), I will, of course, let you know.

In the meantime, if there is anything else I can do, please do not hesitate to let me know.

Sincerely,
Callum Henshall"

Emily threw up her hands. "Unsatisfactory report is right! Where does this leave us? We know no more than before."

"At least we know Claire is probably still living there," Sarah said. "Although I would feel better if he had seen her."

"How rude not to receive him," Viola said. "Surely that was Aunt Mercer's doing and not Claire's."

"I agree," Sarah said. "Unless, perhaps, her experience with . . . a certain gentleman . . . has left her wary of men in general."

"I had not thought of that." Emily looked at her twin. "I am so glad you and the major are traveling there soon, Vi. Surely they won't refuse to see you."

"Let's hope not."

"Are you all packed?"

"Yes. We leave bright and early tomorrow morning."

Emily squeezed her hand. "Have a wonderful time."

"Thank you. I shall write with news as soon as I can."

2

USEFUL COMPANION.
A lady, in her 24th year, anxiously desires a
SITUATION as above. She is a good reader, domesticated,
and industrious. She would be most suitable for
an elderly lady. Salary a secondary object.
—Advertisement, *The Times of London*

The next day, when the butler delivered the post, Claire eyed the missive hopefully, but it was only a letter for her aunt in a hand she did not recognize.

Claire helped her sit up in bed and then watched as the old woman peeled up the wax seal, read, and then sighed.

"Another charity requesting my support. So many poor, miserable people in this world. Write a reply for me, please."

Claire rose in silent obedience, her aunt's shrewd gaze studying her in disapproval.

"You're even more aloof than usual today. And what a long-suffering expression you wear. I suppose you're still upset about that note the gentleman left. I did not prevent your reading it because I am a mean old bat, but because your father insisted the rest of the family cut ties with you. I am merely enforcing his wishes. Be glad he did not forbid me to shelter you as well."

"Yes, Aunt."

Agnes Mercer narrowed her eyes. "I know you find your life here an odious one, but there are many in your situation who would happily trade places with you. Fallen women often find themselves facing far worse fates. You might have ended up in the Magdalen Asylum, one of the charities I support, or even the workhouse, if not for me."

"Yes, Aunt." She forced herself to add, "And I am grateful."

The old woman harrumphed, clearly not convinced, and handed her the key to her desk.

Claire accepted it and turned. A brass quill and ink holder sat on the desk's surface, along with a wax jack, but paper itself was kept in the drawer. She unlocked it and slid it open. Her gaze strayed to a few letters in the far-right corner, the top one face down with its seal still intact. Might one of them be for her? Aware of her aunt's hawklike eyes, Claire withdrew only paper and closed the drawer.

She spread the blank page before her and dipped the quill, saying, "Ready."

Agnes Mercer began her reply, her voice growing increasingly thin and reedy as she continued. She thanked the charity's governors for their request and gave her stipulations for agreeing to make a donation. Claire could have written it without the woman's prompting, as she had written similar responses on her aunt's behalf many times before.

Claire finished the last line in silence and stood to take it to the bed for her aunt's scrawly signature. But the woman had fallen asleep.

How unusual. She always made sure the desk drawer was locked and the key returned to her before dismissing Claire or allowing herself to nap. It was so unexpected that Claire watched the woman's thin, flat chest to make sure it rose and fell, which it did, with weak regularity.

Claire would surely be caught if she unsealed the letter

to read, but perhaps she might write a brief one of her own. Dare she?

Claire sat back down at the desk, gingerly slid the drawer open just enough, and pulled forth another sheet of paper. Glancing over her shoulder to assure herself her aunt still slept, Claire dipped her pen in the ink and began another letter.

Dear . . .

Dear who?

She longed to write *Dear Mamma*. Oh, how she missed her. Thoughts of her kind, gentle mother brought with them a potpourri of memories—encouraging talks and affectionate embraces—along with dry, brittle husks of regret.

As far as Claire knew, the only one of her family who had ever written to her in Scotland was Emily. Then again, Emily had been gone from home when it had all happened and probably didn't know what Claire had done. How foolish and stupid she had been.

Even if Claire wrote to Emily with the hope of a future reconciliation, she knew Emily was not the one she needed to persuade. Mamma was. And Mamma had never gone against Papa's wishes in her life.

Claire thought again of the stern reply to Emily's letter Aunt Mercer had dictated, telling her not to write again. If Emily had ignored the edict and written again anyway, Claire did not know it. The butler or sometimes the footman swept up the post and delivered it to the mistress of the house without delay.

But yesterday Campbell had said there were *others*.

Claire again peered at the small stack of letters on the right, behind extra ink bottles and quills. If they *were* letters from her family, it might be worth the risk. She tentatively slipped her hand inside and, not quite able to grasp them, used her other hand to slide open the drawer an inch farther.

Whiiine.

"Hm?" Aunt Mercer snorted awake. "What are you—?"

"All finished. Ready for you to sign." Claire surreptitiously slipped the extra piece of paper back inside. No use in wasting it for one word. Aunt Mercer detested waste. As Claire rose, she nudged the drawer closed with her hip.

"Lock it and return the key." Aunt Mercer held out her hand, and as always, Claire complied.

After that, Claire left the woman to resume her nap, taking the charity letter down to the hall for the butler or footman to post later. Hearing a small squeak of protest nearby, Claire stepped back and looked down the corridor.

There stood the footman, Fergus, standing close to Mary. The young housemaid backed away until the wall stopped her. He propped a hand on the wall over her shoulder, hemming her in on one side. He leaned down as though to kiss her, but Mary turned her face, ducked, and slipped from his grasp.

Neatly done, Claire thought.

"Come on, Mary," he wheedled. "Ye don't want me to tell the missus I saw that ginger-haired assistant kissin' ye."

Mary hastened away toward the servants' stairs. The footman turned to follow, but Claire called, "That's far enough, Fergus."

Claire said it with all the authority she could muster. In truth, she had little authority in this house, but as lady's companion and a relative of Agnes Mercer's, she theoretically ranked a notch above this impertinent footman.

"Ah, Miss Summers." His eyes glinted to find a new mouse in his tomcat sights. "Jealous, are we? Don't be a shrew. If yer very sweet to me, I might give ye a look at this letter just come."

Another letter?

He stepped closer, a sly smile tilting his lips. "I can see yer interested. So perhaps I'll have two letters' worth."

When Claire remained silent he came closer yet, his smile widening. "Thinking about it, are ye?"

Claire inwardly bristled. She may have fallen for a lord, but she was not about to be seduced by a lecherous, spotty-faced footman.

She held her tongue and managed a small smile of her own. His eyes darkened and he stepped close. The man thus distracted, Claire swiped the letter from his grasp and spun away, much as Mary had.

He swore.

A quick glance told her it was only a note from Aunt Mercer's lawyers. Devious pig.

She handed it back. "You were right; I *was* thinking about something. About whether I should have you dismissed now or wait until after my aunt wakes from her nap."

The sly smile vanished. "Ye don't have that kind of power."

"It's not my power or lack of it that would hand you the sack. A mere mention to my pious aunt of your lascivious behavior would do it."

He blinked. Looked sincerely stricken. "Don't, miss. Please. Just a little jest. Won't happen again."

"Perhaps I will keep quiet if you agree to leave Mary alone. What has she ever done to deserve such behavior?"

For a moment that snakelike gleam returned to his eyes. "Oh, ye'd be surprised."

"And sickened, no doubt."

"Now, now. Not my fault. She's no better than she should be."

Was there any truth to his claim? If so, Claire was in no position to judge another woman's indiscretions.

She lifted her chin. "Either way, she is far better than you are. Watch your step, for I shall be watching you."

A few days later, another caller came to the front door. Claire was in her room reading when the knocker sounded below. She stood and looked out the window, glimpsing a man's black hat and billowing greatcoat, but that was all. She wondered if this one would be sent away too.

Claire returned to her reading.

Aunt Mercer had said she would not need Claire that afternoon, so Claire was enjoying the rare luxury of reading a book of her own choosing. Aunt Mercer did not possess—or allow—many novels, but rereading *The Pilgrim's Progress* was proving more pleasant than being forced to read aloud yet again from Fordyce's *Sermons to Young Women*.

Some time later the housemaid tapped and came in with fresh towels. "Here you are, miss."

"Thank you, Mary. My aunt has a caller?"

"Aye. Some gent's been with her for nearly an hour now."

"One of her doctors?"

"Don't know. Dinna hear his name."

The housemaid turned to go, but Claire asked, "Mary, has Fergus been bothering you?"

The girl tilted her mobcapped head as she considered. "Now ye mention it, he's left me alone for a few days, God be praised."

"I'm glad to hear it."

The maid departed to continue her duties.

A short while later, another knock rattled her door.

Expecting Mary again, she called, "Come."

Instead, when the door opened, Campbell stood there looking awkward.

"A gentleman to see you, miss, in the drawing room."

A gentleman? She instantly thought of the fair-haired Scotsman who had been turned away. Had he come back? Brought news of her family? Why would her aunt allow her to receive a male caller now, when she had refused before?

Claire rose. "Give me a few minutes, please."

The butler nodded and retreated.

Claire tidied her hair and arranged a white linen tucker at her neck, adding needed adornment to the plain grey day dress.

Then she went down to the drawing room, nerves thrumming through her.

She crossed the threshold and drew up short, heart banging against her ribs at the sight of the handsome, elegantly dressed man awaiting her.

Lord Bertram. Here? Now?

"What on earth are you doing here?" she blurted with no attempt at politeness.

"Miss Summers." He bowed. "I have just met with your aunt, as you are probably aware. Surely she mentioned she had written to me."

"She did not. I am astonished to see you. I had no idea she contacted you nor have I any idea why she would."

"No? I must say that surprises me."

"Then that makes two of us. Why did she want to see you?"

He hesitated. "If she did not tell you, perhaps I had better leave it to her to explain. Still a bit of a mystery to me anyway."

Did he assume Claire had wanted to see him? She hurried to correct that humiliating misapprehension. "If you think I asked her to contact you, to interfere in some way, you are greatly mistaken. I had not thought to ever see you again."

He held up his hand, pinkie ring flashing with the movement. "I have no wish to start a quarrel. In fact, I am glad to see you looking well and living in such a . . . respectable house. Is the old woman kind to you?"

A denial was on the tip of her tongue, but she bit it back. She would not seek this man's pity.

She squared her shoulders. "You said you came to meet with my aunt. Why did you ask to speak to me?"

"I merely wanted to assure myself you were well. I confess I have thought of you often. I regret what happened between us, and I also regret it is not in my power to make amends. I hope you will allow me to at least apologize."

She was so flabbergasted by his overdue apology that she could barely fashion a reply. Finally, she managed, "Say what you like. It changes nothing."

When Lord Bertram left, Claire marched directly to her aunt's bedchamber. She found the woman propped up by pillows atop her made bed. She was dressed—with help from the lady's maid—in a favorite Sunday frock with her ruby cross pendant at her neck and a lap rug over her legs.

She looked at Claire with interest. "You saw him, then?"

"I did and was astonished to find him here at all, let alone at your invitation. I did not realize you were acquainted with the man."

"I was not. Never met him till today."

Claire frowned in confusion. "To my recollection, I have never mentioned his name. So how . . . ?"

"Your father named the man in one of his letters."

"Why did you wish to see him?"

"Several reasons. To satisfy my curiosity, first of all. He is handsome, I grant you. Well-spoken. Titled. I can see why he turned your head. Yet he is also in a great deal of debt."

"How do you know that? I doubt he would offer such information."

"He did not, nor did he deny it. I looked into the man's situation. Not bad for an old woman confined to her bed, ey?"

Claire was too befuddled to be impressed. "Why go to the trouble? What were the other reasons you mentioned?"

"I am . . . not prepared to say as yet."

At the vague answer, irritation flared, as it often did in her aunt's presence, and for once, Claire failed to hold her tongue.

"What, did you invite him here to remind me of my stupidity? My humiliation at his hand? I assure you no reminder was needed. I repent of it daily."

Agnes Mercer's eyes glinted. "Ah. So the mouse has a voice after all. Not the insipid milk-and-water miss I've known these last two years. I am glad to see some spark in you."

"Are you? When you have chastised and suppressed my every expression except docile compliance?"

"Careful, my girl. I don't like that sharp tongue aimed at me, but you will need that spirit and courage when I'm gone."

The thought brought unease and even fear. Claire admitted, "I don't know where I'll go after you die."

"What about after *you* die? I know where I hope to go."

"Are you not certain? With all your churchgoing and donations and piety?"

"Pff. That gets me nowhere. The only reason I can hope for heaven is this." She lifted the cross on its gold chain.

"Your necklace?"

"Don't be daft. What it symbolizes. The cross alone renders sinners acceptable to God."

"Do you include yourself in that number, or only me?"

"I am in the same boat, my girl. But you are still at sea." She waved her veined hand. "Now, enough of that. Have you given any thought to where you might go?" Her lips quirked. "While alive, I mean."

Worry pinched Claire. "I have thought about it but have made no decision as yet."

"Your mother won't have you, you know. Your father made his wishes clear."

"As you've often reminded me. Speaking of the future, I hate to ask, but I will need some money. Most companions are given an annual allowance."

"An allowance? Ha. You have had a roof over your head, a warm bed, and meals prepared for you. You've been given proper clothing. Not to mention spiritual instruction from my minister. Far more than most in your situation would expect. I'd say you've already received more than adequate compensation."

All the old shame washed over Claire, paired with heavy defeat. She hung her head. "I am sorry. I do appreciate having a home here." *But for how long?*

Another wave of her hand. "Enough idle chatter. Off with you, now."

Claire swallowed. "Do you not wish me to read to you?"

"Not today." She tapped her whiskery chin. "I have a great deal to think about."

3

. . . Died in this city, Miss Jane Austen. Her manners were most gentle, her candour was not to be surpassed, and she lived and died as became an humble Christian.

—Obituary, *Salisbury and Winchester Journal*

The day after Lord Bertram's visit, Aunt Mercer sent for her lawyer as well as her doctor. The doctor prescribed something new to ease her discomfort and offered to take the prescription directly to the apothecary on his way home. Her aunt must be declining, for he had never offered before. They'd always had to dispatch Fergus to do so.

"I am sorry, Aunt," Claire said, noticing her tight expression. "I did not realize you were in such pain."

Agnes Mercer was typically stoic, but she admitted, "It is getting worse, I own."

Less than an hour later, the apothecary himself delivered the prescribed draught. Recalling Fergus's accusation about Mary and the "ginger-haired assistant," Claire wondered why that young man had not made the delivery as usual.

When the apothecary had gone, Claire asked, "Shall I give

you some now, Aunt?" She stood at her bedside, ready to pick up bottle and glass.

"Not yet. Any word from my solicitor?"

"No. Have you pressing business with him?"

"Do not pry. It does not become a lady."

Her . . . a lady? Aunt Mercer must be confused as well as in pain.

"What can I do for your present comfort in the meanwhile? A glass of wine, perhaps? Or shall I read to you?"

"Nothing, nothing. Just sit with me."

"Of course."

Claire sat at her bedside. After a moment's silence, she attempted to distract the woman from her discomfort by asking about her past.

"How did you come to live in Edinburgh?"

"Your father never told you?"

Claire shook her head.

"My mother was born here—your great-grandmother. After she married my father, they lived with his family in England, near Warwick."

"I noticed you don't have a Scots accent."

"Mamma had that drilled out of her by Papa's family. My sister and I grew up speaking like our English relatives and neighbors."

The old woman paused to gather her thoughts.

"Mamma always missed Scotland, though, and longed for home. And I thought, someday, should Papa go first, I would take her there, let her revisit the Auld Reekie of her childhood. Alas, her health failed, and moving her was not possible. I took care of them both in their old age and infirmities. And for my pains, Papa left me everything. My sister—your grandmother—had married, but I never did, so he wanted to provide for me. When my parents were both gone, I used that money to come here in Mamma's stead. To see the Old

Town of her youth, the castle and Holyroodhouse, and the beautiful New Town as well. I liked it so much I stayed. The strict Scots religion suits my temperament."

Claire could not disagree.

She remembered again the letter Aunt Mercer had sent to her when she was five and twenty. In it, she'd hinted that as Claire had reached such an age without benefit of marriage, she might like to come to Edinburgh and set up housekeeping with her—two spinsters living together. At the time, Claire had been offended, yet that letter had given her the courage to show up at her door unannounced.

Her aunt's story began to wane as the pain clearly worsened. When Mr. Dumfries from Dombey & Dumfries arrived at last, Aunt Mercer shooed Claire from the room, commanding her to shut the door securely behind her.

Claire obeyed. Despite her aunt's brusque manner, Claire felt sorry for the suffering woman and offered a prayer on her behalf, hoping God might hear her, for Agnes Mercer's sake if not her own.

When the lawyer left an hour later, Claire tentatively reentered.

"Would you like that draught now?"

"Yes, please."

After that, her aunt began sleeping more and more.

Meanwhile, Claire waited—an exercise in silent misery. Nerves and fear for the future mounted. Worries stole her peace and made it hard to sit still. To rest. To sleep.

At times, she was tempted to leave now and not wait for the end. But how could she travel anywhere without money for coach fare? Most of the money she'd left home with was gone, and she'd not been paid a farthing in all this time.

If she somehow gathered enough for fare, she would still have to bear the risk and stigma of traveling by public conveyance alone. She had done so only once before, when she'd had no other choice, and was not keen to repeat the experience.

Besides, even had she the money and a traveling companion, where would she go? Aunt Mercer had made it clear her mother wanted nothing to do with her after her disgrace. Her father had forbidden any contact.

How well she remembered the poisoned barbs her aunt had flung at Claire when news had come of Father's death a few months after she'd arrived in Edinburgh.

"You know they blame you, don't you? Oh yes. For the apoplexy brought on by that horrid ordeal. Not to mention the cold he caught when trying to overtake the pair of you on the road. All for naught. If you think your mother or sisters would take you back, you are grossly mistaken."

Claire had no trouble believing it.

Even Sarah, with whom she had been closest in age and affection, was unlikely to welcome a reunion. She and Sarah had shared a room at Finderlay, their family home in May Hill, and Sarah had watched in shock and dread that night while Claire hurriedly packed a valise, pleading with her to change her mind. How Claire regretted begging Sarah not to say anything until she was safely away.

At the memory, shame pressed hard, weighing her down like a millstone in her middle until she could barely move. Barely breathe. So she remained where she was . . . and waited.

Claire awoke in the night, roused by some sound. For a moment she lay there, ears pricked, listening intently.

Nothing.

Even so, something nudged her from the warm bed. She stepped into slippers and pulled on a dressing gown, then gingerly opened the door.

In Claire's early days there, the creak of her door opening—

for a glass of water or a dash to the privy—had been enough to pull Aunt Mercer from bed, sure Claire meant to sneak out with some other man, her "loose behavior" habitual rather than a onetime mistake.

But now the creak of hinges and squeak of footsteps were met with silence.

Claire tiptoed to her aunt's room. Finding the door ajar, she slowly opened it wider. Inside, the chamber nurse sent by the physician sat slouched in a chair, snoring peacefully. The frail figure in the bed, however, was clearly agitated, gnarled fingers clawing at the bedclothes.

Claire pulled a second chair to the other side of the bed, reached over, and took her hand.

"Shh. Rest easy."

The hooded eyes opened into slits. It seemed to take the woman a moment to focus, to recognize her.

"C-Claire."

"I'm here. Can I bring you anything? Water?"

A hesitation, then a mumbled, "Forgive me."

"It's all right."

A slight shake of her head, a mere tremor on the pillow. "Should have been kinder." Her eyes closed. She drew a shaky breath, then added, "Your father's wishes . . ."

"I know. Never mind that now."

Aunt Mercer might initially have been cold and critical , yet over time she had slowly warmed to Claire—at least to some degree. But she had never before apologized.

Now, seeing the woman's misery, pity softened Claire's heart. She said, "You *were* kind, in your way. You took me in when I showed up on your doorstep. You sheltered me, clothed me, fed me, took me to church. . . ."

"Kirk," the woman interjected, insisting on the local term for church.

Claire bit back a smile. Still correcting her, even now.

"If you are burdened, ask God to forgive you." Over a hard knot in her throat, Claire said, "I forgive you as well."

Claire remained at her aunt's bedside the rest of the night. When weariness overtook her, she leaned forward in the chair, resting her head and arms on the bed. She was still there at dawn, when the nurse woke her with a gentle touch to her shoulder. "She's gone, miss."

Claire straightened and looked to Aunt Mercer's still form. The grey pallor of her face. "May God rest her soul," she whispered, sadness flowing through her. Despite the woman's stern demeanor, Claire had done her best to be a help and comfort to her, and now she was sorry to see her go.

Campbell summoned the physician to verify the death, the lawyers were informed, and the undertaker began preparations. Claire herself stopped the clocks and draped cloths over the mirrors in the house.

In Scottish tradition, they laid out her aunt's body for a wake of a few days' duration. Claire, the lady's maid, and women from Aunt Mercer's church took turns sitting with the body round the clock.

A modest number of people came through to pay their respects. The minister. Several church members. Governors and matrons of the various charitable organizations she had supported. The apothecary and a few tradesmen. Each left with a packet of funeral biscuits.

When the funeral was over, the solicitor came to the house, settled himself in the morning room, and met with each of Aunt Mercer's retainers individually. Most accepted their employer's death without noticeable distress. Mary and Campbell, however, were visibly aggrieved. Claire could understand why Campbell might be upset, having served his mistress for many years. And, at his advanced age, it would be difficult to find another situation. But Mary had not been in service there long. She was young and would have little trouble finding another place. So why had the death hit her so hard?

When Claire's turn came, she entered the morning room feeling nervous.

"Mr. Dumfries."

He looked up from his papers. "Miss Summers. Do be seated."

She sat before the desk, hands clasped.

He began, "Your aunt's will won't be read formally nor acted upon for some time. Several details yet to be sorted. However, I have two small matters to address with you now."

"Will the house be sold?" Claire asked, wondering how long she could stay.

"Probably. Although not yet. The will must first be proved in the Commissary Court, Services of Heirs documents completed, et cetera. I'm afraid I cannot disclose specifics. In the meantime, your aunt instructed that the staff be given notice. She had no wish to go on paying, in her words, 'idle servants who are no longer needed.'"

That sounded like Agnes Mercer.

He went on, "So everyone will be dismissed immediately except for her lady's maid, who will stay on longer to donate her personal effects to charity, and Mr. Campbell, who will watch over the place until a new owner makes other arrangements."

"How soon must I leave?"

"By the end of the week."

Claire gasped. "So soon!"

"I'm afraid so. Have you decided where you shall go?"

Claire shook her head.

"Will you go home?"

"I have no other home."

"If memory serves, your family live in Gloucestershire?"

Another shake of her head. "They did. But the house went

to Father's heir after he died, so they've had to move elsewhere." This much she knew, from the one letter of Emily's she'd been allowed to read.

The kindly man gave her a sympathetic look. "I am sorry."

Claire gripped her hands tightly, hoping to divert the topic before threatening tears overwhelmed her self-control. She prompted, "You mentioned some matters you needed to discuss with me?"

"Aye, just two small things. Your aunt wanted me to give this to you before you go. A small token." He opened an envelope and poured from it a thin gold chain and cross pendant.

Her aunt's necklace.

Surprise flared. "Did she? How . . . unexpected." The cross, carved with scrollwork, had a small red ruby at its center to symbolize Christ's blood shed on the cross. She remembered Aunt Mercer saying, *"The cross alone renders sinners acceptable to God."* Was this a gift, then, or a final reminder of Claire's sin?

"And," the lawyer continued, "she instructed me to give you the overdue allowance you're owed as her companion. Twenty-five pounds a year for two years."

"But—!" Claire caught herself before the objection slipped out. Her aunt had said she'd already received adequate compensation, yet Claire needed the funds and wanted to give this man no reason to change his mind.

At her outburst, he looked up, brow furrowed. "Is the sum less than expected? If it helps, I have taken the liberty of adding interest on the portion not paid last year." He gathered a pile of bank notes and coins from the cashbox and held them out to her.

After a moment's hesitation, she held out her palm. "Thank you, Mr. Dumfries."

With more than fifty pounds, she could let a small room in town and live for some time on that sum. But then her money would be gone, and she would be stranded alone in Scotland. How would she ever reconnect with her family if she remained so far away?

In her heart of hearts, what Claire longed for was to be reunited with her mother and sisters. Yet Claire did not presume she would ever be welcomed back home—even now that "home" was Sea View rather than Finderlay. So what should she do? Where could she go instead?

As Claire rose, Mr. Dumfries asked, "If anyone asks after your whereabouts, what shall I tell them?"

Who would ask? Claire wondered. Aloud, she said, "I can't tell you what I don't yet know myself."

He handed her his card. "I understand. Do please send your direction as soon as you are settled. Just in case."

"Very well. I shall."

4

Wanted
As partner, in a genteel boarding house, a respectable Female who could advance from £50 to £100. Letters (post-paid) to A. B. Boarding House, shall meet with immediate attention.
—Advertisement, *Saunders's News-Letter*

Hearing the front door open, Sarah poked her head from the library-turned-office to see who had arrived. She was in time to see the new-wed couple, James and Emily, pause in the hall as James swept off his hat and drew his wife close for a kiss. Sarah turned and retreated to the desk. A moment later, Emily sailed into the office with bonnet askew and the day's post in hand.

Noticing her sister's furrowed brow, Sarah asked, "What is it?"

"A letter for Mamma from Edinburgh. I don't recognize the handwriting." She handed it to her.

Sarah flipped it over and read the return address above the seal:

Messrs Dombey & Dumfries, Edinburgh

"Lawyers," Sarah declared, rising. "Let's take it to her."

They found their mother in the walled garden beside the house, pulling weeds from a bed of irises and lilies.

Seeing their hurried approach, she rose from the kneeling bench.

"A letter for you, Mamma!" Sarah waved it like a flag. Emily followed at a jog, hand pressed to her bosom.

"Good heavens. What is all the fuss?"

"From Edinburgh," Emily called.

At Mamma's quick frown, Sarah added, "From lawyers, we think."

"Ah." Mamma peeled off her gardening gloves and then broke the seal and unfolded the page, expression grave.

"She has died."

Sarah's heart lurched. "What?"

"Aunt Mercer."

Sarah clutched her chest. "Oh. Of course. You gave me a fright."

"And we are to receive nothing, which comes as no surprise. Here, read it for yourselves."

Sarah read it first.

Dear Madam,

As solicitor to Agnes Mercer, your departed husband's aunt, it is my solemn duty to inform you that she has reached the end of her earthly life and has enlisted my services in managing her affairs. In her original will, she had named your husband as primary beneficiary, as you are probably aware. After his death, she revised her will, and I feel it is incumbent upon me to inform you that none of her assets are to come to you, his wife, as you were not named as a contingent beneficiary. However, she did make one small bequest to you. She instructed me to send to you a volume of Fordyce's Sermons *to*

Young Women, *which she trusts will be instructive to your younger daughters. It shall arrive by separate parcel.*

Yours Sincerely,
Robert Dumfries
Messrs Dombey & Dumfries
No. 19 Thistle Street,
Edinburgh

Struggling to read the letter from beside her, Emily asked, "Is there any mention of Cla—" With a glance at Mamma, she broke off, revising her question. "Of her companion? Or what is to become of her?"

"Nothing." Sarah handed her the letter.

Emily read it, shaking her head, then looked up imploringly. "Mamma, I know you promised Papa, but—"

"That's right, I did. So what would you have me do?"

Emily said, "We could try writing to her again, now that—"

"Again?" Mamma snapped.

"Yes, Mamma," Emily said gently. "As I have mentioned before, I made no such promise to Papa. I have written to her, as has Viola. We've had no response to our recent letters and wonder if Aunt Mercer has kept them from her. Now that the woman is gone, she might actually receive a letter we send."

Sarah added, "That's assuming she is still living in Aunt Mercer's house. They won't have sold the property already, surely?"

"Unlikely," Mamma agreed.

Emily said, "Viola and Jack are on their way to Edinburgh now, and they plan to call at Aunt Mercer's during their trip, so—"

"To what purpose?" Mamma asked.

"To learn how Claire fares. To assure her of our love. I hope she is still there when they arrive."

"Your father would not have approved."

Emily frowned. "Come, Mamma. Has Claire not been punished enough?"

"Emily . . ." Sarah warned.

"It was never about punishment," Mamma replied, voice rising. "At least, not for me. It was about shielding the rest of you."

"Let us not argue about all that now," Sarah said. "Let's decide what to do."

"Viola won't reach Edinburgh for some time yet. A letter might arrive more quickly, thanks to the Royal Mail."

"How will a letter help?" Sarah asked. "Claire may need more than a letter. She may need tangible help—somewhere to live. Funds to live on."

"We must do something," Emily insisted. "I will write to Claire, in hopes the letter reaches her, or might be forwarded on to her. Sarah, perhaps you might write to the lawyer? For if Claire has already left, he might have a forwarding address."

Emily turned to her, eyebrows high in expectation.

"Very well. I shall write to Mr. Dumfries and ask. Unless . . . do you object, Mamma?"

Her mother sighed heavily. "I suppose not. Just to make sure she is all right."

Claire began gathering her belongings in preparation for departure. She supposed she would have to find cheap lodgings for a few days until she worked out what to do.

Two years ago, she had left home with only one valise, at Lord Bertram's request. He'd said hefting a trunk from Finderlay at midnight was sure to draw a servant's notice. How hastily and ill-advisedly she had packed. At least she had taken the time to change from the ball gown she'd worn that last night of the house party into a carriage dress of dark blue, the better to conceal herself in the shadows. She had also brought a nightdress, dressing gown, slippers, and one evening dress (sure she and her new husband would share romantic dinners) as well as stockings, a hairbrush, and teeth-cleaning supplies.

Upon arrival in Edinburgh, her great-aunt had examined her clothing, instantly declared the low-cut evening gown of fine muslin scandalous, and insisted Claire donate it to a poor seamstress she knew who could make it over into two shifts and perhaps even a petticoat. Aunt Mercer commissioned the same seamstress to make over one of her own grey day dresses to fit Claire, complete with a plain linen tucker for added modesty. Then, when news came of her father's death, she also ordered a dress in black, modest and mournful enough for afternoon calls or services at the kirk. Later, when the weather turned cold, she had provided a hooded cloak and sturdy half boots as well.

Claire had worn the black and grey dresses in rotation since her aunt's death, and longed to shed herself of both.

She was torn between not wanting to take any of the dreary, practical garments her aunt had provided and the reality that she would be foolish to leave behind warm clothes. Springtime in Scotland was often chilly and rainy. And who knew where she would be once autumn and winter rolled around once more?

In the attic, Claire found a second small valise, too old to be of much value, to hold her boots and cloak. She packed everything she would not need until her imminent departure, and left out only her toiletries and nightclothes.

Mary came in as she packed.

Surveying the partially filled cases, the housemaid's face stretched in dismay. "Yer leavin' already?"

"Not yet. Just getting ready."

Mary stepped closer. "Please, miss. Take me with ye when ye go."

Claire glanced over in surprise. "You don't even know where I'm going. *I* don't even know."

"I don't care where. Just . . . please."

Claire straightened, studying the girl's troubled face. She said gently, "You're young, and you work hard. You'll have no difficulty finding another situation."

Mary shook her head. "I canna. Not round here. I doubt anyone will take me on."

"Why not? My aunt may have neglected to write you a good character, but I shall write one myself."

"Thank ye, miss. But findin' a new place takes time. And I've nowhere to stay meanwhile."

"Why not go home? Your father lives nearby. Is that right?"

"I canna do that. Anywhere but there."

Claire was taken aback by the panic in the young woman's voice, the tight terror in her expression.

"Why?"

"My da', he . . . No, I won't. I'd go the workhouse first."

The workhouse? Claire shivered. Her father must be harsh or even abusive.

She gently pressed the girl's shoulder. "Once I decide where to go, we shall talk again. Agreed?"

"Aye, miss. Bless ye, miss."

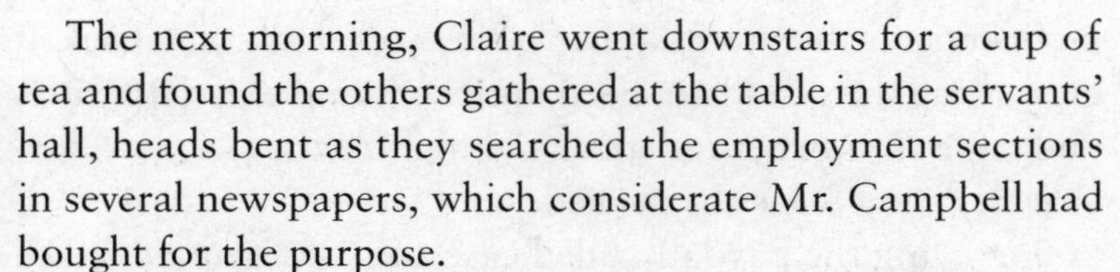

The next morning, Claire went downstairs for a cup of tea and found the others gathered at the table in the servants' hall, heads bent as they searched the employment sections in several newspapers, which considerate Mr. Campbell had bought for the purpose.

Campbell himself thought he might retire and live with his sister when his duties were done. But Mrs. Kerr and her kitchen maid, the lady's maid, Fergus, and Mary would all need new situations.

Mary could read simple text, but she read very slowly, so Campbell sat beside her, helping her review the notices. The girl seemed to listen only half-heartedly, resting her cheek on her hand.

Should Claire search for a new place as well? Perhaps she could find another situation as a companion—if the lady did not inquire too deeply into Claire's background. No one would hire her to chaperone and safeguard a young lady, not with her past. But perhaps an elderly spinster or widow might take her on now that she had experience. She should have thought to ask Aunt Mercer to write her a character reference.

Noticing Claire hovering nearby, Campbell seemed to guess her thoughts. He handed her two of the broadsheets. "We've finished with these, if you'd like to take a look."

Not sure she would be welcome at the servants' table, Claire took the papers and teacup to a chair in the corner. Setting the teacup on the nearby sideboard, she began to read.

She saw no situations for a lady's companion, but another advertisement caught her eye.

GOVERNESS WANTED

Wanted, a middle-aged person of respectability, as a tutoress in a private family. She must be fully competent to teach the English and French languages grammatically, together with the other usual branches of Education.

Letters, post-paid, addressed A.E.T. Post-Office, Exeter, and stating qualifications and references will be duly attended to.

Exeter was not terribly far from her family's seaside home in Sidmouth. The thought of being in the same county as her mother and sisters appealed to her. She doubted she would ever see them again if she remained in distant Scotland. But if she relocated to Devonshire . . . ?

She read the advertisement again and inwardly quailed. No. She was neither middle-aged nor fully competent to teach French. The little French she had learned in the schoolroom would prove insufficient to the task.

Besides, who would trust her when she had displayed such a lack of judgment? Once, all she had wanted was to be a wife and mother and raise a happy brood of children. Now she felt disqualified to even educate someone else's offspring.

With a heavy sigh, she turned to the next broadsheet and skimmed until she reached the *Situations and Help Wanted* section.

Suddenly, an advertisement in the middle of the page came into focus as though haloed by light.

WANTED

As partner, in a genteel Boarding House in Devon, a respectable Female, who could advance from £50 to £100. Letters (post-paid) addressed to W. H., Boarding House, Sidmouth Post Office, shall meet with immediate attention.

Fifty pounds . . . Claire's pulse accelerated. The amount of her allowance. Was this a sign?

Sidmouth was where her mother and younger sisters were now living. Emily might be glad to see her, but the others? Surely young Georgie wouldn't despise her. She was less certain about Viola and Sarah. And their mother? A chill crept over her. They would probably be offended at her presumption in moving so near to them after her disgrace.

Yet time was running out. What other options did she have? Yes, she might keep to her original plan of renting a small apartment somewhere until her money ran out. But at the thought of living alone in some cheerless pair of rooms, loneliness gnawed at her. She longed for her family, and prayed that somehow, someday, they might all be reconciled.

She read the notice again. Considering her fall, could she honestly pretend to be a "respectable female"?

No.

Even so, this opportunity seemed too good to ignore. If she did not respond, would she come to regret it?

Claire rose, planning to retreat to her room to think it over. The old butler followed her into the passage. Taking something from his pocket, he said quietly, "Miss, I thought you might like to have this. As you know, the mistress ordered me to destroy or lock away the few letters that came for you. I managed to retrieve this from her desk before the lawyer came and took the rest of her papers."

He handed her a letter, and Claire recognized Emily's handwriting. Was it the one letter her aunt had allowed her to read? No. This one was still sealed. "Thank you, Mr. Campbell."

"I am sorry about the others."

"I know. Not your fault." She patted his arm, and he returned to the servants' hall to continue helping Mary.

As soon as he'd stepped away, Claire broke the seal, unfolded the letter, and read the lines from her sister. Her breath caught. Emily had written to invite her to her wedding. One of her sisters had by now married, and she had not known it! Had not sent along her congratulations and warmest wishes. Claire's heart twisted. What else had she missed during these last two years?

That news settled it. Taking the broadsheet with her, Claire went up to her aunt's former room, sat at her all-but-empty desk, and composed a letter.

She wrote hurriedly, thinking, *What if another woman writes first, or offers the full one hundred pounds?*

And if *W. H.* did accept her as a partner, what sort of working and living arrangement would they have? Would he expect her to serve as housekeeper or . . . what? How vulnerable it made her feel to put her fate in yet another man's hands. Would W. H., whoever he was, prove more trustworthy than Lord Bertram had?

Oh, God, she prayed, *if this is meant to be, please make a way.* Even as she prayed, she worried she had forfeited the right to ask God for anything.

She decided her next step would be to walk to the coaching inn and learn how much the fare would be for such a long journey.

Even if she could afford it, would moving to Sidmouth bring the longed-for reconciliation with her family or widen the divide?

5

PAWNBROKER AND SILVERSMITH
No. 2 Grace Church Street
Lends money on plate, watches, jewels,
wearing apparel, and household goods.
—Eighteenth-century trade card

When she returned from the coaching inn, Claire took the young housemaid aside.

"I have made a decision, Mary. I will be leaving Scotland for the south of England. If all goes as hoped, I shall not be returning, so . . ."

"Pair-fect. May I go with ye?"

Claire had imagined the girl would refuse to go so far from home, especially permanently.

"Are you certain you wish to travel all that way?"

"The farther the better."

She certainly seemed determined.

Claire added, "Another thing. I plan to enter a partnership in a boarding house there, if someone else does not claim it first. I cannot guarantee a place for you."

"There's sure to be a lot of work runnin' a boarding house. And ye know I'm a hard worker."

"I do know. But it won't be up to me. I am uncertain of my own reception, let alone yours."

"If there is no place for me there, I shall find another."

Claire asked, "Have you any money? You would need to purchase coach fare. I cannot pay for us both and still have enough left to invest in the partnership."

"Da' takes most of my wages, but I have a bit put by. How much would I need?"

"I went to the Crown this afternoon. The fare to London will be at least ten pounds inside and seven outside, not including baggage fees and meals along the way. And then there's the fare from London to Devonshire."

"So much! I can ride outside. And we could pack a hamper of food to save money. I'm sure Mrs. Kerr will oblige us."

"She left this morning."

"Oh." Mary hesitated. "Well, Mr. Campbell is a good sort. He won't mind."

Claire nodded. "That will help, although food shan't be our greatest expense. You go and fetch every farthing you have, and I will do the same. Bring it to my room and we shall count it all and pray for a loaves-and-fishes miracle."

They met again a few minutes later. Setting aside the fifty pounds for the partnership, Claire counted what remained of the money she'd brought with her, the interest Mr. Dumfries had given her, and Mary's meager pile of coins. Her heart sank. Even with their funds combined, there was not enough.

"Please, miss. If I havena enough, I'll pay ye back. I promise. Don't leave me behind, I beg of ye. I need to get away."

The tears pooling in the girl's eyes dissolved Claire's reserve. She patted Mary's hand. "Let me see what I can do. I have one more idea."

Would God forgive her for what she was contemplating? Aunt Mercer certainly would not.

Claire had never stepped foot inside a pawnbroker's shop before, although she had certainly passed them on occasion. Following directions from Fergus, Claire approached the nearest such establishment, identified by three golden balls dangling from a wrought-iron bar over its door. The sign beneath read *Duncanson and Edwards, Pawnbroker*.

When she entered, the smell of dust and disuse met her. The proprietor looked up from a display case filled with jewelry and watches, silver spoons, shaving mugs, silk stockings, and more.

"Good day, madam. I am Mr. Duncanson. How may I be of service?"

Embarrassment heated her face, but Claire forced herself to set aside her pride and approach the counter. "I find myself in need of funds. It's something of an emergency or I would not part with it." She laid the cross pendant and chain on the man's counter.

He raised a glass to his eye and studied it, then asked, "Loan or outright sale?"

"I would dearly love to retrieve it one day. What are your terms for such an arrangement?"

"Ten percent interest per month. After the first month, the interest rate doubles. If you return for it, pay back the loan plus interest, it's yours. If you don't return within a year and week, it's mine to sell as I please."

Claire pressed dry lips together. "I understand."

"I canna give you what it's worth, but I could lend you fifteen pounds."

"Is that all?" Incredulity flared. "That's a real ruby!"

"Afraid so."

She was tempted to refuse until an image of Mary's distraught face appeared in her mind's eye. She swallowed, then asked, "And you will keep it safe?"

"That I will, madam. Store it proper and all."

"Very well."

He wrote out a ticket and handed it to her.

She did not tell him she needed the money for a journey, nor how far she intended to go. He might assume she'd never return for the necklace and sell it tomorrow. She had no idea whether or how she would ever be able to claim it, but at least this arrangement meant it was possible. To sell it outright so soon after inheriting the gift would seem even more wrong. Either way, Aunt Mercer would not be pleased.

The woman had told her the cross was her way to heaven, but at the moment, Claire would settle for Sidmouth.

The next morning, Claire and Mary rose early and hurried to the Crown. From there, they traveled by Royal Mail from Edinburgh to London. The fast, sleek mail coach carried four inside passengers and a few more on top. For safety and propriety, she had purchased inside fare for Mary as well.

Claire wore her only carriage outfit, the same one she had worn upon her arrival in Edinburgh two years before. Meanwhile, Mary wore Sunday best and a shabby straw bonnet, and helped Claire with the baggage and food hamper.

During the long journey, the two ate the food they had brought along, trying to minimize expenses, but Claire had neglected to account for perquisites for the guard and coachman. And the small glasses of cider she'd bought for her and Mary when thirst became too strong to ignore cost more than she would have imagined. She thanked God for the extra coins in interest Mr. Dumfries had provided.

Once they arrived in London, they were forced to spend the

night at an inn, because the last stagecoach to Sidmouth had already departed. To save money, Claire and Mary shared a room.

In the morning, they purchased seats on a stagecoach that would stop in Exeter and other towns along the way. The stagecoach was larger and slower than the mail coach, holding six inside passengers and a ragtag assortment of folks of every description on its roof.

As the baggage was loaded and the horses' harnesses given a once-over, the guard lifted his horn and blew the signal to board. A tall, well-dressed man paused at the coach door, standing aside to allow the ladies to enter first. His skin stood out as a rich, dark brown amid a sea of white faces. His hair was darker yet.

An elderly, bespectacled woman with a small dog tucked under one arm teetered on the first step, and he quickly offered a steadying hand. "Allow me, madam."

She climbed inside and thanked the man for his assistance.

A moment later her young companion came hurrying over. "Sorry, ma'am. There was a line for the privy, and worse, they were out of newspaper. Only corncobs."

"Hush, Miss Henderson. Not everyone wishes to hear the private details."

Feeling her cheeks warm, Claire stole a glance at the man and noticed him bite back a grin.

Inside, the passengers settled themselves on the two facing benches: Claire, Mary, and Miss Henderson on one narrow bench, the older woman, her dog, and the man on the other.

The man addressed the younger woman, offering in a polite, slightly accented voice, "I would be happy to trade places, if you would rather sit here?"

Miss Henderson only glared at him and gave a terse little shake of her head.

The horn blew again, and the coach lurched into motion, and soon they were on their way out of the city.

The pug wriggled until he loosed himself from his mistress's arms and hopped from her wide lap onto the man's trim one, tail wagging.

"Greetings, little friend." He gave the dog a pat on the head.

Tongue lolling in a doggy grin, the creature panted and then gave a happy yip.

"Good heavens," the older woman exclaimed. "Augie rarely warms to anyone so quickly. And he is an excellent judge of character!"

Claire glanced at the man, and the two shared private, amused smiles.

Beside Claire, the younger woman harrumphed, and Claire's smile faded. What an unpleasant girl.

Then she looked over at Mary and saw that she was also staring at the man, mouth slack. Claire supposed the young maid had rarely seen a darker-skinned person. In short order, Mary shifted her slack-lipped stare to the old woman.

Claire followed her gaze to the woman's thick spectacles, tinted a dark green. Claire had assumed the eye shades were like those she'd seen in newspaper advertisements, to be worn by sportsmen and travelers.

Mary leaned close to Claire and whispered in her ear, "Can she not see? Is that why she's talkin' to him?"

Claire looked again. Were the lenses meant to hide blind eyes rather than to shade them? She had not thought so, as the woman had awaited the coach alone. Then again, she'd stumbled when climbing inside. Claire gave a noncommittal shrug in reply.

The woman asked the man, "Have you ever had a dog?"

"Yes, when I was young. Though not as friendly as this fellow."

The woman clucked her pleasure and went on conversing with her seatmate, telling him how much she was looking forward to returning home after her visit to Town.

Miss Henderson leaned across the space between the benches and said, in a poor attempt at a whisper, "Can't you see he's a . . . not someone to speak to?"

Was a lack of eyesight the reason she was being polite to the man? Claire hoped not.

The woman replied, "What are you talking about?"

Miss Henderson raised her voice to be better heard over the road sounds. "He's black."

The man held out both hands, studying them. In a calm voice, he said, "I think brown would be more accurate."

The woman frowned at her companion. "Of course I can see him. I am not blind. I am perfectly aware that I am conversing with a very pleasant man. . . ." She turned to him and asked, "From India, I believe?"

"Originally, yes."

"These glasses . . ." She tapped the frame. "I have recently undergone a procedure for cataracts and am supposed to shield my eyes for a few more days."

Ah. Claire nodded her understanding.

"Please forgive my young companion her rudeness. I suppose not everyone finds people from other places fascinating, but I do." She looked at Claire. "Don't you?"

"Oh, I . . . y-yes," Claire faltered. "Although I have little experience, unless one counts Scotland."

She gave a self-conscious chuckle and was relieved when the man smiled in return.

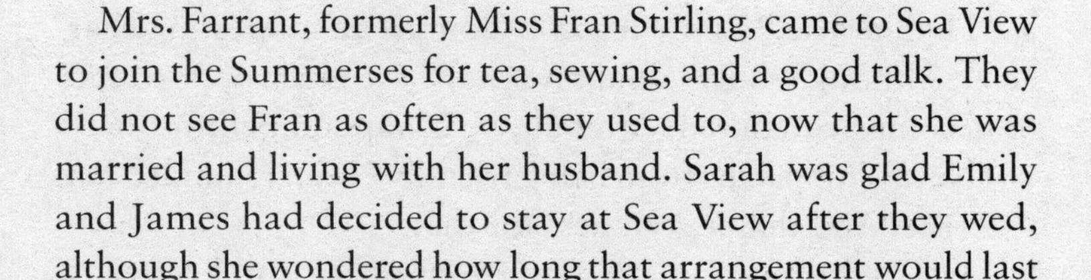

Mrs. Farrant, formerly Miss Fran Stirling, came to Sea View to join the Summerses for tea, sewing, and a good talk. They did not see Fran as often as they used to, now that she was married and living with her husband. Sarah was glad Emily and James had decided to stay at Sea View after they wed, although she wondered how long that arrangement would last when the young groom had to make the long trip to Killerton five or six days a week.

"So, Fran," Mamma asked, "how are things going now that you are a housewife instead of a boarding-house keeper?"

"Good, good. Yet to you, my friends, I confess I sometimes miss it. Things are rather quiet with only Leslie to look after."

"What can you tell us about Broadbridge's new owner?" Sarah asked.

"I met him only briefly, for the transfer of the deed. The property agent handled the negotiations."

Fran sipped her tea before going on. "He seemed a gentlemanlike man, perhaps in his late thirties. And if it is not too gossipy to repeat, my former cook—who has agreed to stay on with him, by the way—saw him arrive with a 'strange' woman." Fran waggled her brows.

"Strange, how?" Georgiana asked.

"A foreigner, apparently. Dark skin, dressed in long, many-colored scarves or some such."

"Probably a sari," Emily said, being the most well-read among them. "Perhaps she is from India."

"His wife?" Mamma suggested.

"I don't know. He did not say anything about a wife to me. And Mr. Hammond himself seems as English as they come, down to his auburn hair and even a few freckles."

"Perhaps he is a nabob returned from India with a fortune and an Indian bride," Emily theorized. "Is he handsome?"

Fran tilted her head in recollection. "Yes, rather. Regular features. Good teeth."

"High praise," Emily teased. "Sounds an interesting character. Although sadly I doubt we shall have much opportunity to become acquainted. After all, he is our competitor now."

"Never stopped us from being friendly," Fran reminded her.

"True. And thank goodness for that."

Mr. Gwilt came in with a fresh pot of tea and a letter. "I

took the liberty of collecting the post on my way home from the shops. Addressed to you, madam." He handed it to their mother.

With a glance at the handwriting, Mamma said, "From Viola." She handed it to Emily. "Here, you read it." Emily opened it and read aloud:

"Dear Mamma, Sarah, Emily, and Georgiana,

You have probably already heard by now, but in case you have not: Aunt Mercer has died.

The major and I arrived in Edinburgh without mishap and went directly to her house. There, we met two ladies carrying out bundles of clothing and other personal items—donations to their charity, they said.

From the elderly butler who came to the door, we learned that Claire is no longer in residence. All the staff besides himself and the lady's maid had already been dismissed and needed to quit the house. The maid will stay long enough to tidy up the place and will soon be leaving as well. Evidently the butler will keep an eye on the house until it is sold.

I told him I had written to let my sister know we were coming and asked if she had received my letter.

He looked abashed and said, 'I don't think so. The mistress was tetchy about the post. And Miss Summers said nothing to me about receiving visitors. I doubt the mistress would have allowed it, truth be told.'

That got Jack's back up, I can tell you. I could see he was about to say something like, 'I would like to see her try to stop us.' . . . Until I quickly reminded him that Aunt Mercer's interference had come to an end.

The butler could not or would not tell us where Claire had gone, even when the major offered him a financial incentive for his trouble.

Even so, I pressed him, asking if he was certain Claire had said nothing about where she was going, or mentioned going home. He replied, and I quote, 'No, ma'am. In fact, she said home was the one place she could not go.'

He did give us the direction of Aunt Mercer's lawyer, and we visited his office the same afternoon. Mr. Dumfries was at first hesitant to share any details, client confidentiality and all that, but when he learned I was one of Claire's sisters, concerned for her well-being, he decided no harm would be done by divulging that Claire had been given an allowance before she departed, so at least we know she is not destitute. Like the butler, Mr. Dumfries insisted he had no idea of her future plans, although he requested she write to let him know when she was settled.

We have asked the lawyer to assure Claire of our assistance and support should she contact him again. There seems little else we can do for now. We continue to Loch Katrine tomorrow before we start the journey home. Loch Katrine, you may know, was made famous by Walter Scott's 'The Lady of the Lake.' I thought you (Emily especially) would find that interesting.

Yours with love,
Viola"

Georgiana looked at each of them, expression troubled. "'Home was the one place she could not go'? Why would she think that? How sad!"

Mamma, Sarah noticed, fidgeted in her chair. She balled the linen napkin on her lap before smoothing it out again.

"So we know nothing more than we did before," Emily said, "except she left . . ."

"Sounds like she had to leave."

". . . and is not coming home."

Oh, Claire, Sarah thought. *Where have you gone?*

Mamma rose and said briskly, "Well, as Viola said, there is little else we can do. We tried."

"We can pray for her, surely."

"That goes without saying." At the door Mamma turned back. "I pray for each of you every day of my life and shan't stop now."

And her strident voice did nothing to disguise the sheen of tears in her eyes.

6

> Many gentlemen in their morning walks have attempted to introduce a sort of shooting dress, parading in a short coat of any light colour, and with Kerseymere gaiters coming up to the knees.
>
> —*Le Beau Monde* magazine

The bespectacled woman and her companion had alighted in Exeter, but the well-dressed man continued on with them to Sidmouth. The coach set them down in the stable yard opposite the London Inn. There, the man retrieved his case, bowed to them, and departed on foot.

After asking the porter for directions, Claire and Mary walked a few streets over and across the marketplace to a three-story house with a parapet on the roof.

On the right, a wrought-iron fence enclosed an outside stairway leading down to the basement servants' area.

On the left, pots of dried sea grasses and a similar wrought-iron rail framed the few steps that led to the front entrance. On one side of the door sat a small bench, and on the other hung a sign: *Broadbridge's Boarding House*. The name struck a chord in Claire's memory. Although at the moment she was too nervous to stop and work out why.

Mary had become nauseated during the last stage of the trip and even now appeared pale and shaky. Leading her to the bench beside the door, Claire said, "Here, sit down."

When the girl had done so, Claire set their cases at her feet, straightened, and smoothed her bodice, pulse racing. Here was her chance to reside and earn her own livelihood in Sidmouth, without presuming on her family. Would she be too late?

Drawing a deep inhale, Claire knocked. Waited. No response.

She knocked again.

Finally, she heard footsteps approach from within and the door latch click. She held her breath. What manner of man would W.H. be?

When the door opened, the figure who appeared was not a man at all, but a woman—a slight, dark woman with a sharp nose, black hair parted in the middle, and dressed in draped fabric like a large shawl or robe.

"Yes?"

Claire had assumed W.H. was a man. Had she been mistaken?

She forced a smile. "I am Miss Summers. C. S.? I wrote about the partnership in the boarding house."

The woman's shrewd gaze moved over Claire, from the top of her bonnet to her hemline.

"Are you W.H.?" Claire asked. "Have I come to the right place?"

Those same dark eyes narrowed. "I think not."

Claire's stomach dropped. "Am I too late?"

"Your services are not required, madam. He has me."

"Oh. I . . . see." Claire's throat burned, and she blinked back tears.

"Good day." The woman shut the door and none too gently.

For a moment Claire stared at the closed door, heart sinking, then turned and met Mary's frightened eyes.

"What now?" Mary asked.

"I don't know."

A whistled tune caught her ear. Claire turned and saw a man striding toward the house, a trim man of perhaps forty, with fair skin and auburn side-whiskers showing beneath his flat wool cap. He was dressed in a light double-breasted coat atop close-fitting leather breeches. Over his lower legs, he wore canvas gaiters, or "spatterdashes," for protection against wet brush. She recalled her father dressing in similar fashion to go out shooting. This man carried no gun, however, but rather a long, pointed stick.

"May I help you?" he asked. "Have you come to inquire about a room?"

"No, I . . . I'm sorry. Are you W. H.?"

"If you mean William Hammond, then yes. This is my establishment."

She swallowed a nervous lump and attempted a smile, hoping to make a good first impression. "I am Miss Claire Summers. C. S.? I wrote about the partnership and have brought the fifty pounds. Though perhaps I am too late."

"Too late?"

She gestured toward the door. "The woman who answered my knock. Has she already accepted the partnership?"

He frowned, clearly perplexed. "Who are we talking about?"

"She did not give a name. Dressed in a brightly colored, em, sari, I believe?"

One corner of his mouth twitched in grim humor. "Ah. Sent you away, did she?"

"Well, she made it clear she was here before me and has a prior claim."

"Indeed she does. But not as my business partner."

"Oh?" *Then a prior claim as what?* Claire wondered.

He angled his head to regard her from beneath the brim of his hat. "Please tell me you do not also possess a jealous, hot-blooded nature?"

Claire lifted her chin. "Certainly not. I am an Englishwoman."

He barked a laugh. "Of course you are." He looked over and noticed Mary. "And who is this?"

"Mary is a skilled housemaid."

"I did not advertise for a maid."

With a glance at Mary's pale, anxious face, Claire lifted her chin a fraction higher. "Perhaps not, but you did advertise for a respectable female, and respectable females do not travel unaccompanied."

"I see. Well. Come inside and we shall discuss it."

He opened the front door and, after scraping off his shoes, led the way inside. As she followed, she noticed that although he was of average height, his shoulders were markedly broad.

They entered a long entry hall with a narrow table beneath a mirror, pegs along one wall, and three doors on the other. Stairs at the far end led to the floors above.

He stowed his stick and hat in a closet, then gestured them through the first open door. The modest room held a table bearing the remnants of breakfast, a small settee, and a cluttered desk positioned to take advantage of the sunlight from an east-facing window.

"Pardon the disarray," he said. "We use this morning room as informal dining parlour, sitting room, and office. Guests eat in the formal dining room next door. We have only a few guests at present, but hopefully business will return to previous levels soon."

Tossing his gloves upon a pile of papers, he opened his mouth, hesitated, then with a glance at Mary said, "Perhaps your maid might wait in the hall while we discuss things?"

"Aye, sir." Mary bobbed a curtsy, retreating back into the hall and pulling the door closed behind herself.

When she had gone, he began. "As I said, I don't know that I wish to hire a housemaid."

In reply, Claire ran a gloved hand over the fireplace mantel, held up a dusty finger, and then gestured to the crumb-speckled table. "Pray, do not be offended, but the place is not as clean and neat as it should be. An experienced maid will be a great asset."

"The woman who owned this place before me made do with a cook and scullery maid."

"Then clearly that woman did a great deal of housework herself, and you do not."

"Very true." He gestured for her to be seated in a chair facing the desk.

She complied, and he sat as well. Now at closer range, she noticed faint freckles in the lighter skin beneath his green eyes, and deep parenthetical grooves from nose to lower cheek. The left groove was more prominent due, she guessed, to a habitual lopsided grin.

Trying to sound businesslike, she asked, "So what is your part in this partnership?"

"My part? I bought the place, which cost far more than fifty pounds, I assure you."

"And once you take on a partner, you intend to have no part in the day to day?"

"As little as possible."

"Then why, may I ask, did you buy a boarding house?"

"No, you may not ask."

Claire opened her mouth to protest but then changed tack. "You mentioned hoping business will return to previous levels soon. Has the place been closed?"

"Briefly, after the former owner married and while we made some needed refurbishments."

We? Again Claire wondered about the woman who'd answered the door.

"It has taken time to settle in and grow accustomed to things here. Therefore I have been somewhat lax, as you've noticed. I am also tardy in announcing the reopening under new management. One of our guests was already acquainted with the place from previous stays. The other is an acquaintance of mine. I trust we shall begin operating at full capacity now you're here."

Nerves kneaded her stomach like cat claws. "I am to fill it?"

"Yes, as well as to help manage it. Why do you think I wanted a partner?"

"For my fifty pounds."

He shook his head. "That is so you feel invested in the place, a sense of ownership. And in return you will have an equitable share of the profits—once there are any." He lifted a hand. "But let us not get ahead of ourselves. I have a few questions for you before we finalize this arrangement." He entwined his fingers on the desk. "First of all, you are younger than I expected. Have you any experience?"

None. Zero. Claire took a breath and endeavored to keep her voice steady. "Not direct experience, but I grew up in a genteel home, and due to my mother's poor health, I often acted as hostess to overnight guests, and presided over many fine banquets and parties."

"This is a boarding house. We shall have no fine banquets or parties here."

"All the better," she said with a confidence she did not feel. "How much easier to oversee more modest domestic arrangements."

She clasped gloved hands together to disguise their tremble. Had she convinced him? Or would he reject her and Mary both? "Perhaps you ought to describe my proposed duties."

"In simple terms, you would oversee the guests' experience

here—the cleanliness and comfort of their rooms, the quality of their meals—and make sure all is satisfactory. You shan't have to actually cook. The former cook agreed to work for me."

That was a relief. Claire had no experience in the kitchen beyond making tea and toast.

He drummed his fingers on the desk. "What else . . . ? Guest correspondence and perhaps some bookkeeping as well. Does that sound feasible?"

Claire bit her lip. "It does. Though I will, of course, need a more thorough explanation of how you want things done."

He waved the suggestion away. "Plenty of time for that later. The former owner has offered to come over and walk through things if and when I found someone."

"Excellent. I have another question. How do you propose we explain our relationship? People may assume we are . . . that is, that I am your . . ."

"Partner in more than business?"

Embarrassment heated her neck. "Well . . . yes."

"Rest assured the boarding house is the only reason you're here. I like my privacy. I have set up a bedchamber and study for myself over the former stables. Quite separate. Quite proper. That should help alleviate your concerns as well as those of any busybodies."

"Good."

The same dark woman came to the morning room door and poked her head in, and Claire saw that she was rather pretty when she wasn't scowling. Perhaps *she* filled the place of *"partner in more than business."*

Her gaze landing on Claire, that sour-faced scowl returned, blotting out her beauty.

"So. You are letting her stay?"

"I am."

"I told you I could help you."

"You have an important responsibility of your own. In fact, should you not be upstairs now?"

She huffed and whirled away.

Claire felt ill at ease to witness the tense exchange, as well as curious, but he did not explain.

Instead, Mr. Hammond rose and gestured for Claire to precede him out of the room. "Come, I will show you around."

"Does that mean we are going forward?"

"It does."

"Well then." Claire opened her reticule. "I hope you understand I cannot provide one hundred pounds. In fact, fifty is practically all I have left, due to unforeseen expenses on the journey here."

"Ah yes, there are always inevitable extras while traveling."

"Are there? I have not much experience with travel."

"And I have far too much."

She drew out the notes.

He hesitated, then laid out a flat palm. "I have never taken money from a woman before."

"And I have never entered into any such arrangement before."

He nodded and pocketed the notes. "New ground for us both, then."

In the hall, he invited Mary to join them and briefly showed them the guest dining room on the same floor. Then he led them up the stairs to the first floor, pointing out the small parlour, simply furnished guest rooms, water closet, and bathroom with a single tub. He frowned at the dirty mirror and pile of wet towels on the floor.

"It's odd how you don't notice the state of things until you see it through a visitor's eyes." He turned to the housemaid. "Mary, was it?"

"Aye, sir."

"Miss Summers was right. You are hired."

"Oh, thank ye!"

"We had better continue up to the attic, then. Several bedchambers there for you to choose from."

They ascended the next flight of stairs together. At the top Claire noticed two doors to the left of the stairs and a line of doors to the right.

"These two on the left are for guests who want more economical lodging and don't mind the stairs. The first two rooms on the right are occupied, but those farther down are open. Mary, why don't you take a look and pick one for yourself."

As Mary disappeared through an open door down the passage, one of the closer doors burst open and a small figure flew out and hurled itself at Mr. Hammond. He crouched at the last moment and swept the child into his arms.

"Papa! I heard your voice."

"Did you have a good nap, my little pumpion?"

He has a daughter. . . . Claire realized with surprise.

The little girl nodded, dark hair swinging around a face the color of creamed coffee.

"Say 'good day' to Miss Summers."

Dark eyes swiveled to Claire. "Good day."

"This is Mira," Mr. Hammond said, expression warm with paternal pride as he grinned at the child of perhaps four or five years of age.

Was the woman she had met this child's mother? With the girl's coloring, it was certainly possible, even probable.

That woman herself appeared in the doorway. "Come, Mira. We should change your frock."

Mira nodded and said something Claire did not understand as her father set her down.

The woman gazed at the girl with approval. Then with a sly glance at Claire, she admonished, "English. She does not speak Tamil."

Mira turned back to Claire. "Sonali is teaching me some words in her language, but I speak English best."

Charmed by her big eyes, pretty face, and ready smile, Claire was instantly taken with the little girl. Far less so with the woman. Perhaps she was not the girl's mother, unless *Sonali* meant *Mamma* in her language.

As if guessing her thoughts, Mr. Hammond said, "I believe you have already met Miss Patel. Sonali, this is Miss Summers, come to help manage the boarding house."

Miss Patel gave her a terse nod of acknowledgment, then turned the girl toward her room. Mira sent them a cheerful wave, and the two retreated from sight.

When the door shut behind them, Claire asked quietly, "Is . . . is she your . . . ?"

"She serves as Mira's nursery-governess."

"Oh. From India?"

"Yes. I've settled them in rooms up here, almost like a traditional English nursery and schoolroom. That way, we leave all rooms on the lower floors for guests."

"And Mira's mother?"

He grimaced. "She died, over a year ago now."

"I am sorry," Claire said, and after an awkward pause, she changed the subject. "And where will I sleep?"

"I thought the housekeeper's room belowstairs would be best. Closer to the kitchen and common rooms. I believe that is where the former landlady slept."

The housekeeper's room? Oh, how she had fallen. Aloud, she said, "Very well."

On the way down, they took the servant stairs toward the back of the house.

"I mentioned my apartment over the stable block. I had the old coachman's and groom's quarters renovated into a bedchamber and study for myself." He paused on the first floor and pointed to a nondescript door. "I reach them through here. There is also access from the former stables, although I keep that door locked."

"And if a guest arrives with horses?"

"The former owner didn't offer stabling. Too expensive to keep a groom. She sent people to the livery opposite the London Inn. I do the same. Mr. Lake and his son are very accommodating."

He started toward the next landing, then turned back. "By the way, I insist upon privacy. I shan't enter your room and I ask that you not enter mine."

That seemed rather harsh. She said, "But surely, should your daughter need you . . . ?"

"My daughter is not your concern."

He must have noticed her pull back, for he winced and qualified, "I only meant . . . Sonali cares for my daughter. You are here to manage the boarding house."

"I see."

He tilted his head to one side. "Why? Have you experience with children?"

"No." Realizing she'd answered more vehemently than intended, she added more gently, "That is, I do have four younger sisters."

"Ah. In Scotland?"

"No," she said again, and did not expand on her reply.

He waited a moment, his green eyes sparking with curiosity. Or was that attraction she saw reflected there? Surely not. At least, Claire hoped not.

They continued belowstairs, where he took her to the kitchen and workrooms and introduced her to the cook, Mrs. Ballard.

The rotund, pleasant woman gave her a friendly smile. "Nice to meet you. Miss Summers, is it? You know, there is a Summers family here in Sidmouth. Perhaps you are related?"

"It is . . . quite possible," Claire replied, avoiding Mr. Hammond's gaze.

"Mrs. Ballard does not live in," he explained, "but she comes every day to cook for us."

The woman nodded. "That's right. I come early to prepare breakfast and stay till dinnertime. The scullery maid does the washing up after I'm gone."

"Do you live nearby, Mrs. Ballard?" Claire asked.

"Yes. Not far from the mill. Mr. Ballard and I have a nice little place near the river."

"Well, I shall look forward to working with you."

Mr. Hammond then led Claire toward the opposite end of the basement and opened a door on the left. "And here is your room."

She stepped inside to better view it. The room had windows that looked into an outdoor stairwell at the front of the house, gracing the space with natural light. It was a larger room than she'd had at Aunt Mercer's, with built-in cabinets, small table and chairs, dressing chest, washstand, bed, and side table. It reminded Claire of the housekeeper's room in her childhood home, which had served as bedchamber, parlour, and storeroom for expensive items like sugar and tea.

From the doorway, he said, "Rather humble, I realize, considering your genteel past. Still, I hope you will be comfortable."

"I am sure I shall be. Thank you." She wondered how quickly his concern for her comfort would evaporate if he knew the whole of her past.

7

> The idea of seeing the sea—of being near it in
> calm, perhaps in storm—fills and satisfies my
> mind. I shall be discontented at nothing.
> —Charlotte Brontë, letter

After Claire had spread fresh linens on her bed and put away her few belongings, she went up to the attic to make sure Mary had all she needed. Mr. Hammond had given them the rest of the day to get settled, and Claire thought she might feel more settled after she saw Sea View again. So while Mary opted to rest, Claire decided to go for a walk.

Claire had briefly resided at Sea View with her family three years ago, shortly after her parents purchased the seaside property as a second home. Papa had hoped the sea air would improve his wife's health. Instead, after only one stay there he had died.

And it was her fault.

Pushing the guilty thought aside, Claire tied on a bonnet and left by the tradesmen's entrance near her room, taking the outside stairs up to the street level. She walked through the marketplace and turned south toward the sea.

Reaching the esplanade, she walked west, past the indoor baths and lodging houses. Past the library, an open field, and a pretty thatched cottage. With each step that brought her closer, her pulse quickened.

When she reached the promenade's end, she glanced diagonally up Glen Lane, and there it was, on a rise. Sea View. A fine, big house built at an angle to better face the sea, fronted by a long, covered veranda. She was relieved to see the chairs on the veranda were empty. She was not quite ready to be recognized or to make her presence known.

With no one about, she felt free to tarry there and let her eyes rest on the place. What an idyllic haven it seemed to her. A place without bad memories, unlike the family home in May Hill.

She and her sisters had come here with such anticipation that first time, eager to see their new seasonal retreat in the increasingly fashionable resort town of Sidmouth.

It had taken two vehicles to transport them all. They had used their own traveling coach and hired a post chaise as well.

Emily had barely paused for breath during the entire journey, pointing out landmarks they passed, reading aloud excerpts from a Sidmouth guidebook she had purchased, musing about how soon they might be able to attend a ball at the assembly rooms and how many handsome beaux they might meet. Finally Papa had gently asked her to be quiet for a time, out of consideration for Mamma's nerves . . . and no doubt his as well.

Soon after arriving at the house, Papa and the servants had helped Mamma settle comfortably in a room on the ground floor. Then Papa offered Claire, as eldest, the first choice of the bedchambers upstairs. He had probably thought she'd take one of the larger rooms with an ocean view, but instead she had chosen a modest room next to the one Sarah preferred. The two had shared a bedchamber at Finderlay and wanted to remain nearby for late-night talks and for morning help with each other's fastenings. Sarah was only a year younger, and she and Claire had been close. Her chest tightened. How she missed Sarah, missed them all.

They'd enjoyed every minute of that happy first stay at Sea View. Strolling on the beach, wading in the waves, exploring the surrounding hills and moors. Sitting on that very veranda to enjoy the fresh air or playing games on the lawn.

As Claire stood gazing up at the house, lost in memory, she became aware of a tapping sound approaching from behind. Turning, she saw a man of sixty or so, walking with the probing assistance of a cane—that and his dark glasses suggested he was blind. Then again, she had been briefly fooled by the woman on the coach.

"Here, allow me to get out of your way," she said, to alert him to her presence as she stepped to one side.

"I thank you, ma'am." He paused and sent a friendly smile in her direction. "Standing here as you are, I suppose you are admiring the view?"

"Yes, although not of the sea. Of the house across the lane."

"Ah. Sea View. Are you to stay there as well?"

Her mouth fell ajar at the question. Had he somehow divined her heart's desire?

"W-why do you ask?"

"I have resided there these many months. Lovely place. Lovely people. I recommend it to you. Best guest house in Sidmouth, although I may be biased."

Guest house? Claire's mind reeled. She could hardly credit it. Aunt Mercer had predicted her mother and sisters must be living in reduced circumstances after Papa's death, but she would not have guessed this.

"And the people who own it. Are they . . . ?"

"Mrs. Summers and her daughters. Excellent family, kind and hospitable. I would be happy to introduce you, if you'd like."

"Oh, no need. I am . . . at Broadbridge's."

"Ah. Pleasant too, from what I hear. The former landlady is a friend of the Summers family, though I don't know anything about the new owner. I suppose you have met him, staying there as you are?"

"I have, yes."

"And what do you think of him? A good fellow?"

"I hope so. It is a bit too soon to know for sure."

He nodded his understanding, then cocked his head to one side. "Do you know, your voice sounds vaguely familiar to me. Have we met?"

"No, sir."

She'd been told she and Sarah had similar voices. Had he noticed? Thankfully he could not see her, or he would likely also notice a resemblance to Emily. She did not want a veritable stranger to walk into Sea View and announce that the black sheep of the family was back in town.

When she remained silent, he said, "Well then, I shall bid you good day. And if you change your mind about Sea View, tell them Simon Hornbeam sent you." He tipped his hat and walked on, and Claire hurried back the way she'd come.

When Claire returned to Broadbridge's, Mr. Hammond invited her to join him, his daughter, and Miss Patel for dinner in the morning room, while Mary would eat belowstairs with the scullery maid after helping to serve their guests. Claire thought it a bit odd that Miss Patel would join the family for meals. Was not a nursery-governess more servant than family? Then again, wasn't she?

Instead of the sportsman's attire he'd worn earlier, Mr.

Hammond was now dressed in a dark green frock coat over light waistcoat and pantaloons, stockings, and polished black leather shoes. He looked very handsome and every inch the English gentleman.

The food was already on the table, so there was no time to change, and she had sadly few dresses to change into anyway. With a self-conscious smile Claire hung her bonnet on a peg and entered the morning room. He pulled out a chair for her at the oval table near the fireplace, and she sat down.

As he took his own seat, he said, "I know in many households a child Mira's age would take meals in the nursery or schoolroom, but I enjoy her company."

Miss Patel ate in stony silence throughout the meal, while Mira chatted cheerfully with her father, recounting a story Sonali had read to her, asking when they might go to the beach, and telling him about a seagull that had perched on her window ledge. . . .

"All right, little *kaddu*," he gently interrupted. "Now, how about you use that eloquent mouth of yours to eat some dinner, hm? You want to grow big and strong, do you not?"

She shrugged. "My shoes are already too small."

"Are they? Then we shall have to buy new ones."

When the little girl stopped talking long enough to eat something, Claire attempted to fill the silence by asking, "Have you been in Sidmouth long?"

He shook his head. "A few months."

"Where did you live before?"

"Several places."

"And have you owned such a property before, or had you a different profession?"

He set down his fork with a clank. "Different. But I prefer not to talk about my past, professionally or otherwise, if you don't mind."

Miss Patel smirked at her from across the table.

"Oh." Claire blinked, feeling chastised. "Very well. I was only making conversation."

"No need. Relax and enjoy your meal." He gave her a small smile that did not reach his eyes.

After they had eaten, Mr. Hammond led Claire into the dining room to introduce her to their two guests, who sat lingering over coffee.

"Mr. Filonov. Mr. Jackson. I'd like you to meet Miss Summers. She will be helping to manage things here."

The first man instantly stood and bowed his fair, silvery head.

The second man, with a balding pate and waistcoat buttons strained over a paunch, reluctantly rose with a groan. "Sorry. It's the dew-beaters." He lifted one large, thick-soled shoe in evidence. "Aching today, they are."

Mr. Hammond explained, "Mr. Jackson is a salesman. Stays here several times a year."

"That's right. I travel all over this area."

"And what is it you sell?" Claire asked, more out of politeness than genuine interest.

"Bobbins, miss. For lacemaking. I'll show them to you one evening, if you'd like."

Claire was immediately on her guard. *Show me his bobbins indeed*. "I . . . Well, thank you, but I shall be rather busy, I'm afraid."

Mr. Hammond turned to the first man. "And Mr. Filonov is an artist. Many artists come here to paint the scenery, you know. He came all the way from Russia."

"Goodness."

"Is true. Dere is real beauty here," Mr. Filonov said with a noticeable accent, his *r*'s lightly trilled and his *th* more like a *d*.

"Well, a pleasure to meet you both," Claire said. "Do let me know if there's anything I can do to make your stay more enjoyable."

Mr. Jackson gave her a greasy grin. "I shall keep that in mind."

Did a lewd suggestion lurk beneath the man's words? Claire hoped not. She decided to give him the benefit of the doubt and smiled from one man to the other. "Though you might need to wait a few days until I am more familiar with my responsibilities. Good night, gentlemen."

Together she and Mr. Hammond walked out. She glanced over and noticed his brow furrow.

In a low voice, he said, "Mr. Filonov is unfailingly polite. I don't know Mr. Jackson as well. If he gives you any trouble whatsoever, please let me know immediately."

Claire's heart warmed at his concern. "I shall."

8

Friendship is certainly the finest balm
for the pangs of disappointed love.
—Jane Austen, *Northanger Abbey*

The next day, Claire awoke before dawn to the clanking of pots and pans from the kitchen down the passage. Mrs. Ballard and her scullery maid certainly got an early start on the day.

With a little groan, Claire rose, washed, and laid out the grey day dress Aunt Mercer had made over for her.

Mary knocked softly and entered, coming down as promised to help with her stays and fastenings. What would Claire have done without her? She supposed she would have had to swallow her pride and ask the cook or scullery maid for help, at least until she could acquire a pair of wraparound stays like Mary wore.

After Mary had finished and gone to the kitchen, Claire climbed the servants' stairs to the main floor and went through the door into the public area.

As she walked through the hall striped with morning sunlight from tall windows, something metallic glinted at her from the deep red Turkish carpet. With a sigh, she bent and picked it up, glad again she had brought Mary along. Hopefully, between them, they could keep the house in good order.

She eyed the object as she straightened. A coin, yet unlike any coin she had seen before: shiny silver and engraved with strange symbols.

Had a guest dropped it? Perhaps Mr. Filonov? She did not know what Russian coins looked like. Then again, the tiny palm tree among the other symbols did not seem Russian.

She carried it into the morning room. The coin might be valuable, so Claire hesitated to leave it on the desk in plain sight. On impulse, she opened one of the drawers, intending to place it inside. Instead what she saw there made her hesitate, hand outstretched.

A piece of paper with handwriting on it stuck out from under a stack of stationery. It looked like a partially written letter, although not in a language she recognized.

Setting the coin in the drawer, she tugged the page free and studied it. Were these words or symbols?

She saw varying swirls and what appeared to be *u*'s with dots in the middle, as well as curvy *j*'s like upside-down interrogation marks.

What in the world? She recalled Mr. Hammond sitting at this desk the day before. She also thought of his refusal to tell her about his previous profession. What was he involved in?

In the next moment, she heard Sarah's practical voice in her mind, calmly advising her not to jump to conclusions. This could mean anything or nothing.

It might not even be his handwriting. She thought again of Mr. Filonov. English was clearly not his native language. He might have come into the morning room to find paper and ink to begin a letter, and then laid it aside, unfinished. She remembered hearing somewhere that Russian was written in a different alphabet, so it was possible.

Another idea occurred to her. She had no idea what the various Indian languages might look like in written form, but perhaps this was something Sonali had written.

Other possible explanations came to her as well, and none of them were frightening.

Then why did she feel uneasy?

Footsteps sounded in the hall, and alarm shot through her. She shoved the paper inside and slammed the drawer shut.

Sonali Patel stepped over the threshold and paused, staring across the room at her, suspicion gleaming in her kohl-lined eyes.

"What are you doing, Miss Summers? Poking about? Mr. Hammond guards his privacy, you know."

"Just tidying up a few things."

"If you say so."

Mira and her father entered behind her, hand in hand. Claire stilled in anticipation. Would Sonali accuse her?

Instead the woman's glower vanished as she turned to smile at the man. "Good morning, Mr. Hammond. Does not our Mira look charmingly today?"

The little girl was dressed in a green-and-gold sari much like Sonali's.

He grinned down at his daughter. "Indeed she does."

Then he raised his gaze to Claire, still standing frozen behind the desk.

"Miss Summers. Everything all right?"

"Y-yes."

Sonali said, "She was searching your desk, to 'tidy it,' she says, but I wonder."

"I simply found a coin and placed it in the drawer."

He waved dismissively. "My private desk is upstairs. Either of you are welcome to use this one—or tidy it." One corner of his lips quirked. Then he said, "But first, let us have breakfast."

He glanced toward the table, smirk fading. "Although it has not yet arrived."

"Is that not one of her duties?" Sonali pointed at Claire with round-eyed innocence.

"Yes," Claire blurted. "I shall go down and offer my help." She turned and hurried out, eager to be useful—and for a respite from Miss Patel.

After breakfast, Claire helped Mary clear the tables in both morning room and dining room. Then Mr. Hammond set Claire to work at the morning-room desk with ledger, tradesmen's bills, laundry lists, a few lodging inquiries from potential guests, and the registration book.

He, meanwhile, retreated upstairs to his private study.

Claire sorted the bills and listed the amounts owed in the ledger, a few of which were overdue. Not, she gathered, from lack of funds, but from lack of an organized system.

Then she opened the registration book and flipped through backward with interest, past the recent, fairly empty pages, to pages upon pages filled with information for guests coming and going. What might they—she—do to attract more guests once again?

A short while later, Mr. Hammond paused at the open door, dressed much as he had been when she'd first arrived, stick in hand. "Off for a jaunt."

She held up her forefinger. "Before you go, may I ask . . . Do you know why the previous owner sold the boarding house? Was it not profitable?"

"On the contrary. It was quite profitable."

"And that's why you bought it?"

"No. Well, partly. After she married, she simply decided she could not manage both this place and her husband's home."

"You mentioned she would be willing to advise me. When might I speak with her?"

"I will ask."

"And what is her name?"

"Fran Farrant. Although her maiden name, Stirling, was on the original deed."

Claire looked up. "Fran Stirling?"

"Yes, do you know her?"

No wonder the name Broadbridge's had struck a chord in her memory. This had been Stirling's boarding house—the place she had bought after she left service as Mamma's lady's maid.

But Claire was not ready to explain that connection to him. How might Stirling receive her? Would she be willing to help? Doubts assailed her.

"I once knew a Fran Stirling," Claire said. "Could be a different woman."

"Where did you know her?"

"In Gloucestershire."

"Hm. Well, this woman has lived in the area for several years, I believe. Her husband, Mr. Farrant, remodeled the old coachman's quarters for me. His home and workshop are only a few miles from here. I shall walk out that way and see if she is available." He nodded to her and turned away, whistling.

When he'd gone, Claire looked back down at the pile of paperwork, spirits sinking. He had got a good bargain. Her fifty pounds, her labor, and more leisure time for himself.

Reminding herself of all she hoped to gain by being there, she resolutely returned to her tasks.

A short while later Mr. Jackson stopped by on his way out, cases in hand. "May I show you my bobbins now?"

"Oh, em . . ." Claire hesitated. He could not intend anything untoward right there in the office, could he? "Yes, if you'd like."

He eagerly came forward, laid one case on the desk, and opened it, revealing dozens of smooth, slender sticks perhaps four inches long with necks for thread, the ends tapering to either a sharp or rounded point. Most of the bobbins were plain, but a few were decorated with rings or patterns: hearts, diamonds, flowers, even words.

He held up one with a mottled brown-and-tan finish. "This one is stained with aqua fortis to look like tortoiseshell. Most of these are of turned wood. But these here are of bone. See the intricate carvings?"

He held up another that bore a saying: *When I am gone and far at sea, forget not love to think of me.* "I sell lots of this kind to fishermen and sailors for their sweethearts."

"Very nice. Do you make them?"

"Not so skilled, I'm afraid. I sell them for the craftsmen, oldsters mostly, unable to make the rounds. Yet I am glad to be a small cog—or a small bobbin, as it were—in such a noble art."

His pride and enthusiasm shone on his face and in his voice. Claire realized she'd been wrong to assume the worst—he really had wanted to show her his bobbins!

He opened his second case. "I also carry pins, small bobbin winders, and now and again I have the good fortune to sell one of these fine bobbin boxes made by a coffin maker in Branscombe."

"Goodness. Quite a complete selection."

His full cheeks rose and lips pursed in a poorly concealed smile. "You are too kind."

An hour or so after the salesman left, Claire went belowstairs to ask Mrs. Ballard about a bill from the greengrocer she could not reconcile. Finding the scullery maid mopping the floor all the way from the kitchen to the meat safe and back stairs, Claire decided not to trespass upon the clean, damp tiles. She turned the other way and went into her room for an apron, planning to help Mary give one of the neglected guest rooms a thorough cleaning.

She glanced through her windows, and movement on the outside stairway caught her eye. There came Mr. Hammond with stick, muddy shoes and gaiters, and an equally muddy dog trailing behind. The dog was snapping at the stick as though it were a rat or a juicy bone. Mr. Hammond descended the stairs, the scraggly dog yipping at his heels all the way.

Thinking of the freshly mopped floors, Claire hurried to the tradesmen's entrance to forestall him.

He pushed open the door a few inches before she blocked his way, pressing against the door with determined hands. "You're muddy!"

"I know. That's why I thought I'd come in down here instead of soiling the carpet upstairs."

"The passageway is being mopped as we speak. Please take off your shoes just inside the door. And leave your muddy dog outside."

"Not my dog. Followed me home."

"Then, for heaven's sake, don't let it in here."

"I can try but the little beast seems determined to shadow my every move."

"It's your stick he wants. Leave it out there and he won't follow."

"This is not a mere stick, Miss Summers," he said, as though deeply offended. "It is an *alpenstock*."

From somewhere above, a female voice called, "Chips? Chips!"

The dog paused, ears pricked, and looked over his shaggy shoulder.

"Quick," Claire urged, opening the door to let Mr. Hammond in, sliding out past him to take his place, and shutting the door at her back.

The oddly familiar voice called again, and stained skirt hems and worn half boots appeared at the top of the stairs.

"He doesn't mean any harm. Probably thought the man was offering to play fetch. Chips is a stray. I know he looks a fright, but he's terribly friendly."

That voice.

Claire eased out from the doorway to get a better look.

A young woman stood up there, hand on the railing, bent at the waist to see into the shadowy space below. She was slightly plump, with pleasing curves, windblown hair, and a fair face. A face she knew. Claire's heart squeezed. Could this young woman be her little sister, who had been a tomboyish adolescent when last she'd seen her? The last two years had certainly changed her. She'd lost most of her childish looks and was well on her way to womanhood.

Claire stepped to the foot of the stairs. "Georgie?"

The girl's mouth fell open, and she slapped a hand over it, eyes widening above rough fingernails.

A moment later, the hand fell away, and Georgiana cried, "Claire! Oh, Claire! I knew you'd come. I knew it!"

She flew down the stairs, and Claire set one foot back, bracing herself for impact, afraid the girl would knock her over.

She held out her arms, and Georgiana launched herself into them. Claire had to widen her stance to stay upright. Meanwhile the dog, startled by Georgie's exclamations, bounded up the stairs to escape.

"Why are you here and not at Sea View?" her sister asked.

"I've gone into partnership with the owner."

"Really? We've been so worried since we learned Aunt Mercer died and you had left."

They had worried about her? The thought was oddly touching until she realized she had caused more strife.

"I am sorry to have worried you."

Georgie gripped her hand. "At least you're here in Sidmouth

now. And in Fran Stirling's old place, yet. When did you arrive?"

"Only yesterday. I am still settling in."

Her sister embraced her again. "Everyone will be so happy!"

Over Georgie's shoulder, Claire glimpsed movement on the walkway above and looked up. A woman on the street paused at the railing, gaping down at them, one hand holding a parcel, the other to her chest.

Claire's breath caught. *Mamma*. She almost didn't recognize her, out walking alone, clearly no longer an invalid.

Mamma's hand reached out, then drew back again, only to grip her parcel with both hands, as though a shield. She stood there, staring down at them. One moment. Two. Three. Then she turned and walked away without a word.

Claire's heart sank. Not *everyone* would be happy she'd come.

"I want to tell you something," Georgiana said, pulling back with a sniff.

Claire refocused her attention on her sister.

"I had a dream the night you went away. It seemed so real. I dreamt you tiptoed into my room and kissed me before you left." Georgiana reached up and touched her own forehead at the memory.

Claire smiled, even as tears heated her eyes. "That was not a dream, my dear. I did." She looked up and kissed her baby sister's forehead again. She used to have to lean down. "Georgie, do you know why I left Finderlay?"

The younger girl nodded. "To help Aunt Mercer."

"Well . . . yes. I did do that." So they had not told Georgiana, Claire realized. Was it her place to do so? To disillusion her innocent youngest sister? She was not sure.

Instead, she gently told her, "You don't know how happy it makes me to see you again. It's why I came to Sidmouth. Unfortunately, I won't be able to come to Sea View. I will be busy learning my new responsibilities and managing the boarding house. But you . . . any of you . . . are welcome to come and see me here."

"What about Sundays?" Georgie asked. "Will we see you at church at least? You must have some time to yourself?"

"Perhaps later . . . once I know what I'm doing."

Georgie sighed. "It does not seem right—your not coming to Sea View."

Claire pressed her hands. "But we are together now and can be whenever you'd like to call. Although if I'm busy, I can't guarantee I won't put you to work." She winked.

"Now you sound like Sarah," Georgie said. "Oh! I must dash home and tell them you're here! Good-bye for now!"

"Good-bye." Claire watched her jog up the stairs and disappear from view. Now that Georgie—and their mother—had discovered she was in Sidmouth, it would not be long until all her sisters knew. She wondered how the news would be received.

Claire turned and glimpsed a face behind the small window in the tradesmen's door. Mr. Hammond, witnessing the reunion. Before she reached the door, he had turned and walked away.

Sarah sat in the parlour with Emily and James that afternoon, relaxing and chatting. Saturdays were one of the nights they did not serve dinner to their guests, so the pace around the guest house was more leisurely. During the conversation, Emily often mentioned Viola, clearly missing her twin while she was away.

They had received one more letter from Viola, describing their travels and the beauties of Scotland. Soon she and Major Hutton would return, and the four sisters would be back together again. The only one missing—Claire.

They were all more or less accustomed to her absence by now, although Sarah still missed her keenly. It had been somewhat easier when she'd known where Claire resided and that she was, at least, safe and had a roof over her head. She wondered where Claire was at this very moment. Had she found a new place to live? Was she in any danger?

Oh, why oh why did she have to run off like that? The old lament returned, and with it a thread of resentment pulled at her, but Sarah did her best to ignore it. Surely Claire had come to regret that night even more than she did.

Almighty God, she silently prayed, *wherever she is, please keep her safe.*

Mamma and Georgiana were also gone at present. Mamma had all but dragged Georgiana shopping to have her measured for better-fitting dresses and half boots with soles not worn away from traipsing all over Sid Vale. Sarah expected them back soon.

Mamma returned first. Alone. She fell heavily into a chair beside Sarah's as though her legs would no longer support her. Sarah hoped her mother's health was not deteriorating after doing so well these last several months.

"Mamma?"

Her mother stared ahead, eyes vaguely focused. Emily and her husband looked at each other in concern.

Unnerved, Sarah touched her arm and asked, "Where's Georgie?"

"Hm?"

"You left with her, determined to make her stand still long enough for a fitting?"

"That's right. And I managed to do so. Barely."

"Then where is she?"

"She saw that stray dog she likes chasing some man and went after them. You know Georgiana."

"I do," Sarah replied, her gaze remaining on her mother's troubled face. Had something happened?

At that moment, Georgiana burst into the house and into the parlour, still wearing her cape and gloves.

"You'll never guess. She's here! Claire. In Sidmouth."

"What?" Sarah asked, stunned.

"Is she?" Emily asked eagerly. "Where?"

Mamma, Sarah noticed, remained silent and did not look surprised by Georgiana's announcement.

"At Broadbridge's. She's a partner in the boarding house with the new owner. She said she'll be too busy to call here but we are welcome to visit her there. He must make her work round the clock. At all events, she's here in Sidmouth. After all this time. Is that not exciting?"

Instead of answering, Sarah looked at her mother, whose expression had not changed.

"Mamma," Sarah asked gently, "did you know?"

She nodded. "I saw her with Georgiana."

"Did you?" Georgiana asked, brows high. "Why did you not say anything? Or come down and greet Claire yourself?"

Sarah exchanged a worried look with Emily, then said, "I am sure Mamma was stunned, as we all are. Give her time to grow accustomed to the idea."

"But it's good news, is it not?"

"Mamma?" Emily asked. "Shall we tell her?"

"Tell me what?" Georgie asked, blue eyes wide with innocence.

Mamma rose abruptly. "I have a sick headache and am going to bed. Let me think on it. Tomorrow will be soon enough."

9

[He] spent a good part of his later life trying to
prove Lord Palmerston was a Russian spy.
—Raymond Jones,
The British Diplomatic Service 1815–1914

During dinner that night, Mr. Hammond raised the topic of divine services the next day. "There are a few churches in town, but if you'd like to attend the parish church, you could go with Mira and me. Sonali prefers not to, but you would be most welcome to join us."

"I shall think about it."

Near the end of the meal, Mr. Hammond took Mira upstairs himself, as the girl was overtired and pleaded for one of his bedtime stories. When they had gone, Claire and Miss Patel finished their desserts in awkward silence.

As soon as she could, Claire excused herself, saying she would just peek into the dining room and make sure their guests had all they needed. Before she left the room, she retrieved the partially written letter from the desk drawer.

She met Mr. Filonov as he was coming out of the dining room.

"Good evening, sir. I found this letter in the morning room. Not in English. Might it be yours?"

She held it out to him.

He gave it a brief glance. "Not mine. And not Russian," he said, rolling the *r*. "But sank you for reminding me. My sister shall expect a letter soon."

He smiled, bowed, and went upstairs.

She turned back toward the morning room just as Miss Patel was exiting. The woman would probably accuse her of prying again, but Claire decided it was worth the risk to satisfy her curiosity.

Claire held out the letter. "Do you recognize this?"

Sonali glanced at it. "Did you take that from his desk? He won't like you invading his privacy."

Not his private desk. "I found it in the morning room. Is it yours?"

"Why would you ask me?"

"I thought perhaps you had started a letter."

"No." Sonali gave a dry huff. "Who would I write to?" She brushed past her and stalked away.

Later that night, after Claire felt certain all was in relatively good order and in readiness for the morrow, she retired to her room, planning to read for a time and then go to bed.

A soft tapping at her window startled her. Hand to her throat, she looked out through a crack between the shutters, glad she was still dressed.

Though dim outside, enough light shone from the windows above to illuminate the person standing there. Fran Stirling.

Claire hurried to the tradesmen's entrance and unlocked the door.

"Stirling! Sorry—Fran." It was traditional to call a lady's maid by her surname, and the habit lingered. Claire quickly added, "Or should I say Mrs. . . . ?"

"Farrant. But Fran is perfect. Actually, I prefer it. I'm still not fully accustomed to my new name."

"Do come in." Claire gestured toward her room, then stopped herself. "You know the way far better than I."

Fran entered the former housekeeper's room—*her* former room, looking around with interest.

"It's much as I left it, although less cluttered."

Claire grinned. "Give me time."

"Do you like it?" Fran asked.

"I do. I like the windows and the cheery yellow walls."

"I painted those myself."

"Please be seated. Shall I put the kettle on?"

"No need. I had some tea after our dinner."

"We did as well."

Fran nodded. "Thought so. I waited until I was fairly certain you'd be done for the night before I came over."

"Did you walk? Mr. Hammond mentioned you live a few miles away."

"Not quite that far. But no. Leslie—Mr. Farrant—brought me. He's happy to have a pint at the inn while he waits."

"Sounds a kind man."

"He is. He works hard and is excessively good to me."

"How long have you been married?"

"A few months now."

"I am happy for you."

"Thank you. And I am . . . concerned about you."

Claire laughed a little bleakly. "That makes two of us."

Fran looked from Claire to her surroundings. "How strange to see you in this room. Quite different from the bedchamber you and Sarah shared at Finderlay."

"True. But this room is larger, and the company more pleasant, than I had in Edinburgh."

One of the woman's dark brows quirked. "Is it? Do you find Mr. Hammond's company . . . pleasant?"

Heat rushed over Claire's face. "I did not mean him in particular. Your company, for example, is very pleasant. Oh! And I saw Georgiana today. She was pleased to see me, although surprised."

"I understand. Mr. Hammond stopped by our house earlier to tell me he'd taken on a partner who could benefit from my advice. When he mentioned your name, I was astonished."

"I can well believe it. And he was right, I need all the help I can get." Claire looked down at her clasped hands. "I hope you don't think it wrong of me to come here. To Sidmouth, I mean. I would not presume to show up at Sea View after . . . everything. But I could not stay away forever. I had to try. And after our great-aunt died, well, I had to move somewhere."

Fran nodded in sympathy, yet her eyes remained troubled.

Claire hung her head. "I know Mamma won't approve. In fact, I saw her today too. From a distance."

"She knows, then? I wondered."

Claire gestured toward the windows. "She stared down at me from the top of the stairs and then turned away without a word."

"That must have been painful." Fran took her hand. "But remember, this is difficult for her too. She told me your father made his wishes quite clear."

"I know." Claire blinked back tears and forced a smile. "Now, enough talk of woe. What is your advice for me?"

Fran pressed her hand and released it. "Next time. It's late, and you've already had a full day. I had to come and see you when I heard the news, but I shall return when you are well rested and so am I. There is a lot to learn. Tomorrow is Sunday. Would Monday suit?"

"Definitely. I shall look forward to it."

On Sunday morning, Claire washed and began dressing, doing as much as she could on her own, donning a clean shift, petticoat, and stays.

Leaving her stays unlaced, she slipped her black dress over it, all the while waiting for Mary to assist her.

No Mary.

She put on her stockings and shoes. Pinned up her hair.

Still no sign of the girl.

A look at the mantel clock told her she was running out of time.

She pulled on a spencer to cover her undone fastenings and hurried up the stairs, all the way to the attic. She was breathing a little hard by the time she reached Mary's room, although not as much as she might have been, thanks to her years living in Aunt Mercer's tall, terraced house.

Claire knocked softly, and upon hearing a grumbled "Aye?" she entered. Mary was still abed.

"I'm sorry, Mary. I thought you would be dressing for church." *And coming down to help me as usual*, she added to herself.

"What time is it?" Mary murmured.

Claire told her.

"I'm not goin' to kirk. Mrs. Ballard said I could sleep an extra hour on Sundays."

"I did not realize. Sorry to wake you. Em . . . could you lace me up while I'm here?"

Mary sat up sleepily. "'Course, miss."

Claire turned, and in a matter of a few minutes, she was fully dressed.

"Thank you." She slipped her spencer on again and began doing up its buttons, turning toward Mary as she did so. "Now, go back to sleep."

But Mary already had.

On her way downstairs, Claire walked through the first floor, planning to make sure the bath-room had enough towels.

As she did, she passed Mr. Filonov's room and, hearing someone speaking, paused outside the door, wondering who he might be talking to so early.

The voice was low, and Claire could not make out the words. She leaned closer and realized their guest was speaking in a foreign language—his mother tongue, no doubt. But to whom?

Perhaps he was talking to himself, an artist's eccentricity. Or perhaps he was dreaming and didn't realize he spoke aloud.

She was about to walk on when a second man spoke in the same language—at least the intonations seemed similar. This second voice sounded younger and quite familiar, despite the unfamiliar words.

Footsteps approached the door from within, the voices drawing nearer. Claire quickly hurried to the bath-room, looking over her shoulder just as the door opened.

Mr. Hammond emerged, said something to the older man that sounded like "Spah-see-bah," and stepped into the corridor. The artist responded with another foreign phrase and shut the door behind him.

Seeing Claire in the nearby doorway, Mr. Hammond paused and looked at her as though waiting for her to speak.

Should she say something? Or pretend she had not heard?

She made do with, "Mr. Filonov is Russian—is that what you told me?"

"From St. Petersburg, yes."

She slowly nodded, watching his face as he watched hers. He offered no further explanation, so she decided not to press him.

Claire had no idea why a boarding-house keeper in the south of England would speak Russian. She thought again of the coin and letter she had found. *And perhaps other languages as well.*

He consulted his pocket watch. "Almost time to set off for church. Have you seen Mira?"

"Here I am, Papa!" Mira came down the stairs, Miss Patel holding her hand. Today Mira was once again dressed as a traditional English miss: printed cotton gown, short spencer, and a bonnet tied under her chin. In gloved hands, she held a small prayer book.

Once she'd delivered the girl to her father, Sonali retreated back up to the attic.

Father and daughter started down the stairs to the front hall. He glanced back. "Will you be joining us, Miss Summers?"

"You two go ahead. I will . . . catch up."

She did not want to walk with them. To draw attention. To potentially cause rumors that might further injure her family. And if she went alone, she could always turn around if her courage failed her, which it very well might.

Claire followed at a distance, and upon reaching St. Giles and St. Nicholas, tarried until the Hammonds had disappeared through its doors. She had no intention of sitting with them. No intention of sitting with anyone she knew.

As she stood there on the churchyard path, Claire's heart pounded hard. Could she do this? Should she? There was little doubt her family would be there—especially as it appeared Mamma was no longer too weak to leave her bed. Claire half wished and half feared to see her again.

She had no desire to make a spectacle of herself or to upset anyone. Yet she needed this—needed God's presence and the comfort of corporate worship, even as she felt unworthy to join the faithful.

The door opened again as another straggler entered, and from inside, she heard the chords of an organ prelude. Palms perspiring in her gloves, Claire timidly entered behind two elderly women and slipped into a pew on the left, near the back.

Looking down the row, Claire realized she had most likely seated herself among the poor widows and spinsters. Yet who was she, after all?

She thought of the Scripture about the Canaanite woman to whom Jesus said, *Let the children first be filled. . . .* And the woman answered, *Yes, Lord; yet the dogs under the table eat of the children's crumbs.*

That's how she felt. Unworthy to sit at the Lord's table, but still longing for its crumbs.

Several older women in the same pew sent her curious, even disgruntled, glances. She had probably taken someone's usual place. Claire kept her eyes averted, trying to ignore their stares.

The parish clerk announced the psalm they were to sing, and the congregation soon raised their voices in worship.

As the people around her sang, Claire braved a look forward and to the right. As she did, her gaze fixed on a familiar profile. Her heart lurched. Sarah. She would recognize her close-in-age sister anywhere. The serious expression, upturned nose, and prominent, pursed lips.

And beside her? Mamma. Her shoulders and back straight, her head high. Mamma was obviously in better health than when Claire had left home, thank God.

Yet her gratitude was tempered by the realization that Mamma would not be pleased to see her at church. To see her anywhere.

Aunt Mercer's caustic words winnowed through her like an icy wind. "*Your father declared you were dead to him. He forbade your mother to even speak your name. You will never be welcomed back there. Never . . .*"

Claire's heart seemed to shrink to a cherry stone inside her. Her own father, considering her dead. Her own mother, unwilling to allow her back into their lives. Yet could she blame them, really?

No.

Claire became aware of someone watching her. Not the old tabbies sharing her pew, but Mr. Hammond, seated across the aisle and a couple rows ahead. His eyes met hers, then followed her gaze to the women near the front.

What did she see in his expression? Had he guessed?

She had not told him her family lived in Sidmouth, although he had witnessed her reunion with Georgiana. And she had not told him they offered competing lodging—a fact she had only recently discovered. Would he be angry when he learned of it?

She decided to ignore his scrutiny. Pretend to, at any rate. After all, he kept his past hidden as well.

The vicar rose to lead them in prayer, and Claire was relieved when Mr. Hammond shifted his focus to him.

Despite her best efforts, Claire's eyes drifted again to the front of the church during the service. She recognized Georgiana on Mamma's other side, and next to her another woman. When the young woman turned to her neighbor, Claire recognized Emily's pretty profile in a pert, upturned bonnet, leaning near the gentleman beside her in some whispered confidence. She recalled the brief letter Campbell had given her after her aunt's death—the few cheerful lines from Emily inviting Claire to her wedding.

This dark-haired man with a handsome profile must be her new husband. She wondered how Sarah felt about one of their younger sisters marrying before her. Claire was not quite certain how she felt about it herself. Then again, everyone had long assumed beautiful Emily would marry young, and most likely to Charles Parker. That last prediction, it seemed, had proved wrong.

She saw no sign of Viola, no woman with her face hidden behind a veil. She supposed Viola still avoided public outings.

Claire looked toward the vicar as he began the sermon and did her best to concentrate.

Later, as the benediction ended, Emily's husband whispered something in her ear. Emily giggled in reply, and Georgiana turned to see what was so funny. When Georgiana looked over her shoulder, her gaze landed on Claire across the nave, and her eyes grew large and bright with excitement. She grinned and waved.

In the next instant, Sarah pulled her hand down and leaned near Georgie, apparently whispering urgent warnings. Then Sarah turned their youngest sister almost forcibly toward the front. Georgiana frowned at Sarah, then with a glance at Mamma, seemed to reluctantly acquiesce.

Claire rose abruptly. Murmuring apologies to the women whose knees she pushed past, she exited the pew.

Others turned to look. Claire stared straight ahead, feigning nonchalance as she walked toward the porch. But as soon as she slipped out the church doors, she ran, fleeing through the churchyard.

What had she been thinking to attend?

10

> She has no money, no connections, nothing
> that can tempt him . . . she is lost forever.
> —Jane Austen, *Pride and Prejudice*

By unspoken agreement, the family went into the parlour after church and shut the doors, something they rarely did, as guests sometimes used the informal sitting room as well.

Mr. Gwilt knocked, poked his head inside, and asked, "Shall I bring tea, or . . . ?" Looking uncertainly from face to troubled face, he broke off and closed the door behind himself without another word.

Emily's husband looked uncertain as well. He rose and said, "I think I shall let you ladies talk in private, but if there's anything I can do to help, please let me know. May I bring anyone anything?"

The women all shook their heads.

So James alone went to partake of the cold collation left on the sideboard for family and guests to eat at their leisure before or after church. Sarah's stomach churned at the thought of food, and apparently none of the rest of them had any appetite either. Not even Georgiana, most surprising of all.

"What is going on?" her youngest sister demanded. "Claire was there. Our Claire. And you all sat there like lichens on gravestones. Looked as grim as gravediggers too. Sarah shushing me. Mamma staring straight ahead, pretending not to notice." She turned to Emily and accused, "Even you just sat there."

Emily raised her hands in defense. "I did not know what else to do. We were in church, after all. Hardly the place to shout someone's name. Or to run to her, although I was very much tempted."

"You've changed," Georgie observed. "Is that what marrying does to a woman? I liked the old speak-first-think-later Emily better."

"I wanted to spare Mamma's feelings. I did not wish to cause a scene, to embarrass her or the rest of us."

Mamma gazed across the room. "I can't believe she came to church, as bold as brass. What did she think would happen?"

"Hardly bold," Sarah defended. "She sat in the back and left before the service ended."

Emily said, "I planned to speak to her afterward. I had no idea she would run off like that."

"Why did she?" Georgiana asked.

"Perhaps she realized she'd made a mistake in coming."

"Why should it be a mistake?" Georgie stood and propped her hands on her waist. "What are you not telling me?"

Becoming aware of all their gazes upon her and the expectant silence, Mamma came back to herself and looked around at her three daughters. "Will you tell her, Sarah? I can hardly bear thinking about it, let alone describe it to my youngest child. And no need to go into gratuitous detail, if you please."

Gratuitous detail? Sarah knew few details, let alone gratuitous ones. She did not want to be the bearer of such news.

Especially to sweet, trusting Georgiana. Had no desire to see the carefree innocence snuffed from her eyes. But the duty fell to her, and the wave of guilt that always accompanied those memories swamped her anew. For she alone had known what Claire intended to do and had not stopped her or raised the alarm.

Sarah licked lips that were suddenly dry and began. "You were told Claire went to Scotland to serve as companion to Papa's aunt. That was not strictly true."

"Then where has she been these last two years?"

"She did live with Great-Aunt Mercer, but that was not why she left Finderlay." Sarah raised a palm to forestall the flood of questions she saw building on Georgiana's face.

"Let me start at the beginning. I don't know if you will remember, but the Parkers hosted a house party of nearly a fortnight's duration in honor of a visiting friend. You were too young to be invited, I was in mourning, and Viola chose not to attend. Only Emily and Claire went, as the party was mostly for young people, and Mamma's health was not good at the time.

"During the party, Claire formed an attachment with a young man, the guest of honor. On the last night of the party, he convinced her to run away with him. She came home at, I don't know, half past eleven. I was already in bed. I woke up as she was changing into traveling clothes and packing. I asked what she was doing, and she confessed all. She was giddy with excitement and not thinking straight. I tried to talk her out of such a rash course, to make her see reason. I did not understand why the pair needed to elope. Claire was of age. Why such a hurry that they could not wait three weeks for the banns to be read and then marry in church?

"At all events, she seemed to be floating above the ground, inhabiting some distant sphere, and I could not pull her back to earth. I warned her she would break our parents' hearts, but she said they would forgive all once she married Lord Bertram."

Mamma groaned.

Sarah had done her best not to mention the abhorred name, but it had finally slipped out.

She went on, "Claire begged me not to tell anyone until they were safely away. She was six and twenty at the time and convinced it was her last chance to marry."

Georgie grimaced. "I don't think I like where this is going. . . ."

"I don't blame you. I don't know all the details, but apparently the man changed his mind. When Papa learned that Claire was gone and confirmed with Charles Parker that his guest had left in the night, Papa was, as you can imagine, justifiably furious. He took off in our coach-and-four, hoping to overtake them, but he failed. He assumed they had chosen the fastest route to Gretna Green and would return the same way, but he did not find them. Of course, Papa did not know that the man had abandoned Claire somewhere and gone back another way, no doubt to avoid just such a confrontation.

"When Papa returned to Finderlay, he was exhausted and chilled through. He took ill and, as you know, suffered his first apoplexy soon after. From Charles Parker, he learned that Bertram had briefly returned to May Park for the rest of his belongings and that he had not married Claire after all."

"But why?"

Emily spoke up. "When Charles was here after Christmas, I asked him about it. He told me about Bertram returning to the house. It seems he cried off when he learned Claire's dowry was far smaller than he'd believed. Charles tried to tell him it was his duty as a gentleman to marry her anyway to spare her reputation. Still, he would not be moved."

"The snake!" Georgie exclaimed, throwing up her hands. "Why am I the last to learn of this? I am not a child!"

"If it makes you feel any better," Emily said, "Viola and I only learned of it last summer."

"Well, you should have told me too." She sank back into her chair. "Go on, Sarah, please."

"Papa wanted to pursue Lord Bertram and force him to marry her. Unfortunately his ill health prevented him from doing much more than writing a few letters. Letters that went unanswered."

"Then how did Claire end up at Aunt Mercer's?"

"I don't know, exactly. Apparently she was too ashamed to come home unwed. After a few days away, in the company of a man not her husband, her reputation was ruined, whatever may or may not have happened between them. I would guess she used what money she had to travel on to Edinburgh, hoping our relative there would take her in."

Mamma sighed. "We learned of her whereabouts in a letter from Aunt Mercer saying she had shown up on her doorstep asking for shelter, offering to serve as her companion in exchange for room and board. Your father wrote back and told her that if she was willing, that was up to her, but as far as he was concerned his eldest daughter was dead to him and would not be welcomed back in his house."

"How awful," Georgie murmured.

"Yes, it was."

"I mean, how awful for Claire."

Sarah said quietly, "It was awful for all of us, Georgie."

"But she is the only one who had her life upended by it."

"How can you say that?" Mamma shot to her feet, face stricken. "Your father was so upset by it that he had not one but two apoplexies. The first left him bedridden and stole his speech. The second took his life. I lost my husband, and you, your father. And with him dead, we all lost our home and financial security. Don't try to tell me Claire is the only one who suffered consequences from her actions. We all suffered."

A heated silence followed.

After a time, Emily said gently, "Yes, there were consequences. I lost Charles, for example. For a long time I thought I should break my heart over it. Then I learned he was not the man for me. James is. Something good came from it too."

"And I lost my big sister," Georgie said. "For two years. Now she is here. Why can we not forget the past and go on? She is family."

"You may forget the past all you like," Mamma said. "I do not have that luxury. Before he lost the power of speech, your father extracted a promise from me not to harbor her or even speak her name. Sarah was in the room at the time. She can attest to it."

Sarah nodded grimly, the dreadful memory revisiting her. "If it helps at all, Papa was concerned about the rest of us. He wanted to protect us from disgrace as much as possible."

Sarah did not repeat all he had said. But she remembered.

"Her reputation is ruined beyond repair. Painful or not, she must now be dead to us. The position of eldest daughter falls to you, Sarah. Eugenia, you must promise me not to aid her in any way, nor correspond with her. Do I make myself clear? We have four other daughters to think of. . . ."

Soon after that, he had his first apoplexy and was less able to communicate, which frustrated him to no end. He became bitter and snappish. Two months later he suffered a second attack and died.

Georgiana seemed to absorb the details slowly and did not look satisfied.

"Mamma, she is still your daughter. Don't you care what happens to her?"

"Of course I care! If your father thought a few words could banish one of my children from my heart, then he had no idea what a mother's heart is. It is called maternal instinct for a reason! Even so, I won't pretend I did not share his disappointment over what she had done—and his anger at that man. That goes without saying. I was livid with that scoundrel, and disappointed in my daughter, whom I'd raised to protect her virtue and reputation. I was also disappointed in Charles Parker for inviting the man into our neighborhood. Disappointed with your father for being unable to do anything about it . . ."

"And disappointed with me, for not preventing it?" Sarah asked softly.

Mamma looked at her. "I suppose I was. I know the bonds between sisters are tenacious, but that was taking loyalty too far. I was also disappointed in myself. So wrapped up in my own ailments that I was not even aware of the romance building between one of my daughters and a veritable stranger. I did not rouse myself to join the party. Did not urge your father to attend.

"And how I worried when we learned that jackanapes had returned without her and we did not know where she was. Had she any money? Was she in mortal danger? As much as I disliked your father's aunt, I was relieved when she wrote to tell us Claire was there with her. Safe.

"No one told me parenting would be so difficult. When you girls were little, I foolishly thought I would train and nurture you for, oh, twenty years or so, and then you would marry and live contentedly on your own and my time for parenting would be over. Perhaps for some women that is so but not for me. Don't mistake me. I don't resent it. I love you and am blessed to be your mother. I hope you know that."

"Do you still love Claire?" Georgie asked.

Mamma's eyes filled with tears. Voice hoarse, she said, "Of course I do."

Sarah felt tears prick her own eyes in response.

After a few moments of silence, Emily said, "Forgive me, Mamma, but I long to speak to Claire. Heavens! She has not even met my husband yet, nor Viola's, although that will have to wait until she and the major return. Perhaps it is better we don't overwhelm her with too many new people at once."

"I want to go too," Georgie said, rising eagerly.

"You promised to go sea-bathing with me today," Mamma said, an oddly plaintive note in her voice.

"Oh. That's right." Georgie sat back down. "At least I've already talked to her once. Do be sure to tell her I send my love and hope to see her again soon."

Emily nodded. "Sarah, will you come?"

With an uneasy glance at Mamma, Sarah said, "Perhaps you and James would rather go alone?"

"Actually, I wish you would come. I feel strangely nervous."

"So do I," Sarah admitted, then paused to consider. She had not verbally agreed to her father's edict but neither had she refused. Was a promise tacitly understood? Sarah was not a wife who had vowed to obey her husband. She was a daughter, taught to obey and honor her parents, yet she was a sister too. And as Mamma had said, sisterly bonds were tenacious.

She looked to her mother, and for a long moment their gazes held. Searched. Then Mamma gave the slightest of nods.

Sarah rose. "I will go with you."

11

> The tariff at a respectable Boarding-House appears to bear the following average: bed and breakfast 3s.; dinner (chop or steak) 2s.; tea without chop 1s.
>
> —*Cruchley's London: A Handbook for Strangers*

Sarah, Emily, and James put on their outdoor things and walked along the esplanade toward the eastern town. It was a warm, sunny afternoon. On the beach, many ladies waited to use the bathing machines, a few young men flew kites, and children splashed and waded while their parents or nurses looked on. The scene reminded Sarah of her and her sisters when they'd first come to Sidmouth, delighted with the seaside. Sarah and Claire, hand in hand, wading in the surf, squealing every time the cold water doused their ankles . . .

At the memory, Sarah's hand closed of its own accord, as if trying to capture Claire's hand once again.

When they reached Broadbridge's, Emily looked to Sarah to knock, and when Sarah hesitated as well, James stepped forward to do so.

Only a few seconds passed before a well-dressed gentleman opened the door. "Excellent timing. I was just passing through the hall. What can I do for you?"

James replied, "Actually, we came to see Miss Summers."

"Ah." Curiosity glinted in his gaze as he looked from person to person. "Of course. Come in. I will see if she is at her leisure." His lips tilted wryly.

Assuming this was the new owner, he might very well resent a social call. He led them upstairs and into the same parlour where Sarah used to take tea with Fran.

"May I tell her who is calling?" Again that crooked grin, as if amused by something.

Emily found her voice. "Mr. and Mrs. Thomson, and Miss Summers."

"Another Summers. I shan't ask if you are related, for it is obvious you are."

James clarified, "Her sisters and brother-in-law."

"Ah. Wait here." He turned and quit the room, closing the parlour door partway behind himself.

A moment later, Sarah heard him call, "Miss Summers, are you at home to callers? I am playing butler now, apparently."

"Who is it?"

"Two sisters and a brother-in-law. I've put them in the parlour."

"Oh. Thank you."

Sarah's pulse pounded as they all turned expectantly toward the door. A moment later, Claire pushed it open and stepped inside. She hovered just over the threshold, hands clasped and expression timid.

"Claire!" Emily hurried forward and threw her arms around her. "You don't know how I've missed you. And how much you've missed! Did you receive my letters? I hope it does not come as a surprise—or at least not an unhappy one—to learn your younger sister is married." She turned to her tall, dark-haired husband. "Please meet James Thomson, my new husband. James, my oldest sister, Claire."

He bowed. "A sincere pleasure. Emily speaks of you often and with warmest affection."

Claire gave an awkward curtsy. "Mr. Thomson. The pleasure is mine." She turned back to Emily. "And yes, I received the invitation to your wedding but only after the date had passed. It was . . . misdirected at first. We always knew you would marry young—as pretty and witty as you are. Did we not, Sarah?"

Thoughts elsewhere, Sarah did not immediately realize Claire had addressed her. She hesitated, then managed a flat, "Indeed."

Sarah did not rush forward with an effusive embrace as Emily had done. Instead she hung back.

Claire darted a nervous glance at her before saying to Emily and her groom, "I am very happy for you both."

Emily said, "Viola was actually the first to marry. Last summer."

Claire's eyes widened. "Was she indeed?"

"Yes. She wrote to let you know she and her husband hoped to visit you in Edinburgh, but they missed you, apparently."

Claire glanced again at Sarah before replying, "I am sorry. I did not receive her letter."

"That's all right. She and the major will return soon, and you shall meet him then."

Claire nodded. She looked ill at ease, which was understandable. And her lightly freckled skin seemed a little pale, without the glow of happiness she'd worn when last Sarah saw her, on the cusp of eloping. Otherwise Claire looked much the same. Still so pretty, with her delicate features and reddish-brown hair.

That rare thread of resentment pulled at her once more, and Sarah decided life was unfair. She felt she had aged more than Claire in the last two years, through the strain of her departure, their father's illness and death, the loss of Finderlay, the move to Sidmouth, and working hard to establish the guest house. And all this not long after the death of her own betrothed.

Sarah stood there, feeling oddly cold. Distant. As if a thin layer of frost had enveloped her heart like an ice-glazed branch.

She became aware of the others watching her.

"Sarah," Claire said tentatively. She took a step forward. When Sarah remained where she was, she drew no closer. "I am glad to see you. And glad for this chance to tell you how sorry I am for the way I left, for asking you not to say anything until I had gone. It was wrong of me to put you in that situation. And I hope, one day, you might forgive me."

In Claire's blue eyes, so like her own, she saw sincerity and regret, magnified by a sheen of tears. A cascade of memories flowed through Sarah's mind, of all their private talks and long walks, sharing confidences and laughter and grief, Claire holding her tight when they'd learned of Peter's death. . . .

Sarah's heart twisted, cracking her resentment and icy reserve.

She stepped forward to meet Claire, enclosing her in her arms. She whispered near her ear, "I forgive you now."

Footsteps sounded behind them, and the two parted to look toward the door. The man who had greeted them reappeared on the threshold and drew up short at the sight of the teary-eyed embrace.

"Forgive the intrusion. I did not realize this was a sad occasion."

Claire gave him a watery smile. "It is not. It is a happy one. Allow me to introduce my family. Well, some of them. My sister Sarah. My sister Emily. And her husband, Mr. Thomson."

"James," Mr. Thomson said, holding out his hand.

The man shook it. "William Hammond."

Claire explained, "Mr. Hammond owns Broadbridge's now and has taken me on as a partner in the business."

Emily said, "We also offer rooms at our home near Fort Field. I hope ours can be a friendly competition."

His eyebrows rose in obvious surprise. "Indeed? Your sister did not mention it."

Seeing Claire's discomfort, Sarah added, "It is a relatively recent development. Needs must and all that."

"Ah. I see."

Meanwhile James continued to study the man, head tilted to one side, expression puzzled. "William Hammond . . ." he repeated thoughtfully. "Your name is familiar to me for some reason."

Mr. Hammond shrugged. "A common enough name, I should think."

"Yes, but I heard it not long ago in connection with Sidmouth." His eyes narrowed in concentration. "You moved here recently, I believe."

"That's right."

"And you moved here from . . . ?"

"I have lived several places. From Aylesbury, originally." He shifted, perhaps uncomfortable with the attention, and shifted the topic as well. "And you, Mr. Thomson. Resided in Sidmouth long?"

"Not long. I came here with the Duke of Kent over the winter and stayed on after his death, having fallen in love with this lovely young lady." He nodded toward Emily.

Mr. Hammond asked, "In the lodging business as well?"

James shook his head. "Only in that it's a family concern. I served as private secretary to the duke and now perform a similar function for Sir Thomas Acland, recently reelected MP for Devon."

"Sir Thomas. Ah. Well . . ." Mr. Hammond drew himself up. "Pray excuse me." He gave a general bow, then turned to Claire. "I shall be in the morning room when you have a minute. No rush." He turned away, seeming suddenly eager to depart. Sarah wondered why.

James watched him go, brow furrowed. "I believe it was Sir Thomas who mentioned a William Hammond to me. I wish I could remember why. Never mind, it will come to me."

Claire said, "I'm afraid I don't know much about him, although I do know he is new to the lodging business, as am I. An unlikely pair, are we not?"

Emily's eyes shone with interest at Claire's words. She probably hoped to find in them a hint of romance—her favorite genre.

"Perhaps Fran might advise you," Sarah said.

"Yes! She plans to begin tomorrow, and I will gladly accept all the advice she can give me. Now, may I offer you tea?"

"No, thank you," Sarah said. "We shan't keep you. We know you are busy settling into your new situation."

Emily added, "But we wanted to assure you of our love and support." She gave Claire another hug. "We are very glad you came to Sidmouth, and hopefully Mamma will come around in time."

Claire glanced down at her clasped hands, clearly pained by Mamma's absence.

"Oh, and before we forget," Emily said, "Georgiana wanted us to pass along her greetings and love. She plans to visit you again soon."

That brought a smile to Claire's pretty face. "I shall look forward to it. You are all welcome at any time."

After seeing her sisters and Mr. Thomson out, Claire stood for a long moment, resting her forehead against the door.

How nervous she had been when Mr. Hammond had told her who had come to call. Having read one of Emily's letters, she was fairly confident that sister would be pleased to see her. She'd been far less certain of Sarah's reception. Her heart had ached to see the initial reticence, perhaps even anger, in Sarah's expression. Claire could not blame her, yet she'd been deeply relieved when Sarah had forgiven her.

And how strangely wonderful to meet Emily's husband and to learn that formerly reclusive Viola had married as well. She had missed so much.

Claire was of course disappointed by Emily's confirmation that Mamma had not "come around," but she thanked God her sisters had.

She took a deep breath and straightened, remembering Mr. Hammond wanted to see her. Was he affronted to learn her family ran a guest house in Sidmouth? She would soon find out. Squaring her shoulders, Claire walked into the morning room as requested.

Mr. Hammond looked up from the desk as she entered. "There you are. Good visit?"

"Yes, thank you."

"Excellent."

"I . . . hope you don't mind . . . about my family's guest house. I only learned of it recently."

"You have been out of touch?"

"Yes."

"And you clearly came here for more than a partnership in a boarding house."

"I came for both. I hope that is not a problem."

He looked upward, as if in serious consideration, yet that humorous quirk tipped his lips again. "I am never sure what to think about the old 'two birds, one stone' adage. Well and good for the stone, far less so for the birds." He returned his gaze to her. "At all events, that's not why I asked you to meet me. I was thinking you might plan next week's menu for Mrs. Ballard. She asked me once but did not appreciate my suggestions of curries and *şiş kebap*."

"What is shish kebab?"

"Spiced meat roasted on skewers. Delicious."

"Is that Indian food?"

"Turkish. Although eaten in India as well, I understand."

She wondered how he knew. She supposed he'd spent time in India and that was how he'd met Mira's mother. Remembering Sonali's warning about invading Mr. Hammond's privacy, she did not ask.

"I suppose I can understand Mrs. Ballard's reticence to serve that here," Claire said. "Very well. I shall attempt next week's menu."

After he left, Claire sat at the desk, her mind wheeling back over the many lavish, delicious dinners they had enjoyed at Finderlay over the years. Closing her eyes, she could still smell the savory aromas and see gleaming dishes of larded sweet breads, pigeon pie, salmon with fennel sauce, haunch of veal roasted to a turn, haricot of mutton, fresh salads, almond cheesecakes, sweetmeats, and more. Her stomach rumbled at the thought.

With these memories in mind, she retrieved pen, ink, and paper and began writing down possible menus. While she was at it, she also wrote a brief letter to Mr. Dumfries, as he'd requested, letting him know where she was living.

On Monday morning after breakfast, she showed the menus to Mrs. Ballard.

The cook sat at the worktable and reviewed them in silence for several minutes, frown lines deepening as she read.

"My goodness, miss. This is exceedingly fine fare for a boarding house. Veal? Duck? Pigeon? I would need a far greater budget, and we'd have to double the daily rates—that's for certain. Has Mr. Hammond agreed to this?"

Claire's stomach churned and bile soured her throat. "These

are only ideas. Never mind. I shall give it more thought and talk it over with Mrs. Farrant. Let's repeat last week's menu for now, shall we?"

"Yes, miss. Very good."

Later that day, Claire sat with Fran Farrant in the housekeeper's room over cups of tea. She gave her the proposed menu and explained Mrs. Ballard's reaction to it.

Fran reviewed it, then looked up with a soft chuckle. "Duck?"

Claire held her head in her hands. She was not off to a promising start.

Fran patted her slumped shoulders. "There, there, my dear. How were you to know? I assure you, your mother and sisters made similar mistakes when they first opened Sea View to guests. Never mind. I shall help. While it's no Finderlay, Broadbridge's can still provide filling, wholesome meals. Not with veal, duck, and pigeon, but with boiled beef, chicken, a great deal of local fish, and mounds of turnips and potatoes, with the occasional green vegetable or fruit. Sound reasonable?"

Claire straightened and nodded.

Fran turned the paper over and slid it toward Claire with an encouraging smile. "Then let's begin."

That evening, Claire opened the door to a couple in search of accommodation—her first guests to register and settle in on her own.

The young man bowed and said, "Mr. and Mrs. Bracegirdle."

The woman on his arm giggled, whether from the surname itself or the newness of hearing herself thus introduced, Claire did not know.

She certainly hoped the young pair were married in actual fact and not simply pretending to be.

"Pray forgive me," Mrs. Bracegirdle said. "I still can't believe that's my name now we're married. How venerable I do sound!" She leaned her cheek against her husband's shoulder, still holding on to his arm as though it were a lifeline.

"You are very welcome," Claire said. "Did you write to let us know you were coming?"

"No." The young lady sucked in a gasp. "Were we supposed to?"

"It's not a problem," Claire hurried to assure them. "We have rooms available."

"Oh, good." The young man blew out a breath between puffed cheeks.

"If you would follow me into the office here, so I can get your details?" Claire led them into the morning room, stepped behind the desk, and opened the registration book.

He said, "We saw the place mentioned in *The Sidmouth Guide*, and thought we might stay three weeks or so, until I ship out again." He shifted awkwardly. "That is, if we can afford it. I'm afraid we don't have a great deal of money. I have my savings, and dear ol' Gran gave us some for our wedding. I hope it's enough."

Claire's heart softened toward the earnest young man. "We have a pleasant room on the top floor that goes for a reduced rate. So if you don't mind an extra flight of stairs . . . ?"

"Not a bit. We're both fit as fiddles." He put his arm around his wife's slender shoulders and pulled her close. "Are we not, my love?"

"We are indeed." The two gazed at each other with such ardent affection that it was almost painful to witness. Claire owned to a kernel of longing and perhaps even jealousy at this display of obvious devotion.

She swallowed it down. "Excellent. The bed-and-breakfast rate for that room is two shillings, if that suits. Dinner is extra, I'm afraid, but Mrs. Ballard makes a generous breakfast. It will easily keep you most of the day."

Apparently doing some quick calculations in his mind, the man brightened. "That will suit us nicely, with a bob or two to spare. Thank you, missus."

Claire retrieved a key from the drawer. "Then allow me to show you to your room."

The next morning, not long after they had breakfasted, the laundress's boy arrived at the basement door with a load of clean laundry for Mr. Hammond. Claire thanked the lad, gave him a coin for his trouble, and carried the clean shirts upstairs.

She did not find Mr. Hammond in the morning room, nor in any of the other public rooms, so she braved the passage to his apartment above the old stable block. Finding the outer door open, and hearing voices within, Claire stepped through and onto a small landing that led to two inner doors—one closed, one open. She tentatively followed the voices to the open doorway.

Inside, she saw Mr. Hammond seated at a desk, Mira on his lap. Claire tried not to be obvious as she surveyed his private study but could not help noticing books with foreign titles on the shelves, maps on the walls, and a painting of a white building with golden domes.

Spread out on the middle of the desk were several small piles of coins.

Mira held out her palm, upon which sat three shiny silver coins. "What's these called?"

"What are those called," he gently corrected. "These two are *piastres* and that one is a *beshlik*."

She set them onto a pile of other silver coins, then held up a gold coin. "And this yellow one?"

"That is gold, my little pumpkin seed. A *foondook*." He picked up another. "And this a *half-myseer*, coined in Egypt and rather rare."

"Pretty," the girl murmured.

Claire hesitated in the doorway, then feigned a smile she did not feel. "Goodness! Look at all those coins. Where did they come from?"

He looked up with a frown, then answered somewhat vaguely, "Oh, I have been collecting them for years."

She said, "Reminds me of the strange coin I found in the hall. The one I put in the desk downstairs?"

"Ah. I forgot you mentioned that. Wondered how it got there."

To his daughter, he said, "These will all be yours one day. But for now, let's put them away for safekeeping." He rose, set Mira on the chair, and moved to the door, effectively blocking Claire's view.

Hand on the latch as if preparing to close it, he said, "Was there something you needed?"

"Only to deliver your laundry, which just arrived."

"Thank you." He accepted the pile. "In future, please leave it for me belowstairs. I shall carry it up myself."

"Very well." Claire walked away, feeling unaccountably chastised by the mild reproof.

12

John Taylor, a local cobbler, made [Queen] Victoria's first pair of shoes and received a Royal Warrant.

—Nigel Hyman, *Sidmouth's Royal Connections*

That afternoon, Miss Patel and Mira returned from some outing, the woman all but dragging the child behind herself in her hurry to enter the house.

With eyes like hard jet beads and her mouth cinched tight, the woman appeared, if possible, even angrier than usual.

"What is it?" Claire asked. "Has something happened?"

Nostrils flaring, Miss Patel replied, "That Mr. Taylor would not make shoes for Mira."

Confusion puckered Claire's brow. "What? Why?"

"Why do you think?" Miss Patel snapped.

"Do you mean because you are not English? But that . . . is . . ." Claire faltered as unspoken words coursed through her mind in a torrent: *Unfair. Unjust. Undeserved.*

Words hurled at her by Aunt Mercer came back to her, striking her like sharp pebbles: *Undeserving girl. Foolish. Fallen. Ruined.* Claire had done something to deserve such contempt. Mira, however, was innocent.

Miss Patel lifted her chin. "When Mr. Hammond returns, he shall have to take her himself."

Indignant, Claire said, "No. I shall take her. Now." Claire thrust out her hand, and after a moment of wide-eyed surprise, Mira slipped her small brown hand into hers.

"He should not have treated either of you so poorly. Where is this shop?"

Sonali told her.

Claire barely stopped long enough to plop a bonnet onto her head before marching out the door, down the steps, and up the street, moderating her agitated pace for the little girl's sake. As they walked, Claire was vaguely aware of perplexed looks from passersby shifting from her to the child and back again, but she ignored them.

As they neared, Mira pointed to the cast-iron, shoe-shaped sign ahead. "There it is."

Claire pushed open the shop door with more force than was strictly necessary. Mira, perhaps startled by this, or not keen to face the cobbler again, hid behind her skirts.

The man on his wooden stool, hammering away at a sole of a boot, paused in his work and turned. He took in Claire's face, straight posture, and fine, if no longer fashionable, attire. "Yes, madam, how may I assist you?"

"I require a new pair of shoes."

"Of course. Happily. What had you in mind? Half boots, heeled shoes, slippers?"

Claire rested a hand on Mira's shoulder, drawing her forward. "A pair of leather shoes for Miss Hammond here."

The man's gaze slid down to the child and his obsequious smile faded. "You again. As I told her mother, or servant, or whatever she was, I am a very busy man with certain standards. I don't make shoes for just anybody." He puffed out his chest. "If you are not aware, I had the privilege of making

Princess Alexandrina Victoria's first pair of shoes, when the Duke and Duchess of Kent resided here over the winter."

"How nice for you, Mr. Taylor. Yet you were perfectly willing to make a pair for me a moment ago, and I am not noble in the least."

"You are English."

"What has that to say to anything?"

The man scowled. "Who are you, anyway? To this girl, I mean?"

Who was she, indeed? "I am a . . . business associate of her father, Mr. William Hammond. He recently bought Broadbridge's Boarding House. Perhaps you have not yet met him."

"Her father, you say?"

"Yes. A gentleman who has decided to settle here in Sidmouth with his daughter. A fine welcome this is."

"A nabob, is he?" The cobbler's lip curled. "Come home from India with a fortune and a *kutcha-butcha*?"

Claire did not know what the term meant, but it certainly sounded derogatory. "That is none of your concern. All that matters is that his daughter needs a new pair of shoes."

Changing tack, Claire said, "Apparently we shall have to go to a different shop where everyone is respectfully and promptly served. I believe there are several shoe and boot makers in the area. And when we find such an establishment, we shall recommend it to all our family, friends, and numerous guests. Come, Mira." She took the girl's hand, prepared to depart.

As she turned, she saw the man's eyes widen and his expression transform. He rose and raised both hands in supplication. "Now, madam. Please. I do beg your pardon. I did not fully understand the situation. I will make this young . . . lady . . . a fine pair of shoes. Far better than you could get elsewhere."

Claire hesitated, not wishing to appear too eager. Then she said coolly, "Very well."

In short order, measurements had been taken and materials and color decided upon.

When they left the cobbler's, Claire blew out a relieved breath. Back on the street, she spied a confectioner's shop. "How about something sweet? I think we both deserve a treat after that ordeal, don't you?"

"Yes, please!"

In the shop, Mira chose a small bag of lemon drops. Thankfully the shop clerk had no qualms about serving them. Claire, having consulted the meager coins in her reticule, decided against something for herself after all. Mira offered one of hers, and Claire popped the tangy morsel into her mouth. "Thank you, my dear. Generous of you to share."

Exiting the confectioner's, Mira tripped, and before Claire could catch her, the girl lost hold of her bag and several lemon drops went rolling onto the walkway.

In a flash, a man came to their aid. He lowered himself to his haunches and picked up the bag. "What a pity. Ah, but good news. Still two left." He handed it to Mira.

Claire recognized him then—the man from the stagecoach. In his mid to late thirties, the striking man had coffee-brown skin, black hair, and very dark eyes.

As he looked at the child, his grin faded into a quizzical look, and he tipped back his beaver hat to better study her face. "I say. I have not seen you before. And I would have noticed." He smiled at the girl, his teeth startlingly white against his deep brown skin. "Would it be terribly presumptuous to ask your name?"

Suddenly shy, the girl clutched Claire's hand and crowded close to her side, even as her eyes studied the stranger with interest.

"Mira," she said softly.

"And I am Armaan. A pleasure to meet you, Miss Mira.

You remind me of someone I once knew. Someone I miss very much indeed."

He rose, and Claire noticed again how tall and handsome he was. His gaze slid past Claire, then returned for a longer look. "Ah. This lady I have seen before. We traveled on the same coach."

"That's right. A pleasure to see you again."

"Likewise. Are you enjoying Sidmouth?"

"For the most part, yes. And you?"

"Much the same. I enjoyed visiting London, but Sidmouth is home . . . at least for now."

Behind them, an aproned shopkeeper cleared his throat, and Armaan stepped aside.

"Well. I shall bid you both good day."

He tugged his hat brim and walked on, and Claire was not quite sure if she was relieved or disappointed that he had not asked her name as well.

On their return to Broadbridge's, Claire almost collided with a woman in the marketplace. "Pardon me," she said. Then, seeing who it was, she drew back in surprise.

"M-Mamma," Claire faltered, a catch in her voice.

Mamma appeared to be startled as well. "I . . . did not expect to see you. I thought you would be busy at Broadbridge's."

"Just out on an errand." She glanced down at the little girl holding her hand. "This is Mira, Mr. Hammond's daughter."

"Mr. Hammond is your . . . ?"

"Business partner. He bought the boarding house from Fran and needed help managing the place."

"I see."

Unsure what to say, Claire stammered, "Are you . . . in good health? You look remarkably well, I must say."

"I have improved, thankfully. The sea air, long walks, and sea-bathing have done me good."

"I am glad."

An awkward silence followed. Mamma fidgeted with her reticule, then said, "I am . . . relieved you are also well. However, your father would not be pleased you are here."

At the words, Claire's chin began to tremble. "I remained in Scotland as long as Aunt Mercer lived, but then I had to leave. I suppose I could have gone elsewhere, but I missed you all terribly. I came here hoping to restore our relationship."

Mamma huffed and pushed a loose hair from her face. "I cannot go against his wishes." Anger sparked in her eyes. "I may have failed to protect you, but I have other daughters to think of now. I'm sorry. Excuse me."

Her mother walked away, weaving rather unsteadily through the crowd of shoppers.

Mira tugged her hand. As Claire looked down, a tear fell onto the cheek of the motherless girl.

After dinner that evening, Miss Patel took Mira upstairs for a bath. When they'd gone, Mr. Hammond turned to Claire, looking quite serious, even somber.

"Sonali told me what happened today—the cobbler refusing to make shoes for Mira. Thank you for speaking up for her. It's maddening you had to, but I appreciate your help."

"I felt I had to. I can't remember the last time I was so angry."

"I understand. Naturally it angers me too, that my child should be treated unfairly. Yet this is not the first time, and it shan't be the last, unfortunately."

"How is Mira, do you think?"

"She seems untroubled, thankfully. I talked to her about it and tried to encourage her. I believe people here will eventually come to know us and accept us. Until then, Mira is fortunate to have you as her champion."

"Sonali was upset too."

He nodded. "She has been poorly treated many times—insulted, refused service. I step in when I can, but she sometimes resents my interference."

"Probably resented mine as well," Claire said sheepishly. "I went charging off like some wild-eyed avenger. I hope I did not do more harm than good."

"I doubt it. Though it is often difficult to know what is best to be done. As much as we'd like to, we can't change the whole world."

"Not yet, perhaps," she said. "But hopefully in time."

Her duties done for the day, Claire again left the boarding house for an evening stroll. Reaching the esplanade, she descended the slope to the beach. She stood there, watching the restless grey waves, the white caps breaking into frothy surf and advancing, diminishing, and finally lapping the pebbled shore.

What was it about the seaside? It drew her. Refreshed her. Soothed her weary soul. For a moment Claire closed her eyes, breathing deeply of the cool, moist air and listening to the rhythmic roar.

Footsteps crunched over pebbles nearby, interrupting her solitude. Realizing it was a little late to be out on her own, Claire nervously glanced over. With relief and pleasure, she recognized the approaching figure. "Fran!"

"Good evening, Claire. I stopped by Broadbridge's, and Mary told me you'd gone for a walk."

Claire nodded. "Mr. Farrant having another pint while he waits for you?"

"He was called out on an urgent repair. But yes, I imagine he will soon reward himself with a pint." Fran smiled and looked around the deserted beach, the sun setting to the west over Peak Hill. "You're out here late in the day."

"I like it best when the crowds have gone."

Fran slanted her a knowing look. "And you're less likely to encounter a relative."

"There is that as well. I understand Mamma sea-bathes here during the day, and I would rather not thrust my presence upon her more than necessary. She has made it clear she intends to keep her distance."

Fran gave her arm a sympathetic squeeze.

Claire said, "Thank you again for helping with the menus. Mrs. Ballard was pleased with them, as was Mr. Hammond."

"My pleasure."

Claire returned her gaze to the sea and inhaled another long breath of fresh air. "I have not been to Sidmouth in years. Yet I feel as though I have come home."

"Despite everything?"

"Despite everything."

After a quiet moment, Fran said, "Give her time, Claire."

Tears stinging her eyes, Claire nodded.

"Speaking of time," Fran said, "I find I have plenty to spare these days, should you ever need more help with anything."

"Really? That would be wonderful. Thank you."

Arm in arm, the two walked together back to the esplanade and then up the street. At the marketplace, they parted ways, Fran to reunite with her husband, while Claire turned toward the boarding house.

As she neared, intending to take the outside stairs down to her room, Claire heard something along the side of the house. She stepped closer and looked down the long narrow alley that led to the old stables.

There in the deepening shadows, she saw two men talking in eager, confidential tones. Mr. Hammond and a slight, bespectacled man Claire did not recognize. Why were they standing there in that dim, overgrown lane, all but hidden from view?

The men turned and began walking toward the street. Claire quickly started down the stairs, not keen to be caught eavesdropping.

From above, she heard Mr. Hammond say, "Yes, but let's keep it between ourselves."

And the man replied, "As you wish. I will be in touch when I receive it."

As the man turned away and Mr. Hammond walked toward the front door above, Claire waited in the shadows, all the while wondering, *Receive what?*

13

> The Home Office needed good, reliable
> intelligence—that is why spies were necessary.
> —Sue Wilkes, *Regency Spies*

When she'd finished her own breakfast the next day, Claire excused herself and walked through the dining room to make sure all was in order.

She hesitated upon seeing a man she did not recognize seated with their four other guests. He was of small stature, fastidiously dressed, with thinning dark hair and keen, shining eyes.

Claire bid good morning to Mr. and Mrs. Bracegirdle, busy tucking into a hearty breakfast, then asked the others, "Have everything you need?"

The newcomer looked up and replied in French, "*Délicieux, merci.*"

She wanted to ask his name. But if he were a guest there, should she not know it?

Mr. Jackson rose from the table and picked up his cases. "All finished. Another excellent repast, thank you."

Not wanting to embarrass him, Claire silently caught his eye and pointed to her own neck.

"Oh!" He belatedly removed the table napkin he'd tucked there, now liberally smeared with jam and egg yolk. "Obliged to you."

Although Claire had initially worried about the salesman, he had been perfectly respectful since their first introduction, even kind.

He followed her into the hall. "Have you ever watched the lace makers, Miss Summers? Sitting upon their stools, bent over straw-stuffed pillows, hands flying from bobbin to bobbin?"

"I have not."

"You must stop and admire their skill when next you see one of them. I often do that, especially at one particular cottage on my route. The widow who lives there, we are of an age. She and her daughters often sit outside for the best light and work their magic. She, of course, would never look twice at a man like me, but still, the heart will hope."

"Yes . . ." Claire breathed in sympathy. "It will."

After the salesman had taken his leave, Claire found Mr. Hammond still seated at the table in the morning room, head bent over coffee and a newspaper. Sonali and Mira had evidently already gone back upstairs.

"Mr. Hammond, we seem to have a new guest. One I don't recall meeting . . . ?"

"Ah yes. Jules Lemaire arrived late last night. I did not wish to wake you. I put him in number five."

This was not the same man she'd seen him talking to in the alley beside the house. This newcomer must have arrived even later. She said, "I did not hear anyone knock late last night."

"Well, no. I met his coach at the inn and walked him over here myself."

"A friend of yours?"

"An acquaintance, yes."

"From France?"

"The Netherlands, actually. Brussels. One of its capitals now, thanks to the Congress of Vienna."

"How did you mee—"

"Now, if there is nothing else?" He rose abruptly.

At that moment, the man himself appeared in the doorway. "*Bonjour.*"

"Ah, Monsieur Lemaire." Mr. Hammond smiled. "We were just speaking of you. Please meet Miss Summers, *l'hôtesse.*"

He gave her a crisp bow. "*Enchanté, mademoiselle.*"

"Um . . . *moi de même*," Claire murmured in reply, the smattering of French she had learned as a girl mostly forgotten.

Monsieur Lemaire went on to ask Mr. Hammond a question in rapid French, perhaps assuming Claire would understand.

She excused herself with a quiet "*Excusez-moi*" and slipped away, but not before she heard Mr. Hammond's reply in seemingly fluent French. *Russian, and now French too?*

She told herself she should not be surprised. Many educated people spoke French. Yet the situation troubled her: the late-night arrival of a foreign guest, Mr. Hammond's curt dismissal when she asked how they'd met, and his closely guarded past and study.

Claire told herself to focus on her own responsibilities and not let it bother her. But she found his secrecy increasingly vexing.

Later that day, Claire answered the door to find Emily standing there, a thin volume in her gloved hands.

She said, "I hope you don't mind seeing me again so soon. I fear you shall quickly grow weary of sisters stopping by unannounced."

"Never," Claire replied, although privately she wondered if Mr. Hammond would. She opened the door wider, and Emily stepped inside.

"I have brought you a Sidmouth guidebook." Emily thrust the volume toward her.

Claire thought of the guidebook in the parlour, left there for guests' use, but said only, "Thank you. How kind."

"I thought it might help acquaint you—or reacquaint you—with the area. You were here only a few months during our first visit, and that was years ago."

"I agree. I am sure I shall find it useful."

"I know Mr. Hammond—or even Fran—probably already bought a guidebook for the boarding house. No doubt the older one, published by Mr. Wallis. This is a newer one, published by John Marsh. I suppose those names mean nothing to you, but the thing is, well, can you keep a secret?"

Daily. "Yes."

"I wrote this one."

For a moment, Claire stared in amazement, then she threw her arms around Emily—the little sister who'd always wanted to write a book someday. "How wonderful. Congratulations."

Emily's face shone with pleasure. "I should mention that my name does not appear in it, and Mr. Marsh made several changes before it was printed. And sadly it's already out of date as his library has since closed, but otherwise I think some of the descriptions are rather good."

"I am sure they are, and I look forward to reading it. Now, can you stay for a bit? I was just about to have a cup of tea."

"Yes, if you are sure I won't be a bother."

"Not at all. Though it won't be a silver tea service brought in by a footman. It will be two plain cups and saucers carried by yours truly."

Emily smiled. "Just as I like it."

When the two were seated at the small table in Claire's room, Emily sipped her tea, then asked, "How are things going here?"

"All right so far. Although I am supposed to be thinking

of ways to increase business and have not a clue how to go about it."

"I could help you write a new advertisement. I have written several for Sea View. And writing is my specialty, after all." She winked.

"Yes, please." Claire wasted no time in providing paper and ink.

She and Emily spent several minutes composing an advertisement announcing Broadbridge's new management and the continuation of its excellent service and commodious accommodation.

Then Emily returned the quill to its holder. "Now, tell me about Mr. Hammond. How on earth did this business arrangement come about? And is it only a business arrangement?"

"Yes, of course it is. Don't be a goose!" Ignoring the heat rising up her neck, Claire went on to tell Emily about the newspaper advertisement she had answered.

"Quite brave of you, not knowing what sort of man had written it."

"Brave or foolish? Perhaps I am the goose."

"And what sort of a man *is* the dashing Mr. Hammond?"

"Dashing? Do you think so?"

Emily nodded, eyes sparkling. "I am happily married, yet I still have eyes, have I not?"

Yes, he is handsome, Claire inwardly allowed, but what sort of man was he? That was more difficult to answer. Thinking aloud, she began, "He's a widower. And seems a caring father to his daughter."

"Ah. I noticed him in church with a little girl. So his wife was . . . ?"

"From India, I believe."

"Was he there with the East India Company, like Viola's husband, Major Hutton?"

"I don't know. He's rather private—secretive, even—about his past."

Claire told her about the foreign languages, coins, and guests. His evasive answers when asked about his prior profession. His out-of-bounds study.

Excitement brightened Emily's face. "Maybe he is a spy!"

"No, I don't think so," Claire said, then frowned. "Wait—a foreign spy or a British spy?"

"A British spy, we hope. A foreign spy could be frightfully dangerous if found out."

"What would any spy be doing in a boarding house?"

"Perhaps it is a cover—a place to meet with foreign informants without raising suspicion. Or . . . now that the wars with France and America are over, maybe he has returned to England to start a new life. Oh! Maybe he has assumed a new identity as well. Hammond might not even be his real name."

"Goodness! You have quite the imagination. Then again, you always did. Still reading a great many novels?"

"Yes. Writing one too."

"I am glad to hear it."

Emily drew in a sharp breath. "Perhaps he is even a famous spy, and that's why his name seemed familiar to James—if he did not change it, that is. How romantic!"

But Claire saw nothing romantic about living under the same roof as a man spying for or against his country. In fact, she found the notion quite unsettling.

Emily set down her cup. "Just supposition, of course. Perhaps James will find out more about him."

"I cannot ask you to keep secrets from your husband, but please ask him not to share what I told you about Mr. Hammond. I would not want the man to get into any trouble over my silly suspicions. There is no doubt some other explanation."

At least Claire hoped so.

The next day it rained hard, and Claire guessed it would curtail Mr. Hammond's regular jaunt out of doors.

She entered the morning room with a duster, planning to tidy the desk with its cluttered stacks of correspondence, pen knives, and quills that needed mending. She lifted the registration book to dust beneath it, and a scrap of paper fell to the floor. Had Mr. Hammond been using it to mark his place?

She picked it up and glanced at it. On the small sheet of note paper was a handwritten series of numbers.

834 1151 4479 2667 2742 3067 788. . . .

She frowned down at them. What did the numbers refer to? Amounts due? Debts owed? Something else?

Emily's conjecture that Mr. Hammond might be a spy returned to her. Was it some sort of code? She tried to thrust the outrageous thought from her mind. Even so, Claire hesitated to throw the paper away. She considered tucking it into the desk drawer as she had the foreign letter and coin. Instead she decided to present it to Mr. Hammond and see how he reacted.

Despite his obvious displeasure at her previous intrusion, Claire again crossed the passage and pushed through the outer door into his apartment, ready to confront him. She stepped onto the landing and found the door to his bedchamber open. Peeking in, she saw the room was surprisingly neat, especially considering he cleaned it himself.

Next she knocked on the closed door of his study. No answer.

She tried the latch. Not locked. She lifted the latch and tentatively inched the door open. The room was empty. The desk . . . crowded indeed.

Nervously, she tiptoed inside and looked at the papers spread atop the desk: correspondence with foreign postal markings. A Russian newspaper. Maps. A journal opened to a page of his handwriting, the words *Constantinople* and *cipher* coming into view.

A floorboard creaked nearby, and Claire gasped and looked up, hand to her chest, frozen above his desk.

William Hammond stood there, anger sketched on his face. "What are you doing in here? Have I not made it clear this is my *private* study?"

Indignation flared. "You have made it clear. Suspiciously so. Yet have I not a right to wonder about the man I've entered into a partnership with? A man who won't talk about his past or previous profession? Who—"

"You have your own secrets," he interrupted. "I don't pry into your private history."

"Well, I don't leave odd codes lying around."

"What codes?"

She thrust the paper toward him.

He glanced at it dismissively. "It's just a list. Nothing that concerns you."

"Nothing that concerns me? You hide up here doing who knows what and go off somewhere almost daily. . . ."

"I simply like to climb the surrounding hills. For the exercise."

Undeterred, she went on, "You meet privately with strangers and have foreign guests to stay but don't explain how you met them—and that's only what I know about. Very well, I shall just come out and ask. Are you a spy?"

"Am I a . . . ?" He gave a bark of laughter. "No, Miss Summers, I am not a spy. Not now, not ever."

"Then how do you explain all . . . this?" She gestured around his study, at the letters, journal, and maps spread about.

He huffed. "You will find the explanation a disappointment, I fear. There's little intrigue to the truth."

"Go on."

"If you really must know, before coming here I was a diplomat. In various capacities in various places: Austria, Russia, the Ottoman Empire . . . "

"Truly?"

"Yes, truly."

She raised both hands in frustration. "Then why not just say so? Why all the secrecy?"

"I don't like talking about it."

"Why? I would think you'd be proud."

"Not proud. Just the opposite. I don't like who I was then. Driven by ambition. Determined to advance, to attain a better post. Perhaps be appointed envoy extraordinary or even ambassador one day."

"Is there something wrong with ambition?"

"There is when you put it before the wishes of someone you love."

He gazed morosely into the vague distance. Then he looked back at her as if just remembering she was there.

"I regret those years, and that is the main reason I don't talk about them. The other is more about expediency. Why would a diplomat who lived in some of the finest embassies in the world leave it all behind to buy a humble seaside boarding house?"

"A natural question."

He scrubbed a hand over his face. "And one I don't wish to answer five times a day. For answering the one inevitably leads to the other."

"Then why buy a boarding house in the first place?"

"It's a long story."

Claire glanced at the rain cascading down the windowpanes. "I am not going anywhere. And we are unlikely to receive any new guests during this."

He heaved a sigh, then gestured toward a chair. "Very well." When she was seated, he sat down as well.

For a few moments, he rested his chin on one hand and stared at the maps, apparently gathering his thoughts.

He began, "My wife, Vanita, grew up listening to tales of her father's idyllic childhood on the English seaside. He promised to take her there one day."

"Her father was English?" Claire asked in surprise.

"Yes. He went to India to make his fortune, as did many. There he met and married an Indian woman—a young widow with a son. They had Vanita a few years later.

"Unlike many Englishmen, he did not treat Vanita's mother as an unofficial 'lady wife' to be discarded before leaving India. He truly loved her and was devastated when she died."

"How sad."

He nodded his agreement. "By that point, her son had grown and left home to become a soldier. He soon fell out of contact with the family."

"Did you meet Vanita in India?"

He shook his head. "In Vienna. But that's a story for another day. Suffice it to say, her father was not in good health when I met them, and he died shortly after we wed."

"Oh no."

"I promised Vanita I would one day bring her to England in his stead. She wanted our children to grow up in the ideal setting she'd heard about all her life. I tried to caution her about dreams of a perfect life in a perfect England—gently warned her that she might not be accepted in that imagined seaside village she longed to call home. You know how some people can be about foreigners. Especially those with darker skin."

"So I am learning."

"But I put off that promised trip to England, accepting one appointment after another. Sadly, Vanita died before I could fulfill my promise."

"I'm terribly sorry. So much loss." Claire considered, then

asked, "So you decided to bring Mira here after your wife's death?"

He nodded. "Better late than never . . . I hope."

"One thing I don't understand. Of all the seaside towns, some far larger and more fashionable than this one, you randomly chose Sidmouth. Why?"

"Not random at all. Through my diplomatic connections, I had been endeavoring for quite some time to discover what became of Vanita's half brother. I am still trying to find him. For Mira's sake.

"I finally received a reply to my inquiries shortly after Vanita died. I learned that he too had left India. He received permission to accompany a wounded British officer on his return to England. They were thought to be residing in Sidmouth, Devonshire—where the officer had been advised to live for his health."

"So that's why you came here."

"Yes. The boarding house was simply a way to supplement my diplomatic pension."

Claire thought of the Indian man she had met on the coach and again in Sidmouth. "And have you found him here?"

"Not yet. I asked around town shortly after we arrived. It seems there might be a man of similar age and description residing on the other side of town in a place called Westmount. I went there but the servant who came to the door was reluctant to talk to me. He would tell me only that the man was not there presently but was expected back at some point."

"Why would he not say more?"

Mr. Hammond shrugged. "He seemed wary of my motives—what I might want with him. I did not explain the connection. Simply left a message that I would like to speak to him if and when he returns."

Oh, I think he has returned, Claire thought to herself. *And his name is Armaan.*

14

> The British embassy in these days was a centre. . . .
> Dinners, balls, and receptions were given with profusion.
> —Rees Howell Gronow, *The Reminiscences and Recollections of Captain Gronow*

After breakfast the next morning, sunshine replaced the previous day's rain. Eager to get out and enjoy the fine weather, Claire offered to buy the fresh herbs Mrs. Ballard needed for dinner.

As Claire walked through the marketplace on her errand, her gaze was drawn to a cheerful display of potted plants. A local flower seller was offering them at a reduced price, as the season for planting was coming to an end.

She thought of the large ceramic, urn-like pots on either side of the boarding-house steps. They held only ragged displays of dried sea grasses and bulrushes that had likely been there since last autumn. Wouldn't flowers be more welcoming? These had certainly caught her eye—perhaps the bright blooms would draw the eyes of prospective guests as well.

Mr. Hammond had given her the key to a cashbox containing

funds for postage and other household necessities. She did not think he would mind.

Claire made her selections, and the flower seller helped her carry them the short distance to the boarding house, giving her advice on how to transplant the flowers and water them.

When he'd gone, Claire delivered the herbs to Mrs. Ballard and asked where she might find gardening tools. The woman sent the scullery maid to the courtyard shed, and she soon came back with a small shovel and a trowel.

Claire had just returned to the front steps with the tools when Miss Patel opened the door for Mira, who wanted to see what Claire was doing.

"Pretty!" the girl enthused and bent to sniff the flowers.

"I think so too. I thought I'd put them into these big pots."

"May I help?"

"If you would like."

"She will get dirty," Sonali warned. "At least wait until I bring an apron."

"Very well."

She returned with an old apron and tied it about the girl. "I shall wait inside, if you don't mind."

"Not at all."

After removing the dried stems and bulrushes, Claire loosened the soil with the small shovel. Then with the trowel, Mira helped her dig holes for each plant. Claire arranged the plants, carefully settling them into the holes, and Mira helped her press the soil gently but firmly around them.

Mr. Hammond came out of the house, dressed for his climb. "I say. That looks nice."

"I hope you don't mind. They were not expensive."

"Not at all. A definite improvement."

"Are they not pretty?" Mira asked.

"They are indeed. Although you, my dear pumpkin seed, have more dirt on yourself than those flowers do." He looked at Claire. "And you have some on your face too, just there. . . ." He reached out and wiped it from her cheek.

Her skin tingled from his touch, and embarrassment further warmed her face. "Th-thank you." She ducked her head. "If you will excuse me, I need to fetch a can of water for them." She thought she might splash some cool water on her burning face while she was at it.

"Allow me to water them for you," he said. "And while I'm at the pump, I shall wash this little one's hands and return her to Sonali."

Claire thanked him and went down the outside stairs to the basement and into her own room. She washed her hands and face in her washstand basin and looked up at her damp reflection in the small mirror, her cheeks still flushed.

She reminded herself that she had experienced this giddy feeling of attraction once before. She had known Lord Bertram barely a fortnight and had believed herself in love with him. Believed *him* when he said the same and convinced her to run away with him. He had seemed too good to be true . . . and he was.

She had known William Hammond for even less time. Was she being foolhardy and gullible again?

In a small whisper, she warned herself, "Be careful, Claire."

Later that morning, a knock sounded at the door while Claire and Mary were busy in the dining room. Claire went to answer it, hoping for the arrival of new guests. So far her puny efforts to increase business had been to clean up the place and plant a few flowers. Thankfully, there was Emily's advertisement as well, although it had not yet run.

When she opened the door, a potential guest was not who she saw.

The tall Indian man stood there, dressed in gentlemen's attire as before. *Armaan.*

His eyes widened upon seeing her. "Oh. I . . . I have come to speak to a Mr. Hammond. I did not realize you were—"

"His business partner," Claire blurted. She didn't want him to assume she was Mr. Hammond's servant or wife.

She opened the door wider and stepped back. "Do come in."

He wiped his shoes on the mat, removed his hat, and followed her into the entry hall.

"I am afraid Mr. Hammond is out at present. Climbing Peak Hill, I believe."

His dark brows rose. "For what purpose?"

"For the pleasure of it, he says. He likes the exercise."

"Ah. I prefer riding. Or swimming."

"May I give him a message?"

"Only that I called. I understand he wishes to speak to me for some reason. Why he should, I have no idea, as I have never met a William Hammond, as far as I recall."

"And your name is Armaan . . . ?"

"Armaan Sagar."

Claire resisted the urge to reveal the truth, knowing it was not her news to tell. Especially with Mr. Filonov in the nearby morning room, humming to himself as he read the St. Petersburg news. And Mary in the adjacent dining room, putting away the breakfast china.

"I think you will be . . . interested in what Mr. Hammond has to say."

"Interested?" The man frowned. "Is he selling something?"

"No, no. Nothing like that. You are welcome to wait, although he might be some time yet." Dishes clattered in the dining room, and Claire winced, hoping the girl had not broken anything.

She was not certain Mr. Hammond would want her to install the man in his *private* study. And Mr. Jackson was currently meeting with a lace dealer in the parlour upstairs.

She searched her mind, wondering where gentlemen usually met to talk, then suggested, "Perhaps you might prefer to wait at the Old Ship? Or the assembly rooms at the London Inn? I understand men meet there to play cards."

A shadow passed over his face, and he seemed about to refuse when the service door behind them opened and Mira dashed into the hall, a doll hanging limp in one hand, half a biscuit in the other. "Miss Summers! Miss Summers! I tore Dolly's dress. Please, can you repair it?"

Noticing their visitor, the little girl stopped abruptly and pressed herself to Claire's side, her eyes fixed on the man with wary curiosity.

The man, too, seemed arrested and again lowered himself to the girl's height, though there were no lemon drops to retrieve this time. His gaze traced Mira's face, his eyes warm. "Good day, little one. A pleasure to see you again."

From somewhere above, Sonali called, "Mira! Come!"

Claire gently turned her toward the stairs. "I am sure Sonali would mend it for you. Why not ask her first? If she cannot, I will see what I can do."

"Very well." Mira bounded up the stairs.

When Claire looked back at the man, she found him standing once again, still staring in the direction the girl had disappeared.

"You will think me foolish, but seeing her reminds me of home. Of the family I once had." Almost to himself, he added, "And lost."

"Not foolish at all. Quite understandable." *More than you know.*

He explained, "In London, I saw many people like myself. Not here."

A thought pinched his features, and he turned his focus to her, studying Claire inquisitively. "When we met before,

I thought you seemed familiar. But now . . . Mira called you Miss Summers, did she not?"

Claire hesitated, fearing what he might have heard about her, then replied, "She did."

"I wonder if you are related to the Summers family here in Sidmouth. I see, or at least imagine, a resemblance. In fact, you look like Emily Summers, now Mrs. Thomson, sister to Major Hutton's wife."

Claire nodded. "Viola, yes. I am their eldest sister."

"Ah. I have heard her mention another sister in Scotland but not here."

"I had just arrived from Edinburgh when we met."

"That explains it. Though I wonder why you are . . ." He glanced around the hall, then cleared his throat. "I have no wish to pry. Actually, I might wish to pry, but I shall resist." A corner of his mouth turned up.

"Thank you."

Again the service door opened, and Mrs. Ballard appeared. "Miss Summers? I need you belowstairs. Mary has broken another cream pitcher."

"One minute."

"I can see you are busy," Mr. Sagar said. "I shall await Mr. Hammond at the . . . Old Ship, did you say?" The half grin faded. "Very well, that is where I shall be."

Sometime later, Mr. Hammond returned from his climb, looking satisfied, if winded, his color heightened by the exercise.

Claire met him at the door.

"Armaan Sagar came by while you were out. The morning room and parlour were occupied, so I suggested he wait for you at the Old Ship Inn."

A frown line appeared between his brows. "The Old Ship? Why?"

"I was not sure where two men would meet to talk. And you've told me to stay out of your study, so I did not ask him to wait there. Have I made a mistake?"

She took in his anxious frown with mounting concern. "What is it? What's wrong?"

"I don't like the thought of him there, surrounded by rough men in their cups. Not everyone is small-minded, of course, but that place has a reputation for lawlessness."

"In that case, perhaps you had better change and go over there."

"How long ago did he set off?"

"Fifteen, maybe twenty minutes."

Another frown. "I had better go as I am."

"Good heavens. You are making me nervous."

"Probably worrying for nothing. Still, if he's there to meet me, I feel responsible."

No, I feel responsible, Claire thought, stomach twisting.

Setting aside his gear and replacing his hat, he added, "If he does encounter incivility, perhaps I can help defuse the situation. I have some experience in peace negotiations, after all. I trust it will serve me well now."

He turned and stalked out the door. For a few moments, Claire remained where she was, thoughts and fears whirling. Then she realized she would get nothing done standing there wringing her hands.

Grabbing her bonnet off the peg, Claire hurried out, tying the ribbons haphazardly under her chin as she jogged down the steps and strode up Back Street. She consoled herself with the thought that it was early in the day so the patrons would not yet be inebriated. She hoped.

Nearing the Old Ship Inn, she heard raised voices before she'd even reached the door.

Rude, jeering voices.

Oh no.

"Are 'ee lost, laddie? No lascars here."

"Look at 'is fine clothes. You in a play? Convincin' costume fer the role of gentleman, but yer the dashed wrong color."

Laughter. And not the friendly sort.

Mr. Hammond's voice. "Come now, gents. This man has lived here—what, more than a twelvemonth? Practically a local."

"An incomer like 'at will n'er be one of us."

Mr. Hammond persisted, "Mr. Sagar served His Royal Majesty in India, alongside many other brave soldiers. He deserves your respect. Come, let us have peace."

"I'll give you peace. A piece of my mind. And my fist."

Another voice entered the fray. "Now, you lot. No fighting in here."

Voices rose to an angry pitch, followed by a loud crash. A table being pushed over? Then came the sound of shattering glass.

Lord, please. Claire stood there, rooted to the spot. This was all her fault. She'd only meant to help. She could not go in, could she? Should she?

She was about to when she noticed a man and woman strolling up the street arm in arm. A woman she recognized—Viola, and without a veil! And with her was a tall, broad-shouldered man with burn scars on half his face. This must be her husband, Major Hutton.

Surprise and relief flooded Claire. "Viola! Oh, thank God. Come quick."

They hurried forward, Viola looking eager, hand outstretched.

"Claire! We were so worried when we didn't find you in Edinburgh. We returned last night and were just on our way to see you." Searching her face, Viola frowned. "What's wrong?"

"They are fighting inside."

"Nothing new there," Viola's husband grumbled.

"But Mr. Hammond is in there, and Mr. Sagar."

At that, he jerked his head around, a fierce scowl on his scarred face.

"Armaan is in there?"

Claire nodded. "I'm afraid so. It's him they're fighting about. And it's my fault."

"The devil it is. You both stay here. I mean it."

"Be careful, Jack."

But he had already charged inside.

Instinctively, Claire stepped closer to her sister and gripped her hand.

"The major will protect him," Viola assured her. "Armaan once saved his life."

Claire hoped it would not come to that. And she hoped he would somehow protect William too.

William . . . Where had that come from? Why was she thinking of him by his Christian name? It was only the stress of the moment. He was Mr. Hammond, her employer in effect, and she would do well to remember that.

Another crash. A moment later, Viola's husband emerged, one arm supporting Mr. Sagar, whose lip and brow were bleeding.

Mr. Hammond followed, or rather was pushed forcibly from behind by an aproned, irate landlord.

"Out with the lot of you. And don't come back."

"Our apologies, my good man." Clothes rumpled but apparently unharmed, Mr. Hammond pulled out his purse and handed the man several gold coins, which he quickly pocketed.

"In that case, sir, you are welcome back anytime."

When the publican retreated, Claire rushed forward. "Are you all right?"

Armaan shook off the major's arm. "Yes, yes. Only a bloodied lip and a bottle to the head. I've had worse."

"And doled out worse," Major Hutton said, mouth quirked and a hint of pride in his expression.

Claire noticed the scraped skin of the major's knuckles.

Viola noticed at the same moment and grasped his hand, studying the damage critically. "Oh, Jack, I told you to be careful."

"I was. But that troublemaker's nose will forever be crooked, I fear."

"He had it coming," Mr. Hammond said with a decisive nod. He stuck out his hand, a clear bond having formed during the melee. "William Hammond. I would gladly serve beside either of you any day."

"Jack Hutton," Viola's husband replied, grasping his hand.

"Major Hutton," Armaan clarified. "And I am Armaan Sagar. I understand you have been looking for me."

William's green eyes glinted. "I have indeed." He shook Armaan's hand and added, "After you have patched yourself up, come back to the boarding house, if you would. I have news for you."

With a glance at Claire, Armaan asked, "Good news or bad?"

"Both, I suppose."

"I shall be there in one hour."

Claire spoke up. "And this is my sister Viola."

Mr. Hammond bowed. "A pleasure, madam."

Claire was tempted to stay and talk with Viola, but she also wanted to return to the house with Mr. Hammond and make sure all was in readiness for Mr. Sagar's call. So after a heartfelt embrace and a quick introduction to her sister's husband, Claire excused herself, agreeing to a long-overdue visit in a day or two.

On the walk back, Claire kept glancing at Mr. Hammond, striding beside her. "Are you truly all right?"

"Yes, I am completely unharmed, except for some drunken pushing and shoving."

"Good."

When he was silent, she looked at him again and saw the muscles in his jaw clench. "And before you ask . . . no, I was not able to defuse the situation with my so-called skills in negotiation."

Impulsively, she reached over and squeezed his arm, instantly noticing how firm it felt. "Even so, you were brave to rush into the fray to rescue your brother-in-law."

Glancing over at her, he tucked her arm more securely to his side. "I suppose he is my brother-in-law. I had not quite thought of it in those terms. Thank you, Miss Summers."

And she knew he was thanking her for more than a reminder of his relationship to the man.

True to his word, Mr. Sagar once again came to Broadbridge's door an hour later. He had changed clothes and sported a bandage on his brow and a lip already scabbing over.

Claire greeted him. "I am glad you came back. I wish to apologize. I truly did not know that suggesting you wait there would prove so perilous."

"Less perilous than it would have been, thanks to Mr. Hammond."

"And the major." She led him inside. "Mr. Hammond wishes to speak to you in his study. Far safer and more private, I assure you."

She led him through the entry hall and up the stairs. As she opened the door that led to Mr. Hammond's apartment at the back of the house, she explained, "Mr. Hammond has taken rooms over the stables. More separate, you understand. More . . . respectable."

"His idea, or yours?"

"His. He was already sleeping there when I arrived."

"I see. Very proper, our Mr. Hammond."

She sent him a wry look. "Very *private*, our Mr. Hammond."

"Does he not keep horses?"

"No. Nor does he employ a groom. When guests arrive with their own horses, he sends them to the livery stables on Fore Street."

At the end of the passage, Claire reached the door that led to Mr. Hammond's private domain. She took a deep breath and knocked. A moment later, Mr. Hammond opened it. Would he send her away?

"Welcome, Mr. Sagar." He turned to her. "Miss Summers, good. Perhaps you ought to hear this as well."

He opened the door wider and gestured them both inside.

Surprised but pleased, Claire stepped through.

"My bedchamber and study." He pointed briefly to each door, then led them into his study and invited them to sit in the two chairs before his desk.

Claire sat down and smoothed her skirt.

Mr. Sagar, however, remained standing as though at attention. "Can you tell me why I am here, sir?"

"I wished to speak with you."

"Why? We have never met before today, I don't believe."

"No, but my wife told me a great deal about you."

"Your wife?" Again, he sliced a confused look toward Claire and quickly away.

"Your sister. I should say, half sister."

The man stilled and his entire body stiffened. "What?"

"Vanita. I married Vanita."

"Little Vani . . . ?"

"She was two and twenty when we married."

Armaan stepped clumsily forward. "Are you sure we are speaking of the same person?"

"Yes, if your widowed mother married George Aston."

Feeling blindly for a chair, Armaan slowly sank into it. A moment later he rose again, clearly agitated. "Where is she? Is she here?"

He started toward the door, but William rose and hurried around the desk to stop him.

"Sadly, no. That is the bad news I warned you about. Vanita died more than a year ago, our newborn baby with her."

Claire's stomach twisted at this mention of his double loss.

Meanwhile, Armaan stood there, shock and even anger rippling over his face. He huffed. "And the good news?"

"I hoped it was obvious. My daughter, Mira, is Vanita's child. Your niece."

For a long moment, Armaan stared intensely at Mr. Hammond, brows drawn low.

"My niece?"

"Yes. You are her last close relative from Vanita's side, as far as I know."

"I can't believe it," he breathed. Then he asked, "Vanita died . . . in childbirth?"

Mr. Hammond flinched, then looked away from the man's intense gaze. Instead he stared down at the stacks of paper on his desk. "No. The plague took her and the child both, when we were in Constantinople."

Armaan flopped back down in the chair and laid his head in his hands. "Poor Vani."

"Yes," her husband bleakly replied.

Armaan looked up at him. "And poor you, if you loved her."

"I did. I love our daughter as well."

Again, Armaan pressed his hands to his forehead. "I saw Mira on the street. I thought she looked familiar. I felt I *recognized* her. I told myself I was being foolish. It was only my . . . aloneness telling me that."

In silence, Armaan sat there, clearly pondering, then he

said, "So when you moved to Sidmouth and learned I was here—an astounding coincidence, you must allow—you decided to inform me of our connection?"

Mr. Hammond came and stood beside him, placing a tentative hand on his shoulder. "No, my brother. I came to Sidmouth *because* you were here. I had been trying to find you for some time. After Vanita died, I finally received word that you had moved to Sidmouth. I brought Mira here in hopes of finding you."

"Truly?" Armaan looked up at him, mouth ajar.

"Truly. Imagine my disappointment when I went to Westmount only to be told you were not there. The man who answered the door was not keen to confide your plans to a stranger. He would only tell me that you had left but were expected to eventually return."

Armaan nodded. "I went to stay with the major's father for a time. I hope it is not rude to say that living with a new-wed couple can make a single man feel quite . . . Well, I think we were all ready for a change. Later, I went to London, a city I had long been curious to see. Do not mistake me, I am fond of the major's family, yet they are not mine. I lost all my family, to distance, at least, if not death. Or so I thought."

"You were informed of your mother's death?"

Armaan nodded. "Vanita sent a letter through the company post. I had joined up to the great displeasure of my extended family and former friends. My mother's marriage to an Englishman had not endeared us to them either. Vanita and I had been outcasts of a sort even before I chose to serve alongside the British. After our mother died, well . . . I did not blame Mr. Aston for leaving India and taking his daughter with him."

"You knew they were leaving the country?"

"Yes, Vanita wrote again to tell me. She asked to see me one last time, to say good-bye in person. To my shame, I waited too long to act."

William Hammond met his gaze. "Where Vanita is concerned, I know that feeling all too well."

"Do you? Please. Tell me everything about her—about your life together."

Mr. Hammond nodded and again looked down as he gathered his thoughts.

"I remember the first time I saw her—a dinner at the embassy, seated with her father. How striking she was with her lovely face, dark hair, and deep brown eyes. She looked beautiful, although not happy.

"The ambassador's wife introduced us, and Mr. Aston invited me to join them at their table.

"Mr. Aston and I conversed easily, but his daughter remained subdued.

"He explained that she was disappointed. He had been promising to take her to England for years, to see the country where he grew up."

Mr. Hammond looked at Armaan. "I gather that after you left home and your mother died, Vanita focused all her love and affection on her father. She drank up the stories of his childhood in England. His idyllic boyhood at his parents' cottage by the sea.

"Yet considering the long voyage from India, Mr. Aston decided to disembark along the way and spend some time on the Continent before going on to England. One of his reasons was to show his daughter more of the world, giving her time to improve her English and learn society ways and manners.

"Personally I thought her English and manners were already excellent and said as much.

"In reply, Mr. Aston invited me to join them for dinner at their hotel the next night, to further our acquaintance. I later attended a concert with them, and a party as well.

"Then Mr. Aston asked to meet with me privately. I assumed he wanted to ask what my intentions were toward his daughter, perhaps to probe into my background and financial situation. When I met with him, he did ask a few questions along those lines. He could see I admired Vanita and encouraged me not to wait to pursue her even though we were not long acquainted.

"That's when he confided the other reason he'd come to Vienna—to consult with a physician who'd been recommended to him. He'd seen the fellow again that very day and the prognosis was not good. Cancer. He had not long to live and wished to see his daughter well settled before he passed. Your sister traveled with a companion, but still he shuddered to think what might befall two unprotected women left alone in a foreign land.

"I asked if she had no other family. He mentioned you, her half brother, saying you and Vanita had fallen out of contact."

Armaan nodded. "To my shame."

"Mr. Aston admitted he had also lost contact with his few remaining relatives in England after so many years abroad. He thought it unlikely any of them would accept Vanita as family. He also feared some distant relatives he barely knew might try to overturn his will in their favor instead of Vanita's.

"Despite the difficult circumstances and our brief acquaintance, I truly fell in love with your sister and she with me. I was a paid attaché by then, so I could afford to marry. Her father offered a generous marriage settlement—and a provision for you as well, by the way.

"I acquired a license and we married in haste so he could witness our wedding and be assured his daughter would be taken care of. So he could die in peace.

"Vanita was, of course, devastated when he died. I did my best to comfort her. I, too, promised to take her to England one day, but first I had to make something of myself. Succeed in my career. I estimated a few more years was all it would take."

His lips twisted. "That estimate proved to be overly optimistic.

"I admit I briefly worried that marrying Vanita might hinder my chances of securing a higher appointment. For prejudices exist, even abroad. Yet she won people over with her charm and impeccable manners, her keen sense of humor and beautiful smile. . . ." Mr. Hammond gazed over their heads, eyes soft in memory, a gentle expression on his face.

Claire's heart burned with longing. Oh, to be so loved.

A moment later his expression sobered. "But I gave her precious little reason to smile in those final months.

"Whenever she asked about England, I put her off. I always had a reason. Mira was born and we could not travel with an infant. Then when Mira was older, an opportunity for advancement proved too tempting to pass up.

"Finally, when Vanita let me know she was expecting our second child, I began making inquiries into situations in England.

"In the meantime, I was appointed secretary of the Ottoman capital in Constantinople. I could not turn down such an opportunity. I assured Vanita that after our second child was born and grew old enough to travel, we would move to England, as I had long promised.

"Instead, she contracted the plague." He shook his head, lips trembling. "She and the infant died. A son . . ."

Tears filled Armaan's eyes. "I am sorry."

William nodded, eyes bright with unshed tears. Claire's eyes filled as well.

"So was I. But it was too late. She never made it to the English seaside she'd longed to see."

Armaan slowly nodded. "So you came here in her stead?"

"Yes. She did not extract such a promise from me. But when I realized how quickly she was failing, I vowed it. Our little girl would be brought up in an English village as her father had been. As Vanita had dreamt about her entire life.

"A few months after the funeral, I received a letter from my contacts detailing your presumed whereabouts. After the quarantine lifted, I resigned my post and began making arrangements to travel here to Sidmouth."

He ran a weary hand over his face. "I should have been a better husband to her, put her desires before my ambitions. I will not blame you if you despise me."

Armaan seemed to give this due thought, then said, "I do not despise you. We both disappointed Vanita in our own ways. Perhaps we might help each other make peace with the past."

When their conversation ended, Mr. Hammond walked with Claire and Armaan back through the passage to the main house.

He asked, "Would you like to see Mira again, now you know?"

"You read my mind, sir."

"Not *sir*. William, please."

"Very well, and you must call me Armaan."

He nodded. "Come with me, Armaan."

Mr. Hammond led the way up to the nursery. When they arrived, they found the girl on her own, playing with her dollhouse.

Mr. Hammond said, "Mira, there is someone I would like you to meet."

As before, Armaan Sagar sank to his haunches to face Mira at her level. This time, however, curiosity had been replaced by something deeper.

"Good day, Mira. Do you know who I am?"

The little girl said softly, "Armaan."

"And what else?"

Confused, Mira shook her head.

"I am also your uncle. Your *amma*'s brother. Your . . . *mamu*."

"*Mamu* . . ." the little girl breathed in reverent reply.

"Yes, *bhanji*."

"*Bhanji*?" Mira repeated. "What is that?"

"This means *niece*. For that, my dear, is what you are to me. And I thank God for that. And for you."

For a moment the little girl stared, uncertain. She glanced at Claire, then at her father, and at his reassuring nod, Mira tentatively reached out and touched Armaan's face. "I never had an uncle before. I am glad you are mine."

Sonali came in then, returning from the water closet or wherever she had been. She stopped abruptly at discovering others in the nursery. Her gaze flicked from Mr. Hammond to Claire, then latched onto the newcomer with guarded interest.

"I only stepped out for a moment."

"That's all right," Mr. Hammond said. "We have just brought Mr. Sagar to see Mira."

"Why?"

"He is her uncle. Vanita's half brother."

The woman's mouth fell open, and her eyes brightened. "Armaan? Can it be? Vanita spoke of you often."

"Thank you. I am gratified. I'm afraid I don't know your name."

Mr. Hammond spoke up. "Forgive me. This is Sonali Patel. Former companion and friend to Vanita, and now nursery-governess to Mira."

She smiled at him, and Armaan bowed.

"Miss Patel. An honor."

When he straightened, Claire noticed Armaan survey the woman, eyes warm in obvious admiration. Yes, the woman could be charming when she wished to be. Claire only wished she made the effort more often.

Sonali added, "Of course, you don't know of me. You had already left to enlist in the company army when I joined the household. Still, I heard all about you. Vanita was most fond of you and missed you terribly."

"I missed her as well. I regret not staying in contact with her."

"Yes. You should have."

Surprise flashed in Armaan's eyes, and he briefly ducked his head. "You are right. But I am very glad to meet her daughter now. And her friend."

Mr. Hammond said, "You must visit us often, Armaan. As often as you like. No need to wait for an invitation. For you, the door is always open."

"Thank you, William. That is most kind."

15

> Her needlework both plain and ornamental was excellent, and might almost have put a sewing machine to shame.
> —J. E. Austen-Leigh, *A Memoir of Jane Austen*

A few days later, Sarah left Sea View carrying a brown-paper parcel and a fabric bag containing several of Claire's possessions she had saved. She had not brought Claire's girlhood sampler that she had rescued from the rubbish heap, because she still hoped Mamma might one day have a change of heart and hang it with the others.

She walked east along the esplanade past Fort Field on the left, boats and beach-goers on the right, the wind off the Channel tugging at her bonnet. Ahead stood Wallis's Marine Library with its veranda shaded by a striped awning. On one of the benches there she spied charitable Mrs. Fulford and returned the woman's wave.

Not far past Mr. Hodges's Medical Baths and Billiard Room, Sarah turned inland toward the boarding house, passing the marketplace on her way.

At Broadbridge's, Claire greeted her warmly, then self-consciously removed her apron as she invited her inside.

"No need to take that off on my account," Sarah said. "I wear one daily for my tasks at Sea View." She added, "I brought a few small things for you." She handed over the parcel. "Some biscuits and tarts I made."

"You made them? I am impressed."

Sarah shrugged. "I've learned a great deal this last year. I daresay we all have."

"Please join me for tea," Claire said. "Mrs. Ballard already has a kettle on, and it will take just a few minutes to steep."

"If you can spare the time."

"I could use a respite. I've been up since dawn helping Mary beat carpets and sweep floors before guests awoke. The place had not been thoroughly cleaned since Fran left."

"And Mary is . . . ?"

"A young maid, formerly in Aunt Mercer's employ. She came with me from Edinburgh, and thankfully Mr. Hammond agreed to give her a place here."

Sarah followed her sister down the back stairs and to her room, a generously sized bedchamber, work area, and sitting room in one.

"Make yourself comfortable. I shall return directly."

In a few minutes Claire reentered, carrying a homely ceramic teapot, cups, and saucers on a tray. When the tea had steeped, she poured milk and tea into their cups. Sarah noticed no sugar on the tray. Claire evidently remembered how she took her tea—the same way she did.

Claire helped herself to one of each pastry and tasted the tart first. Her eyes widened. Covering her mouth with her hand as she finished chewing, she exclaimed, "These are delicious!"

"Thank you. Baking has become a new pastime of mine. I enjoy it. Speaking of pastimes . . ." Sarah reached into the fabric bag. "I've brought one of your old sketchbooks and some drawing pencils."

Claire accepted them. "Goodness. I have not sketched in far too long. Thank you, Sarah."

"You are welcome. We were not able to bring everything when we moved, but I did save these in case you should want them one day." She handed over a leather volume with gilt border. "Your prayer book. And these embroidered gloves and fichu. You were always such a fine needlewoman." She handed them over as well.

Claire ran a finger over the decorative stitches and then rested her hand on the prayer book, keeping her head bowed.

In a small voice, she said, "It must have been difficult when Papa died—losing him and Finderlay too. Having to move."

Sarah drew a long breath as she considered her reply. "It was difficult. I can't pretend otherwise. Nothing was the same after you left. Papa was furious—with the pair of you and with himself too. Nor can I deny the situation . . . the distress . . . contributed to his attack." Sarah went on gently, "But we were always going to lose Finderlay at some point. You mustn't feel guilty for that. And in hindsight, I cannot regret the move. Oddly, I think we are all happier in Sidmouth than we were in May Hill. Well, except perhaps for Mamma. Yet her health has improved since coming here. So as much as she misses Papa, I don't think she regrets the move either."

Claire nodded her understanding and lifted the items from her lap. "Thank you again for keeping these for me."

"Oh! There's one more thing. Most of the family jewelry was listed in the entail and had to be left behind. But I saved these earrings."

Claire accepted them. "I remember these! A gift for my eighteenth birthday." The dainty gold earrings each held a tiny red garnet. "I am happy to have them back. Do you know . . . they remind me of a necklace Aunt Mercer left to me."

"I am surprised she left you anything. I had always gathered she was something of a dragon."

"She was—at least at first. But she softened toward the end."

Sarah studied Claire's profile, then asked, "How did you spend your time there?"

"In penance, I suppose you might say. Serving Aunt Mercer, attending services at the kirk, reading Fordyce's sermons and anything else she or her minister assigned."

"Sounds awful."

"Not awful. Merely dull. Bleak. Boring. Yet I had a roof over my head, food, and warm clothes. I was not deprived, except for affection. And as Aunt Mercer often reminded me, my life there was a better fate than I deserved."

"I am not so sure about that," Sarah said, then glanced at Claire's neck. "You don't wear the necklace?"

"I'm ashamed to say I had to surrender it to a pawn dealer to pay for Mary's and my coach fare."

Sarah felt her brows rise. "I have never ventured into such an establishment. How did you even know where to find one?"

"I asked for directions. Thankfully it was not far from Aunt Mercer's house."

"What was the necklace like?"

"A scrollwork cross with a small ruby at the center on a thin gold chain."

Sarah asked a few more questions about the novel experience: if she had received a fair price for the necklace and if the proprietor had given her a receipt or claim ticket, et cetera.

Claire answered her, then said, "I only had the necklace for a few days, but I'd seen it around Aunt Mercer's neck nearly every Sunday for two years. I was sorry to leave it behind. Coming here, however, was more important."

Sarah nodded and squeezed her hand. "And we are very glad you did."

When Sarah returned to Sea View a short while later, she went into the library-office and sat at the desk, pulling forth paper, quill, and ink. For a moment, she hesitated. Then, reminding herself of what he'd said in his previous letter, she began to write:

Dear Mr. Henshall,

In your last letter, you said that if there was anything else you could do for us, to not hesitate to let you know. I hope you will not regret that offer after receiving this second letter from me.

I fear I am becoming greatly in your debt, but I wonder if I might request another favor. . . .

After her duties were finished for the evening, Claire lit a lamp in her room and sat down with the sketchbook Sarah had returned to her. The book contained mostly empty pages, but at the front were several sketches she had done years before. How strange to see them again, these moments of the past captured like flies in yellow amber, like butterflies pinned in place.

And, oh, the memories that accompanied the simple images.

A favorite teacup.

A small vase of flowers Georgie had picked for her . . . from their neighbor's garden.

An attempt to sketch from memory the face of Sarah's betrothed after he was gone. Not terribly successful.

Viola's hands. At the time, her hands were all her reclusive sister had allowed Claire to draw. Yet hands had proven rather difficult.

A watercolor of an orange tabby that kept coming to the garden door. Despite Mamma's refusals to let the cat inside,

Emily and Georgie had conspired to sneak out bowls of cream to the charming creature.

A still life of Papa's pipe atop a favorite book.

Claire smiled even as tears stung her eyes. She lightly ran a finger over the lines, then closed the sketchbook and set it aside.

The door creaked open, startling Claire. Hand to her chest, she searched the darkness until Mira's small form appeared.

"Miss Claire? I had a bad dream."

"I am sorry to hear that." She spread her arms, and the girl hurried into them. Claire held her close and patted her back. When she had calmed, Claire said gently, "You really should not wander around alone in the dark, though. Don't forget Sonali is in the room next to yours."

"She got cross the last time I woke her."

"I am sure she does not mind. Not if you are scared. Come. I will take you back."

Mira nodded. Claire picked up her candle lamp and led the girl upstairs.

Sonali stood outside her bedchamber door with a candle of her own. "There you are, Mira! I worried when I came to look in and you were not there."

Claire said, "She had a bad dream."

"I see," Sonali replied a little stiffly. "Well, come, let's go back to bed." With a curt nod to Claire, the woman put a gentle arm around the little girl's shoulders and shepherded her into her room.

The next morning Claire rose early, washed, and dressed. Mary popped in to lace her stays and fasten the back of her dress as usual. Together they helped with breakfast, carrying up the serving dishes for the sideboard and family table: fresh bread rolls and butter, cold ham, and boiled eggs. Mrs.

Ballard said she would send up the hot coffee and tea in a few minutes.

Finding everything ready ahead of schedule, Claire took the sketchbook and drawing pencils into the morning room, where the light was better.

The pencil quickly and naturally slipped into position, as though only a few days had passed since she'd drawn something instead of two years.

For lack of a more inspired subject, she began sketching the items on the desk: brass wax jack, ceramic ink well, bone-handled seal, and powder jar.

A short while later, Mira bounced in, doll in arms. "What are you doing?"

"Just drawing while I wait for everyone."

"Can you draw me?"

"I'm afraid I am not very good at drawing people."

"What about Dolly?" Mira held up her doll with its painted porcelain face atop a soft body.

"I suppose I might be able to draw your doll." Claire began sketching.

Mira lifted the doll's miniature dress hem with a pout. "It's still torn. And Sonali says she is too busy."

"I am sorry, Mira. I would be happy to mend it, but I'm afraid I don't have my own sewing things. Perhaps I could borrow some."

"What's this?" Mr. Hammond came in at the tail end of this conversation.

"Miss Summers promised to repair Dolly's dress, but she has no sewing things."

"Really?"

Claire's face heated. A lady without her own sewing supplies? Unheard of. She had not actually promised the girl yet felt embarrassed even so.

Thinking of her sisters, Claire said, "I am sure I can borrow something until I have a chance to buy my own." *And the money to do so*, she added to herself.

But Mira had already moved on to the next topic, like a bee swiftly flying from one flower to the next.

"Miss Summers is drawing. See?" She pointed to Claire's sketch pad. "May I learn to draw too?"

"I don't see why not. That is, if Miss Summers does not mind."

"Not at all. I have an extra drawing pencil and can give her one of these pages. Perhaps after breakfast?"

After they had eaten, Claire sat beside Mira and provided her with paper and pencil. The little girl set to work, little tongue protruding.

Mr. Hammond came to stand over his daughter. "And what are you drawing, *kaddu*?"

"Us. You, me, Dolly, and Miss Summers."

The stick figures were indistinguishable, except that the tallest wore a hat. Self-conscious, Claire said, "You mean Miss Patel, surely."

The girl shrugged. "I can draw her too."

Later that day, after luncheon and several hours spent on various projects around the house, Claire returned to the morning room to work through the latest tradesmen's bills.

Mr. Hammond came in while her head was bent in concentrated effort to decipher a hard-to-read invoice. "Mira mentioned you don't have your own sewing things. Is that right?"

She kept her head down and hoped he would not notice her flush of embarrassment. "Not presently, no. I neglected to pack a workbag when I left home—I mean, Scotland."

"Will this do?"

She looked up and saw he held a satinwood sewing box with domed lid and swing handle, painted with a country landscape. He set it on the desk before her.

"This is lovely," Claire said. "Almost too lovely to use."

She opened the lid and found the pink silk–lined interior filled with small scissors, pins, needles, threads in various shades, and much more.

"This will do very well indeed."

"It was my wife's. No use letting it sit idle. I also have several yards of fabric she meant to one day turn into garments, if you have any use for those."

"That is uncommonly generous. Thank you."

Miss Patel walked in. She stopped and glared at the box before Claire. "That is Vanita's."

"I know. Miss Summers has need of it."

"It should go to me. Or perhaps to Mira when she is older. Not to a *gori* like her."

"Her skin color has no bearing here," he said. "Besides, you have your own."

"Of course I have. But this one is special."

Claire lifted the box, unsure whether to hand it to the woman or the man. "Here. I can do without. I shall ask my sisters for needle and thread."

Mr. Hammond's gaze remained on Miss Patel. "It is mine to give, and I give it to Miss Summers."

Glancing uncomfortably from one raised chin to the other, Claire said, "Suppose I just borrow it? It will be Mira's one day, but for now I shall repair her doll's dress with these supplies."

The woman's eyes glittered with resentment. Then she said, "Very well."

Mr. Hammond took a deep breath and forced a light tone Claire doubted he felt.

"I had better go down to the kitchen," he said, probably hoping to extricate himself from the tension in the room. "Mira is helping Mrs. Ballard make sugar biscuits, and I promised to rescue her in half an hour." He grinned. "Rescue Mrs. Ballard, that is."

When both women looked flatly back at him, his grin faded, and he turned and exited in silence.

After Mr. Hammond left, Claire expected Miss Patel to stomp out after him, or to sullenly return to Mira. Claire was tempted to suggest the latter so she might enjoy a little peace. Instead, Miss Patel lingered.

"Perhaps you think I overstep. But I am more than a servant to this family. I don't like Mr. Hammond to forget it. Or for you to treat me as beneath you."

"I hope I don't. It was never my intention."

"I was with Vanita's household for many years. After her mother's death, I became her maid and confidant. We were not of the same caste, yet we became friends. When she and her father made plans to leave India, she asked me to travel with them as her companion and lady's maid, to stay with her always. I agreed."

That's loyalty, Claire thought, wondering if she had misjudged the woman. Or had Sonali been like Mary, desperate to leave a difficult situation?

Claire said, "That was quite a sacrifice on your part."

Sonali shook her head. "My own family was not . . . Our home was not a happy one. My father was cruel to my mother. My brothers cruel to me, the mere girl they saw as their slave. So while I was sorry to leave my *amma*, I was relieved to go."

She reached out and ran a finger over the sewing box. "I was with Vanita when she met Mr. Hammond. Stood with her as bridesmaid when she married him. Held her hand when her father died. Assisted the midwife when Mira was born. I was there in Turkey when the plague struck. Cared for Mira in another part of the embassy to keep her safe. So I was not at Vanita's bedside when she and her baby died. That I regret. I should have been there for my friend who was like a sister. My *didi*.

"Mr. Hammond asked me to stay with them even after Vanita died. To help with Mira. I did so. For I love Mira and . . . admire him. And when he decided at long last to honor his promise to bring the family to England, I thought I would become a member of that family too."

Claire stared at her dumbly, the pronouncement striking her like a blow to the stomach.

Sonali shook her head. "But no. Even now more than a year has passed, Mr. Hammond keeps me at arm's length, becomes, if anything, more distant.

"I see how he looks at you." She pressed a trembling hand to her chest. "I have already lost Vanita. Now I shall lose him and Mira as well—be cast aside and treated as a mere servant once again."

At the woman's confession, vinegary unease pooled in Claire's mouth. She choked it down. "I am sorry. That must be quite disappointing."

Did Mr. Hammond look at her with admiration? Claire decided it would be wiser to focus on the other things the woman had said. "If it helps, I think he does esteem you as a . . . family friend. I know he appreciates all you do for Mira. When I first arrived, he made it clear I need not concern myself with his daughter, for she was already well cared for."

"That is something, I suppose. Though not enough." At that, Miss Patel turned and swept from the room.

Claire sat back and expelled a long breath of relief.

After luncheon the next day, Claire sat across the desk from Mr. Hammond as the two went over a list of needed repairs and other maintenance items for the house.

Mira drew at the cleared table while Sonali sat nearby, embroidering a headscarf.

Someone knocked, and Mr. Hammond rose to answer before Claire could do so. A moment later, he returned with Armaan Sagar, come again to visit his niece. Mira rose to greet him.

He brought her a small parcel of lemon drops like those she had lost on the street upon their first meeting.

"Thank you, *Mamu*."

He looked to the papers, pencils, and few pieces of colored chalk at her place at the table.

"Did you draw these?" he asked, walking closer to peruse the childish pictures.

Mira followed. "Yes! This is me and Dolly. And this is me and *Amma*. I tried to draw her face, but it's too hard for me. And this one is all of us: you, me, Papa, Miss Summers, and Sonali."

"Well done. And this one is me?"

He pointed to a tall black stick figure.

"Yes. You wear dark clothes like Papa. But I had to use color for Sonali. She is like a rainbow."

Armaan glanced at Miss Patel and quickly away again. "I agree."

Mira slid the paper toward him. "Now you draw something."

"What shall I draw?"

"Something from India. I have never been."

"In that case, I wonder if you've ever seen an elephant?"

The girl shook her head, eyes wide. Claire listened with interest as well.

"Of all the animals in the East, the elephant is the largest. More than twelve feet high." Armaan took up the drawing pencil and began sketching as he talked. "The legs are short and stout, and the tail is curly like a hog's. It has large ears and a long trunk, which is strong but also nimble, able to retrieve the smallest nut from the ground. Elephants also have two long tusks, which protrude like so. One they keep sharp as a weapon, the other they blunt to gather food. They are remarkably intelligent. The *hotteewallies* train them to serve the nabobs and rajas, but I preferred to see them in the wild, coming down from the mountains to drink and swim in the river. They are excellent swimmers."

"I would like to see an elephant," Mira breathed in wonder.

"Perhaps someday you will. When I was in London, I learned they keep one in a menagerie there." He shook his head. "Though seeing a magnificent beast in captivity would not be the same."

Claire went and fetched refreshments for their visitor, bringing enough cups for all of them. The men enjoyed a pleasant conversation over hot tea and sugar biscuits while Sonali listened, Mira made another drawing, and Claire finished her list.

When the clock struck the hour, Mr. Hammond looked from Armaan to Sonali and rose. "I shall take Mira up for her nap today. I promised to read her another story anyway. You stay and finish your tea."

After the two left, Claire rose as well, having some tasks to complete before dinner. "And I should get back to work. A pleasure to see you again, Mr. Sagar."

She'd intended to go outside and water the flowers, but noticing someone's coat had fallen from the pegs in the hall, she walked over and picked it up.

Through the morning room's open door, she heard Sonali say, "You are not fooling anyone, you know. Wearing English clothes and speaking in an educated accent."

"It is not my intention to fool anyone."

"Then why do it?"

"I have not worn traditional clothing in more than twenty years. When I left home, I wore a uniform, first as a soldier and later as translator in the office of the governor. That's where I became acquainted with my friend, Major Hutton."

"Pff," she scoffed. "Do you really think he is your friend. Truly?"

"I do, absolutely. He risked his life for me, and I would do the same for him. And if I speak as an educated Englishman, it is because I attended a British school for several years. Vanita's father saw to my education. Mr. Aston was a generous man, you must admit."

"True."

He added, "And your English is excellent as well, I noticed."

"Out of necessity. I grew up speaking a different language than your family—Tamil. I learned to speak English in Mr. Aston's household. He preferred it."

"I see," Armaan replied. "And as far as my clothing, it was difficult enough to find someone willing to make an English suit of clothes for me here. Do you think the local tailor would agree to make a *dhoti* or *kurta*?"

"I suppose not. Yet I still wear *saree* and *choli*."

"And you look lovely in them."

"Th-thank you." She gave a nervous little laugh. "Can you imagine me in English dress?"

After a brief hesitation, he replied, "I could, but there is no need. You look well as you are."

As silently as possible, Claire slipped from the house.

16

The life of spies is to know, not be known.
—George Herbert, *Outlandish Proverbs*

Sarah sat with her mother and three of her sisters—Emily, Viola, and Georgie—in Sea View's parlour, chatting over tea and needlework, or in Emily's case, pen and notebook.

Sixteen-year-old Georgiana sat half-heartedly picking out some threads she had stitched incorrectly, her mind clearly elsewhere.

Mamma still expected her youngest to finish a sampler as a rite of passage for a young lady, a project Georgie had been working on for many months now.

Sarah's own sampler, along with Viola's, hung in Mamma's room. She had not yet hung Emily's, which would win no awards. And Claire's was upstairs in Sarah's trunk, where Sarah had hidden it, bringing it with her during the move. Neither the sampler nor Claire herself were where they should be.

Despite this glum thought, it was good to have Viola back with them after an absence of several weeks. She described with animation their wedding trip: the roads, the delays, the inns good and bad, the scenery, the beauties of Lake Windermere in Cumbria, and the rugged peaks and lochs of Scotland.

A wistful longing seeped into Sarah's soul as she listened. She tried to tell herself that she was merely missing Claire and wished her eldest sister could be there with them. But she knew, deep down, it was more than that.

As Viola described the clear water of the lochs, Sarah saw Callum Henshall's sea-green eyes, looking at her with warm admiration. When Viola talked about the beauty of the highlands, she saw his handsome face, with sunlight bronzing his high cheekbones. When she spoke of the lovely music they had heard at Scottish inns along the way, Sarah recalled listening to him play his Scottish *guittar*. She also recalled his bravery in rescuing stranded townspeople during the flood, and how her breath had hitched when his hand touched hers.

All the memories were not good ones, however. She had not responded well when he suggested she might carry her desire to organize and be useful into a new life as mistress of her own home. And before his departure, when he'd asked to write to her, she'd responded with a hasty, *"To what end?"* She could still see him flinch. At the time she'd told herself a clean break would be better, easier, for them both.

She had come to regret it. If only Scotland were not so far from Sidmouth. . . .

"Sarah?"

"Hm?" Yanked from her reverie, Sarah looked up to find her mother staring at her over half-moon spectacles.

"Did you hear me? I asked if you had spoken to Fran recently. I had hoped she would join us today."

"Oh. I hoped so too. She is probably busy at home." Sarah had guessed they would see Fran far less often after she married and moved to her husband's home two miles away. How infrequently would a woman see her family if she lived four hundred miles away?

Eager to shift the focus from herself, Sarah turned to Emily. "And where is James off to? I saw him leave the house, but I did not think he was going to Killerton today."

Sir Thomas had given James the use of a horse and two-wheeled carriage to travel to and from his country estate. James stabled the horse at Westmount with the major's horses.

"He is not," Emily replied easily. "Sir Thomas asked him to do something else today. To meet with some local man, apparently."

"Someone here in Sidmouth?"

"James did not divulge details, and I am learning, slowly, not to pry. Some of his work is confidential. Government secrets and all that. Though I doubt this meeting is anything so important."

"Interesting. Well, I'm sure he'll tell us if he can." Sarah returned to her sewing.

After a time, Georgie grumbled, "I wish Claire could join us. After all, this was her home too."

Sarah said gently, "Only briefly."

Emily turned to their mother. "I know you might not want Claire to come here to the house, but perhaps we might all take tea together at the York Hotel. Would that be so terrible?"

"Your father was adamant she not rejoin the family."

"That's not fair."

"He thought it best. He wanted to protect this family from scandal and protect all of your futures."

Emily said, "I hardly think that matters much anymore, considering our reduced circumstances and the fact we keep a boarding house."

"Guest house," Mamma corrected, as she always did.

Undeterred, Emily went on, "Besides, Viola and I are already married. And Sarah could be if she wanted."

Sarah ignored the comment.

"Perhaps," Mamma allowed. "Yet there is still Georgiana's future to consider."

Georgie's eyes flashed. "After what happened to Claire? I have no intention of even *thinking* about men!"

"Please don't despise all men because of what happened," Sarah said. "There are still honorable men in the world."

Emily waggled her eyebrows. "Thinking of any man in particular?"

Sarah dipped her head, neck heating. "Heavens, no."

"There is also Sea View's reputation to consider," Mamma said. "Guests want to stay at reputable establishments kept by people of good character."

"I don't think there is much risk of harm to Sea View now. The only risk I can think of is if someone from home heard the rumors and came here to spread them around. That seems unlikely."

"Remember, Claire is not asking to live here," Viola said. "She has a place at Broadbridge's. But she would dearly like to spend time with us. It's why she came to Sidmouth."

"I think Claire should be welcome to call on us, at least," Emily said. "I would love to have her join us here for our weekly gatherings."

"I would like it as well," Sarah said. "But that is up to Mamma."

They all looked toward their mother.

"I shall need to think about it. For the present, I will honor your father's wishes in this manner."

"Mamma!" Georgie dropped her sewing. "What is there to think abou—"

"Of course you do." Sarah gently spoke over the outburst. "Take all the time you need. I know it was a shock, Claire showing up like this."

"Indeed it was."

Removing her spectacles, Mamma rose a bit shakily and

retreated to her bedchamber, her footsteps accompanied by the terse whispers of her three younger daughters.

Sarah, however, followed their mother into her room and shut the door behind her.

"Mamma, I want you to know that whatever you decide I will stand with you. I cannot speak for the others, but—"

"Ha. Your sisters have made it plain they would welcome her back here with open arms, and I truly can't fault them." She looked into Sarah's face, her own features pained. "And you, my dear, dutiful daughter, must search your own conscience and do what you think is right." Her voice grew hoarse. "Do not blindly stand with me, a conflicted widow torn between duty to my husband and a heart longing to take my firstborn into my arms. . . ."

"Oh, Mamma." Sarah embraced her, hoping to comfort her, at least a little.

After luncheon, Claire helped Mary carry down the serving dishes. Then she gathered clean towels and started up the servants' stairs toward the water closet and bath-room. As she reached the first floor, she saw Mr. Hammond leading another man into the passage that led to his apartment.

"My study is through here. We shall not be disturbed or overheard there."

She only glimpsed his visitor's profile, yet the tall, dark-haired man seemed familiar. Was that not Emily's new husband? What could Mr. Hammond want with him? And why were they meeting where they would not be overheard?

Claire had thought Mr. Hammond's secret keeping was over.

Apparently not.

Secretive or not, surely the two men were not up to anything nefarious, were they? When they'd met, Emily's husband had mentioned he worked for a local member of Parliament. Mr. Hammond had reacted to that news by abruptly taking his leave. Why now was he meeting with him? And in private yet?

Had Mr. Hammond told her the truth about his diplomatic career—one he had supposedly put behind him? She hoped whatever they were meeting about would not endanger Emily's husband or his career. Did she owe it to her sister to make sure?

Curiosity and concern gnawing at her, Claire turned and went back downstairs. Leaving the towels in her room, she slipped out the tradesmen's entrance, up the outside stairs to street level, and then walked through the narrow alley beside the house toward the unused stables.

Glad to find the sliding door unchained, she gingerly pushed on the door, which barely budged, iron fittings heavy and perhaps rusty with disuse. She shoved again, harder, and this time the door begrudgingly slid open with a groan of complaint. She paused, straining to listen over her pounding heart. Had they heard?

When no alarm was raised, she slipped inside, the musty smells of old hay and manure assaulting her. Instantly struck with the need to sneeze, she pressed a finger beneath her nostrils and breathed through her mouth.

Thankfully, the urge passed. Claire waited for her eyes to adjust to the dim light and then crept across the hay-strewn floor toward a flight of narrow wooden stairs along one wall. Looking up, she saw a line of light seeping from under a door at the top. Male voices seeped through as well. She could not, however, make out the words.

Gripping the rickety railing, she slowly ascended. Nearing the door, she stopped to listen. Closer now, the voices were clearer.

"This must remain confidential—a secret project."

"I don't do that sort of thing anymore," Mr. Hammond replied.

"But you could."

"Perhaps. Where did they come from?"

"Hidden in a captured French ship and only recently discovered."

Claire listened in consternation. What were they talking about? Was he a spy after all? No. He had denied it, and quite vehemently. She believed him, did she not?

"The war is over," Mr. Hammond said.

"We have thought so before. Castlereagh thinks it best to learn all we can, to be better prepared the next time or even avert another war. Are you willing?"

"I might be," Mr. Hammond replied. "How soon?"

"I could have them delivered under guard as early as next week."

"Not sure I like the idea of armed guards traipsing past our guests. Perhaps they might come through the old stable below us and use the back door there. More discreet."

Claire held her breath, imagining both men turning toward the very door that concealed her. Hopefully Mr. Hammond wouldn't show his guest out that way now.

"As you think best. May I tell Castlereagh to proceed?"

"Will it be dangerous? I have a daughter to consider."

"Unlikely, although I suppose that depends on what you discover, and if anyone wants to keep us from learning what's in there. I doubt anyone would bother with something so complicated for a mere laundry list."

"Oh, you might be surprised," Mr. Hammond said, and Claire heard that familiar wry humor in his tone. After a moment he added, "Let me think on it."

"I am away most days, but I will be in church on Sunday."

"Very well. I shall give you my decision then."

Mr. Hammond had told her he had been a diplomat in

Austria, Russia, and the Ottoman Empire. What would that have to do with something found in a French ship now? And how could a boarding-house proprietor help avert a future war?

Claire tiptoed quietly down the stairs and out the stable door, pulling hard to slide it closed. *Secret project. Confidential. Dangerous? Armed guards?* What were they involved in? And what sort of trouble would she be in if she were caught eavesdropping?

Claire had made it to the front of the house and down the basement stairs when she heard the front door open and footsteps on the pavement above. She looked up in time to see Mr. Hammond's visitor emerge and walk away. Definitely Emily's husband.

Claire returned to her tasks even as her mind continued to mull over what she'd heard.

She wished now she had not sneaked up there. If anyone was guilty of spying, it was her.

A few hours later, weary from her labors and worries, Claire went back down to her room to tidy herself for dinner. She halted in the passage, surprised to see Mr. Hammond standing there. Her stomach knotted. Had he somehow learned of her eavesdropping?

A moment later, she noticed something else. On the floor near her door sat a leather-covered traveling trunk with brass studs and clasp. A pile of folded fabric lay on top.

"I hope you don't think me terribly rude," Mr. Hammond said, "but I notice you wear the same few dresses in rotation. Don't misunderstand me; you always look neat and pret . . . uh, perfectly presentable. This is not a criticism. Dash it, I'm making a muddle of this." He scrubbed a hand over his jaw, then gestured toward the trunk. "There on top are the yards of fabric I mentioned, should you want to make something for yourself. Vanita wore primarily English clothes, so hopefully something is appropriate, though there may be silk for a sari as well."

"Thank you."

"I also realize you are busy—up early, up late—and have little time for sewing. So I asked Mary to help me carry down the trunk as well. It contains Vanita's clothing. I have not looked inside since she . . ." He cleared his throat. "If there is anything that would suit you, please feel free to wear it or make it over for yourself as you like."

Sonali's disapproving face appeared in her mind's eye as Claire said, "But surely Mira will want these for herself one day?"

"She won't grow into them for at least ten years. You have sisters. Tell me, when Mira is a young lady of fourteen or fifteen, will she be interested in wearing her mother's gowns, a decade out of fashion?"

Claire chuckled. "Probably not."

"I would have carried it all the way in for you, but I promised not to enter your room, if you remember. A silly promise now, I think."

She looked up at him sharply.

"I did not mean . . . That is . . ." He grimaced and started again. "I only meant that the promise I extracted from you when you first arrived, 'I shan't enter your room and I ask that you not enter mine,' was boorish of me, I realize now. As if you would."

She *had* entered his private study, although not his bedroom, if that's what he'd meant. Her cheeks warmed at the thought, and she made no reply.

"Well." He straightened. "Shall I drag it inside before I go? Or will you take it from here?"

"I am sure I can push it the last few feet. Or Mary will help me. Again, I thank you. Very considerate."

She was tempted to ask him about Mr. Thomson's visit, but courage failed her, especially in the face of his kindness. She *would* ask him, though . . . soon.

When he had gone and Claire was sure she was alone, she adopted an unladylike crouch and shoved the trunk over the threshold and into her room. The way was harder going when the trunk came into contact with the carpet, but she managed to wrestle it against one wall.

She was not sure she would feel comfortable wearing one of his wife's dresses—and Miss Patel would certainly not approve—but perhaps she could make something from the lovely fabrics on top. She picked up a length of light blue lawn and another of spotted cambric. She would not attempt a complicated dress with layers and flounces and fancy trimming. In the past, her mother had hired modistes to make those sorts of gowns for them. Nevertheless, Claire thought she might be able to make a simple day dress with a gathered waist and lacing or a few buttons at the front for ease of dressing. And with the white cotton lawn, perhaps a second nightdress.

She studied a smaller piece of sturdy cotton twill. Maybe she could make short wraparound stays with it. Mary was sometimes late coming down to help her dress. Stays Claire could put on herself would help a great deal. Making a pair really ought to be her first priority . . . if only she knew how.

Next, Claire spread out several yards of figured sarcenet silk in a vibrant yellow-green. Not a color she would normally choose, but still a lovely material.

In her eagerness, Claire had left the door open, and Mary appeared on the threshold, eyes alight as she took in the rich and varied fabrics on Claire's bed.

"How lovely," she breathed. "Are ye gonna make somethin'?"

"I hope to."

"Wish I knew how to sew."

"You never learned?"

Mary shook her head. "Mam died when I was a bairn."

"I am sorry to hear it. Then your clothes . . . ?"

"Secondhand dealer."

Claire thought, then said, "I noticed your wraparound stays when we shared a room on the journey here. I'd like to make myself a pair. Might you lend me your spare to use as a pattern?"

"'Course, miss. Happily."

"I appreciate that. And I'm no dressmaker, but if you'd like to learn to sew, I would be happy to teach you, when our work allows."

"Truly? How kind ye are. Like the sister I always wanted."

The words both pricked and comforted. Claire squeezed the girl's hand. "That is the nicest thing you could say to me, Mary. Thank you."

17

Uninvited guests seldom meet a welcome.
—Aesop

The next day dawned grey and rainy, so Mr. Gwilt lit a fire in the library and Emily and Mamma sat in armchairs near the hearth, Emily writing and Mamma sewing.

Sarah sat at the desk, reviewing the reservations for the upcoming weeks in the registration book. As she did, she made notes of which rooms to assign and calculated the number of people they would serve at meals so she could provide that information to their cook, Mrs. Besley.

She looked over at the others and said, "We are expecting four new guests ten days from now: A Miss Craven and a Mr. Craven, as well as a Mrs. Harding and her maid."

"Mr. Craven?" Emily looked up, a deep frown marring her pretty face. "Not Sidney Craven."

Sarah consulted the original letter. "Why, yes."

"I did not confirm rooms for those people!" Emily insisted. "I would not have accepted their request. Who did?"

"I believe I wrote that letter myself," Mamma calmly replied. "You have been rather busy of late, what with your novel and new husband."

Emily blushed, pretty looks restored. "I suppose I have been distracted. In the best possible ways."

"Now, what is wrong with the Cravens?" Mamma asked.

"They are friends of Lord Bertram."

Mamma flinched. "I have asked you all not to say that name."

"It cannot be helped in this instance," Emily replied. "I don't know who Mrs. Harding is, but Mr. Craven and his sisters came here last summer with . . . that man. The sisters were tolerable, I suppose. But Mr. Craven was quite rude."

"Well, we've survived rude guests before and we shall again," Mamma said. "It's too late to turn them away now."

"At least there are no Bertrams mentioned in the request," Sarah said.

"True," Emily agreed. "We definitely do not want that man here."

Sarah rose. "Let's make sure our best rooms are especially clean. Perhaps fresh flowers for the ladies?"

"Good idea."

"I shall confer with Mrs. Besley about meals."

Mamma rose as well. "Actually, Sarah, let me do that. I think we might be wise to serve a somewhat finer menu to these particular guests."

"You are kinder than I am, Mamma," Emily said. "I'd serve that man fish heads and tripe, were it up to me."

"It is not kindness, Emily. It is strategy. The happier they are with their stay, the less likely they will circulate a bad report among people we know."

Claire entered the morning room a few days later and sat at the desk, girding herself to face the unpleasant task of balancing the accounts. But instead of the account book, a collection of new art supplies lay atop the desk: a fresh sketch pad, several pencil-shaped sticks of colored chalk, and a set of watercolor paints and brushes.

She glanced up and found Mr. Hammond watching her expectantly.

"I cannot accept these. You've given me too much already. Or are these for Mira?"

"Of course you can accept them. It's just a few art supplies the stationer had on hand. I hope they prove useful."

"I'm sure they would, but I—"

"And Mira will enjoy sharing them with you. We can call it a gift for you both, if you prefer."

"I do. Thank you." Claire was mortified to feel tears fill her eyes and threaten to spill over.

For most of the last two years, she had been starved of affection and deprived of caring gestures. Now, in the span of a few days, Emily, Sarah, and now Mr. Hammond had brought her unexpected, undeserved gifts.

Regarding her with mounting concern, he said, "I did not mean to upset you. If I've done wrong, or these are the wrong things, I can take them back. . . ."

"No, they are perfect. Truly."

"Good." He crossed his arms. "You know, I've had a thought. Mr. Filonov is an artist. Perhaps he might give you a lesson or two. I'm not saying you need it. But as he's here, you might gain some benefit, or at least enjoy seeing his work."

"I have no pretensions of becoming a bona fide artist," Claire replied. "I began drawing and painting the occasional watercolor for the simple pleasure of it. Even so, I would enjoy seeing his work."

"I will mention it to him. I am sure he would be pleased to show you."

That evening after dinner, he asked Mr. Filonov to bring his coffee into the morning room and join them there.

"Why don't you tell us something of your background, how you came to be an artist."

Their guest nodded and sat down, and Claire refilled his cup.

"Sank you." He sipped, then began, "I was student at Imperial Academy of Arts in Sankt Petersburg, and earn scholarship to study in Europe: Rome, *Napoli*, Capri. . . ." He kissed his fingertips and said something that sounded like "Ochen harasho."

"When scholarship ends, I return to Russia. Stay for many years. Now I come to England. Paint seascapes and landscapes. Sell some too." He grinned at her. "So don't worry—I pay my bill."

Claire assured him she was not worried and went on to ask several questions about his travels and favored mediums.

Then, taking advantage of the opportunity, she asked, "And how did you meet Mr. Hammond?"

"Ah. We met at . . ."

He looked to William, who supplied, "A party for the British ambassador."

"Da." The man nodded. "I was honored to be invited but also . . . intimidated—is right word? I am not good at parties. Many people. My English, not so good."

"I think it's excellent," Claire said sincerely.

"I improve since then. Mr. Hammond showed me great kindness. He spoke French and a little Russian, and I was grateful. Less like, what is saying, fish outside de water."

She nodded, and with a glance at Mr. Hammond, noticed him shift uncomfortably.

"He came to Russia for special project. Training new attachés—is correct?"

Mr. Hammond winced. "Something like that. Enough

about me. I believe Miss Summers would rather see some of your work, if you are willing."

"Of course, of course!" He rose. "Most welcome."

She and Mr. Hammond followed him up the stairs to his room.

Inside, they lit lamps and Claire looked through Mr. Filonov's sketches in pencil, pen, and chalk. Then he showed her several oil paintings propped against the walls: moody, muted seascapes and landscapes of the surrounding area. One was a view of Sidmouth from a height east of town.

"Where did you paint this?" she asked.

Mr. Hammond peered over her shoulder. "That is from Salcombe Hill."

The artist nodded. "Mr. Hammond take me there."

"Lovely," Claire murmured.

Mr. Hammond's gaze shifted to her. "Indeed."

Claire thought back. "I vaguely recall walking there with one of my sisters. Though that's years ago now."

"Then you shall have to see it again sometime."

She glanced away, unable to meet his direct gaze. "Perhaps I shall."

On Sunday, Claire donned her usual black dress and followed behind Mr. Hammond and Mira on the way to church. Again she quietly yet firmly refused Mr. Hammond's request that she sit with them. And when Georgiana sidled up to her and whispered, "Come and sit with us," Claire shook her head and sat in the same pew she'd occupied before.

Mamma and Sarah walked by without a word, although Sarah squeezed her hand in passing. Mr. Thomson and Emily followed. Emily hesitated upon noticing her and seemed about to stop and talk, but her husband gently took her arm and ushered her forward to their pew with a quiet word in her ear, perhaps to avoid drawing attention to themselves.

Viola appeared next. She paused at the end of the pew and glanced along its length, evidently to gauge if she and the major could squeeze in, but the pew was full. Claire gave her an apologetic look.

She heard a whispered exchange behind them, and a moment later Major Hutton positioned a wheeled invalid chair next to the end panel beside Claire.

The chair's elderly occupant patted the major's hand in thanks and waved him on his way. Then she turned a beaming smile on Claire. At first Claire tensed, expecting disgruntled looks or mutterings from her pew-mates, but none of them objected. In fact, a few actually smiled at the old woman who'd joined their row.

Regardless, Claire was relieved when the service began and everyone looked toward the raised pulpit at front. She did her best to concentrate, even as she wondered who the woman was. She also tried not to stare at the Hammonds or her family.

When the service concluded, the elderly woman in the chair reached over and took her hand. "You are Miss Claire Summers, I know. Viola has told me much about you."

She wished she could say the same. "Thank you, Mrs. . . . ?"

"Denby. Jane Denby."

"I'm afraid I am new to town," Claire said, "and am not yet acquainted with my sisters' friends."

"We shall have to remedy that. I hope you will come and take tea with me at the poor house one day soon. I can't promise the tea won't be weak and the biscuit tin empty, but I can promise a warm welcome."

"Sounds lovely. I will even bring some tea and biscuits, if you'd like."

"Just the tea, I think. Your sister Sarah often brings us baked goods. Such a dear."

Sarah came down the aisle at that moment, and the sisters held gazes. Claire said, "I have always thought so."

Then others began greeting Mrs. Denby, clearly a popular person. Claire excused herself and slipped from the pew.

As she left the church, she glanced over and noticed Mr. Thomson and Mr. Hammond in a quiet conversation that ended with a shaking of hands.

18

PROFILE MINIATURE PAINTER
Profiles neatly finished, shaded in water colours
. . . Children in colours, and full-length, 5s.
—J. H. Gillespie, printed handbill

A few days later, Mr. Hammond said he would be busy in his study most of the afternoon. Finding the house quiet and her tasks completed, Claire went down to her room. As she opened her shutters to let in more light, she noticed men wearing Hessian boots with swords at their sides march past. Military men were a fairly common sight in Sidmouth, so Claire gave them little heed and sat down at her small table with the satinwood sewing box.

She had meant to make herself a new dress straightaway, but as Mr. Hammond had said, she was up early and up late most days as it was, and the project seemed overwhelming to her. She had progressed no further than sketching out the basic design. Where would she spread the fabric to do the cutting? And what if she made a major mistake and ruined the gifted material? Perhaps she should ask Sarah for help. Or begin with something smaller.

She had made a good start on her wraparound stays, which the French called *corset à la paresseuse* or "lazy stays." Contrary to the name, constructing and stitching the undergarment had proved to be more work than she'd anticipated. She still needed to add boning and gussets, but even so, the project was coming along well.

In the meantime, she had grown thoroughly weary of her few frocks. Mr. Hammond's words, *"I notice you wear the same few dresses in rotation"*—though kindly delivered—revealed others were aware of her limited clothing as well.

Her gaze strayed to the trunk against the wall. Mr. Hammond had said she should feel free to wear anything that suited her or to make something over for herself.

She remembered the almost-strangled look on his face—the repressed emotion, the tight voice—when he'd said, *"Vanita's clothing. I have not looked inside since she . . ."*

Claire had not yet looked inside either, but surely he'd expected her to by now.

Curiosity rising, Claire opened the trunk. She carefully began extracting the garments within and laying them on her bed—a spencer, two chemises, and two day dresses.

She paused to consider the day dresses. One was of gauzy white muslin, which did not seem practical in her situation. The other was of a sturdier green cambric with dainty embroidered flowers on the bodice. A flounce had been sewn to the hem of the skirt and a wide strip of shiny satin ribbon stitched at the waist. After studying it, Claire decided she could easily remove the flounce and waist trim. At the neckline she could wear the fichu Sarah had returned to her. These changes combined would hopefully render it less recognizable for Sonali's sake as well as Mr. Hammond's. Claire had no wish to provoke the one or sadden the other by parading around in a gown that had obviously belonged to Vanita.

Claire set aside the green day dress to alter and returned to her perusal of the trunk. She pulled out an evening dress of ivory silk embellished with tiny seed pearls. Lovely. Too lovely. She would not dare wear it. Beneath it lay a matching reticule, a few pairs of stockings, and a marigold-yellow embroidered sari and matching skirt.

One final item lay nestled on the bottom. A small tissue-wrapped parcel. A jewelry case, perhaps? She unwrapped it and found a framed miniature portrait.

Claire lifted it closer. For a moment she thought the subject was Mira. But as she studied the image, she realized the figure depicted was an adolescent girl or young teen. She wore a sari like Sonali's and a beaded veil over black, center-parted hair. A jewel adorned her forehead, and gold earrings dangled from her ears.

This must be Vanita Aston when young. She wondered if Mr. Hammond knew the miniature was in the trunk, and guessed not.

Rising, she carried it upstairs and across the passage to his apartment. There she hesitated, then knocked on the outer door.

A few moments later, Mr. Hammond opened it a mere crack.

"Ah, Miss Summers. Um . . ."

He glanced over his shoulder. At what? A visitor? The aforementioned guards? She thought again of the soldiers she'd seen marching past. Delivering the secret project, whatever it was?

He slipped out through the narrow opening and quickly shut the door behind himself. "Everything all right?"

"Sorry, I did not realize you had a guest. I just found something in the trunk I thought you should have."

She extended the portrait, face up.

He stilled, expression transfixed. He slowly reached out and accepted it gingerly. Reverently.

"I forgot this was in there. I packed in a hurry, without much forethought."

"Your wife, I assume?"

He nodded. "Yes."

His chin trembled. He turned his face, but not before she saw the tears in his eyes.

"Forgive me," Claire said. "I should not have given it to you so abruptly, without warning."

"No. It's not . . . It is only the surprise of seeing it again."

He paused, throat working, and she knew he was fighting for control. After an audible swallow, he continued. "It's the only portrait I have of her, painted when she was quite young. I meant to have another commissioned after we married. I meant to do a lot of things. . . ."

His shoulders shook. Claire reached out to lay a hand on his arm but stopped herself before touching him. "Again, I apologize. I shall leave you."

She turned and retreated. At the opposite door she glanced back and saw him still standing there, shoulders hunched, apparently gathering himself before returning to whatever—or whoever—awaited him inside.

Two days later, alterations complete, Claire donned the modified day dress, feeling supremely self-conscious as she did so. She looked at herself in the small mirror in her room. It was a rather plain dress, except for the small embroidered flowers on the bodice. And with her own fichu knotted like a neckerchief, the ends dangling over her chest, those adornments were barely noticeable.

She began her workday as usual by helping Mary carry up the breakfast things for guests and family alike.

"Pretty dress, miss," Mary said.

"Thank you."

Sonali came into the morning room. Mira sometimes insisted, Claire knew, on charging over to her father's room in the mornings and walking down with him. So Sonali entered alone.

Sonali looked at Claire, gaze riveted on the dress and a scowl upon her face.

She muttered something in a foreign tongue, then said, "That is Vanita's dress. Why are you wearing it?"

Claire's stomach sank. "I am sorry. I did not intend to upset you. I selected the plainest of her dresses and thought I had changed it enough that it would not be obvious."

"I embroidered those flowers myself. I would recognize them anywhere."

"I had no idea. You may have the dress. I shall change and give it to you."

Sonali shook her head and threw up her hands. "What would I do with it? Vanita wore English clothes. I do not."

Claire studied the woman's agitated profile. "I hate to see you so unhappy. Is there anything I can do to help?"

"Leave."

Claire's head jerked back as though slapped, and she chastised herself for inviting the rebuke. She turned to go, but Sonali called her back.

"No, wait. That was unkind."

Claire took a deep breath to summon self-control, then managed to speak calmly and gently. "Do you regret coming here with the Hammonds? Do you wish to go somewhere else?"

"If I am unhappy here, I should just leave—is that it? Easy for you to say. You are brave and white, with the means to travel. You want me gone."

"No! I am only trying to understand why you stay if you are so miserable." She lowered her voice. "You mentioned you . . . admired Mr. Hammond. But if that is not to be . . . ?"

"Of course I stay. An unmarried woman, alone? A foreign woman, with little money of my own. What else can I do? When he asked me to come with them to England, I thought . . ." She shook her head almost violently. "He says I misunderstood. He only asked me to remain for Mira's sake. To help keep alive memories of her *amma*, whom I knew so well."

"You are given a generous wage, I believe? Or allowance, if you prefer the more genteel term."

"I do," she snapped. "Yes, I have been paid to care for Mira so he can climb his precious hills and hide away in his study. I have made his life easy. Too easy. He uses me when it is convenient."

Claire winced. "Please don't phrase it like that. If someone overheard, it could be misconstrued. I have never seen him treat you with anything other than respect and propriety. Do you say otherwise?"

"No. Despite my efforts, he is cold to me. You alone seem to warm his blood. Yet I wonder, Miss Summers, if you are truly the 'respectable female' he advertised for?"

Claire stilled. Had the woman somehow discovered her secret? "What do you mean?"

Sonali raised her head high and looked down her long nose. "What truly 'respectable' lady would answer such an advertisement? Would live under the same roof as an unmarried man and do such menial tasks, and not possess her own sewing things!" She turned and stormed off.

When Miss Patel had gone, Claire took several more calming breaths and prayed for both the woman and herself. She stepped into the hall and drew back abruptly to find Mr. Hammond and Mira standing there. How much had he overheard?

He tucked his chin and gave her an apologetic look. "Sorry. I did not intend to eavesdrop, but I heard some of that as we came downstairs."

She nodded in acknowledgment, wondering what he would say.

He gestured his daughter into the morning room. "I see

Mrs. Ballard has made your favorite muffins. Why not go in and start with one of those? We shall join you in a moment."

Mira hurried to comply.

When she had gone, he heaved a sigh. "I did not realize I was inviting trouble when I asked Sonali to come here with us. Nor that she believed I might marry her after we'd both mourned a suitable period. I have tried, gently, to discourage her."

"You knew she hoped . . . ?"

He grimaced. "I noticed the gradual change a few months after Vanita died. I pretended not to notice her hints at first. Lingering after dinner, standing closer than before, the seemingly accidental touches in passing or when handing Mira into my arms. I hoped it would pass when she realized I did not reciprocate. It has not."

Another grimace. "Perhaps it was selfish of me to ask her to remain for Mira's sake. Yet Mira had already lost her mother. I did not want her to lose Sonali as well."

"I understand."

"If she were any other servant, treating others rudely as she does, I would have dismissed her long ago. But she was Vanita's friend. And as far as what she said about you . . . I can only apologize on her behalf and assure you that her bitter words reflect poorly on herself, not you."

Claire managed a halfhearted smile and excused herself, saying she would go down and see if the coffee was ready.

As she walked away, she wondered how quickly his gallantry would fade if he knew there was at least some truth to the woman's words.

After Sonali's explosive reaction to seeing her in one of Vanita's dresses, Claire once again looked through the pile of folded fabric and considered making a new dress for herself. The project still seemed too daunting.

She decided she would begin with something smaller. A

simple dress for Mira. If she failed, at least the attempt would waste less fabric.

She borrowed one of the girl's current frocks from the laundry for size, sketched a rudimentary design, and set to work.

Emily tapped on her window while she was sewing, and Claire rose to open the door to her. Her sister invited her to take tea with them at the York Hotel. "Perhaps tomorrow? I'm not sure who all will be able to join us, but Viola and Georgie certainly. Maybe Sarah, too, if we can pry her away from her to-do list."

"What time?"

"Whenever it is easiest for you to get away."

"I usually take a respite in the early afternoon, if that suits."

"Perfectly."

Claire agreed, and the plan was arranged.

At the appointed time the next day, Claire changed into her blue carriage dress and stopped by the morning room to remind Mr. Hammond she was going out. His gaze lingered briefly on her dress, but he said nothing.

Claire then left the house and walked the short distance to the York Hotel on the seafront.

Emily had said nothing about Mamma coming, so Claire was not especially nervous. It was only tea with her sisters. Not a court-martial to try her for desertion.

Claire walked into the hotel and found the door to the dining room. She stepped over the threshold and stopped midstride. Her mother sat at a table with her sisters. Seeing her enter, Mamma shifted in her chair, looking uncomfortable. Sarah appeared similarly uneasy.

Emily rose and pulled out the last empty chair for Claire before a waiter could do so. "You're here. Excellent. Come and join us."

"Are you . . . sure it's all right? I hope this is not a shock to you as it is to me, Mamma."

"No, Mamma agreed to come."

"Please sit down," Mamma said, with a glance around. "No need to draw unwanted attention."

Claire sat, feeling uncertain and out of place.

Viola said, "We've ordered tea and cake, but if you prefer something else . . . ?"

"No. Sounds fine."

Georgiana said, "I still don't understand why we could not all take tea together at Sea View, but the cakes here *are* delicious."

"I have told you why," Mamma said in a quiet undertone.

Heart burning, Claire spoke in an equally hushed voice. "I am sorry, you know. I never imagined it would come to this. I truly thought he loved me and planned to marry me."

Mamma huffed. "I don't doubt you are sorry. I am sorry as well, but it does not change what happened."

"To Papa, you mean? I know you blame me for his death. Aunt Mercer told me so."

"She never!" Viola exclaimed, incredulous.

"Shh. Let's keep our voices down," Mamma warned. "This is not a conversation for a public place."

"But you won't let her come to the house," Emily reminded her.

A waiter delivered tea and slices of cake to their table. When he had departed, Mamma sipped her tea and leaned in to make her low voice heard.

"I will not sprinkle sugar on the facts. God may be merciful, but our actions, our sins, always have consequences. We may not like it, yet that is the way the world works."

Claire sighed. "Perhaps I should have married Harrison Welch as Papa wished, then none of this would have happened."

Georgie turned to Viola beside her and whispered, "Who's that?"

"The son of Papa's friend, Mr. Welch. Papa wanted her to marry him."

Mamma's lips tightened. "That boy turned out to be a grave disappointment to his parents."

"We have that in common," Claire murmured.

"Then, why did Papa want her to marry him?" Georgie asked.

"We did not learn until later that he was not all we believed him to be. Your father thought if she married his friend's son he would keep her close. He did not like the idea of her marrying some stranger with a house in London or some far-off estate. But he would not have wanted to see her miserable, which she would have been, if half of what I've heard about Harry Welch is true."

A fashionably dressed, middle-aged woman stopped at their table.

"Good day, ladies. A pleasure to see you."

"Good day," Mamma returned the greeting, although not very eagerly.

The woman's gaze swept the table and landed on Claire. "Have a friend visiting?" she asked.

Mamma's smile seemed forced, but hopefully the woman did not notice. "Y-yes."

When Mamma failed to make the introductions, Sarah said, "Lady Kennaway, please allow me to introduce our sister Claire."

Claire dutifully rose and curtsied. "A pleasure, my lady."

"Likewise. Ah. Now I see the resemblance. I don't believe we've met before."

"No," Claire replied. "I have only lately come to Sidmouth."

Sarah hurried to explain, "She had been caring for an ailing relative in Edinburgh, until her recent death."

"I see. Most admirable. Well, I won't keep you. Enjoy your reunion."

After she left, Mamma hissed, "Now, that's enough of the past. Let's speak of topics more appropriate to our surroundings."

Sarah obliged by asking Claire how things were going at the boarding house, and how often she saw Fran.

Claire, in turn, asked how long they had been hosting guests at Sea View and how it had all come about. She also asked what advice they would give her, still relatively new in her situation at Broadbridge's.

When Viola raised the subject of Mr. Hammond's surprising connection to the major's friend Armaan, Claire explained that Mr. Hammond had come to Sidmouth, at least in part, in hopes of meeting his wife's half brother. She also described the sweet bond between Mr. Hammond's young daughter and her uncle Armaan.

Viola nodded and said, "Mr. Hammond brought her to Westmount the other day. Such a sweet little girl. Oh, before I forget, I brought her a little something. Just a little ribbon with a silk flower I saw at the market. I thought it would look well in her hair." She handed over a small paper-wrapped parcel. "Armaan is happy about it as well. How wonderful to discover connections to a family he thought he had lost."

Claire swallowed a hard lump. "Yes."

A short while later, tea drunk and cake eaten, the ladies rose to depart. As they did, Claire said softly to Mamma, "I know you don't wish me to come to the house, but perhaps you might call on me at Broadbridge's as my sisters have done? Would that be all right? I miss you."

Mamma held her gaze, throat convulsing. "I . . . shall think about it."

"Thank you." Claire longed to reach out and touch her mother's hand but resisted.

19

Uninvited guests are often most welcome when they leave.
—*Aesop's Fables*

After taking tea with her family, Claire returned to Broadbridge's and went upstairs to Mira's room to give her Viola's gift.

She paused in the doorway, surprised by the sight within. Sonali sat on a chair, while Mira sat on the floor, back resting against the woman's legs. Sonali was massaging Mira's hair, and from the girl's drowsy lids and half smile, she seemed to be enjoying the experience.

"That looks pleasant," Claire said.

Sonali's head snapped up, and Claire was taken aback to see tears in her eyes. Blinking them away, the woman opened her mouth, then seemed to think the better of whatever retort she'd been about to deliver. She looked back down at the child and simply said, "Mira likes it."

Mira nodded her agreement, then quickly stilled so the massage would continue. She said, "*Amma* used to do this for me."

Claire raised the package. "This is for you, Mira, a gift from my sister Viola. I shall leave it here on the dressing chest."

Duty completed, Claire lingered, still curious. "Is that oil you are rubbing in?"

"Of course."

"And do you do this for your own hair as well?"

"Why do you ask?"

"I have noticed how lovely and shiny your hair is. I suppose now I have learned your secret."

Sonali glanced up at the compliment, then raised one shoulder. "No secret. Many Indian women do this. Mothers pass it down to daughters. It is tradition."

"Did your mother do that for you?"

The woman glanced up again and her eyes flattened. "No." She quickly looked away.

Claire feared she had offended her and she'd say no more, but a moment later, Sonali added, "Though some of my earliest memories are of sitting at my grandmother's feet as she massaged my hair. Sometimes we talked, sometimes we sat in peaceful silence. She added crushed hibiscus flowers to her oil. The smell still reminds me of her."

"What kind of oil are you using?"

"The last of the apricot oil I brought with me, mixed with oil of castor beans."

"Castor oil? Ugh."

"Foul to the taste, perhaps, but good for the hair and scalp."

"Then do you wash it out?"

"Later. For now, we braid the hair and let the oil absorb. We shall wash it in the morning."

"Did you do this for Mrs. Hammond as well?"

"Yes, and she for me." Tears misted her eyes once more, but she wiped them away with an oily hand. "After she married, sometimes her husband performed the service for her—at least while the two were newly wed."

Claire felt her neck warm and did her best to banish the image of Mr. Hammond massaging his wife's hair.

Sonali added, "When he grew too busy and began working all hours, I resumed the task for Vanita."

"I am sure you miss her. What a grievous loss for you all."

Sonali nodded. "Thank you. You are kind to include me in that sentiment."

After a moment of companionable silence—rare in this woman's presence—Sonali asked, "And you, Miss Summers. What traditions did your mamma pass down to you and your . . . several sisters, I believe?"

"Oh." A rush of rejection and shame rose up in her, but she pushed it aside like a moth-eaten curtain and looked further back into her memories, to the time before she had broken her parents' hearts. "Yes. I have four younger sisters. Two already married, which makes me quite the old maid. Growing up, Mamma taught us how to sew and embroider. How to behave in church, and how to pray. From her example, we learned to be charitable to all, generous with those less fortunate, and gracious hostesses."

"Ah. Perhaps that is why you are so good with the guests here."

Claire blinked at the unexpected compliment. "I hope I am. Mamma was all a genteel lady should be. I regret not following her example more faithfully."

Sonali's keen gaze sharpened. "You made mistakes?"

Claire was torn between honesty and self-preservation. She wanted to improve her relationship with this woman but did not yet trust her not to use anything she said to disparage her to Mr. Hammond. Claire settled on, "Of course. Have we not all made mistakes?"

Sonali nodded. "At least your mother was a good example."

"True," Claire agreed, wishing again she could earn her worthy mother's forgiveness and reclaim a place in her life.

She tilted her head to study Miss Patel's expression. "And your mother? Was she not a good example?"

Sonali opened her mouth to reply but then, with a glance at her young charge, said, “I will only say that I loved her, but she was weak and let men take advantage of her. I shall not do the same.”

That evening after dinner, Sarah and Mamma sat in the drawing room together. Georgiana was in the parlour with Mr. Hornbeam, who was attempting to teach her how to play chess. Blind though he was, the man had an excellent memory. His opponents called out their moves as they made them, and Mr. Hornbeam kept track of the positions in his mind, dictating his own moves in response. He usually won.

Sarah recalled with fondness that Callum Henshall had been the first to offer to play chess with the man during his stay at Sea View—to cheer him after a disappointing visit from his selfish son. Just one of Mr. Henshall’s many considerate acts.

Emily and Mr. Thomson came in from the veranda and bid them good-night before retiring for the evening.

“Before you go up,” Mamma said, “tell us more about our guests arriving tomorrow—besides their unfortunate taste in friends, that is, and Mr. Craven’s rudeness.”

“Very well.” Telling James she would follow shortly, Emily sat down with them while he continued upstairs.

“Would I have ever met the Cravens?” Sarah asked. “I don’t recall doing so.”

Emily shook her head. “I met them last summer at a ball in the assembly rooms. You did not go. I went with Mr. Stanley and his sister, remember? Oh! But you may have seen Mr. Craven. He was the batsman who struck Viola with a cricket ball at the visitors-versus-fishermen match.”

“That was an accident, surely.”

“Yes. Although his flippancy afterward was less forgivable.”

"That man is coming here?" Mamma frowned. "Unfortunate, indeed."

"I can think of a few other words for it."

"Well, thank God Viola was not seriously injured. Now, go on. Tell us about meeting them."

"I recognized Lord Bertram from Charles's house party, and he recognized me. He was quite civil and introduced me to Mr. Craven and his sisters. Mr. Craven asked me to dance and made me rather uncomfortable—lingering hands, leering looks, innuendo. I am not sure if he knows for certain about Claire, but Lord Bertram must have said something about her for Craven told me he'd 'heard of the beauty of the Summers sisters.' I did not like learning we had a reputation among strangers, though I did not know why at the time. I even danced with Lord Bertram, who was at least more polite."

"You danced with him?" Mamma looked pained.

"I would never have done so had I known what happened between him and Claire."

"Again, we can be grateful he is not coming to Sea View," Sarah reminded them.

"True," Emily agreed, "although his friend may be worse. I asked Charles about Mr. Craven when he was here. He called the man a libertine."

Mamma shook her head in disgust. "And his sisters?"

"One of the Miss Cravens took me aside after I danced with Lord Bertram and whispered a warning in my ear, telling me not to trust him. She said, 'He flirts with many women he has no intention of marrying.'"

"Was she referring to Claire?" Mamma asked, clearly anxious.

"I don't know. But considering she said, 'many women,' perhaps she spoke in general terms."

Mamma groaned into her handkerchief.

Sarah asked, "And how did you respond to Miss Craven's warning?"

"Rudely, I'm afraid. I thought she was insolent or must be jealous of Lord Bertram's attentions toward me. Now I see her warning was just."

"Well." Sarah patted her hand. "Tomorrow you shall have a chance to make amends."

Claire attended church again that Sunday and sat in the same pew near the back. Once again Mrs. Denby gestured to Major Hutton to place her wheeled chair at the end of Claire's row. Claire shared a smile with the woman and then with Viola before she and her husband continued on to the front.

After the service, Mrs. Denby reached over and squeezed her hand. "How are you keeping, my dear?"

"Fairly well, I think."

The older woman leaned near and sank her voice. "I am sorry to see you separated from your family like this, but I hope we might be friends."

"I would like that. Thank you."

Viola and the major came to collect Mrs. Denby, but the sweet woman said, "Perhaps Miss Claire might walk me home, if she would not mind?"

"Oh, I . . . would be happy to," Claire replied.

"Good. That way, you can see where I live and then visit me again when you have the time."

Claire nodded, and noticed Viola send the woman a grateful look.

A few minutes later, Claire pushed the wheeled chair down Church Street and then up narrow Back Street. They passed the post office and several shops. Outside the Nicholls lace shop, a young woman sat on a stool, bent over the plump pillow on her lap, bobbins shifting nimbly in her hands. Claire thought of Mr. Jackson's admonition to pause and admire the skill of the lace makers. She would have walked past to complete her task, however, had Mrs. Denby not said, "Can we stop a moment?"

"Yes, of course."

Together, the two watched the young woman work. The speed at which her hands moved the many bobbins was impressive indeed.

Mrs. Denby said, "My mother, sister, and I made sprigs like that. It does my heart good to see her make lace as we used to do."

Mrs. Denby politely greeted the young woman and introduced Claire, and then the two moved on. When they were out of earshot, Mrs. Denby said, "And please don't think poorly of her for working on Sunday. Times are hard for lace makers."

Mrs. Denby then directed her to follow the next street until they reached a neat brick building, much nicer than she would have expected. Inside, rooms opened off a central corridor. As they started down it, Mrs. Denby said, "I am in number three."

Claire pushed her to the door marked *3*. The woman lifted the latch with gnarled fingers, and Claire guided the chair inside a tidy, sparsely furnished room.

When she was settled, Mrs. Denby reached out and took Claire's hand. "I lost my mother and sister years ago and still miss them. I can only imagine how you must be feeling. Yet never forget, where there is life, there is hope, and I shall be praying for all of you."

"Thank you, Mrs. Denby."

On Sunday afternoon, the Summerses' unwelcome guests arrived somewhat earlier than expected. A carriage halted on the drive, and a liveried footman hopped down to help the occupants alight before Mr. Gwilt could hurry out to meet the coach.

Mamma and Georgie were still out on one of their long walks. Perhaps, Sarah thought, that was for the best. She asked Emily if she would prefer to be absent as well, but Emily squared her shoulders and said, "I shall not hide in my own home."

As the new guests approached, Mr. Gwilt opened the door for them. First to enter were two women, past the first blush of youth but still pretty and elegantly attired in carriage dresses and smart hats.

After them came a slender man dressed in all the accoutrements of a dandy: cravat pin, quizzing glass, and gold-tipped walking stick that set off his well-tailored suit to ornate perfection. He looked vaguely familiar, but Sarah doubted she would have recognized him from the cricket match had Emily not told her.

Behind him trudged a grim-faced woman burdened with a load of bandboxes and other cases. The lady's maid, Sarah guessed. Mr. Gwilt was quick to offer his assistance to her as well as to the footman now lugging in the trio's baggage.

Sarah managed a smile. "Welcome to Sea View."

Emily said, "How astonished we were to receive your letter asking to stay here." Her words were perfectly polite, her tone less so.

If Mr. Craven noticed, he gave no sign. Instead his eyes lit with interest. "Ah, a pleasure to see you again, Miss Summers." He swept off his top hat and bowed.

"That is no longer my name. I recently married. I am Mrs. Thomson now."

The light in his eyes dimmed. "Pity."

"Not at all, I assure you."

"For me, I mean."

With a glance at her pretty sister, Sarah supposed they had

their answer as to why such fashionable people would choose to stay at Sea View rather than the York Hotel or London Inn.

One of the ladies gave a discreet cough, and Mr. Craven turned and gestured toward them. "You may remember my sisters, Caroline and Persephone."

"I too have recently married," the older of the two, Caroline, said. "To Welford Harding, the shipping magnate. Perhaps you have heard of him?"

"I am afraid not," Emily said. "But congratulations."

"Well, do come in and we shall get everything settled," Sarah said, gesturing toward the door of the office.

Once inside, Sarah selected keys to rooms across the front of the house, with views of the sea.

Mrs. Harding said, "I should have the best room, as I am the only one among us married, and first in precedence. And do put Herriot, my lady's maid, close to me."

"Very well. I shall put you in Scots Pine. It has a smaller, adjoining room that should suit your maid well." Sarah did not enjoy putting unpleasant people in the room named for Mr. Henshall, but she refused to let her heart rule over matters of business.

"And Miss Craven, I will give you the Oak room. It also has an excellent view. And Mr. Craven, you shall be on the other side of Mrs. Harding."

Sidney Craven gave a teasing pout. "I had hoped for a room next to Miss Emily's, but alas, my hopes are for naught now."

Emily's eyes flashed. "My husband would object most vehemently should you trespass anywhere near our room, I assure you."

He smirked. "I do so like a challenge."

Indignant on Emily's behalf, Sarah was tempted to slap the smug look from his face and barely managed to keep her countenance.

Mrs. Harding rolled her eyes. "Don't mind him. He's a rake. Most men are, sadly."

Even so, Sarah felt compelled to say, "Emily's husband is an expert swordsman, and his blade is never far from his side."

Mr. Craven raised both hands. "Consider me duly warned."

Yet he did not appear at all chastised. In fact, a mischievous gleam shone in his eyes.

Sarah wondered, for the first time, if she should insist Georgiana begin locking her door at night. Perhaps she would as well.

They did not customarily serve dinner on Sundays, but they had decided to make an exception for these guests. That evening, they were a table of eight, with Mrs. Harding, Miss Craven, and Mr. Craven along with Mr. Hornbeam, Emily and James, Mamma, and Georgiana. Sarah took her turn helping Jessie and Mr. Gwilt serve the meal.

Sarah had suggested Emily and James might like to have dinner in their room to avoid Mr. Craven, but Emily had lifted a pert chin. "No, thank you. I want to show off the handsome and far-superior man I married."

When they were all seated, Caroline Harding looked around the table and said archly, "Are we to dine with your entire family? What a privilege."

Her brother muttered, "Now, Caro . . ."

Emily feigned a smile. "If you would prefer a tray in your room, we would be happy to provide one."

"*Is* this your entire family?" Miss Craven asked.

Ignoring her, Mamma began ladling soup from the large tureen at her elbow while Emily began the introductions.

"This is our mother, Mrs. Summers. Sarah, you have met. Our sister Georgiana. And this is my husband, James Thomson."

"And this is Mr. Hornbeam," Mamma added. "Our friend and longtime guest."

Emily gestured to the sideboard, where Mr. Gwilt and Jessie were preparing to lay the next course. "And Mr. Gwilt helps us in many ways, as does Jessie."

"Ah, we are to be introduced to the servants as well. How unexpectedly charming are these boarding houses one reads about."

"Guest house," Mamma corrected as she served the final bowl of soup to herself.

"But these are not all your sisters," Mrs. Harding said.

"No. Viola is married now, and she and Major Hutton live nearby." Emily looked pointedly at Mr. Craven. "The one you struck with a cricket ball last summer, as you may recall."

"And the other?" Mrs. Harding persisted.

Emily and Sarah exchanged uneasy glances across the table. Mamma, Sarah noticed, set down her spoon, soup untouched.

"Do you mean our oldest sister, Claire?" Georgie asked. "Are you acquainted with her?"

Mr. Craven replied, "Only by reputation."

A commotion sounded from under the table, and Mr. Craven winced and muttered, "Oof."

"Are you all right?" Georgie asked.

"Em . . . yes. Just kicked . . . the chair leg."

"She does not live here with you?" Mrs. Harding asked.

"Here in Sea View? No."

"How surprising, when you all seem so close."

Miss Craven asked, "Has she married, like the other sister you mentioned?"

"No." Sarah's pleasant expression felt stiff on her face.

"And may we ask where she lives?"

"Why?" Emily asked a touch sharply. "Why are you so interested?"

"We are not. Only attempting to make polite dinner conversation."

Georgiana looked from her sisters to her mother and back again, the pause noticeable. "Is it such a secret?"

When no one answered, she took a rather large bite of crusty bread, perhaps to keep herself from saying more.

When the silence grew heavy, Emily explained, "Claire only recently came here from Scotland. She lives at Broadbridge's now, in the eastern town. A partner in a boarding house."

"Really? How . . . interesting. Lodging must run in the blood."

"Pray, what took her to Scotland?"

No one answered immediately. Instead Sarah, Emily, and Mamma stared at one another, gape-mouthed. Mr. Thomson laid his hand atop Emily's. Mr. Hornbeam sat there, shielded behind his dark glasses, alert, silent, listening. Georgiana busily chewed her bread. Glancing around at her stupefied family, she rolled her eyes, and chewed all the faster.

Sarah answered before she could. "She lived with our great-aunt, who was quite elderly and frail. Served as her companion through her final days."

Finished at last, Georgie added, "Very good of her. Though we all missed her terribly."

Mr. Gwilt and Jessie removed the soup bowls and began the next course.

"Again, I wonder why you ask," Emily said, a sheen of defiance in her eyes. "Have you ever even met her?"

Mrs. Harding picked at her food and said, "No, but one of our friends is acquainted with her. Lord Bertram?"

Mamma dropped her fork with a clatter.

Emily said, "I am acquainted with him as well, as you may recall. A friend of our former neighbor's."

"I do not claim any acquaintance with that man," Mamma said, a decided bite to her tone. "Nor do I wish one."

"But why?" Persephone Craven asked, limpid eyes wide. "He is most charming. Not to mention a viscount."

Mrs. Harding said, "Now, Persephone, having a title does not make the man a saint."

"I don't know why you are set against him."

"Not at all, my dear."

Emily tipped her head to one side. "No? Yet I distinctly remember you warning me about Lord Bertram at a ball last summer. You advised me not to trust him."

"Did you, Caro?" her brother asked.

"Yes, did you?" echoed her sister, looking ready to cry.

The woman waved a dismissive hand. "I simply mentioned that he flirts with many women without serious intentions."

Mr. Craven shrugged. "Nothing unusual there."

And Sarah knew that Claire had been one of those women.

At Broadbridge's that evening, they hosted a very welcome dinner guest.

Armaan Sagar and Major Hutton had paid a call that afternoon, having been passing Broadbridge's on some errand. Mr. Hammond invited the men to stay for dinner. Major Hutton politely declined, saying his wife was expecting him, but Armaan accepted.

So while Claire helped Mary serve the boarding-house guests in the dining room, Armaan waited with Mr. Hammond in the next room, the two men chatting over small glasses of arrack.

Miss Patel came down with Mira, and Claire followed them into the morning room, a basket of bread rolls in hand.

Mr. Sagar rose and bowed. "Miss Patel. Miss Summers. A pleasure to see you both again."

The little girl hurried to him. "And me?"

He picked her up. "Far more than a pleasure. A blessing." He spun her around until she giggled.

"Please stop," Sonali said. "You will upset her digestion."

"Very well." He set Mira in a chair and took a seat beside her at the oval table.

Since Claire had not known in advance they were to host a special guest, the dinner was rather ordinary—soup, fish, vegetables—but the company and conversation were excellent.

As they spooned their soup, Mira's gaze remained fixed on her uncle.

"Do not stare, Mira," Miss Patel said gently. "It is not polite."

"I don't mind," Armaan assured her.

"I like to look at him," Mira said. "He reminds me of *Amma*."

"And you remind me of her," he said.

"What do you remember about her?" Mr. Hammond asked.

"Many things. Seeing your daughter—her bright eyes and inquisitive face—ah, how the memories return to me! Vani asked so many questions. So interested in everything. She begged to know what I was learning in school. Read all the books she could find. Such a clever girl! But Vani did not like monsoons. She would come running and beg for stories until the worst of the wind and rain had passed. . . ."

The conversation continued, with questions about the British school he attended, what his mother was like, his reaction to being presented with a new half sister. But they carefully skirted the topics of his departure from home and his military experiences to keep the conversation light.

After dinner, Mira begged him to play a game of spillikins, and he agreed. The girl eagerly retrieved the narrow case of fine wooden sticks.

The game was a simple one: Players attempted to pick up a single stick from a tangled pile without moving any of the others. If successful, that player had another turn, and the one with the most sticks at the end won.

While they played, Mr. Hammond was called away by Monsieur Lemaire, and Claire excused herself to help Mary put the dining room to rights for the following morning. After carrying a few things down to the kitchen, Claire came back upstairs to replace the cloth on the dining room table. As she spread the fabric, she overheard some of the conversation from the next room.

Miss Patel said, "I was amazed you stayed for dinner when your British officer did not. I thought the poor sepoy would follow on his heels like a loyal hound."

"You assume I am poor?"

"Are you not? I suppose you earned the king's shilling as a soldier, but I expect that money is long gone."

"Not that it is any of your concern, but I, in fact, am not poor. My father left an inheritance for me as well as providing for my mother."

"Indeed?"

"Yes, she married Mr. Aston for love, not financial need. And, as Mr. Hammond has recently made me aware, Vanita's father also left a small legacy for me."

"Really?" Claire heard surprise and perhaps chagrin in the woman's voice.

A moment's silence followed while Claire smoothed the final wrinkles from the cloth. Then Armaan appeared in the adjoining doorway.

"Ah. There you are, Miss Summers. Please do join us again, when you are able."

Claire did not mistake the look of appeal in his dark eyes. "Very well. If you are sure."

"Definitely."

When Claire sat down with them again, Miss Patel sent her a brittle smile. "Mr. Sagar was just telling me about his inheritance." She turned back to him. "And what will you do with it?"

"I once thought of buying a property like this one. But I have little experience in domestic matters. I can understand why Mr. Hammond took on a female partner."

Armaan gazed warmly in Claire's direction, while Sonali kept her focus on him.

"You would actually leave Major Hutton?"

"We are not inseparable. I volunteered to travel with him from India to ensure he received the best care during the voyage and here in England. But he has recovered now and has a home and wife of his own. He does not need me as he once did. Of course, he says I am always welcome and he could not do without me. I know better. Besides, I want that too—a home and wife of my own."

Sonali's mouth softened, and when she spoke again, her voice sounded small and young. "Do you?"

He nodded. "To that end, I have been pondering my future. What I might take up. Where I might live. In London, I dined at the Hindoostane Coffee House and stayed at a lodging house owned by a couple from Madras. Most inspiring."

Regret shimmered in Sonali's eyes. "So you . . . might move away?"

He shrugged. "I have yet to decide. For now I will enjoy this time with my newfound niece, an undeserved gift from God."

20

Bright star, would I were steadfast as thou art.
—John Keats

Over the few days they had been in residence, the Cravens claimed the formal drawing room as their personal domain. They spread their magazines and fashion plates on every surface. They left books and boxes of bonbons on the side tables, and their own lap rugs over the arms of the chairs.

The Summers family primarily used the less formal parlour, so it was not a great imposition—at least without other guests to accommodate at present. And Sarah realized it was probably best to keep some distance between them.

So while Sarah sat with Mamma going over the week's shopping list and Emily sat writing nearby, she was surprised when Mrs. Harding appeared in the parlour doorway.

"Good day, ladies. Might I join you for a moment? I'd like to have a word."

The women exchanged uneasy glances and then gestured to a nearby armchair.

Mrs. Harding sat, looking elegant in a fine afternoon gown, posture straight. "May I be frank, Mrs. Summers?"

"If you must, Mrs. Harding."

"Firstly, I admire you."

"Do you? Why?"

"It takes great strength of character to do as you have done. I admire anyone who remains steadfast to her convictions, even when personally difficult. You are to be commended."

Though Caroline Harding was some two decades younger than Mamma, she possessed a regal bearing and sophistication that made her seem older.

Mamma said, "Shall I ask what you are talking about, or do I not want to know?"

"Your eldest daughter, of course."

Mamma visibly stiffened, and Emily set down her pen.

"As I said," Mrs. Harding went on, "I am not personally acquainted with her, but I spoke to Lord Bertram not long ago, and he mentioned a recent trip to Scotland. For some reason, he visited that elderly relative of yours. He did not say why. He also saw Miss Summers while he was there."

Emily and Sarah shared astonished looks. This was news to them. Was it even true?

Mrs. Harding continued, "Apparently there has been a falling out between you. Even so, we naturally assumed she would come here after the old lady's death."

"You assumed wrong."

"Yes, and I must say I was impressed to hear it. The initial reason she went to Scotland may not be widely known—although some people know or at least suspect. But that is not the point. It is the principle that is paramount, as you clearly understand. I realize I am your junior, Mrs. Summers, yet if it is not too impertinent, please allow me to advise you to maintain the break in your relationship—to throw off your unworthy child from your affection forever, as difficult as it must be."

"I think that is quite enough, Mrs. Harding," Sarah protested.

But the woman went on as though Sarah had not spoken. "I do condole with you. It is a grievous affliction you suffer under. I sincerely sympathize with you and all respectable members of your family. May it comfort you to know you are doing what is right. In the eyes of society and of God."

"You speak for God, do you, Mrs. Harding?" Emily asked dryly.

"Of course not. I only remind you all of the standards of Scripture and of polite society."

"What Scripture is that, exactly?"

"Emily . . ." Sarah cautioned.

"You may think me unfeeling, but I do understand. As women, we may feel such judgment is harsh, yet we cannot pretend it is not true. It is the way of the world."

Mamma sighed wearily. "It is as I have often told my daughters. We may not agree with or like that women are held to a higher standard, but we ignore that reality to our peril."

"Exactly." Satisfaction glimmered in the woman's eyes. "How wise you are." Mrs. Harding rose. "Thank you for hearing me. I shall trespass upon your privacy no longer."

Mamma nodded, looking shrunken and dejected.

Mrs. Harding departed the room, and Emily followed her out. Fearing what might happen, Sarah followed Emily.

In the hall, Emily confronted Caroline. "Why are you doing this? The last time we met, I thought you must want Lord Bertram for yourself. But we are both married now, so why go to such lengths to prejudice our mother and encourage her to keep shunning Claire?"

Mrs. Harding demurely folded her hands. "I felt compelled to speak. Your sister has come to Sidmouth and is trying to wheedle her way back into your family's good graces. Probably Lord Bertram's as well."

Sarah gasped. "Claire came to Sidmouth to reunite with us, not him. She is finished with him."

"Are you certain? Or did she beg your great-aunt to invite him to Edinburgh in hopes of rekindling a relationship?"

"She would not do that." Emily frowned at Caroline, revelation sparking in her brown eyes. "Your sister wants him for herself—is that it? I remember Persephone all but begging Lord Bertram for a dance last summer. You are married now, and she is not getting any younger. Better a man without honor than no man at all?"

Mrs. Harding lifted her nose in the air, nostrils pinched tight. "He may not be perfect, but who is? Either way, Persephone has set her cap at him. She feels she will never be happy until she is his wife. As her sister, I cannot bear to see her miserable. I still believe she probably will be after she marries him, or at least after the honeymoon period has ended. But no more miserable than she is now. I love my sister and would do anything for her."

Emily stepped closer, standing almost nose to nose with the woman. "I love my sisters too. Every last one of them. And you had better—"

Sarah grabbed Emily's arm to interrupt before the conversation devolved into threats. She asked, "Have you some reason to think Lord Bertram means to come here? Does he even know Claire is in Sidmouth?"

"I certainly would not tell him. Nor would Persephone. I cannot, however, speak for our brother."

After a few days, Claire had managed to cut, pin, and sew a simple frock for Mira—bodice and skirt—although she was still struggling with the sleeves. Realizing she had enough of the same fabric remaining, she also started a miniature, matching frock for Mira's doll.

Someone knocked on the basement door. Claire rose and opened it to find Sarah there, basket in hand. "I was in the market and thought I'd stop by."

Claire invited her inside. "I am always happy to see you. Though I still hope Mamma will come with you one of these days. Any progress there?"

"Sadly, she seems more resolved than before." Sarah's face clouded. She opened her mouth to say more but instead turned her attention to the sewing things spread on the table. "What are you making?"

Claire explained her project, and her troubles with the sleeves. Sarah offered to help, and the two sat down and sewed together, very much like old times.

Later, after everything was finished and Sarah had gone, Claire wrapped the two frocks in tissue and wrapped a second parcel as well, carrying both up to the nursery.

When she presented the first to Mira, the little girl squealed in delight and immediately began to change Dolly's dress.

Sonali was less pleased. She begrudgingly admitted, "I have learned to embroider but am not skilled in dressmaking."

"Nor am I. But my sister helped me. Together, we worked it out."

Sonali nodded. "As I said before, you are braver than I."

Claire shook her head and said earnestly, "You are the courageous one. You left your home, your country, to travel halfway around the world to a new land, a new culture. *You* are far braver than I am."

Sonali searched her face, measuring her sincerity. "You think so?"

"I do."

Claire handed over the second parcel, which contained Vanita's yellow sari and skirt, as well as the length of fine silk. "And here are a few things from Vanita's trunk I thought you might like to have."

Sonali pulled back the tissue and fingered the fine fabric. "I remember these," she said, almost reverently.

Claire stepped to the door and turned back. "And if you'd

like help making something with that, let me know. I'm sure we could manage it together."

That night, Claire helped Mary clean up after dinner as usual and then played a game of spillikins with Mira. Mr. Hammond excused himself but paused at Claire's elbow and asked to have a quick word with her before she retired. She hoped he did not disapprove of her making a dress for his daughter and her doll when she might have been doing something more productive around the house.

When it was Mira's bedtime, Sonali gently but firmly took her upstairs, despite the girl's pleas for one more game. After they had gone, Claire put away the sticks and removed a few lingering teacups and dessert plates, planning to take the remaining cake downstairs.

The new-wed couple came into the house looking windblown and a little sunburned, but otherwise happy.

Claire greeted them. "Did you have a good day?"

"We did. Fell asleep on our beach rug or we'd have been back sooner."

She noticed the young husband's gaze linger on the cake before shifting away.

Knowing they were getting by on limited funds, Claire smiled and said, "You are just in time. I hope you will help us finish this date-and-walnut cake. And there's tea as well. No charge. You'll be doing me a favor—one less thing to put away."

"If you're certain. I confess I am rather hungry."

"Me too," his wife said. "Must be the sea air."

"Do sit down and help yourselves."

When they were seated side by side, Claire went downstairs and brought up a plate of cheese, bread, and cold meat as well, setting it before them without fanfare.

"When you're finished, just leave everything here, and I will tidy up later."

"Thank you, missus."

Claire went upstairs. She first peeked into the parlour, where she saw Monsieur Lemaire and Mr. Filonov bent over a game of cards, quietly speaking together in French.

Mr. Jackson sat alone, organizing his bobbins by the looks of it. He glanced up with a friendly grin. "Ah, Miss Summers. Any chance of more tea?"

"Of course, Mr. Jackson. I shall bring it up in a few minutes."

Finally, after she'd delivered a fresh pot of tea, Claire went in search of Mr. Hammond.

She saw Mary coming down the attic stairs in her dressing gown.

"I thought you'd gone to bed," Claire said.

"I did but I need to use the water closet again."

She wondered if Mr. Hammond had retired early or had returned to his study. "You have not seen Mr. Hammond lately, have you?"

"Aye, miss. He's up on the roof again."

"The roof?"

She nodded. "With one of them spyglass things. Goes out through one of the empty rooms up there."

"Does he? Interesting. Thank you, Mary."

Curious, Claire lit a candle from the landing lamp and went up to the attic, past Sonali's, Mira's, and Mary's bedchambers. Noticing weak light seeping from an open door at the end of the passage, Claire investigated.

Inside, a candle lamp sat burning on a small table near an open sash window. She looked outside and saw Mr. Hammond standing at the far end of a narrow roof walk, bent over a telescope mounted on a three-legged stand. Moonlight outlined his form, cheek creased and one eye squinted to focus with the other.

She set down her candle and climbed through the window to join him on the roof, which was enclosed by a low-railed parapet. She had seen the parapet from below but had thought it an architectural feature for ornamentation, not as protection for someone venturing onto the roof. She wondered how stable it was.

"Here you are," she called.

He glanced over. "Ah, Miss Summers."

"Mary told me you were up on the roof again, using a spyglass. And here you told me you were not a spy." She sent him a teasing grin, even though she was not certain he could see it in the dim light.

"I am still not a spy," he replied, waving her forward. "But come and have a look."

She gingerly crossed the roof. "What are we looking at?"

"Polaris, also known as the North Star."

He stepped aside and gestured toward the eyepiece.

Being shorter, she did not to have to lean down very far to place her eye to the instrument.

"Where?"

"The brightest star in current view. Just left of center?"

"Ah. I see it."

As she stood there, gazing at the star, she grew increasingly aware of his presence beside her, his stillness. She glanced up and caught him studying her profile.

Pretending not to notice, she asked, "Is it true sailors navigate by the North Star?"

"I believe so. At least in the northern hemisphere. I've never been to the southern hemisphere, so no matter where I've traveled—Vienna, Constantinople, St. Petersburg—I could always find the North Star in the night sky. Even when everything else around me was different, it remained unchanged. Constant. Rather like God, I suppose." He gave a self-conscious laugh.

Claire asked, "You believe in God?"

"Does that surprise you? You know I attend church."

"Not everyone who attends believes." She thought, then added, "I suppose I'm not questioning whether you believe in God's existence so much as wondering if you still . . . revere Him after your loss?"

"Ah. God may have allowed it, but He did not cause Vanita's death. The plague did. I don't blame God. I blame myself. Vanita did not want to go to Constantinople. But as I told you before, I put my ambition ahead of my wife's wishes, as I did too often."

For a long moment, he stared up at the starlit sky without aid of the telescope, and she guessed he was seeing more memories than stars.

Then he glanced at her. "And you, Miss Summers? What is your view of God?"

Her stomach fell. Why had she asked? She could not decline to answer when he'd simply reciprocated with the same question.

"I don't have any trouble believing God exists. Yet when I think of Him, I cannot help picturing my own father and hearing his voice."

"What does it sound like?"

"Disappointed and disapproving."

"Your father was not a kind man?"

"He was. When I was young he doted on me, his firstborn. He would have welcomed a son, especially with the estate entailed down the male line, but he never treated me as less important. He praised me for being clever and laughed at my every joke, far more than the quip deserved. I had no doubt he loved me and approved of me. Then."

"What happened to change that?"

Tread carefully, she warned herself. "I did, I suppose. I grew older and more interested in gowns and balls than spending time with my father. But the first real friction began when he decided I should marry the son of his oldest friend. He was not happy when I refused."

"Were you well acquainted with the young man?"

"Yes. His family lived fairly close to us, and his father often brought him along when he visited. As a boy Harry was polite to adults but bullied anyone younger or weaker. As we all grew older, he visited less often, although we still saw him at the occasional party or village fête. He became more charming. Even chivalrous. Yet I still could not like him. Let alone marry him."

"You did not believe he'd truly changed?"

Claire shook her head. "No. I saw glimpses of the same boy beneath the new polish. At all events, when I refused to marry him, Papa changed toward me. First, he expressed his disappointment, and when I continued to refuse, he grew angry."

"Simply for refusing to marry a man you did not like?"

She nodded. "Though that was not the worst of my offenses." *Careful, Claire.* What was it about the starlit darkness . . . and this man . . . that made her want to bare her soul?

He tipped his head to one side, clearly waiting for her to continue. When she remained silent, he said, "If you want to tell me more, you will find I am a good listener."

Again she chastised herself for saying as much as she had. A part of her longed to confess. The other part feared the consequences. She was, after all, supposed to be a respectable woman.

"Forgive me," she said instead. "I have been prattling on. What about your father? Did you get on together?"

"Yes, thankfully. He was gentle, honest, and caring. A clergyman."

"Have you brothers or sisters?"

He shook his head. "Only child. At least, the only one to survive infancy, sadly. So my father doted on me as well."

"Did he want you to follow him into the church?"

"Not necessarily. He spent most of his career as a perpetual curate until he finally secured a modest living of his own. He did not want me to struggle financially as he did. Despite his rather humble profession, he had high enough connections to see me educated and later appointed to the Foreign Office at a relatively young age, thanks to the patronage of an acquaintance.

"I'm sure it was difficult for him and Mamma when I moved far away. Nevertheless they were thoroughly supportive. We corresponded, although they wrote far more often than I did. I justified that I was busy with important work and they would understand. I regret that now."

"Are your parents yet living?"

"Unfortunately, no. They've been gone several years. I did manage to visit them shortly before my father died. Or more accurately, my patron insisted I visit them between appointments when word of my father's declining health reached him. I am glad I heeded him. My parents were delighted to see me. So proud—making sure every delivery boy and visiting apothecary knew I was their son, and insisting our ancient cook prepare all my favorite dishes. Made me utterly ashamed of my neglect. I told them stories of my travels, of the dignitaries I had met. Brought them coins and trinkets from foreign lands. You would have thought I'd brought them priceless treasure."

"You did. You brought them their son."

He grimaced. Not the reaction she'd anticipated.

"My father was quite frail by then, though he did rally a bit while I was there. I asked if there was anything I could do for them. Mamma patted my cheek and assured me all was well.

"Thankfully our cook, Mrs. Petrova, had no such qualms and told me about the unpaid bills to physician, greengrocer, coal merchant, and more. I settled the accounts and gave Mrs. Petrova a letter of permission to draw from my bank as needed. Gave the same instructions to the banker."

"That was considerate of you."

He shrugged. "Too little, too late, in my view. I would have stayed longer, but I received word that my superior had abruptly resigned due to health problems of his own. I was asked to step in *ad interim* until his replacement could be appointed. I hoped the permanent appointment would come to me, but it did not.

"My father died not long after I left. My mother soon followed. Mrs. Petrova wrote to me with the news. She said maybe it was a blessing my mother did not linger long after her husband of more than forty years. I don't know. I have heard that often happens, that one spouse seems to lose their will to live after the death of their husband or wife."

"Yes, although not in my mother's case," Claire said. "She used to be an invalid. You'd never know it now." She raised a hand. "Don't mistake me—I'm not saying Papa's death improved her health. She credits the sea air, long walks, and sea-bathing."

He nodded. "I think I agree with her. Speaking of long walks, I plan to hike up Salcombe Hill tomorrow morning. Care to join me?"

She hesitated. "I would like to, but someone must stay and oversee things here."

"Come, Miss Summers. We managed without you before you arrived. Not well, but we managed. The place won't fall to ruin in a few hours. Besides, Mr. Filonov plans to go along, so no need to worry about propriety."

"Very well, then. I would enjoy that." She turned to go, then remembered something. "By the way, you asked to see me before I retired?"

He nodded. "I simply wanted to thank you for taking the time to make Mira a dress, and one for her beloved Dolly as well. I did not want to praise you too highly with Sonali there, yet I did want to thank you."

Her heart warmed. "It was my pleasure."

21

> The idea of walking for leisure . . . resonated with artists in the 19th Century. Painters, poets and writers turned to woods and mountains to connect with their surroundings.
>
> —Jolan Wuyts, *Europeana*

Claire rose at dawn the next morning to get an early start on her tasks. She sorted a load of clean linens from the laundress, exchanged the towels in the water closet and bath-room, and helped the kitchen maid lay breakfast for guests and family. Mary was not feeling well and joined them rather late, apologizing profusely.

After that, Claire reviewed the registration book. No new guests were expected that day, and hopefully none of their present guests would need anything while they were gone.

At breakfast, Mr. Hammond made a request of Sonali. "Miss Summers and I will both be out for an hour or two this morning. Would you mind listening for callers?"

Claire tensed, awaiting a sharp retort. But Sonali remained silent as her dark gaze slid from him to Claire and back again.

He added, "Perhaps Mira might draw here at the table for a time so you would be closer to the door?"

"Oh yes!" Mira clapped. "I want to try the new colors."

Claire expected Sonali to protest that it was not her responsibility.

Instead the woman said evenly, "Very well."

"Thank you. We're not expecting any guests but it's possible someone may walk in looking for a room. I've left the key to number six on the desk, just in case."

Sonali nodded and finished her tea.

Claire was surprised at her acceptance but made no comment.

After cleaning up the breakfast things, Claire put on sturdy half boots, a bonnet, and a long pelisse over her day dress, as Mr. Hammond had warned her it might be windy and cooler on the hilltop. Then she went up to meet the men in the hall.

In his shabby brown suit, Mr. Filonov put her in mind of a pack mule carrying a heavy load: easel, canvas, folding stool, and a case of art supplies. She offered to carry something for him, and he handed her the collapsed easel. Mr. Hammond carried the heavier stool.

Mr. Hammond, dressed in his usual kit, led the way, stool under one arm, walking stick in the other. They took the Byes footpath along the River Sid, then crossed the wooden bridge near the water mill.

They walked along the road for a time, passing a wagon loaded with produce and a man in a donkey cart. Eventually they diverted from the road and took a narrow path, which grew steeper as they went.

As the path curved and the foliage thinned, the sea below came into view. Breathing heavily, Mr. Filonov stopped and said, "You go on. I will paint here."

They helped him set up his stool and easel before continuing onward and upward.

Mr. Hammond strode in front of her, occasionally swinging his stick at some unsuspecting bush or sapling growing along the path.

After a time, Claire called, "May I go first for a while? You are taller and blocking my view."

He turned to face her, then stepped to the side of the trail. "Of course, madam. Would you like to borrow this?" He held out his walking stick, which seemed to her an affectation.

"No, thank you. I am not yet feeble enough to need a stick." She grinned at him, hoping he would not mind her teasing.

"Feeble, am I?" he replied with a crooked half grin of his own. "Well, I am older than you are, after all."

"Exactly. And I would not want to deprive you of your crutch."

A sparkle lit his eyes, which she credited to her playful gibe. He gestured her ahead of him with a lift of his hand and a little bow. "Watch how you go."

She swept past him, feeling oddly triumphant, and led the way up the path as it wove between shrubs and brambles. She called over her shoulder, "Now the view is much better!"

From behind her, he said, "I disagree. I find the view from here pleasant indeed."

Claire's mouth slackened and her cheeks warmed from more than the exertion. Had he meant . . . Surely not. She considered delivering a set down, but at that moment something fell across her face.

She shrieked and stopped midstride, swiping at the web that had draped itself over her like a filmy veil. Something crawled down her neck, eliciting another shriek of alarm. "Get it off! Get it off!"

"What is it?" Mr. Hammond hurried forward, dropping his stick as he came.

"A web. I think a spider crawled down my neck. Look. Is it still there?"

He took his time inspecting her—neck, bodice, waist—then he braced her shoulders and turned her the other way. "If there was a spider, it probably jumped for its life when you shrieked like that. No, wait, here it is."

She felt him graze her back as he flicked it off. She shuddered.

Then he turned her once again toward himself, studying her. A translucent string hung from her bonnet, and he carefully peeled it away, then dipped his head to look beneath the brim to better search her face.

"All gone?" she asked.

He reached out and gently cupped her jaw, tilting it one way, then the other. Then he brushed light fingertips down her nose and across her cheek.

"Find something?"

Humor danced in his eyes. "Only a few freckles."

She huffed and pushed away from him. "Not very gallant to mention them—especially when you have some too."

He picked up the stick from where he'd dropped it and once again offered it to her.

She looked from it to him. "Are you telling me that's why you carry a stick and swing it about?"

He nodded. "To clear the path. That, and in the event we should meet with some wild animal unhappy to be disturbed. Unlikely, yet I prefer to be prepared."

She was about to accept the stick and carry on, but recalling his comment about enjoying the view from behind, she gestured him ahead, saying, "In that case, after you."

He hesitated. "About that. I apologize for what I said earlier. When you shrieked, I feared it was in anger! I suppose I was accustomed to teasing Vanita like that, but I do not have the right to treat you with the same familiarity. I hope you will forgive me."

Sincerity now shone in his green eyes, capturing her gaze like another sticky web. She had a difficult time looking away.

"You are forgiven. And I suppose I share the blame as I teased you first."

"True, although only to criticize my age and infirmity." He winked and continued on in an exaggerated hobble before lengthening his stride once more.

There was certainly nothing infirm about the man. In fact, he appeared to be in excellent physical condition.

When they reached the summit of Salcombe Hill, Claire paused to catch her breath. The view stretched before them to lofty Peak Hill and beyond, much as she remembered and just as Mr. Filonov had depicted it in his painting. Sidmouth lay below them, a hodgepodge of roof lines, chimney smoke, and there, the church tower. The esplanade ran parallel to the town beach with its rocky outcroppings, all the way to grassy Fort Field. On the far side of the field, she could just make out Sea View. It seemed very far away. Almost unreachable. Tears sprang to her eyes at the thought.

She became aware of Mr. Hammond beside her, his expression concerned. "Is something wrong?"

She shook her head. "The wind makes my eyes water."

Inhaling deeply of the brisk breeze, Claire pushed aside her sadness and admired the scenery. "It is beautiful up here."

Feeling his gaze on her once more, she turned and found him watching her.

"I completely agree."

That night, tired from rising at dawn and the strenuous walk, Claire went to bed early and quickly fell into a deep sleep.

At some point, her door creaked open.

"Miss Summers?"

Claire struggled to waken. "Y-yes?"

"Is Mira with you?"

"What?" Startled, Claire looked at her caller with wide eyes and recognized Sonali, holding a candle lamp.

"Is she not in her bed?" Claire asked.

"No. I thought she might have come down here again."

Claire rose on her elbows, then sat up in the dark, reaching her hands to search beneath the bedclothes.

"She is not here."

"Oh no."

"What time is it?" Claire asked as she climbed from bed, her thoughts becoming clearer.

"About half past four."

She slipped her feet into shoes and reached for her pelisse instead of a dressing gown, pulling it on over her nightdress.

"Perhaps she has gone to her father. Have you looked in his bedchamber?"

"Not yet. He made it clear he does not wish me to trespass there."

"We shall go together."

Leaving her room, Claire remained close to Sonali, who held the light as they went up the stairs and across the passage to the apartment over the stables.

The outer door was ajar, and Sonali pushed it wide with her free hand. The two inner doors, however, were closed. Light shone from beneath the study door. Sonali hung back while Claire walked resolutely forward and knocked.

After a moment's hesitation, Mr. Hammond called out a tentative, "Yes?"

Claire opened the door, surprised to find Mr. Hammond at his desk, dressed in trousers and shirtsleeves, shirt open at the neck.

"What are you doing up?" she asked. "It's half four in the morning."

"Is it? I was working on . . . something, and lost track of

time." At that, he closed the leather cover of his portfolio as though to shield the documents from view.

"Mira is not here with you?"

"With me? She should be in bed."

"She was," Sonali said, joining Claire in the doorway. "But something woke me, and when I looked, I found her bed empty."

He frowned, then rose with his candle lamp. "I'll look in my bedchamber. Perhaps she went there."

They followed him to the next room and found it unoccupied, the bed not slept in.

He turned back to Sonali. "You said something woke you. What was it?"

"I don't know. Perhaps a door closing."

He paused to light another lamp and passed it to Claire. "Let's search the house before we panic—or wake the others."

"Yes," Claire agreed. Then, to reassure herself as much as them, added, "We're sure to find her somewhere."

"Let's spread out. Sonali, please start on the top floor. I'll start belowstairs, and Miss Summers, perhaps you could begin by searching the public rooms. If we don't find her, I'm afraid we shall have to wake the guests. When we've searched everywhere, let's meet back in the hall—hopefully one of us with Mira."

The women nodded and the three parted ways, Sonali up the stairs and him down the back stairs, while Claire looked first in the water closet, bath-room, and parlour, then went down a flight of stairs to look in the dining room and morning room.

Nothing.

Taking a deep breath to steady her nerves, she walked back up and knocked at Mr. Filonov's door. He answered a few moments later, hair awry and dressing gown hastily donned.

"I am sorry to disturb you. We can't seem to find Mr. Hammond's daughter. You have not seen her, have you? Please do not be offended, we are asking everyone."

"I have not. How upsetting! Please look all you like."

He opened his door wide, and Claire quickly swept the candle's light over the room, then looked inside the wardrobe and under the bed.

She did the same in Monsieur Lemaire's room to the same result.

Sonali came down the attic stairs with Mary trailing behind.

"No sign of her," she said. "Mary woke the Bracegirdles and Mr. Jackson as well. No one has seen her." Miss Patel shook her head, dark eyes large and luminous. "I fear it is my fault. I complained once when she woke me in the night. I never thought something bad might happen."

Claire squeezed her hand.

Mr. Hammond came up from belowstairs with the cook. Mrs. Ballard was still wearing her outside things, clearly having just arrived for her day's work.

She said, "If that little lamb had come to the kitchen, the top would be off the biscuit tin. There's no sign she came down there."

As they gathered in the hall as planned, Claire's gaze fell to the front door and her stomach cramped.

It stood ajar a few inches, the key still in the lock.

She pointed. "The door is open."

They all turned toward it as though at an unwelcome intruder.

Claire said, "I locked it before I went to bed. I know I did."

Yet the door could easily be opened from the inside.

Mr. Hammond ran a hand through his hair. "If she left the house, where would she have gone? While it is still dark, for heaven's sake? And alone. At least, I assume she is alone."

"All the guests are accounted for."

Claire's mind scanned through the possibilities. Where would Mira go? The shops were closed, and she had not yet made any friends here in Sidmouth. . . .

Except one.

"Armaan," Claire whispered. "Perhaps she went to find her uncle."

"Why would she do that?" Mr. Hammond asked. "Westmount is all the way on the other side of town."

"Does she know the way?"

"I took her there once. I suppose it's possible she remembers. Still, I can't fathom why she would go there now."

"Have you another idea?"

"No. Let's go and see." He retrieved a coat from the hall closet. "If nothing else, we'll enlist Armaan and Major Hutton in our search. I don't even know if there's a constable in town or where to find him." He shrugged into his coat. "For once, I wish I had a horse."

"It is not so far," Claire assured him. "We shall walk quickly." She was glad now that some instinct had told her to don a pelisse over her nightclothes.

Mr. Hammond turned to Sonali, still in her dressing gown. "Stay here and keep watch. She may not have gone to Westmount at all and may wander back, or someone else might bring her home."

Sonali nodded. "I will watch for her. And pray."

"And I had better get breakfast started for the guests," Mrs. Ballard said.

Claire and Mr. Hammond left the house as the faint glow of dawn began to warm the top of Salcombe Hill.

"I think the footpath would be faster," she said.

He nodded his agreement, and the two started off at a brisk pace, walking north from the marketplace toward the parish church, passing quiet houses and shops still shuttered. From the church, they took the footpath that led across Fort Field—

a back way between the eastern and western towns, and the path her family took to church.

They walked on, tense and barely speaking.

Breaking the silence, she said, "I wanted to come along and help find her. I am sorry if it was presumptuous of me."

"Not at all. I am glad you are here." He took her hand and squeezed it. Hard.

Their footsteps quieted as they moved from cobbles, to gravel, to the damp grass of the field. What might have been a leisurely stroll of ten minutes was accomplished in half the time. When they reached Glen Lane, they turned onto a wooded drive.

"There it is," he said.

Nearing the house, Claire was heartened to see a single light in one of the lower-floor windows. Advancing purposefully to the door, Mr. Hammond knocked loudly, despite the early hour. A few moments later, the door was opened by a man in a stained apron.

"Is my daughter here?" Mr. Hammond blurted. "Mira Hammond, Armaan's niece?"

"No, sir. Not that I know of. And I'm the first to wake in this house."

Again, Mr. Hammond squeezed her hand. In Claire's anxious haze she'd barely realized he still held it.

Roused by the commotion, Major Hutton stalked to the door behind the servant, a frown scoring his brow. "What is it, Chown?"

"I am sorry for the intrusion," Mr. Hammond said. "We are looking for my daughter."

Viola appeared at the major's side, cap on her head, dressing gown tied around her. "Mira's missing? Oh no!"

"Mira's missing?" Armaan echoed, joining them, expression tight with concern.

"I'm afraid so."

"Let's mount a search," the major said. "Chown, fetch Taggart. Breakfast can wait."

Viola reached across the threshold for Claire's hand. "Come and wait inside. We'll all be ready in a minute or two."

The rapid clopping of hooves and crunching wheels distracted them from that aim. They all turned to look as a heavy wagon came up the lane, moving much more quickly than a farm vehicle typically traveled, apparently on an urgent delivery.

Armaan and Chown stepped outside to join them as a wagon loaded with milk cans turned into the drive.

"It's only Mr. Pym," Chown said. "Though he's early this morn."

The dairyman waved, then pointed to the bench beside him . . . where Mira sat sobbing.

"This yer girl?" Mr. Pym called. "Found her wandering, lost. Said she needed to go to Westmount."

William and Armaan ran to the wagon, Claire struggling to keep up.

"Is she all right?" William called.

"Crying her heart out. Not hurt, though."

"Thank God," William breathed.

Claire thanked God as well.

William reached up to help his daughter down, but before he could, Mira launched herself into her uncle's arms, crying all the harder. "I thought I could find you, but I got lost."

William turned back to the dairyman, patting his pockets. "I rushed out without my purse, Mr. Pym. I shall make it up to you later. I sincerely appreciate your assistance."

"No need. Glad to help the little miss."

After handing over the Huttons' delivery of milk, cream, and cheese, the man continued on his way.

Viola ushered them all inside Westmount's sitting room while the major stoked the fire. Armaan lowered himself into an armchair, Mira still clinging to him, and held her on his lap.

Mr. Hammond knelt before his crying daughter and rubbed her back. "Mira, whatever is wrong?"

After a few more sniffles, she loosed her hold on Armaan's neck and turned toward him. "I had a bad dream about *Amma*. She had no face. I woke up and could not remember what she looked like. I had to come, to see my *mamu*." She turned back to Armaan and raised a small hand to his cheek.

Armaan laid gentle fingers over hers and gave Mr. Hammond an apologetic look. "I am sorry."

"Nothing to apologize for. Miss Summers guessed Mira might come to you."

Armaan met Claire's gaze a long moment before looking away. "Most wise, our Miss Summers."

William Hammond tenderly gathered his daughter in his arms. "Mira, please promise me you won't leave the house on your own again. You've had us all frightfully worried."

"I'm sorry, Papa."

"You are forgiven. I just thank God you are safe. Anytime you want to see your uncle, you tell me, and I will bring you here myself. Agreed?"

Mira nodded into his neck.

Viola spoke up. "In fact, please come for dinner. Perhaps in a day or two?" She looked from the Hammonds to Claire. "All of you. We would love to see you again."

Claire looked at Mr. Hammond, wondering how he would respond.

He met Claire's gaze, then glanced again at his daughter. "We would like nothing better, thank you."

The major insisted on sending them home in his carriage, which Taggart had already hitched and sat in ready to serve as coachman.

A short while later, Mr. Hammond handed Claire inside, then helped his daughter in after her. Mira immediately climbed onto Claire's lap and nestled close.

Mr. Hammond stepped in and shut the door. "I can take her, if you'd like."

"No need. It is my pleasure. And such a relief to have her back safely."

"I wholeheartedly agree."

Claire wrapped her arms around the little girl.

Mira murmured, "Papa's arm too."

He looked from his daughter's face to Claire's. "If Miss Summers does not object."

"I . . . don't."

He slid nearer, lifting his arm and gingerly draping it over Claire's shoulders, holding them both close.

How strangely good it felt to sit with them like that, like a little family, Mr. Hammond's warm and protective arm encircling them.

When they reached Broadbridge's a few minutes later, Sonali rushed out to greet them. Mr. Hammond descended first, then reached back to help Mira down.

Seeing the little girl, Sonali fell to her knees and threw her arms around her.

Claire heard a string of words in a language she did not understand, then in English, "I know I grumbled before, when you woke me in the night. I promise never to do so again. Oh! I am so glad you are safe."

Mrs. Ballard bustled out like a clucking mother hen and ushered them all inside for hot coffee and a hearty breakfast.

As they sat down together, Mr. Hammond offered up thanks for far more than the food.

When they had eaten, Mira and Sonali returned to their beds, and Mr. Hammond went to sleep after being up all night. Before retiring, he'd kindly suggested Claire sleep for a few more hours too, but she was wide awake by then and had responsibilities to attend to. Instead, she asked Mrs. Ballard for a large cup of strong tea and set to work.

22

> We spent a very pleasant Day, and had a very good Dinner, tho' to be sure the Veal was terribly under-done, and the Curry had no seasoning.
>
> —Jane Austen, "Lesley Castle"

Viola came by Broadbridge's later that afternoon to make sure all was well with Mira, and to reiterate their dinner invitation for the following day. She added, "Please do invite Miss Patel to join us as well."

"Oh?" Claire said. "I did not realize you were acquainted with her."

"I am not. Armaan gave me a little hint that she is a family friend and might appreciate being included."

"She might, although I believe Mr. Hammond plans to ask her to watch over the boarding house while we are out."

"I thought of that. I hope it was not too presumptuous, but I talked to Fran before coming over. She has offered to oversee things here for a few hours. That is, if you and Mr. Hammond don't mind?"

"I am sure we'd both be grateful."

Viola glanced around. "I would be happy to invite Miss Patel personally, if she is available."

"I believe she is upstairs in the nursery, but I will pass along your invitation." Claire wondered how the woman would respond. She also wished she had a prettier dress to wear—and one she had not worn several times already. Oh, how differently she would have packed two years ago had she foreseen the circumstances she would find herself in! Claire might be tempted to wear another gown from Mrs. Hammond's trunk if she did not fear Sonali's censure.

She became aware of Viola watching her in concern. "What is it?"

"Hm? Oh, it's silly, really. Just wondering what to wear."

Viola patted her hand. "Don't give it another thought. Emily plans to bring a few gowns to you tomorrow."

"That is not necessary. I did not intend to beg for charity."

"Nothing charitable about it. She only intends to return the dinner dresses she borrowed from your things after you left."

Claire grinned. "Well, in that case, I shall be happy to accept."

That evening, after the guests had been served their dinner, Claire joined Sonali and Mira in the morning room.

A moment later, Mr. Hammond entered, looking well-rested and freshly bathed and dressed, his auburn hair still damp, rendering it a shade darker than usual. In his hand, he carried a small tissue-wrapped parcel.

"I am sorry, Mira," he began. "I should have given this to you long before now. It was in a trunk I had not even looked in since the move. This is the only portrait I have of your *amma*. It was painted when she was quite young, so I don't know if it will help you remember her, but you should have it."

He handed it to his daughter and waited as she pulled back the paper. Claire leaned over to share a look as Mira stared down at it. The miniature was much as Claire recalled. The adolescent with large, dark eyes, wearing jewelry and a beaded veil over her hair.

Mira's little face wrinkled in some confusion or perhaps disappointment. "She is a girl. Not *Amma*. *Amma* did not dress like that."

Sonali came over and stood behind her chair, bending to see. "Ah!" She drew in a sharp breath. "That is the Vanita I first met, before she began wearing English clothes."

Claire observed, "You look like her, Mira."

"I do?" The little girl stood on her chair to look at herself in the mirror over the mantel.

"Be careful," Sonali warned.

Mira sat back down and again studied the miniature. She shook her head. "*Amma* looked more like Uncle than this girl."

"When you knew her, yes," her father said. "I believe you are right."

Sonali scoffed, lip curled. "But he is so dark. And . . . masculine."

"And handsome, you must admit," Claire added with a streak of mischief. "And their eyes are similar, don't you think?"

Sonali looked at the image again, gaze softening. "Perhaps."

Mr. Hammond glanced from one woman to the other, bemusement creasing his brow.

Claire said, "Oh! Before I forget. You are invited to join us for dinner at Westmount tomorrow night. Mr. Sagar asked especially that you be included in the invitation."

"Did he indeed?"

"Yes. And Mrs. Farrant has offered to come and watch over things here, so we can all go." She glanced from Sonali to Mr. Hammond and back again. "If you agree."

Was that a hint of a smile on the woman's face? "How kind. I . . . suppose I could."

The next day, the Bracegirdles departed with effusive thanks for her generous hospitality. Claire was sorry to see the young couple go and wished them safe travels.

Later, Mary came upstairs and interrupted Claire while she was tidying the bath. "Your sister's here, miss."

"Which one?"

"Don't know. Looks like ye, though."

Claire looked Mary over. "Are you feeling better?"

The maid's face reddened. "Aye, miss, thank ye. And thank ye for doin' my mornin' chores."

"That's all right." She patted the girl's arm and headed toward the stairs.

Claire went down and found Emily waiting for her in the morning room, garments over her arm and a small bag in hand.

"You will probably think me a terrible sponger, but I helped myself to two of your dresses when Papa ordered your things boxed up and donated." She winced. "Perhaps I should not have told you that part. It's no doubt painful to hear. I'm sorry he was so cruel about everything."

"I gave him cause, after all."

"Pish. In any case, I think they still look rather well. I hope you don't think them terribly out of fashion."

"And I hope they still fit."

"Of course they will. You are more slender than ever. I suppose it's all the work you do here."

And all the bland food at Aunt Mercer's, Claire thought but didn't say it.

Emily added, "Sarah and I both saved a few of your belongings without Papa knowing. I don't know if Viola or Georgie did."

Claire nodded. "Sarah brought over a sketchbook, earrings,

and a few things I embroidered. I doubt she took any of my gowns. She was still in mourning then, besides being taller."

Emily squinted in memory. "I believe she kept something else as well, though I don't recall what at the moment. Never mind. Shall we see how these fit?" She lifted the dresses, followed by the bag. "I brought a set of underthings, as well as satin shoes, in case you could use them."

"I could, yes." Claire led the way down to her room.

"And after you choose which one to wear tonight, perhaps I might help with your hair," Emily offered, laying the clothes on her bed.

Claire took her hand. "Thank you, my dear. I am sorry I did not turn out to be the model older sister you once thought me."

Emily squeezed her hand in reply. "Nonsense. You were and are the best eldest sister a girl could want."

That evening Claire went upstairs wearing one of the dinner dresses Emily had brought to her, which still fit and, according to Emily, suited her well. The gown was a pale celestial blue with a fluted border of white crepe.

Mr. Hammond came down the stairs, striking in evening attire. His skillfully tailored dark coat framed broad shoulders, while a sleek brocade waistcoat drew attention to his trim abdomen. His side-whiskers had been neatly trimmed, and his hair appeared freshly cut for the occasion.

He hesitated upon seeing her, his gaze sweeping over her in frank appraisal, and if the warm admiration in his eyes could be believed, Emily was not the only one who thought the gown suited her.

"New dress?"

"Old dress, but I have not worn it in some time. Emily brought it over for tonight."

"It looks well on you."

"Thank you."

She retrieved her cloak from the hall closet and pulled on her gloves.

Miss Patel came down the stairs with her young charge. She had dressed Mira in a gown of pretty rose satin, the hair ribbon from Viola, and the new shoes. Sonali herself wore a traditional sari embellished with golden threads and floral embroidery.

Mr. Hammond bowed. "Good evening. How lovely you three look. I am the luckiest man in Devonshire."

"You look handsome too, Papa!" Mira exclaimed.

Indeed he did.

At the appointed time, the Huttons' carriage drew up in front of Broadbridge's, Taggart once again on the coachman's bench.

Together they walked out to meet the carriage, and Mr. Hammond assisted one lady in after another. His gaze lingered on Claire, and he gave her hand a warm squeeze before releasing her.

She noticed Sonali watching them as she entered, but the woman looked away without a word—or the scowl Claire expected.

When they arrived at Westmount, Armaan stepped outside to greet them and help them alight. The Huttons stood at the door, wearing smiles of warm welcome.

For a moment, Claire could not tear her gaze away from Viola's bright, lovely face. She had never seen her sister look so happy, never imagined such a transformation possible for her formerly snappish, self-conscious, and reclusive sister. Had love done that?

Soon they were all ushered inside. Viola slipped an arm through hers and squeezed. "I am so glad you are here."

And Claire guessed she'd meant not only for dinner, but there in Sidmouth as well.

"Now, I hope you've all come to enjoy the company and not fine cuisine," Viola said, "for our Mr. Chown is no French chef but rather a former military mess cook. He has learned a great deal and improves daily. Even so, you might be wise to moderate your expectations."

When they were all seated, the man in his stained white apron brought out a covered soup tureen. He set it *not* at the head of the table but in front of Armaan. With an air of ceremony, he lifted the cover, watching Armaan's face expectantly.

"Take a whiff of that, gov, and tell me what you smell."

Armaan leaned closer and sniffed as directed, then sniffed again. "Lemon and . . . ginger? And something else . . . ?"

"That's too-mare-ic. The grocer suggested it."

Viola asked, "And, em, what sort of soup is it, Chown?"

"Curry of rabbits, ma'am. Found a recipe. Thought it would make a nice change, considering Mr. Sagar and his guests."

"Our guests," Major Hutton corrected mildly, perhaps noticing his friend's unease.

"Thank you, Chown," Armaan said. "A kind gesture."

William Hammond smiled. "I love a good curry. And this smells delicious."

Armaan ladled out bowls of the fragrant stew, and then passed the bread basket.

When they had all been served, they cautiously sampled small spoonfuls, except for Mr. Hammond, who took a hearty bite.

"Well? What say you?" Chown asked.

"It's quite good," Armaan replied.

"I like it," Mira said.

Her father nodded. "So do I."

Chown looked at Miss Patel, and Claire held her breath. Across the table, Armaan seemed to do the same.

She set down her spoon. "It lacks cumin and coriander and would benefit from more cayenne pepper—"

At Armaan's sharp look, she quickly amended, "But not everyone likes spicy food, so for a gathering such as this, it is . . . practically perfect."

Chown beamed.

Armaan relaxed, and Claire exhaled in relief. The meal continued, and thankfully the cook had not attempted an entire menu of unfamiliar dishes. Even so, the veal had not been roasted long enough and the vegetables rather too long.

As Viola had said, however, the company was excellent, and the conversation pleasant. That is, until Armaan raised the uncomfortable topic of her time in Edinburgh.

"Were you introduced to any unusual dishes in Scotland, Miss Summers?"

"Oh, I . . . Not really. Not unless you count haggis and cock-a-leekie soup. We ate quite plainly."

"No Scotch collops or clootie dumpling?" Mr. Hammond asked.

"Um. Not that I recall."

He looked slightly disappointed. "And what took you to Scotland? I don't think I've heard."

Claire blinked, not eager to lie, especially not with a sister who knew the truth sitting right there at the same table.

Thankfully, Viola spoke up on her behalf. "My sister served as companion to our elderly great-aunt until her recent death. We are glad she has come home to us at last."

Interest and suspicion flickered in Sonali's eyes, or perhaps Claire's guilty conscience caused her to imagine it.

Mr. Hammond seemed about to ask a follow-up question, but before he could, Viola elbowed the major, who blurted, "And how goes your work for the Foreign Office?"

William Hammond stared at him in surprise, mouth slack.

A moment of tense silence followed.

Then Major Hutton revised his question. "That is, I . . .

understand you once worked for the Foreign Office in a diplomatic capacity. Is that right?"

"Yes, for several years." Now Mr. Hammond was the one answering awkward questions. "But I recently resigned."

"That's right. I remember you telling me. Forgive my stupid question."

"Not at all."

Viola, an adept hostess, directed the conversation onto another topic, but Claire was left wondering what sort of work or "secret project" Mr. Hammond might still be doing for the Foreign Office. Or had Viola's husband simply blundered in his attempt to change the subject?

After dinner, instead of separating, men and women gathered in the candlelit drawing room, which held comfortable furnishings and a pianoforte.

Armaan turned to Viola. "Will you play some of your beautiful music for us?"

When Viola hesitated, he added, "I know you prefer not to play in company, but—"

"I shall play," Viola said. "*If* my sister will sing. She has a fine voice."

"Oh, I . . ." Claire wanted to demur, but seeing the entreaty in Viola's eyes, she found herself replying, "If you'd like."

"Excellent." Armaan beamed, and then seated himself between Major Hutton and Miss Patel.

Mira climbed up beside Sonali, and William sat on his daughter's other side.

The sisters consulted quietly, selected an old piece they both knew, and began the song.

> "I go where glory leads me,
> And points the dang'rous way;
> Tho' coward love upbraids me,
> Yet honor bids obey . . ."

Oh, the memories that flooded through Claire to find herself singing with her musical sister once again. Although reticent with strangers, Viola had often played for family during evenings at home. And Claire had happily sung with her while their parents looked on with pride and pleasure.

> "But honor's boasting story
> Too soon those tears reprove,
> And whispers fame, wealth, glory:
> Ah! What are they to love!"

As she sang of glory and love, Claire's vision filled with more images of the past. Then, recalling her surroundings, she risked a glance at the assembled company.

From across the room, she met William's gaze, his eyes simmering with admiration. But could he ever love anyone as he had his wife?

23

A really effective cipher is literally worth
far more than its weight in gold.
—François de Callières,
The Practice of Diplomacy

When they arrived back at Broadbridge's, Sonali took a sleepy Mira straight up to bed. Claire and Mr. Hammond hung up their outer things and stepped into the morning room.

Fran Farrant rose from where she sat sewing near the hearth. "Good dinner?" she asked.

"Yes, very. Thank you for coming over so we could all go."

"My pleasure. Anytime." Fran gathered her things and bid them farewell, planning to meet her husband at the nearby London Inn for a ride home.

Mr. Hammond followed her out, no doubt offering some compensation for her trouble.

When he returned, Claire asked, "Shall I make tea?"

"No need. I have had plenty." He gestured her into the chair drawn up to the fire and sat in another close by.

She asked, "How are you even familiar with the Scottish foods you asked about at dinner?"

"Ah. While in Constantinople, I served under Sir Robert Liston—ambassador and Scotsman. He often mentioned how much he missed food from home."

"I see." Claire hesitated, then asked another question. "What did Major Hutton mean about your work—current work, apparently—for the Foreign Office?"

"I was afraid you'd caught that. Hopefully others were not so quick." He shook his head. "I am admonished by one of your brothers-in-law to remain discreet, while another blurts it out at a dinner party."

"Sorry about that." Claire knew it was at least partly her fault. The major had been trying to shift the focus away from her time in Scotland. "I hope you know you can trust me."

"Well, as both your brothers-in-law and likely their wives already know, I don't think much harm can come from telling you. But I do need to ask for your discretion."

"Of course."

"Mr. Thomson recently came to me on behalf of his employer, Sir Thomas Acland. Sir Thomas had been contacted by the Foreign Office, who, aware I was living near him in Sidmouth, requested he approach me about a special project. They want me to decipher a cache of French dispatches found in a ship captured near the end of the war—the hidden compartment only recently discovered.

"These dispatches are written in a code our Foreign Office had not seen before. Not the Great Paris Cipher that Scovell unlocked during the war. A different code. It makes sense—once the French learned we had their cipher, they would have lost no time creating a new one. This one is a proper diplomatic cipher, but more complex than the one we used under Sir Robert."

"That's what you've been working on in your study all hours?"

He nodded.

"I thought a diplomat would be involved in, I don't know, embassy parties, treaties, negotiations. . . ."

"Not all the duties are so lofty. As an attaché, I handled the passport work, composed, corrected, and copied papers, and studied the local language. I like mastering languages, but most of the other tasks were tedious. Later I was asked to learn to encipher and decipher the coded messages used in dispatches to protect government secrets. Others loathed the work, yet I liked it and, if not vain to say, excelled at it. Soon I was ciphering and deciphering codes much more rapidly and accurately than anyone else. I was charged with creating a new cipher to improve security should our dispatches fall into enemy hands. I did so with relish. I was then asked to train others in the new system, first in one mission, then another: Vienna, The Hague, St. Petersburg. I found the work engrossing. Perhaps it sounds odd, but my brain loves a challenging puzzle. It's almost addictive."

He ran a hand over his face. "After we had Mira, I often worked late into the night, sometimes sleeping a few hours in the chancery instead of going home to my wife. I felt guilty about it but continued on, finally gaining recognition for my work. Fool that I am, I believed that's what was important.

"I thought I had given it all up when I came here. I was astonished when Mr. Thomson asked me to complete this project. The foreign secretary thinks it might help us be better prepared in the future, should another threat arise. No guarantee, of course, but I was convinced the work might prove worthwhile—at least, more worthwhile than chatting with guests and answering boarding-house correspondence."

He looked at her, expression uncertain. "Do you think I was wrong to agree? I don't want to revert to the man who put work above all else—above family, worst of all."

"It is not my place to say."

"I'm asking your opinion."

Claire considered. "I admire your abilities and your patriotism. And unless it prevents you from being an attentive father to Mira, then . . ."

"If it does, I hope you will bring any neglect to my attention. Mira must be my priority. Will you help me? Make sure I don't lose sight of what is truly important?"

Claire wanted to repeat that it was not her place. She was only there to assist in managing the boarding house. But . . . she wanted it to be her place, so she stammered, "I . . . I shall try."

Claire felt honored by his trust, even though she knew she did not fully deserve it.

After breakfast the next morning, Mr. Hammond was the first to excuse himself. Claire followed him into the hall.

"I've had an idea," she began. "Probably a strange one, but an artist might be able to paint a new portrait of Vanita, a composition based on the miniature as well as on Mira's face and Armaan's."

"An artist like you?"

"Heavens, no. I am not that skilled. But perhaps Mr. Filonov?"

"Hmm. Interesting. I suppose it would not hurt to ask what he thinks."

They found him in the dining room, lingering over a cup of tea and a copy of the *Sankt-Petersburgskie* newspaper. Claire explained the idea to him.

The man considered, then said, "I never attempted it before, so cannot promise good result. Yet I should like to try. Intriguing notion."

They began that very afternoon.

Mr. Filonov sat with sketch pad and pencil in the morning room, where he judged the light to be best. On the table beside him sat the miniature portrait. On stools before him sat Mira and Armaan.

He looked at the little girl and explained, "I shall begin by sketching, and try to draw your *amma* as you remember. Miss Mira, when you think of her, how is she dressed?"

"Like Miss Summers. In English clothes."

"Good. And her hair?"

Mira screwed up her face. "I dunno. Papa?"

"Um. At home, she wore it in a plait over her shoulder, like Miss Patel often does. And she pinned it atop her head when going out."

The artist turned to Sonali. "Miss Patel, if you will oblige us?"

"But my hair is darker than hers was."

"I shall make allowances."

Mr. Hammond brought another chair forward, and Sonali self-consciously sat with the other "models," arranging her long, thick braid over one shoulder.

"Da. Perfect." The man sketched for a time, then looked up with a smile. "You are all part of dis project now, you see?" He continued sketching.

After a few minutes, he consulted the miniature and asked, "Miss Mira. When you look at your uncle, what reminds you of *Amma*?"

Mira gazed carefully and admiringly at Armaan. She placed a hand on his cheek, much as she had at Westmount. "His eyes."

"Anything else?"

"His lashes are long and dark like *Amma*'s."

"Well done. And his nose?"

Mira shook her head, giggling. "It's too big! His whole face is big. But I like it."

"Excellent. And his coloring?"

"His what?"

"His skin and hair—are they like *Amma*'s?"

When Mira shrugged, Sonali answered in her stead, "He is darker."

Mr. Filonov sketched for some time in silence, now and again consulting the miniature or pausing to study the faces before him.

Finally, he held out his sketch to Mira. "Is only a beginning, but tell me . . . does it look at all like your *amma*?"

"Yes!" Mira replied. "Except her eyes, her eyes were more . . ."

"More what . . . ?" he prompted.

"Happy." She turned to her father. "Were they not, Papa?"

"I suppose they were. After all, when you saw her eyes, she was looking at you. And who could not be happy then?"

Mr. Filonov made a few adjustments. "Very good. All for now. Next comes easel, brush, and paint."

There were fewer people around Sea View's dining table that night—intentionally so.

Meals with Mr. Craven and his sisters were unpleasant affairs that strained Mamma's nerves and Emily's self-control. When they had initially discussed the idea of serving dinner to these guests every night, Mamma had told Sarah the decision was hers. Sarah, who had always been the most determined to make the guest house a success, now questioned that decision.

She waited at the sideboard, prepared to help Mr. Gwilt serve, while Jessie stood ready to clear away.

At the table sat Mrs. Harding, Mr. Craven, Miss Craven, and Simon Hornbeam.

When they began serving the first course, Mrs. Harding glanced up at Sarah in question.

"Are we not to have the pleasure of your family's company tonight?"

Mr. Craven smirked. "Something we said?"

"My mother is not feeling"—*equal to another meal with you*—"very well. She is having dinner in her room with Georgiana."

"And the beautiful Emily?" he asked.

"She and her husband are dining at Westmount tonight."

"Afraid you must make do with my company," Mr. Hornbeam said with an easy grin. "And of course Miss Sarah's, Jessie's, and Mr. Gwilt's. At least it's roast beef and Yorkshire puddings tonight. You are in for a treat."

Miss Craven managed a polite smile, perhaps realizing too late the man could not see the gesture.

Her brother, meanwhile, poured liquid from a pocket flask into his water glass and downed it in a single swallow.

Mrs. Harding sipped her soup, then eyed Mr. Hornbeam with interest, her scrutiny rather bold, free of concern of being thought rude.

"Mr. Hornbeam, is it?"

He turned toward her voice. "That's right."

"And you have been a guest here for some time?"

"Since last summer. My grown son was due to meet me here but went to Brighton instead. I find Sidmouth suits me. Sea View and the Summers family suit me as well."

"Have you no one waiting for you at home, wherever that might be?"

"I am a widower, so no. My son has visited yet prefers the company of his fashionable friends, which I know is only to be expected. And I have retired from my career, so I am at leisure to stay as long as I like. Or as long as Miss Summers will put up with me."

"You, dear sir, are always welcome," Sarah assured him.

He smiled in Sarah's direction before adding, "Although,

if God and a certain woman favor me, I may one day marry again."

Sarah knew he referred to his friend Miss Reed. Having known each other in their early years, the two had become reacquainted right there in Sea View after last year's flood.

Mr. Hornbeam turned back to his dinner companion. "And would it be rude to inquire about Mr. Harding?"

"Not at all! Dear Welford is busy with his shipping interests. Travels a great deal between London and Bristol. If you are interested in investing in one of his ships, I would be happy to give you his card."

"Thank you, madam, but no need. My money is right where I want it. What's left of it, that is, after my son's last visit." He chuckled, and she politely joined in.

"And your son, sir? How old is he?"

"One and thirty."

"Ah. Just the right age for Persephone here."

"Caroline, please."

Sadness flickered over his features. "As much as it wounds my father's heart to say it, I could not recommend my son as a good match for any young lady. At least, not at present. I hope in time he will mature into a man of sense and responsibility, though I have seen little evidence of either so far."

"Do men ever really mature?" Mrs. Harding asked with a pointed look at her brother.

"Some of us do, yes," Mr. Hornbeam replied, then directed his next words to her younger sister. "Don't lose heart, my dear. There are still many good men in the world. One who would make you a good husband, I don't doubt."

Persephone spoke up. "Do not worry about me, sir. I already have just such a man in mind, as my sister knows full well. A viscount."

"Ah, I see. And is he kind and honorable? Does he treat you with gentlemanly respect?"

The young lady blinked, expression uncertain. "Well. I . . . I am sure he would, given the chance. Once he'd truly committed to a woman."

Mr. Craven snorted.

Caroline Harding shot him a scowl before returning her attention to Mr. Hornbeam. "And during your stay here, have you become acquainted with all the Summers sisters, including the elusive Miss Claire?"

"No. I have not had that pleasure." Puzzlement furrowed his brow, and he added almost to himself, "That I know of."

Persephone said, "I don't know why you are so worried about her, Caro. He had his chance and did not take it."

Sarah dropped a serving dish lid with a clatter and bit her tongue to keep from saying something she'd regret.

After a sharp glance in Sarah's direction, Persephone turned back to her sister. "You spoke to him recently. Did he say something that led you to believe he had revised his opinion of her?"

"No. Not specifically."

"I thought he decided not to join us in Sidmouth this year. Did he not send his regrets?"

"He was uncertain of his plans when I spoke to him."

Slouched in his chair, her brother said, "That reminds me. Received a letter from the old boy."

"Did you?" Mrs. Harding asked. "Why did you not tell us?"

Her brother raised his glass in mock salute. "Just did."

"Well, what does he say?"

Mr. Craven opened his mouth to reply, then with a glance at Sarah, shut it again. "Let's discuss it after dinner, shall we? We don't want our roast beef and Yorkshire puddings to grow cold. After all, Mr. Hornbeam here says they go down a treat."

Persephone pouted. "But I want to know if he's coming."

So did Sarah.

"Patience, sister."

Miss Craven no doubt hoped the man had changed his mind about coming to Sidmouth. Sarah sincerely hoped he had not.

Now resolved, Sarah faced Mrs. Harding and announced, "It is not our custom to serve dinner to guests on Saturday and Sunday evenings. We made an exception in your case because of our mutual acquaintance with Charles Parker. However, after tonight, we shall resume our usual schedule. Thank you for understanding." She forced a smile despite Mrs. Harding's frown.

Sarah turned back to the sideboard feeling satisfied. She had not made the decision out of spite but had put her family's comfort ahead of pleasing these particular guests, who, she guessed, would not be pleased in any case.

"Perfectly understandable," Mr. Hornbeam replied. "Family and rest are important, and the hotels in town serve excellent food as well."

Sarah thanked him and made sure he received the best cut of roast beef.

24

Public Subscription Rooms, Sidmouth. John Marsh has the honour of respectfully announcing to the Nobility and Gentry . . . a Concert of Vocal & Instrumental Music.
—Advertisement, *Exeter Flying Post*

Emily and Viola visited Claire again on Sunday afternoon to ask her to accompany them to a concert in town the following night.

Emily added, "Although I should mention Mr. Craven and his sisters might be there. I don't believe you've met them, but you have a . . . mutual acquaintance in a certain lord. And they seem rather curious about you."

"No, I don't know them. How odd. Thank you for inviting me, but I had better stay here."

"It would not have to spoil the concert," Viola said. "Just meet them and move on."

"It's not only that," Claire said. "I should not abandon my duties here so soon after spending the evening at Westmount."

"But I know you would like the music," Viola insisted, "and we would very much like your company."

Claire was about to decline again when Mr. Hammond wandered into the morning room.

"Mr. Hammond, please convince her," Emily pleaded. "Claire loves music. Not as much as Vi does, but a great deal. And she has had so little enjoyment the last few years."

"What are we talking about?" he asked.

Emily raised an advertisement cut from the *Exeter Flying Post*. "There's to be a 'concert of vocal and instrumental music' tomorrow night, but Claire does not think she should leave the boarding house to join us."

"Indeed she should. I thoroughly agree. I will be here and will happily watch over things."

"Don't you wish to attend yourself?" Claire asked.

"Me? Music?" He shuddered theatrically. "Abhor the vile stuff." He winked, then added, "I have work to do and can easily accomplish it down here. Please do go, Miss Summers. You have been working hard, and I appreciate your efforts. Broadbridge's is already a better and more hospitable place, thanks to you."

Satisfaction warmed Claire, and Viola beamed.

"See? You must go now! The major and I shall collect you in our carriage."

"Very well, I am outnumbered. Thank you all. I shall no doubt enjoy it."

Mr. Hammond sat at the desk while Claire walked her sisters out. In the hall, Emily stepped close and lowered her voice. "I do think it will be a pleasant evening, despite the possibility of having to endure that man's friends."

Claire's stomach knotted. "I suppose it is inevitable I should meet such people eventually. But I appreciate the warning."

When it was time to change for the concert the following night, Claire donned the second dress Emily had returned to her. The high-waisted gown was of fine gauze over a white slip with a bodice of pale rose satin. The full, short sleeves were slashed with the same satin. Over her bare arms, she wore white over-the-elbow gloves.

Mary helped with her hair, pinning it up and adding silk roses. Claire put on her long-lost earrings and wished once again she'd not had to pawn her aunt's necklace.

When the maid finished, Claire said, "Thank you, Mary. And how is your sewing coming along?"

"Well, I think. I've been practicin' on the scraps ye gave me."

"Good. Being able to help with mending will add to your qualifications should you ever seek another place."

"Aye, miss. And one day I could sew for my family. If I had one."

"That too."

Viola and Major Hutton dropped off Emily and Mr. Thomson first and then came for Claire in their carriage. She could have easily walked the short distance, but they'd insisted on driving her there. From the livery, they walked together to the assembly rooms, where they surrendered their cloaks and hats and went to find seats. Claire sat between her sisters, while their husbands sat on their opposite sides.

The Sidmouth band played a few opening numbers, and then the visiting musicians performed a stirring program. Viola had been right. Claire enjoyed the fine music. It nourished her soul like rain and sunlight revive a plant kept in the dark too long.

She reached over, took Viola's hand, and whispered, "Thank you."

Tears shimmered in Viola's eyes, and she held tight to Claire's hand and did not let go.

Another memory struck Claire then. Of sitting beside a young Viola, six years her junior, at the Finderlay pianoforte and gently positioning her small fingers on the keys—fingers that had soon outpaced Claire's skill, thanks to lessons from a music master and hours of practice. Now Claire gratefully squeezed those same fingers once again.

At the concert's conclusion, they all rose and mingled with others in attendance. Emily, James, and Jack spoke to a fine-looking older gentleman and his wife, while Viola introduced Claire to a Mrs. Fulford and Mrs. Robins, acquaintances from her charity work.

After a brief chat, they turned away, planning to rejoin the others, and instead came face-to-face with an unfamiliar trio: two elegant women and a well-dressed man.

The older of the two women greeted Viola. "Good evening, Mrs. Hutton. If you recall, we met at Sea View when you visited your mother and sisters."

"Ah. Mrs. Harding. That's right. We met in passing."

The woman gestured to her companions. "And this is my sister, Miss Craven, and my brother, Mr. Sidney Craven."

Her glittering gaze landed on Claire. "And who is this, pray? If I am not mistaken, I notice a marked resemblance to your sister Emily."

Viola squared her shoulders. "Allow me to introduce my sister Miss Claire Summers. Claire, these three are guests at Sea View." Viola turned back to the trio with a cool smile. "I trust you are enjoying your stay?"

"Yes, yes," Mrs. Harding replied. "Although most disappointed not to meet your eldest sister before now."

Confused, Claire faltered, "Why . . . should you be disappointed? I don't believe we have met before."

Mr. Craven spoke up. "Sadly, no. But I have heard your beauty described and am delighted to find those descriptions were not exaggerated in the least."

His praise made her uncomfortable. "Good gracious," Claire said with a weak laugh. "That is too much flattery."

"Not at all. Well deserved, I assure you."

Mrs. Harding said, "We have a mutual acquaintance. I wonder if you have heard from him recently. Lord Bertram?"

Emily's warning echoed in Claire's mind and bile climbed her throat. She swallowed it down and attempted to appear unaffected. "Why do you ask?"

The woman watched her closely, then said, "Oh, just curious if he had contacted you. So difficult to pin these men down! Do you know his future plans?"

"I have no idea. Nor do I care. I saw him briefly in Edinburgh when he visited my great-aunt, but otherwise I have not been in contact with the man in years."

"No? Good. That is, thank you. Good evening."

The trio walked away.

"What was that about?" Claire whispered.

Viola lowered her voice as well. "Emily believes Miss Craven has set her sights on Lord Bertram and fears you may threaten that plan."

"I don't see how."

"Did he truly travel all the way to Edinburgh to call on Aunt Mercer?"

"Yes, although I'm not sure why. He spoke briefly with me as well. Apologized for what happened but certainly did not renew his long-ago addresses. Miss Craven has nothing to fear from me. Now, come. The others are waiting. Let's take our leave."

When Claire returned to Broadbridge's, she found Mr. Hammond in front of the fire in the morning room. Waiting up for her?

He rose when she entered. "I just made a fresh pot of tea, in case you should like some when you returned."

"Thank you. I would." She set aside her outdoor things and joined him in the morning room, sitting in a nearby chair.

He reclaimed his seat, poured for her, and asked, "How was the concert?"

Claire sipped, then answered, "The music was excellent."

"And the company?"

"Of course I enjoyed spending time with my sisters and their husbands."

"Was the concert well attended?"

"Yes. Quite a crush. Viola introduced me to a few of her friends, who seemed pleasant enough."

He regarded her curiously. "But . . . ?"

She looked over at him. "Hm?"

"I must say, for someone who just attended a concert, you seem . . . well, disconcerted."

She looked down, feeling self-conscious, the scene washing over her anew: the awkwardness of talking with friends of Lord Bertram's, their appraising looks, prying questions, and cloying flattery.

"It's nothing, really. I met a few people staying at Sea View. Apparently we have a mutual acquaintance."

"From Scotland?"

Claire shook her head. "From England. They seemed to think I should be familiar with his plans, but I could tell them little. They were . . ."

"Rude?" he suggested.

"Not rude exactly, but I . . . could not like them. I am glad they are not staying here."

She set down her cup and rose. "Well, I am off to bed. Thank you again for the evening off and for the tea."

Claire felt his gaze follow her in thoughtful silence as she left the room.

A few days later, Armaan came to the house again.

Claire greeted him warmly. "Good day, Mr. Sagar."

"Armaan, please."

"Very well. And you must call me Claire. Come in. I know Mira will be delighted to see you."

He stepped inside and she took his hat and hung it on a peg. "I believe she is upstairs with her father. Why don't you wait with Miss Patel while I let her know you are here."

She led him into the morning room, where Sonali sat stitching. "I will return as soon as I can."

On her way up the stairs, she heard Sonali say, "It's first names now, is it? I suppose you admire Miss Summers as Mr. Hammond does. Yet I wonder if she is all she appears to be."

Claire paused, hand tight on the railing, and held her breath.

"Jealousy does not become you, Miss Patel," he replied.

Sonali huffed. "Of course you defend her. But I doubt she is as respectable as she pretends. A supposedly genteel young lady traveling to Scotland alone? Is that not where the English go for the elopements? And now she is here and not living with her family? Most suspicious."

Voice cool and clipped, Armaan said, "Let me make something perfectly plain. Major Hutton is my closest friend. His wife, whom I also esteem, is sister to Miss Summers. If you think I will thank you for spreading malicious gossip about her, you are wrong. I want nothing to do with it. And if you think I would be interested in a mean-spirited woman, even were she the only Indian woman in all of England, you are quite mistaken."

A chair squealed as it was pushed back.

"Mr. Sagar, wait!" Sonali called. "I am sorry, and ashamed. I deserved that rebuke. Please forgive me."

"It is not me you have wronged."

Claire hurried up the stairs, blood roaring in her ears. She felt as ashamed as Sonali claimed to be. For as much as she appreciated Armaan's defense, she knew she did not deserve it.

Some time later, while Mira was occupied with her father and uncle, Sonali came and found her belowstairs.

Claire stiffened, bracing herself for another unpleasant confrontation.

Instead the woman said, "I wish to apologize, Miss Summers. I have been resentful and bitter and mean. In truth, I have felt threatened by you—afraid to lose my place in this family. Yet my uncertain situation is not your fault. I have wronged you, and I hope you will forgive me."

Claire stood there, momentarily rendered speechless. For even if this apology had been prompted by what Armaan had said, the humble contrition in the woman's expression seemed utterly sincere.

Claire laid a hand on her arm, half expecting the woman to throw it off. "I forgive you. And I hope we can be friends."

Tears brightened Sonali's large, dark eyes. "I would very much like that. I have missed having a friend."

When Claire entered the morning room later that day, Mr. Hammond looked up from the day's post. "Ah. Just the person I was thinking of. Sir Thomas Acland has invited me to an evening party at his estate. Probably to introduce me to a few other politicians and local officials. There's a rumor the Russian ambassador and his wife may also be there. Will you accompany me?"

Claire drew up in surprise. "Me? No. I could not attend uninvited."

"The invitation is addressed to myself and a guest of my choosing. I choose you."

Claire's body warmed, heart tingling at his words.

"That is kind of you, but . . . how would we get there?"

"I suppose I will have to hire a post chaise or at least a horse and gig."

And the two of them would journey alone together at night?

As if guessing her thoughts, he said, "Perhaps Mary might accompany us."

Claire replied, "Let me think about it, if you don't mind. When is it to be?"

"In one week."

Claire turned away, mind and stomach churning. She hesitated to accept the invitation for more than propriety's sake. She knew Mr. Hammond was attracted to her and might be growing attached to her. She should tell him everything and walk away. Allow him to find someone else—someone who truly deserved him.

But she did not want to walk away.

The next day, Emily and Viola came to the boarding house again. Emily handed her a piece of embossed stationery that looked strangely familiar.

"What is this?" Claire studied it.

"An invitation to an evening party."

Claire stared in some astonishment at her name on the official-looking invitation. "But how?"

"James added you to the guest list—with Sir Thomas's approval, of course. Do say you'll come. Several gloomy politicians will be there, so we'll need help enlivening the mood, as well as another woman to even the numbers. I have even convinced Sarah to come. Viola and the major will be there too. You could wear the white-and-rose dinner dress again. It would be perfect for an evening party."

Claire admitted, "Mr. Hammond also suggested I attend . . . as his guest."

Emily's dark eyes sparkled. "Did he indeed?"

"I was reluctant to agree, but now that my name is officially on the guest list . . ."

"You'll come! Excellent," Emily said. "I'm so glad. The cabriolet at our disposal has a hood but seats only two."

"So," Viola interjected, "you are welcome to ride with Sarah, Jack, and me, as our carriage is larger."

Claire nodded. "Mr. Hammond said something about hiring a chaise or gig, but I was not sure I should travel alone with him."

"There would be room for him as well," Viola said. "And less room for gossip."

Mr. Hammond came into the room. "Ah. Mrs. Thomson. Mrs. Hutton. A pleasure to see you both again."

"Mr. Hammond. We were just speaking of you."

"All good, I hope?"

Claire explained, "Emily's husband has procured an official invitation for me, and Viola and her husband are offering to convey us both in their carriage to Sir Thomas's party."

"Excellent. That's all sorted, then. Thank you very much. And please do thank your husbands for me."

"The major and I are happy to do it." Viola met his gaze directly. "We want there to be no mistake. My sister is not alone in the world, without the protection of family."

For a moment Mr. Hammond stood stock-still, only the deep lines between his eyebrows giving away his displeasure. "I know that. I would never take advantage, even if she were."

"Good. I am glad we understand one another."

"We do."

Good heavens! Claire thought, mortification heating every pore. What had happened to her shy, reclusive sister? This Viola was a woman to be reckoned with.

Despite the embarrassment, her sister's protective gesture touched Claire's heart.

Later that day, they all gathered in the morning room, including Armaan, ready for Mr. Filonov to unveil his portrait.

The artist pulled back the covering and looked first at Mira. "So. What do you say?"

Mira gasped and pressed her hands to her mouth, then clapped loudly. "It is *Amma*!"

Claire could hardly believe the transformation from pencil sketch to full color portrait. "You are a master, Mr. Filonov."

"Sank you, my dear."

"I don't know how you accomplished it and so quickly," Mr. Hammond said. "I see Miss Summers's dress. Miss Patel's braid. The girl in the miniature, and Mira, as well as Armaan. Yet I blink and look again, and I see my wife, Vanita, as she was."

Mr. Filonov laid a hand over his heart. "You honor me, sir. You are pleased?"

"More than pleased." He sent Armaan a sour look. "Although I am not sure I like my wife having Armaan's eyes." His lip quirked. "I shall endeavor to overlook it."

25

The study of Shells is a branch of Natural History not greatly useful in human economy, yet by the infinite beauties of [its] subjects . . . leads the amazed admirer into the contemplation of the glory of the Divinity in their creation.

—Emanuel Mendes da Costa, *Elements of Conchology*

Sarah walked from the library-office through the hall, tidying as she went. She picked up a pair of discarded shoes from beside the door, as well as a fallen glove, and placed them in the closet.

She heard music coming from the parlour—someone playing the pianoforte. The musician was too skilled to be either Georgiana or Emily. Had Viola come over? Sarah went to investigate.

Instead she found one of their guests, Miss Craven, playing while her sister sat nearby with a cup of tea.

Seeing Sarah in the doorway, Mrs. Harding asked, "You don't mind, do you?"

"Not at all. It's a pleasure to hear. The instrument is played far too rarely now my sister Viola has moved next door."

"Persephone is quite accomplished," the older sister said with almost maternal pride.

Sarah could relate and offered a smile. "Yes. Clearly."

While she was in the room, Sarah neatly stacked a cluttered pile of newspapers and another of magazines.

Miss Craven turned a page of music and began another song.

"Oh, I know this one." Mrs. Harding set down her teacup and rose, coming to stand beside her sister at the piano bench.

After the introductory bars, she began to sing,

> "O where and O where does your highland laddie dwell;
> O where and O where does your highland laddie dwell;
> He dwells in merry Scotland where the bluebells sweetly
> smell,
> And all in my heart I love my laddie well . . ."

Sarah turned and abruptly left the room. She retreated belowstairs and busied herself gathering a basket of pastries, bread, and a fresh pot of currant jam. Georgiana came in as she did so, a ruby smear beside her mouth. She'd clearly been sampling the new batch.

"Good jam?"

"Hm? How did you . . . ?"

Sarah pointed to the spot beside her own mouth.

"Oh." Georgie's tongue darted to lick off the smear. Then she asked, "Going to the poor house?"

Sarah nodded. "Would you like to go with me?"

"I'll walk with you. I want to go to the school again and see Cora."

"You don't fool me," Sarah teased. "I know you want to join their daily game."

Georgie grinned. "That too."

Together the two sisters walked from Sea View down to

the beach. The town stray, Chips, trotted along at Georgie's side, as he often did.

They waved to Mr. Cordey and Bibi, a local fisherman and his daughter, who were busy beside their small cottage, taking down lines of split mackerel they'd smoked near a fire.

Chips bounded over to sniff out a snack.

Sarah and Georgiana walked on, stepping around beached boats and lobster pots, their half boots crunching over the pebbled shore, the call of seagulls in the air.

A young lady in her early twenties strolled toward them, a small basket over her arm. Sarah recognized Eliza Marriott, who lived nearby. They did not know her well but shared a friendly passing acquaintance, especially Georgiana, who spent a great deal of time out of doors, as did Eliza. While Georgie pursued sports of every kind, Eliza focused on one pursuit: conchology. She regularly walked the area beaches in search of interesting seashells.

They stopped to greet her. "Good day, Miss Marriott," Sarah said.

"Miss Summers. Georgiana. Care to see my latest discoveries?"

"Yes, please," Georgie enthused.

In her basket lay several shells of various sizes, shapes, and colors: chalky white to shiny pearl, pale gold to pale pink. Eliza pointed to each one in turn, using names like *conch*, *cockle*, *mitre*, and *limpet*.

"Goodness, they are all so different and interesting."

"I think so. You shall have to call at Temple Cottage and see my entire collection sometime. I have a new penwork casket with small compartments to display them."

"Sounds lovely."

After bidding her farewell, Georgie and Sarah resumed walking.

Around them, fishermen mended nets, children played on

shore, and well-dressed visitors strolled the promenade, greeting friends as they passed.

Georgie gave a contented sigh. “I love it here, don’t you?”

Sarah considered. “I like it, yes. I am not pining for May Hill, if that is what you mean. I think the move has been good for all of us.”

“That’s not the same as loving it, though.”

Sarah shrugged. “Does a place make someone happy, or is it the people one is with, or something else?”

Georgie rolled her eyes. “That’s too deep for me.”

Leaving the shingled beach, they moved up to the packed-earth promenade, which workmen were maintaining with iron-handled stone rollers. Just past the York Hotel, they turned left, following the footpath along the River Sid.

The marshy track was muddier than Sarah had expected. “Perhaps we ought to have gone another way.”

From a side street a youngster came running, playing hoop and stick. His hoop got away from him, and Georgie leapt to grab it before it flew over the bank into the river. With a mumbled word of thanks, the lad took it and ran off again, using the stick to roll the hoop back up the street as he went.

With a rueful look at her sister’s muddy half boots, Sarah encouraged Georgie to walk on. Passing Marsh Chapel, they soon reached the Sidmouth School, its yard enclosed within a brick wall. Through its gate, Sarah saw a group of boys—and one athletic girl named Cora—kicking a ball.

Sarah waved to the schoolmaster. “Good day, Mr. Ward.”

He returned her wave and opened the gate for Georgiana, who joined the children for a rousing game, while Sarah continued on to the poor house.

She stopped to serve bread and jam to two old men playing draughts in the common room, and then went to visit Mrs. Denby.

“I’ve brought you some little treacle tarts,” Sarah said.

"Thank you, my dear." Mrs. Denby smiled and invited her to sit down. Then she studied her through thick spectacles.

"What is it, Sarah?"

"Hm?"

"You seem sad. Or at least, distracted."

"I'm sorry. I hoped my visit would cheer you."

"You always do, my dear. But if you will pardon me poking my nose in, sometimes I think you spend so much time looking after others that you neglect yourself."

"I like to be busy, to serve people."

"I know you do. Though I wonder . . . Are you lonely?"

"Lonely? I have four sisters and a house full of guests. I don't have time to be lonely."

"My dear Sarah, one can be lonely at a crowded party. I know who I am missing—my family, these many years gone. Who are you missing, I wonder?"

Sarah pressed dry lips together. "I don't know what you mean. I missed my sister Claire terribly while she was gone, but now she's here, so I don't . . . Of course, I miss my father, yet that grief has eased."

Still the old woman watched her. "You were engaged once, I believe?"

"That was years ago. I am not troubled by memories of Peter anymore."

"Someone else?"

"I . . . Mrs. Denby, please do try a tart."

The woman laughed. "And with my mouth full I cannot ask more impertinent questions! Yes, I know. I may be old, but I can still take a hint."

"I am sorry. I did not mean to—"

"Never mind. You must forgive an old busybody. You know I care about you, right? I only want to see you happy."

"I do. I am!"

"Well, I have said more than enough on that subject. And

now I will happily eat one of these delicious-looking tarts, if you will join me."

"Very well."

They each lifted a miniature tart as though in a mock toast before taking bites.

"Mm. Delicious. When you marry, your husband will be a very blessed man."

"*If* I marry," Sarah corrected.

Mrs. Denby popped the rest of the pastry into her mouth, then held up both hands as if conceding the point, although the sparkle in her eyes told a different story.

Georgie was still playing with the children when Sarah paused at the school gate. Clearly enjoying herself and in her element, Georgie waved her on.

Sarah waved back and began the walk to Sea View alone.

Simon Hornbeam and Alvinia Reed came strolling toward her, arm in arm. Like Viola, Miss Reed had stopped wearing a veil to cover her scars. She wore a bright smile instead. It pleased Sarah to see the pair looking so happy.

"Good day, Miss Reed. Mr. Hornbeam."

Recognizing her voice, Mr. Hornbeam stopped to talk. "My dear Miss Sarah, I would like you to be the first to know. This lovely lady has accepted me. We are to be married."

"Oh, how wonderful! I am delighted for you both."

"We have yet to decide on a date and where we shall live afterward, but I shall keep you apprised."

"I appreciate that, and congratulations."

When the two departed, Sarah continued on. Instead of going straight home, she diverted to the churchyard. Passing through its gate, she recalled the time she had followed Callum Henshall there, wondering what he was up to, only to discover he was visiting his wife's grave.

She did that now.

From the path, she walked over chestnut- and acorn-strewn grass until she reached the grave, its granite headstone topped by a Celtic cross. She solemnly approached, bowing her head and folding her hands, much as he had done that day. Again she read the inscription:

Katrin McKay Henshall
Beloved Wife and Mother
Forever in Our Hearts

According to the engraved dates, she had been gone nearly four years now, a year longer than Peter. Sarah felt pity for the troubled woman who had come to Sidmouth in search of a cure and instead died there. And what did Sarah feel for the man who'd tried to save her, and who served as caring stepfather to the daughter she left behind? Sarah was not sure but was beginning to realize that despite her efforts to forget him, Callum Henshall would likely be forever in *her* heart.

The following day, Mr. Hammond invited Armaan to join him for a few games at the billiards room. With the men gone and the house quiet, loneliness threatened. To distract herself, Claire wandered upstairs to Mira's and Sonali's rooms.

There she found Sonali standing before a long mirror, adjusting a sari over her shoulder, a sari Claire had not seen her wear before.

"That's the one you were embroidering."

"Yes. I wanted to try it on."

"It looks beautiful on you. That border is exquisite."

"Thank you, Miss Summers."

"Claire, please." She did not wait for the woman to return the offer of given names. Instead she asked, "Is your clothing comfortable? It is certainly pretty."

"It is. Although the stares of others are not always comfortable. I am a strange sight here, dressed in *saree*. Everyone looks, and the looks are not always friendly."

"I am sorry. I would not like to be stared at."

"I am too proud, perhaps. Vanita gave up traditional dress, but I shall not. This is who I am. It would be interesting to try, though I imagine the stays are very constricting."

"Actually, a pair of well-fitted stays can be quite comfortable. A whalebone busk, however, is less so."

Sonali looked up, mischief quirking her mouth. "Should you like to try my clothes, while I try on yours? Just for the experience?"

"Could we?"

"Why not? The house is quiet, Mira is napping, and Mr. Hammond is out."

"Then let's! Give me a few minutes to gather some things."

Claire eagerly descended to her room. There, she selected a gown from Vanita's trunk and one of hers, as well as a bandbox and correct underpinnings from the extra set Emily had given her. Then she hurried back upstairs.

When she returned to Sonali's room, she noticed the woman had draped a long swath of fabric over the mirror. "Let us wait and look together, when we are both fully dressed. Yes?"

Claire nodded. Then Sonali helped Claire unfasten her gown, stays, and petticoat.

Claire stood there, self-conscious in her thin chemise, relieved the mirror was covered.

"First, you will want a well-fitted *choli* or blouse." She helped Claire into a formfitting top.

"Next, an underskirt, I think. For modesty while walking." She helped Claire into one of hers.

"We tuck in the *saree* at the waist and drape it around your back and then again to the front and over your shoulder, folding it like so."

The sari, Claire realized, was at least seven or eight yards long.

"Finally, I shall secure it with pins."

The sari felt silky and featherlight against Claire's body and almost too fine. She was glad for the underskirt and blouse.

Next it was Claire's turn to dress Sonali in English clothes.

"First, a simple shift." Claire helped her into the basic, rather shapeless, underdress. "Now the pair of stays you are dreading."

She wrapped the quilted article around the woman's midriff and began tying the laces in back. Sonali adjusted it so that it better supported her bosom and fit to her waist.

"Too tight?"

"Surprisingly, no."

Claire finished lacing it, then picked up another garment. "Next, a petticoat." Claire held one out and helped Sonali step into it.

"Perhaps stockings should be next. Do you wear stockings?"

"Only in winter."

"Then we shall both forgo them for today's exercise. And which gown will you choose?" Claire first held out her pale blue dinner dress. "I am afraid my wardrobe is limited, so I brought up one of Vanita's as well." She next held up Vanita's ivory evening gown adorned with seed pearls.

Sonali's eyes brightened. "I always admired this dress of hers."

Claire helped her into it and did up the fastenings. It fit the slender woman and suited her well, flattering her coloring.

"Oh, I should pin up my hair in proper English style," Sonali said. "And you should wear yours in one long plait. Perhaps tied with bright ribbon at the end."

They helped each other with their hair. Almost, Claire realized, as sisters would.

Sonali said, "Sit here at my dressing table. You need a bit of *kajal*, or kohl, around your eyes. Look up." Claire did so and fought against blinking as Sonali feathered the stick along her lashes. Despite the light application, her eyes watered.

Then Sonali lifted a shiny necklace and bracelets from a case on the dressing chest. "And here—wear some of my jewelry."

Claire sat obediently while the woman placed the necklace around her neck and fastened the clasp, then slid the bangles onto her wrists.

Claire rose. "And you must wear one of Vanita's hats." She settled it onto Sonali's head, an ostrich plume rising from it at a jaunty angle.

When they were both fully dressed and coiffed, the two stood before the tall mirror on its wooden stand. They grinned at each other. Then, with a flourish, Sonali pulled off the fabric covering.

Claire stared, oddly breathless, at the strange vision of herself. She giggled like a schoolgirl. "Good heavens. What have you done to me?"

"I could ask the same of you. I look like a proper English miss, do I not?"

"Indeed you do. An English rose."

"Although a *little* darker," Sonali added with another grin.

"Perhaps. But a diamond of the first water nonetheless."

Standing side by side before the mirror, Claire impulsively grasped the woman's hand, and the two smiled at each other's reflections.

The door flew open wide, and Mira dashed in. "Here they are!"

In the passage behind the little girl stood her father and uncle.

Startled, Claire's heart banged hard, and Sonali gasped. William Hammond and Armaan Sagar stared open-mouthed from one woman to the other. It was difficult to judge whose gaze lingered longer on which woman.

"What in the world . . . ?" Mr. Hammond murmured.

Mira clapped. "Pretty!"

Claire pulled off the clinking bracelets and Sonali removed the hat. "We were only . . . seeing what it would be like."

"It's quite astounding, the transformation."

"Yes, well. Mira was napping and we thought you'd gone out or we would not have attempted it."

"We had. I invited Armaan back to the house to join us for dinner."

"And he is welcome, of course."

"We did not intend to intrude," Armaan said. "We came up to find Mira."

"And you've found her." Claire turned the girl toward the door and gently nudged her out into the passage with her father and uncle. "Now, please excuse us while we change."

"Don't hurry on our account."

Sonali flashed Armaan a defensive look. "I know what you are thinking. That I criticized you for dressing like an Englishman and now I dress like this. This was a mere novelty. A diversion. I don't plan to make a habit of it."

"Dress however you like, Miss Patel," he said gently.

With a measuring glance from Armaan to Sonali and back again, Mr. Hammond said, "Come, my friend. Let's leave the ladies to it." And taking Mira's hand, he closed the door.

26

Donkeys were a common sight at seaside resorts, giving tourists rides along the beach. They were used because of their quiet disposition and gentle nature, and were usually ridden side saddle.

—The Donkey Sanctuary, Sidmouth

The next day, Mira ran into the morning room, hair dancing around her shoulders. "Papa says we are going to the beach tomorrow. Is that not exciting? And you and Sonali are to come as well."

"That does sound exciting," Claire replied. "I shall stay and watch over the house, but I know you shall enjoy yourselves."

Mira's father walked in after her. "None of that, Miss Summers. I have arranged for Mrs. Farrant to come over again for a few hours so you can join us. I have been promising Mira just such an outing for some time, and I am striving to become a man of my word."

"But I have no wish to go bathing," Claire said, adding to herself, *And certainly not with a gentleman present.*

"Nothing as strenuous as that. Walking along the seashore

followed by a picnic lunch for us and wading and seashell collecting for Mira."

"And may I have a donkey ride?" Mira asked.

"You may. In fact, I think I shall hire one of Mr. Smith's donkeys to transport our provisions."

"The town beach is not far," Claire said. "We could carry what we need."

"I was thinking we'd go a bit farther. Not as far as Ladram Bay, but to the western beach. It has sandy areas, whereas the near one is mostly pebbles."

"I thought men swam there?" Claire did not add *naked*, although she thought it.

He nodded. "In the mornings, yes. In the afternoons, families with children often congregate there."

"I see. Well. Let me think about it."

An hour or so later, she found Mr. Hammond and asked, "May I read something to you?"

"Of course."

She opened her copy of *The Sidmouth Guide*, which Emily had given to her. Aloud, she read, "'The beach extends for half a mile from the River Sid, at the foot of Salcombe Hill, to the rising grounds on the opposite side of the vale. . . . It is furnished with seats and neatly rolled. Here the valetudinary may inhale the refreshing sea-breezes and contemplate the lofty ranges of the hills, rugged and precipitous to the sea, but clothed on the receding sides with cornfields, woods, and houses in beautiful variety.'"

When she'd finished, he replied, "Very affecting. Though I wonder. Do you consider me one of the 'valetudinary'? I promise not to bring my stick if that will improve your opinion."

"No! No one can think you infirm after watching you climb Salcombe Hill without pausing for breath or rest."

His eyes glimmered. "I am glad to hear it. Does reading this excerpt mean you've decided to join our outing?"

"Yes, but that's not why I read it to you. My sister Emily wrote that. Her name does not appear on the guide, but still, I am so very proud of her. Thank you for indulging me by listening."

"The pleasure is mine, and well you should be proud."

The following day, they set off together. Picnic basket, blankets, umbrellas, and Mr. Filonov's art supplies strapped to a docile donkey led by one of Mr. Smith's sons. The artist had accepted his host's invitation to join them and planned to paint as well as partake of the picnic meal.

Mira, meanwhile, carried her own small bucket and shovel. Miss Patel had dressed her in a pinafore and pantalettes so she could frolic more easily than in a long dress. Claire and Sonali wore their customary clothing, and Mr. Hammond wore his usual outdoor attire but with knee-length breeches instead of trousers and gaiters.

They followed the esplanade for a time and then descended, walking westward along the pebbled shore, past bathing machines and fishermen's cottages.

The way narrowed near the jutting headland that divided the beach in two. As they rounded the headland, Claire glanced up at the lime kiln looming on the cliff top above.

Reaching the more secluded western beach, Claire saw two men standing on shore, thankfully clothed. As they neared, she recognized them as Armaan Sagar and Jack Hutton, hair still damp after a swim, towels in hand. Mr. Hammond hailed them, and they paused to exchange greetings.

Mr. Hammond invited the men to join their picnic. Armaan, looking from Claire to Mira to Sonali, cheerfully agreed. Major Hutton, however, politely declined. He bid them farewell and took the cliffside path up toward the lime kiln on his way back to Westmount . . . and his wife.

The adults prepared for their picnic as Mira enjoyed her donkey ride, sitting sidesaddle on the gentle creature, the lad leading them along the shore at a sedate pace. Meanwhile, a few other people arrived and spread their blankets at a distance.

The western beach was largely pebbles, but low tide revealed a generous stretch of damp, packed sand. To avoid the damp, they spread their picnic blankets farther from the surf on smooth pebbles.

Mr. Filonov set up his stool and easel nearby, preparing to capture the scene. He enthused, "Is nothing like painting *en plein air*. Natural light! Fresh air! De views!"

Looking from the sunny beach with its backdrop of red sandstone cliffs to the blue-grey sea, mild waves, and distant sails of passing boats, Claire could understand the appeal.

Sonali settled herself primly on the blankets, a parasol fluttering over her pretty head. Claire and Mr. Hammond laid out the food. Knowing their load would be much lighter once the food and jug of lemonade had been consumed, Mr. Hammond released the lad with warm thanks and coins to seek another customer for his donkey.

Mira was too excited to nibble more than a few bites and soon began to dig in the sand and collect seashells in her bucket.

After the rest of them had eaten and the men were busy conversing, Claire surreptitiously inched up her skirt, removed her shoes, and rolled down her stockings, slipping them into her shoes. She rose and stepped gingerly over the pebbles to reach the sandy stretch. Standing barefoot, she pressed her toes into the warm, damp sand. Heavenly.

Then she joined Mira in exploring rock pools, the two exclaiming over crabs and prawns and starfish trapped there until the tide rose once more.

Her father joined them, and Claire noticed he'd discarded

his coat and removed his shoes and socks as well. In shirt-sleeves and bare feet, he chased Mira down the beach and picked her up, swinging her around to peals of delighted laughter. When he set her down, she splashed him, and he chased her again, back toward Claire.

Mira slipped one hand into Claire's, and her father took the other. "Swing me!" she pleaded.

So together they walked along the shore, swinging the little girl between them at intervals, over the larger waves.

Soon Claire's skirt hems were damp a good six inches, but she decided she did not care.

Eventually Mira ran off to show her uncle the shells she'd collected, while Claire and Mr. Hammond remained near the shore. She looked at him, his wind-tossed auburn hair, pale skin and freckles, and rumpled, rolled-up sleeves, and imagined the rumbustious lad he'd once been. Mischief tickled her breastbone, and she bent to the water and splashed him, much as Mira had done.

"Foul play!" he exclaimed, and retaliated in kind.

The cold water pelted her neck and she gave a girlish squeal, which inspired him to laugh and repeat the act.

She bent toward the water again, intent on revenge.

"Oh no, you don't!" he playfully called, grasping her from behind.

She was immediately conscious of his nearness, the tangy smell of shaving soap, his muscular forearms sprinkled with freckles and golden hairs, wrapped firmly around her.

She spun to face him. Looking up, she found his face perilously close to her own. Her breath caught, and his playful expression changed into something else entirely.

For a moment neither moved.

Then Mira ran over and thrust herself between them. "I want to play too!"

Claire pulled back abruptly, face hot. Had she learned

nothing? Would he think her a loose woman? No doubt Sonali would. But when Claire braved a look toward the blankets, she was relieved to see her and Armaan deep in conversation.

"Look!" Mr. Filonov called, pointing out to sea.

Glad for the distraction, Claire joined the others in turning to discover what he was gesturing at. Then she saw them: several dolphins jumping in the distance, traveling eastward.

"A rare treat," Armaan said. "I have heard dolphins are sometimes seen near Branscombe, to the east, but I've not seen them here before."

They watched until the animals grew small and distant and finally disappeared from view.

"A rare treat, indeed," Claire echoed.

Mr. Hammond nodded. "This entire outing has been a delight, and one we shall have to repeat. However, that seems a fitting end for today, I think."

The others agreed and began packing up their things. As they did, Claire asked Mr. Filonov if she could see his painting, but he demurred, saying it was not yet complete.

After their beach outing, Sonali suffered a headache she attributed to too much sun. Claire urged her to retire early with a cool cloth over her brow, offering to read to Mira and put her to bed herself.

In the nursery that evening, Mira showed Claire where her nightclothes were kept, and Claire helped the girl change and clean her teeth.

She had planned to read a book to her, but Mira had a different idea.

"Will you oil my hair? Since Sonali is not feeling well?"

"Oh. I . . . would be happy to attempt it, although I have never done so before."

"I can tell you how. It's easy. Warm the oil, rub it in."

"Sounds simple enough when you say it like that."

"It is!"

Together they gathered towels, fetched a bowl of hot water from the kitchen kettle, and warmed the oil bottle in it.

Claire sat in a chair and Mira sat on the soft rug at her feet. She draped a towel over the girl's shoulders in case the oil dripped and began combing out Mira's hair and parting it into sections. Tentatively, she tested the oil to make sure it was not too hot. It felt warm and silky to the touch. Reassured, she dabbed it onto the parts she'd made in the girl's hair.

Claire then massaged Mira's scalp. "Is that all right?" she asked. "Too hard? Too soft?"

"Just right. Rub it all the way to the ends."

Claire relished the tender, maternal task. It reminded her of her girlhood. As the eldest, she had often helped her younger sisters, brushing their hair, helping them dress, and reading them stories. Soothing them after bad dreams or minor falls and scrapes. Gently shushing them in church when Mamma was not there to do so. It had all come naturally to Claire. She had always longed to be a mother and raise her own children. Considering she would soon be nine and twenty, that dream seemed about to slip through her fingers, like the fine strands of Mira's hair.

Mr. Hammond came into his daughter's room and stopped midstride.

Noticing him, Mira said, "Papa! You could oil Miss Claire's hair while she does mine."

"Oh, em . . . I would be happy to, but I don't think that would be . . . wise."

"Why?"

"Miss Summers is . . . Well, she's our friend, but she's not quite family." He glanced at Claire, then away again. "And though you cannot see it, she is blushing deeply at the mere mention of such a liberty."

Claire swallowed hard. "Still, kind of you to think of me,

Mira." She risked a glance at him, and if she was not mistaken, he looked rather flushed as well.

He cleared his throat. "I came up to hear your prayers, but I shall return later. I see you are in good hands."

After he had gone, Claire finished running the oil through to the ends and then plaited Mira's hair.

Finished with the task, she washed her hands in the still-warm water and spread a clean towel over Mira's pillow.

Mira knelt beside the bed.

"Do you want to wait for your papa to return?" Claire said.

"No need. Only God needs to hear." The girl clasped her hands and closed her eyes. "God bless Papa and Miss Claire and Sonali. And Mr. Filonov and *Mamu* and Chips the dog. Please tell *Amma* we miss her. Amen."

"Amen," Claire murmured in reply, touched to be included in the girl's prayer.

When Mira had climbed into bed, Claire asked, "Now shall I read to you?"

"Will you sing to me instead?"

"Oh. I . . . What would you want me to sing?"

Mira shrugged. "Anything you like."

"Very well." Aware of Sonali sleeping in the next room, Claire sang quietly,

> "I see the moon, the moon sees me,
> God bless the moon and God bless me:
> There's grace in the cottage and grace in the hall;
> And the grace of God is over us all."

When she had finished, Mira begged for another.

"You're too old for 'Rock-a-bye Baby,' and I'm afraid I don't know any other lullabies."

"Something else, then. What is your favorite song?"

"I like 'Amazing Grace.'"

"Sing that, please."

"Very well. Though that must be the last one, understand?"

Mira nodded.

Softly and slowly, Claire began to sing,

> "Amazing grace, how sweet the sound,
> that saved a wretch like me.
> I once was lost, but now I'm found,
> was blind but now I see."

She glanced up, chagrined to see Mr. Hammond in the doorway, leaning one shoulder against the doorframe, arms crossed over his chest. She stopped singing.

"Don't stop," he said. "That was beautiful."

He joined her in singing the second verse, their voices blending beautifully, and Claire very much feared she was falling in love.

27

Soon after our arrival in Constantinople,
the plague, that periodic scourge of the Levant, made its appearance in the city.
—William Turner, *Journal of a Tour in the Levant*

When the front knocker sounded on Monday, Claire answered it, hoping for a new guest. A thin man of forty-odd years stood there, impeccably dressed, wearing small spectacles, and somehow familiar.

"Good day," she began. "How may I help you?"

"Good day, madam. I am John Wallis, proprietor of the Marine Library. I come bearing a book Mr. Hammond ordered." He lifted the brown paper–wrapped parcel in his hands.

"How good of you to bring it yourself. I believe he is upstairs in his study. You are welcome to step inside while I let him know you're here. Or I would be happy to make sure he gets it."

"I cannot leave the library in my clerk's hands for too long. If you could see that he gets this safely, Mrs. . . . ?"

"Summers. Miss Claire Summers."

"Ah! Any relation to Miss Emily Summers, or I should say, Mrs. Emily Thomson now?"

Claire nodded. "She is one of my sisters."

"I see a resemblance. And are you a great reader as well?"

"I doubt anyone can compare with Emily, but yes, I enjoy reading."

"Then I shall have no qualms about handing this over to you. It's new, you see. Only recently published."

She accepted the paper-wrapped book. "May I ask what it is?"

"The first of a three-volume account of the travels of William Turner, Esquire, a British diplomat, according to the publisher's description. It is entitled *Journal of a Tour in the Levant*."

"Levant?"

"A term for a region in the Eastern Mediterranean, I believe, although I am not well-read on the topic."

"Then perhaps Mr. Hammond might give you a summary after he is finished reading it."

The man nodded. "Excellent notion. I always enjoy a good discussion of books. And a pleasure to meet another Miss Summers. I'd thought I had met them all."

He started to go, then turned back. "By the way, I hope you will visit the Marine Library one day soon. We have many compelling novels, both mysterious and romantic." He tipped his hat and walked away at a sprightly pace.

Watching him go, Claire quietly chuckled. This was the man she'd seen talking with Mr. Hammond in the alley beside the house. She'd suspected some clandestine meeting, and here they had simply been discussing a book Mr. Hammond had wanted—one he wasn't keen to explain his interest in, as he avoided mentioning his previous profession.

Unbidden, the playful scene on the beach played through her mind again—laughing together, splashing, Mr. Hammond's strong arms coming around her, their faces close . . . Had she misread that change in his expression? Only imagined he'd wanted to kiss her?

Claire shook her head at herself. Perhaps she would be wise to avoid reading any of the compelling novels the man had mentioned. She already saw mystery where there was none and read romance in Mr. Hammond's every look and action.

No.

If he *could* ever love another woman as he had Vanita, that woman should be someone without a tainted past. Someone worthy to help raise his daughter. And that someone was not her.

The next morning, after Claire had washed and dressed herself, thanks to the new wraparound stays, she went into the kitchen to help carry up the breakfast things. Mrs. Ballard was there with her maid, but no Mary. Feeling responsible, since she had brought Mary to Broadbridge's, Claire said she would go up and see what was keeping her.

Reaching her room in the attic, Claire knocked softly, and the unlatched door swung open. The housemaid sat sobbing on her bed, face in her hands, shoulders shaking.

"Mary? What is it? Are you feeling unwell again?"

"Aye, miss. I fear I am very unwell indeed."

Claire sat on the narrow bed beside her, the bed ropes creaking under their combined weight. "Do you need a doctor?"

"Not for five or six months yet."

Dreadful realization rushed over her. "Oh, Mary."

She nodded. "I'm that sorry for not telling ye sooner. I suspected as much when I asked ye to take me with ye. Now I'm sure."

"Is that why you were afraid to go home to your father?"

"Aye. I woulda been scared anyway, but with this?" She

placed a hand on her slightly rounded abdomen and shook her head. "We'd both be goners. Da' broke my brother's arm for a far lesser offense."

"Despicable. And the babe's father?"

Mary hung her head.

Claire asked tentatively, "Was it Fergus?"

"No, thank God." Mary visibly shuddered. "Though he certainly tried."

"Then who?"

"Do ye remember Liam? Liam MacBain?"

At her blank look, Mary added, "The apothecary's assistant. He delivered tinctures and draughts to your aunt regular-like?"

"Oh yes! Bright red hair, exceedingly polite."

Mary nodded. "That's him."

"I remember Aunt Mercer chastising him for coming so often with one package of pills or one small vial of whatnot, instead of delivering her weekly supply at once. I suppose now I know why."

Mary dipped a blushing face. "He came as often as he could. We fell in love and hoped to marry when we'd saved enough to live on our own. I know it were wrong, not waitin' fer the weddin'." Her blush deepened.

"Did your father find out?"

"About Liam, aye. Da' came to take a share of my wages and saw Liam kiss me as he left the house. Put two and two together and flew into a rage. He struck Liam over the head and when he fell kicked him hard. A watchman came and broke it up or he'd 'a killed 'im."

"When was this? I don't remember hearing a fight."

"You'd gone to the kirk."

"Did the watchman summon a constable to arrest your father?"

"No, miss. Da' intimidates everyone, so the watchman sent

him off with barely a warnin', though poor Liam was bleedin' bad. Da' left but said he'd find Liam and when he did, he'd be a dead man."

"So what did you do?"

"I wanted us to run away together, but Liam said no. He couldna support me without a job, and he wouldn't see me homeless. He said he would think on what to do and come back the next day after he'd bound his wounds. But Da' came to the shop that very evenin' and beat the apothecary when he refused to tell where Liam was. Took three passersby to pull 'im off the man. Liam sneaked over to see me one last time and told me he was leavin' Edinburgh before anyone else got hurt on his account. He promised to write as soon as he had a new place somewhere."

"And did he?"

"Aye." Tears filled the girl's eyes once again. "And it's so awful. For me, at least." She rose and retrieved a letter from her dressing chest and handed it to Claire. "Here. Read it."

My dearest Mary,

I have taken a place as a surgeon's mate on the merchant ship Clyde. *We're undertaking a voyage for the East India Company, bound for Bengal. I know it's a long way, and a long way from you, but the wages are good, and when I return, I shall be able to afford a place for the two of us and marry you proper-like. I do love you, my girl, more than you know, and I sincerely regret this time apart. Please don't forget me. I promise I shall return for you, God willing.*

Yours forever,
Liam

"Oh, miss! He'll be gone ages! I don't think he realized when he signed on how long he'd be away, and now it's too late."

Sympathy for the girl swelled in Claire, for who was she to judge? "Oh, Mary. I am so sorry."

"Not half as sorry as I am. What am I to do?"

Claire considered. "We have some time yet before your condition becomes obvious. But you should probably talk to Mr. Hammond about it fairly soon."

"I'd die of shame! Could ye talk to 'im for me?"

Claire hesitated. "Very well. I will do what I can, but I can't promise he'll keep you on. Ultimately that's up to him."

"I understand."

"Good. For now, let's go down and help with breakfast."

Later, when Claire told him, Mr. Hammond frowned at her from across the desk of his private study.

"With child?" He shook his head. "I am as compassionate as the next man, Miss Summers, but it is not the done thing. How do we know this Liam MacBain was truly serious about marrying the girl? Perhaps his flight had more to do with putting distance between them. It would not be the first time a man has fled his responsibilities."

Well I know it, Claire thought. "Please. Just read his letter." She thrust it toward him.

He read and then looked up with a furrowed brow. "Let me think on it for a time, will you? Consider what is best to be done."

"Of course."

Claire took her leave. She privately feared he would decide employing a visibly pregnant housemaid would prove too damaging to his respectable establishment. And if so, she could not fully fault him.

Oh, why was the woman always to blame and left to face the consequences alone?

28

Snapping the fingers in Country Dancing and
Reels, and the sudden howl or yell too fre-
quently practiced, ought to be avoided.
—Thomas Wilson, *A Companion to the Ball Room*

The day of the Killerton party arrived. Claire was excited about it until she recalled how eagerly she had looked forward to the Parkers' house party, and that had ended in disaster. She resolved not to do anything at this party she would later regret.

In the afternoon, Claire began dressing herself as best she could in the evening gown of white gauze and satin. She curled her hair with the hot iron and then gathered her long gloves and reticule.

Mary had offered to help her dress, but the Huttons would soon come for them, and the maid had failed to appear.

In desperation, Claire scooped up a handful of pins and a silk rose and climbed the stairs to the attic.

When she entered the maid's room, Mary sat up in bed. "Sorry, miss. I fell asleep sewin'. Awful tired these days."

A quarter of an hour later, dress fastened and hair pinned

high on her head and adorned with the silk rose, Claire made her way downstairs to the hall, hoping she had not kept the others waiting.

Mr. Hammond looked up as she descended, and her breath caught. How broad-shouldered and dashing he looked in evening attire: dark blue tailcoat, white waistcoat, and white cravat over knee breeches with stockings and black leather shoes. His auburn hair had been brushed back from his forehead and gleamed in shades of amber and brandy in the light of a nearby wall sconce.

She felt his steady gaze on her as she descended the remaining stairs, her pulse accelerating with each step that brought her nearer to him.

Worried she might trip, she gripped the railing with one hand, and with the other held her skirt. Reaching the bottom, she looked up and found him staring at her, lips parted.

"Good evening." Candlelight reflected in his green eyes. Admiration shone there as well. "How beautiful you are."

She looked down, self-conscious, and plucked at the simple white skirt. "I wore it to the concert, but Emily assured me it would be appropriate for tonight too."

"It becomes you very well."

"Thank you."

"Here. Allow me." He retrieved her cloak from the hall closet, and after a moment's hesitation, she turned so he could lay it over her shoulders. His hands rested lightly on her upper arms before lifting too soon.

The jingle of tack and horse hooves announced the arrival of the Huttons' carriage. Mr. Hammond opened the door for her, and they joined the major, Viola, and Sarah inside the vehicle, the fit rather tight.

Viola said, "I brought a coral necklace I thought would look well with your dress, should you like to wear it."

She held forth a strand of pinkish-red beads.

"They are lovely. Thank you."

At the same time, Mr. Hammond and Sarah held out their hands to assist. After a brief moment of uncertainty, Claire turned her back toward Sarah, her knees brushing Mr. Hammond's as she did. She would be too self-conscious to have him perform the simple, familiar act—especially with her sisters and Major Hutton present.

Sarah made quick work of fastening the clasp, and Claire turned forward again, breaking contact with Mr. Hammond.

"That does look well," Viola observed.

"Thank you for loaning it to me."

"Keep it as long as you like."

After that, Claire sank back against the cushions, content to listen as the major and Mr. Hammond carried on a conversation about recent parliamentary news, glad the focus had shifted away from her.

When at last they neared Killerton, the carriage turned up a long gravel drive that wove through rural woodland before leading to a torchlit entrance.

Liveried footmen helped them alight, and soon they were ushered into a grand hall dominated by a large, paneled staircase. There they were greeted by their host and hostess and made welcome.

A short while later, they all sat down to a sumptuous meal in the dining room lit by candelabra and an ornate marble fireplace, rows of gilt-framed paintings of ancestors arrayed to the ceiling.

Mr. Hammond sat on one side of Claire, an officer she did not know on the other.

At the head of the table, next to Sir Thomas, sat a vivacious woman dressed in an ivory gown trimmed in gold thread. She had dark, springy ringlets around her face and an accent that reminded Claire of Mr. Filonov.

She laughed and spoke with confidence, and the men around her seemed to listen with avid attention to her every word.

Claire leaned closer to Mr. Hammond and asked quietly, "Who is she?"

He followed her gaze. "The Countess Lieven, the Russian ambassador's wife."

"She appears to be quite popular."

"Indeed. I understand invitations to her home are highly sought after, and she was the first foreigner to be elected a patroness of Almack's."

"Really?" Claire was impressed.

He nodded. "In fact, it is said she is the person who introduced the *wicked* waltz to England through her influence there. Perhaps we shall have an opportunity to dance it this very night." He waggled his eyebrows at her in a teasing manner. "If you are brave enough."

Claire grinned in reply, although she was not certain she was.

After dinner, the ladies withdrew, leaving the men to their port and cigars. Claire excused herself to freshen up in the ladies' lounge.

When she came back down the corridor, the sound of men's voices drew her attention to an open door. There she saw Mr. Hammond in a small parlour with Sir Thomas, Emily's husband, James, and another man, deep in serious conversation. Claire was glad she knew now what Mr. Hammond was involved in, or her suspicions would have been roused all over again.

Back in the elaborately decorated great parlour, the carpets had been rolled up, and as the men rejoined the ladies, the musicians began to play.

Mr. Hammond approached Claire with a gallant bow. "May I have the honor of the first dance, Miss Summers?"

"I would be happy to, but I have not danced in a few years. I'm afraid I don't know the latest dances."

"Nor I. That's why I had a private word with the musicians and requested a few older, more familiar dances."

"That was clever."

He shook his head. "Completely self-serving. I have no wish to make a fool of myself in your company."

"I doubt you could. Are you fond of dancing?"

"I am. There was a fair amount of it at diplomatic parties, although like you, I am out of practice. Shall we muddle along together?"

"Very well."

To tinny music drawn from a harpsichord accompanied by flute and violin, the assembled company began a quadrille in clusters of four couples. The dance commenced with bows and curtsies, followed by a series of advancing and retreating steps, turns, and changing places with the person opposite.

The pattern was a simple one, and soon Claire began to relax and enjoy herself.

After the first set, they all changed partners, and Sarah—who had sat out the first time—danced with the officer who'd been beside Claire at dinner.

Sarah appeared even more ill at ease and uncertain of the steps than Claire had been. She supposed Sarah, who had lost her betrothed, had not danced much in recent years either.

Sarah had watched the couples dancing, feeling wistful and out of place. She found herself thinking not of Peter, whom she had planned to marry before he died at sea, but rather of Callum Henshall. Would she ever have a chance to dance with him?

She thought back to his stay at Sea View, when he'd confessed his wife's depression of spirits and his attempts to cheer her—including asking her to a dance. *"I am a bit of an ox, truth be told, and woe to anyone who stands too close during a Scottish reel! But for her, I would try."*

Despite his efforts, his wife had ended her own life. At the thought, Sarah offered up a prayer for him and for Effie, the woman's daughter.

Sarah noticed Emily approach the musicians to call the next dance. In honor of their former royal neighbor, her sister requested the Duke of Kent's Waltz.

Despite its name, this was a longways country dance in three-quarter time. It was a lovely, stately dance and far more acceptable than the partner waltz now gaining popularity.

An awkward young officer asked her to dance, and taking pity on him, Sarah agreed.

When the music began, they formed a star with another couple. Next, she joined hands with her partner, stepping forward and back in a balance step, before moving down the line and back up again.

Sarah glanced over and saw Claire dancing with Mr. Hammond, looking happy and pretty, and she owned to a shaft of jealousy as well as concern. She hoped this man would prove more trustworthy than the last man who'd made her sister smile like that.

Later in the evening, the Countess Lieven stood, clapped her hands three times, and announced with authority, "We must have a proper valtz!"

The young officer asked Viola to dance, but the major, who had refused to dance until that point, abruptly stood and took her hand, staring menacingly down at the smaller man. "If anyone is to put his arm around my wife, it shall be me and me alone."

"Jack . . ." Viola admonished, but Claire saw the fond amusement in her eyes and the tilt of her lips.

The young man blanched and scurried away to find another partner.

Seeing him heading toward Claire, Mr. Hammond quickly stepped forward and asked Claire to dance again. She agreed, even though they had danced together twice already.

She quietly admitted, "I've not waltzed before."

"Just follow my lead."

Once the music started and the honors had been paid, he turned Claire under his arm, then brought both hands to her shoulders.

"You do the same," he encouraged.

After a quick glance around to assure herself others were similarly positioned, Claire complied. Holding each other by the shoulders, they turned in circles around the room. One, two, three. One, two, three . . . Then, grasping right hands, they stepped forward and back in a balance step, and then again he turned her under his arm. This time as they came back together, he put his right hand around her waist.

She barely resisted a gasp. No wonder the dance was deemed scandalous! He lifted her other hand over their heads, and they continued to turn around each other, all the couples moving about the room in a large circle.

He grinned at her from beneath the arch of their raised hands. "You learn quickly."

Then the tempo increased, and embracing shoulders again, they hop-turned around each other, circling the room, Claire soon breathless and grinning. How exhilarating! And really, surrounded by friends and family, and moving so swiftly, there was surely nothing wicked about the dance. The rapid turning and the swirl of skirts around her ankles made her almost giddy. She felt happy and more alive than she had in a very long time.

"Enjoying yourself?" he asked.

"Yes," Claire answered between panted breaths. "You?"

He smiled into her eyes. "I am, thanks to you."

Knowing they had a long drive ahead of them, the major called for their carriage to be readied well before the midnight supper. Claire, exhausted and content, fell asleep on the way home, her head on Sarah's shoulder, while Sarah rested against the padded carriage wall. Across from them, Viola slept on Major Hutton's arm.

When Claire awoke, only William Hammond was awake, staring out the window at the starlit sky. As if sensing her scrutiny, he looked over and their gazes tangled and held.

"Almost home," he whispered.

And the low, intimate words did strange things to her heart.

They returned to Sidmouth as the moon rose in the east. The Huttons delivered Mr. Hammond and Claire to Broadbridge's before continuing back to Sea View and Westmount.

William held the door for her and helped her off with her cloak, fumbling in the darkness to hang it in the closet by feel and traces of moonlight. Then, facing her in the dim hall, he took her hand and brought it to his lips.

"Thank you for being there tonight."

"My pleasure. I enjoyed it."

The landing lamp had burned itself out. The fire in the morning room had burned to embers, but he managed to ignite a long match from it, then lit two candles and handed one to her.

"Can you find your way?"

She nodded, then realizing he might not be able to see her, said, "I know it by heart."

He reached up and traced gentle fingers over the contours of her face, cheekbone to chin, his thumb coming to rest beneath her lower lip. In a voice low and husky he said, "I know it by heart too."

29

Be not alarmed, madam, on receiving this letter, by the apprehension of its containing any repetition of those sentiments or renewal of those offers which were . . . so disgusting to you.

—Jane Austen, *Pride and Prejudice*

Two days later, Sarah opened the library windows to allow in the fresh summer breeze. She saw a carriage turn from Glen Lane onto Sea View's drive. The fine coach-and-four had a crest on its door and a liveried coachman at the reins.

She stepped into the entry hall just as Mr. Gwilt opened the door to a handsome, well-dressed gentleman. He said, "Good day, sir. How may we help you?"

"I am here to see Miss Summers."

Sarah walked forward. "I am Miss Summers. One of them." And the only one home currently, as Emily and Georgiana had again gone to the school—Emily to read to the pupils and Georgiana to play ball with Cora, a tomboy after her own heart.

"Ah, I should have specified," the man said. "Miss Claire Summers."

Sarah stilled, her mouth parting and pulse quickening. "She is not here. And you are . . . ?"

"Lord Bertram!" Persephone Craven called, gliding into the hall from the drawing room. "How wonderful to see you. Although, I confess, not a complete surprise, as Sidney mentioned he'd had a letter from you."

This was Claire's betrayer, Sarah realized. Here. Now.

He turned toward Miss Craven, face a mask of cool civility, clearly not as delighted to see her as she was him. "Miss Craven." He bowed.

"Come and join us in the drawing room. Sidney will be so pleased to see you."

"Actually, I need to speak with Miss Summers first."

"About what?" Persephone asked, lips in a pout.

"About her . . . her family's health, and perhaps a room. Why don't you go in. I shall join you presently."

"Very well, but don't be long. I shall just slip upstairs first and let Caro know you are here." She hurried up the stairs.

A room . . . at Sea View? Sarah's stomach twisted. Mamma could not bear to hear this man's name spoken. She would certainly not abide having him sleep under their roof.

"I'm afraid we cannot accommodate you," Sarah said. "But there are two good hotels in town."

Mr. Craven sauntered into the hall. "Bertram, old chap. Thought I heard your voice."

"Sidney."

"Come into the drawing room. I have news for you."

"Perhaps for a few minutes, before I"—he shot Sarah a look—"take my leave."

Sarah was not sure if she should be relieved or disappointed that Emily was absent. Emily would no doubt send the man packing with a flea in his ear but would likely create a scene while doing so. Even without her assistance, Sarah hoped to show the man out before Mamma came to see what was causing all the hubbub.

Too late. Mamma stepped from her room into the hall, dressed in a becoming afternoon frock.

"Good day." She gifted the newcomer with a gracious smile. "And who have we here?"

The man turned to face her, lips pressed tight, his Adam's apple rising and falling on a hard swallow. At least he had the decency to look sheepish upon meeting the mother of someone he'd ruined.

"Mamma, this is . . . Lord Bertram."

He bowed. "Mrs. Summers."

Mamma stared at him, clearly stunned. A muscle in her jaw tensed, and her countenance paled to a sickly green.

"I am sorry to intrude like this," he said. "But I trust you will forgive me when you learn why I've come."

The front door opened, and Georgiana bounded in, face flushed and smiling as usual, Emily on her heels.

Georgie looked at the unexpected assembly. "I say. This is quite a welcome! Good day, everyone." She looked from familiar face to familiar face until she came to the newcomer. "And who is this?"

The well-dressed man turned but hesitated, perhaps expecting someone else to introduce him or perhaps fearing her response.

"Lord Bertram," Emily said, her voice low and clipped. "This is a surprise." And her tone conveyed that it was not a pleasant one.

"Bertram?" Georgie echoed, brow furrowing. "Not *that* Lord Bertram?"

He smiled thinly. "I am afraid so."

Mr. Craven stepped to the front door, holding it open. "Come on, old boy. I believe you've outstayed your welcome.

Broadbridge's is where you want to go. I'll give your coachman directions."

Coming back down the stairs, Miss Craven called to her brother, expression stricken. "Sidney, no! He can't go there. He . . . he has not even greeted Caro yet. She will join us directly."

Lord Bertram paused long enough to say, "Please convey my regards. Another time, perhaps."

And the two men escaped out the door.

When they had gone, Mamma looked at her daughters and announced, "Family meeting." She turned to Mr. Gwilt. "Would you mind terribly dashing over to Westmount and asking Viola to join us if she can?"

"Not at all, madam. Happy to." He hurried out to do so.

Sarah sent Miss Craven a weak smile. "Please excuse us."

They gathered in Mamma's room, awaiting Viola. The others sat, but Emily paced. "Perhaps we ought to run over and warn Claire."

"It's no use. He had his coach-and-four awaiting him. We'd have to go on foot or wait for the Huttons' carriage to be readied. We'd never arrive before him."

Viola jogged up the lane and into the house a few minutes later. She joined them in Mamma's room, and once the door had closed behind her and she'd caught her breath, Sarah explained the situation.

Viola's eyes widened. "Why is he here?"

"He came to Sidmouth last summer with the Cravens," Emily said. "Perhaps he has only come to see them again."

"I don't know . . ." Sarah mused. "He did not seem especially keen to see them. Or at least, not Miss Craven. And he seemed to think Claire was here at Sea View. He asked for her."

"Why would he seek her out?" Georgie asked. "This is the snake who convinced her to elope and then abandoned her, right?"

Viola nodded and said, "At the concert, Claire mentioned

seeing him in Edinburgh when he visited Aunt Mercer. She said they spoke briefly, and he apologized for what happened between them but did not renew his addresses to her."

Mamma frowned in concentration. "Then what did he mean when he said, 'I trust you will forgive me when you learn why I've come'?"

"Has he reformed, do you think?" Sarah asked. "Come to rectify the situation? Marry her?"

Emily shuddered. "I hope not."

Mamma's frown remained. She stared vaguely into the distance, looking worried and uncertain.

"Mamma? What is it?"

"I am thinking. Of course I despise the man, but if he's come to make an honest woman of Claire, should we meddle? Claire must have loved him once. Perhaps she still does."

"She was deceived in his character, Mamma," Emily insisted. "Caroline warned me about him, remember?"

"Let's also remember the Cravens have their own reasons for warning us against Lord Bertram," Sarah said. "Miss Craven wants him for herself. We must not credit everything she and her sister say."

"As much as it pains me to say it," Mamma began, "it would be best for us and especially for Claire if they married."

Emily's mouth fell open. "You can't mean it, Mamma! Marriage to such a man would render her miserable for the rest of her life!"

Georgie nodded her agreement. "I don't want that snake for a brother. What awkward family holidays we'd have!"

"I hardly think our pleasure at holidays is the priority here, Georgiana. Now, you girls leave me in peace for a while." Mamma said it almost brusquely, but Sarah saw the torment in the taut lines of her face.

"It's nearly time for luncheon," Sarah reminded her.

"I am not hungry. You go on without me."

The door knocker sounded. Already on her way to the morning room, Claire diverted to the front door and answered it, a cheerful greeting on her lips.

The greeting faded. Her throat seemed to close at the sight of the man standing there.

Lord Bertram.

Again.

She glanced behind him and saw his grand coach-and-four blocking the street. "What are you doing here?"

"I came to see you."

"How did you know where I was?"

"I assumed you returned to your family, so I went to Sea View first. Craven told me you were here."

"I am not welcome at Sea View—thanks to you."

The slightest flinch creased his face and quickly faded. "Perhaps I can remedy that."

"You are two years too late." She began to close the door, but he prevented her with a firm gloved hand.

"Actually, I hope to take rooms here. For it seems I am not welcome at Sea View either."

"No? Then allow me to recommend the York Hotel or the London Inn. I am sure you will find them far more to your taste."

"But you are here."

"You had your chance with me, and you squandered it."

"I know I treated you abominably. I have come to redeem those mistakes."

"Why do I doubt that?"

"I promise you I am in earnest."

"I relied on your promises once before, to my ruination. I shall not do so again."

"I regret what happened between us."

"So you said in Edinburgh. Why come all this way to say it again? It changes nothing."

"But something *has* changed."

At that moment, Mr. Hammond came down the stairs. "Miss Summers . . . Excuse me. I did not realize we had a guest."

"I don't know that we do."

The proprietor looked from one to the other. "Is . . . everything all right?"

"No. This man wishes a room, but I am not certain we should give him one."

"Really? Perhaps I can help. William Hammond, at your service. Had you a reservation, Mr. . . . ?"

"Lord Bertram. No, but I'd like rooms for myself and my valet. Is that a problem?"

Mr. Hammond sent her an inquiring look, then turned back to their visitor. "Apparently so. Unfortunately it seems we cannot accommodate you. Perhaps try the York Hotel?"

Anger rose up and solidified into resolve. She would not cower in this man's presence. If he wanted to stay, so be it.

Claire huffed and straightened her spine. "Actually, I believe we can accommodate him after all. In the attic, perhaps. I understand Mr. Jackson snores like an angry badger, but if this person is determined to stay here, then far be it from me to turn away a paying guest."

She stalked into the morning-room office and threw back the cover of the registration book.

Mr. Hammond followed. She looked up at him, fighting back tears. "Would you mind taking his details? I have pressing tasks awaiting me belowstairs."

Concern shadowed his face. "Of course."

Claire went down to her room, closed her door, and pressed her hands to her face, torn between yelling and crying. In the end, she did both.

An hour or so later, she had all but cried herself to sleep when someone tapped on her door.

"Miss Summers?" Mr. Hammond softly inquired from the other side. "I just wanted to see if you . . . need anything."

Claire sat up, wiping a hand over her damp face. "No. I'm all right. Thank you. I shall be up soon."

"Very well. If you're sure."

After that, Claire did her best to avoid both Lord Bertram and William Hammond, not ready to face the one nor explain herself to the other.

She skipped dinner that evening and instead sipped some warm, salty broth in the kitchen to settle her stomach. She carried up coffee and dessert to the morning room but avoided conversation with the Hammonds and Miss Patel. Then she waited until she saw Mr. Bertram leave the dining room before going in to help Mary tidy up.

Claire was folding up the used tablecloth when Lord Bertram came back into the room.

"Good evening, Miss Summers."

She stiffened. "My lord."

He opened his mouth to say something, but she held up a hand to cut him off, hoping to forestall more awkward conversation—especially with Mr. Hammond and Sonali still in the next room. "W-was the meal to your liking?"

"Perfectly adequate. I wonder . . . Might I have a private word? I was just upstairs and saw the parlour there is currently unoccupied."

Not eager to be alone with the man, Claire hesitated. But better a private conversation than another confrontation like the one in the hall upon his arrival. She wondered how much Mr. Hammond had overheard.

"Very well. Let me finish here and I will join you in a few minutes."

She carried the cloth to the laundry basket with unsteady hands and looked at her hair in a mirror as she passed. Her hair was fine. Her face? Tense and pale.

Reaching the parlour, she closed the door but kept her distance. "Why did you come here—really?" she asked.

"I told you why."

"In Edinburgh, you told me it was not within your power to make amends."

"That was true then."

"If you have changed your mind about marriage, I understand Miss Craven is eager to be the next woman to break her heart over you. You are wasting your time with me."

"I am not interested in Persephone Craven. You are the only woman in my thoughts at present."

"Why?" The word came out almost like a groan. "What is it you want?"

"To marry you properly, in a church, surrounded by your family, as I should have done two years ago."

Foolish hope sparked to life within her before memories flooded in to drown it. She slowly shook her head. "Why the sudden change of heart?"

"I will not deceive you by pretending I have simply changed my mind. I am not so fickle a man. You know the reason I did not go through with it before. Your dowry was not what I had been led to believe."

"That has not changed. In fact, I am not certain I have any dowry after being disowned."

"You—we—have something better."

"What are you talking about?"

"You remember your Aunt Mercer summoned me to meet with her in Edinburgh?"

"Of course."

"She told me she needed to appoint a new heir, since your father had died, and was considering candidates. She went on to ask me a series of questions. I thought it must be a ruse, that she simply wanted to have a look at the man who had eloped with the great-niece now living with her. Or perhaps she wanted to force our paths to cross in hopes of rekindling our short-lived romance."

Had she? Claire wondered. The notion startled her.

"During our interview, she made it clear she knew about my financial difficulties. I anticipated she might offer some incentive to force my hand. Yet she dismissed me that day without doing so and without making any promises, so I assumed she'd decided against me. And considering that you were not exactly pleased to see me, I left Edinburgh not expecting to hear from either of you again."

Claire had never expected to see him again either.

"Then I received a letter through her lawyers. Apparently your aunt *has* named me conditional beneficiary of the majority of her assets: stocks, shares, and over ten thousand pounds."

Claire gasped at the injustice. Not only had this man escaped any consequences for his betrayal, but now he would benefit financially. Why would Aunt Mercer do that? She'd thought the woman had softened toward her near the end, but apparently she had remained determined to teach Claire a lesson.

Mistaking her gasp as a sign she was impressed, he nodded and went on. "A sizable sum, all told. Enough to pay off my debts and then some."

"Congratulations," Claire said dryly, not bothering to disguise the asperity in her tone. "Why tell me?"

"I inherit only under one condition."

She stared up at him, stomach sinking. "Oh no."

"Oh yes. That I marry you, publicly, legally, properly. If not, I get nothing, and it all goes to some charity or other."

"So that's why you're here."

"Yes. As I said, our financial situation was the only reason I changed my mind before. But now with this boon, I can follow through on what I'd hoped to do all along."

When she merely stared at him, stupefied, he pulled a folded letter from his pocket and handed it to her.

"Here. Read it for yourself."

Claire's mind was spinning too quickly to focus enough to read the whole thing. But a few lines leapt out at her.

> *These are my terms: Marry Claire Summers. Make a respectable woman of her. Restore her good name and that of her family.*

Claire stood there, wanting to throw the letter in his face. To flounce away. To refuse with bold, certain finality.

Instead, she remained still and silent, the words before her fading from sight. She saw not the letter, not the man, but rather a woman's face.

Mamma's.

A part of her was tempted. Not because she still loved this man or even liked him, but because marriage to him would go a long way to removing the cloud of shame she'd hung over herself and her family. It would "make a respectable woman of her," as Aunt Mercer had written.

Here at last was a way to make amends to her family, and perhaps finally be forgiven and accepted by her mother.

His quiet voice interrupted her thoughts. "I can see this comes as a shock to you, so I shall give you some time to think it over. I will stay on a few days so we may become reacquainted before you decide."

He turned to go, but she said, "Wait." She stepped closer and lowered her voice. "If you have not gathered, Mr. Hammond is my business partner. He does not know about . . .

why I went to Scotland, and I would prefer to keep that humiliation private."

"Of course."

"Not 'of course,'" she hissed. "For I gather the Cravens know or at least suspect."

"Sorry. Craven never could keep his mouth shut. Don't worry, I can."

After that, Claire made her escape. She put on her cloak, called in at the morning room door that she was going for a walk, and left before Mr. Hammond or Sonali could respond or ask any questions. She hurried from the house, eager to put distance between them.

Again she sought the solace of the seaside, walking along the shore, breathing deeply of the fresh air, and trying to grasp onto a calm she did not feel.

30

Three may keep a secret, if two of them are dead.
—Benjamin Franklin

The next day, Claire sat working at the desk in the morning room when Lord Bertram entered, looking perfectly groomed and without a wrinkle on his fresh suit of clothes, carefully packed and pressed by a dutiful valet.

"Good afternoon, Miss Summers."

"Lord Bertram."

He looked at her expectantly. She moistened dry lips and faltered, "I . . . trust your room is comfortable?"

"Yes. Mr. Hammond took pity on me and gave me a room on the first floor, sufficiently distant from your noisy Mr. . . . Jackson, was it? Although my valet testifies to the accuracy of your description of the man's snoring. Angry badger indeed. Thankfully, I cannot hear it."

Pity, Claire thought.

He stepped closer. "Have you given any thought to my proposal?"

She'd been up half the night wrestling with it. "Naturally."

"Any decision? Or questions you wish to ask me?"

The door knocker sounded, and Claire was relieved for an excuse to rise and excuse herself. "Pardon me."

She went to the door and opened it to Mr. Craven, whom she had met briefly at the concert, along with his sisters.

He beamed at her. "Ah, the lovely Miss Claire Summers. What a delight to see you again."

"Mr. Craven."

"Is Bertram available? I hope to convince him to join me at cards in the assembly rooms, unless he is otherwise engaged?"

No doubt recognizing Craven's voice, Lord Bertram joined them in the hall.

With a glance at him, Claire sweetly replied, "Not at all. Here he is, and quite at his leisure."

"Excellent. Shall we, Bertram?"

Lord Bertram looked at Claire and whatever he saw in her expression propelled him to say, "Why not. Apparently I am not otherwise engaged."

Perhaps having heard the door knocker, Mr. Hammond came down and stood beside her as she watched the two men depart.

Then he led her into the morning room and closed the door, which they rarely did. He asked, "Who is that man? To you, I mean."

Good question. She was not fully sure of the answer herself.

Quietly she replied, "A man I once thought would be my husband."

He drew in a breath of surprise. "You were engaged?"

"Not officially, although he did ask me to marry him."

"You refused?"

She shook her head, the sting of rejection still sharp after all this time.

"He changed his mind when he realized I was not the heiress he thought me."

"And now?"

"His financial expectations have improved. He says he regrets crying off before."

"And how do you feel?"

How did she feel? Torn. Guilty. Wishful. She wished she could tell Mr. Hammond everything, and hear him say none of it mattered, and she should not marry a man motivated by money.

"I am not sure how I feel," she replied truthfully. "But I would be foolish to dismiss his offer out of hand. My mother would, I think, approve of the match, which might better our relationship."

His expression became more somber yet. "How so? Do you . . . need to marry?"

Did he assume she shared Mary's predicament? Heat rushed up her neck and spread to her face at the thought.

"No. I . . . no. Nothing like that. Our brief courtship ended two years ago."

"Ah. That's a relief."

A relief for him, or . . . ?

Perhaps seeing her confusion, he added, "In that you don't need to rush into anything. Or make a rash decision you might later regret."

Oh, if only he knew how many regrets she already had. Claire's sour stomach twisted. She had painted herself an innocent in this partial explanation. How differently Mr. Hammond would respond if he knew the whole truth.

Feeling uneasy and restless, Claire told Mr. Hammond she was stepping out again for a short while. She needed fresh air. A change of scene. She needed . . . She didn't know what she needed.

Instead of the beach, this time her feet traveled north up Fore Street as if of their own accord.

Reaching the poor house near the river, Claire paused only

briefly before entering the brick building. Inside, she passed an elderly gentleman snoring in a chair in the communal dining room before walking down the corridor to Mrs. Denby's room.

Claire knocked tentatively, and a voice bid her to enter. When she did, the woman graced her with a smile and warm welcome.

"Ah! Miss Claire. You came. I am so very glad."

"I forgot to bring tea or anything else."

"No matter. Your presence is the best treat of all. Besides, Sarah gave me a packet of biscuits just yesterday, and now I am doubly glad I resisted eating them all in one go." She held the packet toward her.

When Claire hesitated, she said, "Go on, love. Looks you need something sweet more than I do."

Claire took a bite, and the sweet, chewy pastry soothed her. Sitting down, she said, "I realize we are not well acquainted, but may I ask you a personal question?"

"Yes, my dear. You may ask me anything."

"Have you ever done anything wrong? Anything you're ashamed of?"

Sadness tinged the woman's eyes, and her cheerful mouth turned downward. "Oh, my dear girl. At my age? Of course I have. Many things. Many regrets. But do you know . . . for years, I hid away here. Too ashamed to go out. To go to church. To the shops. To see my old friends. But when I did—thanks to your sister Viola—what did I find? Forgiveness. Friendship. Freedom."

"Really?"

"Yes, my dear. Whatever it is, don't keep it hidden. Burdens only grow heavier the longer we bear them alone. And you are not alone. For we all have sinned and fallen short."

Claire nodded, thinking of the many times Aunt Mercer had reminded her of her sin. "And God is a righteous judge."

"Yes, yet He is also merciful and loving. Whoever believes in Him shall not be ashamed." The old woman pressed her hand with knobby fingers. "I shall be praying for you, dear heart."

"Thank you, Mrs. Denby. I have no trouble understanding why my sisters esteem you so highly."

"The feeling is entirely mutual."

As if on cue, someone knocked on the door, and Viola herself stuck her head in.

Mrs. Denby beamed at her. "Ah, just in time, Viola. Come in and see who else has visited me. Am I not most blessed?"

Viola's mouth parted in surprise. "Claire! I was planning to call on you after this. How are you?"

"Unsettled, truth be told, and found myself in need of a chat with Mrs. Denby."

"I don't blame you at all," Viola said with a fond look at the older woman. "A visit with this dear lady is often just the tonic I need."

The two stayed to talk awhile longer. Then Viola walked out with Claire.

"I truly did intend to visit you this afternoon. Emily and Sarah stopped by Broadbridge's last night, but apparently you had gone out. Today they are busy at Sea View, so I promised I'd call and make sure you were all right. Are you? Is Lord Bertram truly staying at Broadbridge's?"

"He is."

"And has he . . . has he come to . . . ?"

"He's asked me to marry him, Viola. But it's not like it sounds. Aunt Mercer offered him an inheritance if he marries me. He says finances are the only thing that prevented him before, so I should be glad, but I . . . I am finding it difficult to be enthusiastic."

"Oh my. What a quandary."

Claire nodded. "I assume Mamma would wish me to say

yes, that it might . . . smooth things over to some degree. Yet I am torn."

"And no wonder!" Viola took her hand. "How can I help?"

"You have helped—by introducing me to your friend and just by listening. Thank you."

"I am always close-by if you want to talk. Anytime." Before they parted ways, Viola asked, "Should I keep his proposal a secret?"

"Please don't tell Mamma," Claire said. "For if I don't agree, she shall surely disown me all over again."

Later that day, Claire again answered the door. This time, Mr. Craven's sisters were standing on the doorstep.

"Good day," Claire said half-heartedly.

"Ah, Miss Summers. A pleasure to see you again," the elder began. "I am Mrs. Harding, if you don't recall. We met at the concert?"

"Of course. Do come in."

Claire stepped back, and the ladies entered the house, looking around the narrow hall with its modest furnishings with interest.

"So this is where you work, is it?" Mrs. Harding asked.

"I am a partner in this boarding house, yes. Now, how may I help—"

"Partner?" she interjected. "To whom?"

"Mr. Hammond."

"Quite understanding of him to take on a woman of your . . . background. A married man, I trust?"

Claire bristled. "Widowed. Why do you ask?"

"Oh, I would think, considering your history, you would wish to avoid even the appearance of impropriety."

Sonali stepped from the morning room, leading Mira by the hand. How much had she heard? Sonali glanced at the women before continuing up the stairs.

Miss Craven frowned. "I say, who are they?" she asked, not even bothering to lower her voice. "Apparently you will accommodate anyone here."

"That is not just anyone. That is Mr. Hammond's daughter and Miss Patel, a family friend."

"Good heavens." Mrs. Harding appeared scandalized, brows drawn low, mouth parted. "Is Mr. Hammond . . . black?"

"No, ma'am," Claire replied, without change of expression. "He is ginger."

The woman harrumphed. "Well. We have come to visit our dear friend Lord Bertram."

"Of course. Please follow me." Claire led them upstairs to the parlour. "If you will wait here, I will see if he is available."

Leaving the ladies, Claire walked to his room partway down the corridor. She knocked and Lord Bertram answered, his eyes lighting up when he saw her at his door.

"Mrs. Harding and Miss Craven to see you. I've put them in the parlour."

Disappointment darkened his gaze, then he seemed to steel himself. "Then perhaps you might join us?"

"No, thank you. They seem keen to see you. Alone."

"Ah." His expression hardened. "I see. I appreciate the warning."

He stepped into the corridor, shutting his door behind himself. "Are you sure there is no . . . news . . . I might relay to them?"

"Not from me, no."

"So be it." He nodded and walked into the parlour.

Despite her best intentions to move away immediately, Claire lingered outside the parlour door long enough to hear a few moments of their conversation.

"Lord Bertram! What a pleasure to see you. I was so sorry to miss you when you called at Sea View."

"The regret is all mine," he said politely.

"And how kind of you to join us in Sidmouth, as you did last year. We have been looking forward to your company."

"You honor me."

"Not at all. But . . . as a friend. A close friend. May I say something in confidence?"

"I suppose so."

"My lord, you must see. This place, these people, are far beneath you. You don't belong here with them."

Claire turned and walked away, not sure she disagreed.

Sarah and Mamma were on their way into the parlour when Mrs. Harding and her sister returned to Sea View, tossing their coats and hats at poor Mr. Gwilt with barely a glance.

"Ah, Mrs. Summers. We saw your daughter at the boarding house. Quite an . . . interesting establishment. And rather shocking to find her living with a widower. How sad that she continues to disregard the dictates of good society. You are wise indeed to keep your distance."

It was all Sarah could do to hold her tongue. She wanted to defend Claire, to ask the woman if she herself was perfect and had never made a mistake. She wanted to tell her to pack her bags and leave.

Instead she looked at her mother, who appeared more downcast than before.

When the women had gone up to their rooms, Sarah led her mother into the parlour and closed the door.

"Mamma, please don't let that mean-spirited woman influence you. She will be gone soon, and quickly forgotten, but none of us shall ever forget Claire."

Mamma took a deep breath. "You are right, of course. I don't like the woman, but she does represent how many in society would look down on Claire—on all of us—if her past were generally known."

"Do we still care so much about 'society'? We have already lost touch with most of our former friends and neighbors. And those who would shun us because of rumors about Claire or our reduced circumstances have already done so. I don't think they can cut us a second time. And we have made new friends here, who, I believe, would not be so quick to shun us even were Claire's history revealed. You and Lady Kennaway have become friends. Would she cut your acquaintance if she learned of Claire's past?"

"I hope not. The truth is, I can put up with the sly jabs of a Mrs. Harding or even bear Lady Kennaway snubbing me, should it come to that. What troubles me most is the thought of your father being disappointed in me. As a wife, I always tried my best to honor and obey."

"I know you did. But remember he was angry at the time he made those decrees. He was also seriously ill, and not thinking clearly."

Mamma vaguely nodded.

Sarah thought, then said, "Where is he now, Mamma?"

"What? In heaven."

"I agree with you. He was not perfect, for who is? Yet, with the exception of his last difficult months on earth, he was a God-honoring man. A Christian in word and deed. And now, he is with God." At least Sarah hoped he had died on good terms with his Maker.

Mamma nodded again.

Sarah asked, "Do you really think Papa would still want you to ostracize Claire, now that he's gone on to his eternal reward? A reward he is only enjoying thanks to God's mercy and forgiveness?"

"I don't know."

"Remember, there is no more sorrow in heaven, Mamma. His pain has passed, and his anger too, I imagine."

Mamma clutched Sarah's hand. "Oh, Sarah, I dearly hope you are right."

Sarah returned to the library-office. A short while later, Mr. Gwilt handed her a thin rectangular parcel, barely thicker than a letter. Noticing the postmark, she sat at the desk and eagerly opened it.

In a matter of moments, she held the necklace in her hand, just as Claire had described it: a cross pendant with scrollwork and small ruby on a thin gold chain.

She turned her attention to Mr. Henshall's letter that accompanied it.

Dear Miss Summers,

I am pleased to report that I found the shop as you described and was able to redeem your sister's necklace. The proprietor, Mr. Duncanson, was reluctant to hand it over without the original ticket. But as I was armed with your letter and the correct payment in full—not to mention discovering I had been at school with his parson—he became convinced. Please be assured that it was my sincere pleasure to help. No repayment is necessary, but in return I would be grateful for word of your sister and any news of you or your family.

For my part, I can relate that I am once again in Effie's black books. After a recent wedding, the bride's family hosted a céilidh (a party with spirited dancing, pronounced in English "kay-lee"). Effie and I attended, and she was utterly mortified to witness my attempt to dance a Scottish reel. Might I have whooped too loudly, like a "howling wolf or barbarian"? Stomped and clapped and snapped my fingers in a "most unbecoming manner"?

According to Effie, I am guilty of all these unforgivable trespasses and should be banned from céilidhs forever. . . .

Sarah smiled at his self-deprecating humor and carefully refolded the letter to read again later. Filled with gratitude and eagerness, she set off for Broadbridge's.

31

Confession is good for the soul.
—Scottish proverb

Sarah came to Broadbridge's, her usually reserved expression bright with excitement.

Claire invited her inside, and the two sat down together in her room.

"I have something for you," Sarah began.

Claire chuckled. "More biscuits? Or did you find something else I left behind?"

Sarah nodded, lips pursed in a barely restrained grin. With an air of ceremony, she held out her fist, and Claire extended her palm to receive whatever it was.

Sarah opened her hand and from it slithered a pendant on a dainty golden chain.

Claire stared at it in astonishment, then lifted the cross to examine it more closely, barely believing her eyes: Aunt Mercer's cross pendant with its small ruby and thin gold chain.

"How in the world . . . ?"

"When you described it to me and told me how sorry you

were to leave it behind, I wrote to a Scotsman I know who lives not far from Edinburgh. He went and reclaimed it for us."

Claire thought back, eyes widening. "That's why you asked so many questions about the shop and its proprietor!"

Sarah nodded. "Apparently Mr. Duncanson was reluctant to hand it over without the original ticket, but Mr. Henshall can be quite charming and persuasive."

"I am astonished. And very grateful for your kindness, and his. I'm afraid I cannot repay him presently, but . . ."

"Never mind. Mr. Henshall assures me it was his pleasure to do this service for me." She quickly corrected, "For us."

Claire looked at her sister, cataloging with interest her averted gaze and the dull blush creeping up her neck.

"This Mr. Henshall, Sarah. What does he look like?"

"Why do you ask?"

"Fair hair?" Claire prompted. "Well dressed?"

"Well, yes, but—"

"A Scotsman came to the house once and asked for me. I saw him briefly and heard his voice, but Aunt Mercer refused to allow him to speak to me and told the butler to send him away. I've often wondered who he was. Might it have been the same man?"

"Very possibly. I wrote to him at Emily's urging and asked him to call and discover if you were in good health. We were all concerned when you did not reply to Emily's and Viola's letters. He wrote back that he'd tried to call but had been turned away."

Claire nodded. "Sadly accurate. And how are you acquainted with this man?"

"He was a guest at Sea View. Our first, actually—he and his stepdaughter."

"He is married?"

"Widowed."

"Ah. He must think a great deal of you to go to so much trouble."

Sarah glanced down, but not before Claire saw the blush move up from her neck to mottle her cheeks.

Claire said knowingly, "And you clearly think a great deal of him."

"I . . . esteem him and certainly appreciate his acts of service on our behalf."

Claire continued to watch her with interest. Gently, she asked, "Did he pursue a relationship with you?"

"I suppose he did, or might have. I discouraged him."

"Why? Were you unsure of his character? Or still grieving Peter?"

"Neither of those. I am needed here. For Mamma. For the guest house. And you've just come. Are you eager to be rid of me already?"

"Of course not. And to hear Emily describe it, you are due the lion's share of credit—and did the lion's share of work—to get the guest house up and running after all our losses. But Mamma is not an invalid any longer. And Sea View seems to be doing rather well. Surely, now . . . ?"

"I have thought about it. Of course I have. But to grow attached to a man like that, with property so far from here. I would lose you all forever."

"Not lose us, surely."

"Then rarely get to see any of you. You are more familiar with the journey than I am. Is it one you would want to undertake often?"

Claire sighed. "Not willingly, no. Then again, I had to pinch and scrape, and worried at every stop if I would have enough for the next inn, the next fare. I imagine traveling in a private chaise would be a far different experience."

Claire's face heated as she realized what she'd said. She *had* made the journey in a private chaise once. With Lord Bertram. They had not made it all the way to Scotland, but still . . .

As if reading her thoughts, Sarah tentatively asked, "Was

it as we heard? Did Lord Bertram truly abandon you on the way?"

Dread burned Claire's stomach like acid, just as it had that night. She nodded, unable to meet her sister's eyes. "Even before we reached Gretna Green. He bought himself a bottle of brandy that night and drank it to pass the time. Perhaps he was having second thoughts already. I certainly was. I remember him touching my cheek and saying in a slurred voice, 'Fifteen thousand pounds and the face of an angel. . . .'

"When I asked him what he meant, he said, 'Your dowry will come in handy, I don't deny. Debts to settle. White's. Boodle's. The horses . . .'"

"I asked if he was under the misapprehension that I had a dowry of fifteen thousand pounds. He said yes, Charles Parker had told him so.

"I told him he'd misunderstood. Or Charles had. That our father had settled that amount on all five of us, to be divided equally.

"Perhaps I should not have told him about the dowry. At least not until after we had married. I tried to convince him we had come too far, that Papa would help us.

"He seemed somewhat appeased, or so I thought. We spent the night at an inn outside Carlisle. I still believed we'd marry the next day. But in the morning, he was gone."

"Oh, Claire, I'm so sorry. That's terrible."

Claire nodded her agreement. "Thankfully I had enough money to travel on to Edinburgh. I knew I could not go home, that I had forfeited my place there by my own reckless mistakes."

"And his. He must own the greatest part of the blame."

Claire shrugged. "I knew better."

"How strange it must be for you, with that very man staying here now."

"It is strange. He is being polite and discreet, which I appreciate. Yet I feel so guilty."

"About . . . what happened between you before?"

"Well, of course, but . . ." Claire paused to consider, struck with the realization that she felt nearly as guilty about keeping the truth from Mr. Hammond.

"I hope it was not a secret," Sarah began. "Viola stopped by after seeing you yesterday and told Emily and me in confidence that he wants to marry you. We haven't told Mamma or Georgie, who cannot keep a secret, sorry to say."

"I don't mind you knowing. Honestly, I'm not sure he *wants* to marry me, although he says he does. He insists a lack of funds was the only reason he cried off before."

Claire toyed with the gold chain. "I don't know why I'm hesitating. Many men marry for money and many women to repair a reputation."

"Is there another reason you hesitate?"

When Claire did not immediately answer, Sarah asked, "Is it Mr. Hammond?"

Claire looked down and lowered her voice. "Between you and me, I have come to admire him. In other circumstances . . . But I have ruined things by coming here under false pretenses. And by keeping my past mistakes from him. He's bound to learn the truth at some point, and then he'll never look at me as he does now."

"Can you not tell him? Before he hears it from someone else?"

"Perhaps I shall," Claire replied. "Once I find the courage." Silently, she added, *Though if I marry Lord Bertram, I shall not have to.*

After Sarah left, Claire stared at herself in the looking glass. The ruby and gold cross looked lovely at her neck, yet the blue eyes that gazed back at her appeared weary. Drained. What had become of the person she used to be? She stared at the pale woman of eight and twenty years and whispered, "Who are you?"

She had once known who she was and liked who she was: the cherished eldest daughter of Mr. and Mrs. Summers. The older sister to Sarah, Emily, Viola, and Georgiana, who had all looked up to her. Loved, trusted, and valued her. Emily had even wanted to emulate her.

She had been held in high esteem by elderly neighbors and young people alike. Responsible, honest, dutiful. And destined to marry well, or so they'd thought. Able to hold her head high in church, instead of hiding in the back.

Then, after one impetuous mistake, all of that had vanished. No longer valued and cherished, at least not by her parents. No longer worthy of being admired, trusted, or emulated by her sisters. If she accepted Lord Bertram, might she regain some of what she had lost?

One of her own thoughts echoed back to her, *Able to hold her head high in church*. Was that important? Was that even true? She'd once considered herself a good person, acceptable to God and worthy of His love. But had she been, even then? As she stroked the cross pendant, words Aunt Mercer had spoken resounded through her mind once more. *"The cross alone renders sinners acceptable to God."*

If true, Claire thought, then perhaps no one should enter church with head held high. For no one was good enough on their own. And certainly not her.

Then again, as a believer, she was a child of God—a merciful and loving God, thankfully, as Mrs. Denby had said. And in that sense, Claire supposed she could still hold her head high in church or anywhere. Not because she was good or worthy, but because her heavenly Father was.

And a good and holy God did not want her to prevaricate.

She knew then that it was more important to be honest than to try to preserve the appearance of respectability. It was time to stop hiding, as Mrs. Denby had advised. And it was time to apologize to Mr. Hammond. To confess all and let the consequences come . . . even if that meant losing any hope of a future with him.

On Sunday night, Claire again found Mr. Hammond on the rooftop with his telescope. This time she carried her candle lamp out onto the roof-walk, because she needed to see his face.

At her approach, he straightened and turned.

"Mr. Hammond, I . . . I must tell you something."

He stiffened as if preparing for a blow. "Do I want to know?"

"Unlikely, but you will hear sooner or later, and I would rather you heard it from me."

"Has this something to do with Lord Bertram?"

"I'm afraid so."

"Go on."

"First of all, I am sorry. You advertised for a respectable female, and I misled you by replying. I once was respectable. Then, I met him. He said he wished to marry me, but like my own father, his father wanted him to marry someone else. He assured me that once the fact of our union could not be changed, then his father would accept it. I don't know what came over me. I had always been responsible, obedient, and dutiful to my parents. I suppose I was flattered. Swept off my feet. I was six and twenty at the time and starting to fear I'd end up on the shelf. And suddenly here was my chance. Perhaps my last chance. This aristocrat—handsome, confident, wealthy, or so I thought—assured me he loved me. And fool that I was, I believed him. I left my family and put myself under his power. . . ."

Mr. Hammond's mouth slackened. "You eloped with him?"

Claire nodded. "I hastily packed a valise, and we set out together in his coach, bound for Gretna Green." She swallowed. "We never made it that far."

He looked away. "So that's what she meant."

"Who?" Claire's throat tightened, that familiar sense of betrayal slicing through her yet again. Had Sonali said something, told him what she'd overheard?

"That Mrs. Harding creature," he replied. "She passed me on her way out and said something about how broad-minded I must be to take on a woman of your background."

"Oh." Relief that it had not been Sonali warred with the shame balling in her stomach. "If it helps, I don't think it is widely known. Mrs. Harding's brother is a friend of Lord Bertram's, and he confided in him."

Mr. Hammond considered, then asked, "You said earlier that he changed his mind when he learned you were not the heiress he thought you were. Was that true?"

"Yes. He'd heard my dowry was fifteen thousand pounds, but that was the amount settled on all five of us girls together."

Mr. Hammond scrubbed a hand over his face. "Tell me the worst, and let's have done. I gather you are not a maiden?"

Again shame washed over her. She was tempted to evade his question. Yet if there was any hope of a future for them . . . No. There would not be. Not after she told him the truth, which he deserved. Oh, how she wished things were different, that she had waited.

"I wish I could tell you it was not true, that I am still an innocent. But I am not."

He grimaced. "Was it worse than that? Had you a child by that man?"

"No. I don't share Mary's predicament. There but for the grace of God go I. Lord Bertram and I shared a bed on the way to Gretna Green. Please remember, I thought he was about to be my husband. Not that that is an excuse, yet I never guessed he would abandon me as he did. He . . . he was drunk that night, truth be told, and it was not . . ." She winced against the unpleasant memory. "At all events, when I awoke the next morning, he was gone."

He flinched. "What a nightmare. I am sorry. For you, and for your poor family."

"Yes. My father had an apoplexy soon after hearing the news and died a few months later."

"You blame yourself?"

Claire nodded. "And my family blames me too. At least my mother. Poor Mamma."

"So that is the reason for the rift between you."

"Yes. Before he died, my father declared I was dead to him and made my mother promise not to harbor me, help me, or even speak my name."

"That seems harsh. As a father, I can understand his anger and disappointment, but I don't think anything would shake my love for Mira. Though I would find it hard not to throttle the man."

"He probably would have, had the first apoplexy not laid him low before he could."

"And now this Bertram fellow has repented and wants to make things right?"

"Nothing so noble. In fact, it's rather humiliating. My great-aunt—the woman I lived with in Scotland after he abandoned me—has offered him a sizable inheritance, on the condition he marries me."

He stared. "You must be joking."

"I wish I were."

Again he grimaced, whether in disdain or empathy, she did not know.

"I am terribly sorry," she said. "I should not have come to Broadbridge's. I hoped to be reconciled with my sisters in time. Maybe even my mother. I never meant to hurt you or embroil you in scandal. Please believe me."

"You must have known it would affect me. Affect us all. Poor Mira has become very fond of you."

"And I her."

He groaned. "What a dreadful state of affairs."

"If you want me to leave, to break all ties with me, I will understand."

He seemed to consider her words, then said, "Perhaps I should release you. For both our sakes." He looked at her, expression veiled. Unreadable. "What do you want?"

You, she thought, but did not say it. She raised a weak hand and chuckled bleakly. "I want the impossible, I suppose. I want to be forgiven, to no longer be a source of shame to my family. For you to not regret taking me in." Silently she added, *I want to be loved. Forever. By you.*

"Will you marry him?" he asked, looking over the parapet to the lights of Sidmouth below.

"I don't know."

"If you do, that renders the question of whether I want you to stay a moot point."

"And if I don't?"

"I shall keep my own counsel on that for now. Nor shall I try to sway you. I am not a man who makes impulsive decisions."

"I understand. Let me know what you decide."

He nodded. "I trust you will do the same."

Claire offered to oil Mira's hair again in Sonali's stead. She longed for the sweet comfort of the maternal task and imagined it might be her last chance to perform it.

Sonali and Mira were both quick to accept her offer, although Sonali's gaze rested on Claire in some concern before she departed to her own room.

As before, Mira sat on the floor, resting her back against Claire's shins, while Claire rubbed oil into her scalp and hair. The process seemed to soothe them both. Would Claire ever be a mother and minister to her own child in similar ways: bathing, brushing, embracing? Or was this as close as she would ever come?

The thought of motherhood brought dear Mamma to mind. Claire missed her mother's affectionate touch. Would she ever feel it again? Or enjoy the sweet mother-daughter bond they had once shared?

Tears filled her eyes at the thought.

She was startled from her reverie by a soft knock and the appearance of two women at the nursery door. Mary and . . .

"Mamma . . . ?" Claire breathed.

"Here she is, madam," Mary said.

"Thank you."

Mary bobbed a curtsy and disappeared.

Her mother looked back at her. "May I come in?"

"Of course. I was just thinking about you."

"You're crying. Did I cause that?"

"Only indirectly." Claire swiped at her eyes with the back of an oiled hand. "Sorry."

"Don't be. I've been doing a lot of that myself lately."

Mira tilted her head to look up at the newcomer. "Who is she?"

"This is my mamma. We saw her once before, on the street? Mamma, as you may recall, this is Mira Hammond."

"Good evening, Mira. And what are you two doing?"

"Miss Claire is oiling my hair, as my *amma* used to do."

"Your mother did that for you?"

The girl nodded.

"It is a tradition," Claire explained. "Grandmothers, mothers, daughters. Sometimes all three at once."

"What sort of oil are you using?"

"A mixture, but apparently different types are used, olive, castor, apricot . . . We warm it, then massage it into the scalp and hair."

"Is this part of your duties here?"

"No. I offered. I find it pleasant."

"Seeing you like this reminds me of all those years ago at Finderlay, when you were such a little mother, helping with your younger sisters, brushing their hair and reading them stories and teaching them to sew. You did a good job with Sarah and Viola. I am afraid I failed with Georgiana in your absence."

"And Emily?"

"She would rather write."

"I remember those days too. I had no grand aspirations like Emily. I simply wanted to be a wife and mother. Like you."

When Mamma was quiet, Claire said, "We are nearly finished, if you want to talk privately."

"I did want to ask about . . . a certain male guest recently come to stay. I passed him on the stairs."

Claire plaited Mira's hair and rose, helping the girl to her feet as she did so. "Why do you not go to Sonali's room and let her know we're through, hm? I will finish tidying up in here."

When the girl had gone next door, Claire cleaned and dried her hands.

In a low voice, Mamma said, "How difficult it must be to have him here."

"Yes."

"Has he . . . said anything?"

Claire took a deep breath and forced herself to meet her mother's gaze, to watch her expression. To tell her all. She said, "He has asked me to marry him. Properly, this time."

Mamma slowly nodded. "And have you given him an answer?"

"No, but I must soon. He is reaching an end to his patience, I can tell. The lawyers are awaiting my decision."

"Lawyers?"

Claire told her mother about Aunt Mercer's offer to make Lord Bertram her heir on the condition he marry her.

"Scheming woman!" Mamma fumed, then expelled a deep breath. "Although, to be honest, I might once have tried something similar, had I the funds. For your benefit, of course, not his."

"So you . . . want me to marry him?" Claire asked uneasily, bracing herself for an answer. If she did not, would she lose any ground she'd gained with her mother since arriving in Sidmouth?

Mamma hesitated, then said, "You must marry or not as your conscience dictates, and as you think God would have you do."

"I am not certain what God wants in this instance."

Again Mamma nodded. "Discerning His will is difficult, and I have not mastered it myself." She drew herself up. "But now, let me tell you why I called. I had a purpose in coming here, before I was distracted. I've come to invite you to visit me at Sea View. Perhaps tomorrow afternoon?"

Is this really happening? Claire looked at her, heart squeezing and eyes filling anew. "Yes, happily. Thank you, Mamma."

32

Thou anointest my head with oil; my cup runneth over.
—Psalm 23:5

The following day, Sonali asked Claire to keep an eye on Mira while she bathed. Claire agreed, and the two sat drawing at the morning room table together.

Mr. Jackson came in to settle his account, and Claire rose to assist him. Once the salesman had gone, only Mr. Filonov, Monsieur Lemaire, Lord Bertram, and his valet would still be with them.

After handing over payment, he said, "I'm off to Seaton next, but I'll be back in a month or so."

"You will be very welcome, sir. Safe journey and good sales."

"Thank you, miss."

When he had taken his leave, Claire looked back at the table, and Mira was nowhere to be seen. Her stomach sank. *Not again . . .*

She went looking for the girl, only to find her curled up, asleep, on two cushioned chairs in the adjacent dining room, the doors between them open. Mira had not slept well the night before, and she looked so peaceful, Claire didn't have the heart to wake her. Instead she sat on the next chair and laid her shawl over her. Instinctively, Mira reached out in her slumber and latched onto her skirt.

The front door knocker sounded, but before Claire could extricate herself, Mary answered it, her voice echoing in the entry hall. "Good day, Mr. Sagar."

"Greetings, Mary. I'd like to see Mr. Hammond, if he is available."

"You're in luck, then, for here he comes."

Descending the stairs, Mr. Hammond called out, "Armaan, good to see you. Come in."

"Thank you, and thank you, Mary."

Mary's heels tapped away down the corridor, while Claire remained where she was.

In the adjoining morning room, Armaan began rather formally, "I hope you don't think it presumptuous of me, but I've come to ask your permission. As Miss Patel has no father living nor other male relative, and as she lives under your roof, I thought I should ask for your blessing, or at least your permission, before I propose."

A weighty silence followed, a few seconds longer than was polite.

"Propose . . . marriage?"

Armaan chuckled a bit awkwardly. "Yes, of course."

"Forgive me, you have taken me by surprise."

"So I see."

"You have not known one another that long."

"And how long did you know Vanita before you married?"

"Even less time," Mr. Hammond admitted.

"Have you some reservation about my suitability? As you know, I served the East India Company and the office of governor. Major Hutton would no doubt vouch for my character. I may not be presently employed but I am not without means.

Along with the bequest from Mr. Aston, my own father left an inheritance as well. We would not be poor."

Mr. Hammond murmured, "Good, good . . ."

"I realize it will be a loss to you. You and Mira have come to rely on her, I know. And I cannot promise we would stay in Sidmouth. For a time we might live at Westmount. But for a couple like us, perhaps London would be better."

"I don't know. We'd hate to see you go. Has Sonali given you any indication that your offer will be looked upon favorably?"

"At times, she seems to favor me. Other times she is more aloof. Therefore I own to some nerves. I esteem her, and we have a good deal in common. Whether that is enough, we shall have to see."

"Well, far be it from me to interfere. If you believe you are the man to make her happy, then you have my support."

"She is not a woman well accustomed to happiness, though I would like to change that."

"A worthy aim. All the best to you."

"Don't congratulate me yet. With Sonali, one never knows."

"True. But I hope she does accept you."

"Thank you, sir. Er . . . William." Armaan stepped from the morning room into the hall. Mira whimpered in her sleep as he passed, and he poked his head through the dining room doorway. Seeing Claire, he paused, then looked back toward the adjoining room.

He stepped inside. "You heard?"

"I did. Forgive me. It was not my intention to eavesdrop. Mira fell asleep, and I had not the heart to wake her. Sonali is most fortunate to have gained your regard."

"I am honored you would think so."

Claire noticed Mr. Hammond did not join them. Was he avoiding her?

Armaan looked down at Mira and offered, "If you want to lay her in bed, I would be happy to carry her up for you."

"Thank you. I would appreciate that. She had a restless night and could use a good nap."

He deftly slid his long fingers beneath Mira's sleeping form and lifted her into his arms. The little girl's eyes cracked open, and she murmured a contented "*Mamu*" before closing them once more.

Claire followed behind as he climbed one pair of stairs and then the next. As they passed the bath-room, Claire noticed the door was open, so Sonali must have finished her bath. When they reached the attic, Claire heard Sonali softly humming in her room, probably brushing her long hair.

Continuing on to the nursery, Armaan laid Mira gently down on her bed. After watching to make sure she remained asleep, he straightened.

He looked at Claire, hesitated, then said softly, "Perhaps you think it strange that I should pursue Sonali when she has been rather rude to me at times. Even bitter."

Claire wasn't sure how to reply, and at her silence he continued, "But you see, I was once bitter too. Bitter about the supposed friends who resented me serving with the British and came to kill me. They beat me severely before Major Hutton interfered." He glanced down at his wrists, and she glimpsed pale scars.

Noticing her gaze, he said, "Mine are nothing to his."

He pulled at his cuffs and went on. "For a time, I was consumed with hatred. I rehearsed every injustice, every punch and kick and evil word spat at me. Then I realized I was not hurting them—they were not chastised by my bitterness. I was the only one who suffered.

"Eventually, I learned to stop dwelling on the past and to be thankful for the good things in my present life. God has replaced those false friends with a real friend in the major. His father and brother have all but adopted me as one of their family, and now Mr. Hammond has as well. I have a niece and friends, a place to call home for as long as I choose, sufficient funds to secure a place of my own if and when I decide to, and perhaps even someone to share my life with, should she agree.

"In Sonali, I see someone who has also suffered loss, disappointment, and prejudice. I see the hard shield she holds high to protect herself from a hostile world. I wonder how she might change, perhaps even thrive, if someone were to love her, to vow to protect her and stand by her, no matter what."

Claire said softly, "A woman could grow accustomed to that."

He drew a deep breath. "I hope so."

"Well then. What's stopping you?" Claire urged. "She is right next door."

Half an hour later, Sonali came to find her, hair loose and damp after her bath, eyes and smile gleaming.

"I am engaged, Miss Summers. To Armaan Sagar!"

"Oh, Sonali. What excellent news. I am so happy for you. So happy for you both."

"Are you? Then, I thank you. I am sorry I have been rather . . . peevish. I thought he liked you."

"As a friend, yes. And I like him as well. I hope you will be very happy together."

"I hope so too. I have not been as kind to him as I should be. Yet I shall endeavor to deserve him."

"I am glad." Claire pressed the woman's hands, and, seeing the joy glimmering in her dark eyes, felt her remaining reservations fall away. "God bless you both."

"Oh, *didi*." Sonali beamed. "He already has!"

Claire went back downstairs and found Mr. Hammond still in the morning room, seated at the desk, head in his hands.

Concern flared. "Are you all right?"

He looked up. "You tell me."

"You have heard the news?"

His features tensed and his eyes flattened. "What news?"

"About Sonali and Armaan? She has accepted him. They are engaged."

"And you . . . ?"

"Me? I am happy for them."

"I meant, are you to be congratulated as well?"

She swallowed. "I have not given Lord Bertram an answer but have promised to do so by tomorrow."

"Why wait?"

"I . . ." Again Mamma's face appeared in her mind. She had told Claire to follow her own conscience, but if saying yes would help her reconcile with her mother . . . ? She glanced at the mantel clock. "At present, I am expected at Sea View. My mother has invited me."

His expression softened. "That is excellent news. Unless . . . Is her change of heart due to Lord Bertram's proposal?"

"No, I don't think so. But I—"

"*Mon cher* William." Monsieur Lemaire swept into the morning room, valise in hand. "I come to say, *À bientôt*! I take my leave now." Seeing Claire, he bowed. "*Merci, mademoiselle. Pour tout.*"

"*De rien*," Claire murmured in reply, and left the men to say their farewells.

Claire donned bonnet and gloves, her hands trembling as she did so. Then she walked to Sea View.

Had her mother truly invited her in? Claire hoped she had not misunderstood.

Reaching the house, Claire knocked, not presuming to enter unannounced, and a small man answered the door.

"Ah. You must be the Miss Claire I've heard so much about." He bowed. "Robert Gwilt at your service." He ushered her inside and took her bonnet and gloves.

From across the hall, a voice called, "Claire."

Mamma, using her given name. It sent a shaft of longing and hope through her.

"Yes?" she replied rather breathlessly.

"Come and join me in my room, if you would."

"Of course."

"Shall I bring tea, madam?" Mr. Gwilt asked.

"Maybe later."

Claire had expected her sisters to be there too. But only Mamma greeted her. Was this not to be the reunion Claire had longed for, after all?

Claire followed her mother into her bedchamber.

"Sit down here, if you would," she directed. "I would like to try the mother-daughter tradition I witnessed at Broadbridge's."

"Oh. Very well." Palms damp, Claire sat awkwardly on the floor, her mother in the chair behind her.

"I have taken the liberty of warming some olive oil. I trust it will serve the purpose. After all, I imagine that is what they used in ancient times, when anointing a beloved brother or sister—or in this case, daughter—for forgiveness or restoration."

When the first drop of warm oil touched Claire's scalp, tears filled her eyes and rained down her face. She was powerless to stop them, did not wish to stop them. How cleansing. How healing.

Her dear mother anointed her head with oil and began massaging it into her hair like a blessing, like an embrace, like a benediction.

Thank you, Lord, Claire silently prayed. *I truly, deeply, thank you.*

An hour later, hair freshly washed and still damp, Claire readied to depart. Only then did Mamma ask, "Have you given that man an answer yet?"

Claire shook her head. "To be honest, Mamma, I don't want to marry him simply so he can pay off his debts. But if you wish me to, if it's what I need to do to—"

"No. Do not marry him to please me or anyone else."

"Truly?"

"Yes, truly." Mamma put her arms around Claire and drew her close. "God has been working on my heart. Sarah too, truth be told."

Claire drank in the affection, relishing her mother's embrace.

Then Mamma sniffed and released her, adding with a grin, "Besides, Georgie has declared she does not want him for a brother-in-law."

A relieved chuckle bubbled out of Claire. "Well, that settles it, then."

The next morning as Claire helped Mary carry up the breakfast things, the maid leaned close and whispered, "Have ye told Mr. Hammond yet?"

"I have."

"And must I leave?"

"He has not yet decided, as far as I know. Either way, I will help you all I can."

"Thank ye, miss."

They found the morning room strangely empty.

"Have you seen him today?" Claire asked.

"Earlier, aye. He left the house dressed for one of his walks."

Sonali and Mira soon arrived and joined her at the table. Claire had little appetite but sipped tea and nibbled toast to bide her time.

After breakfast, Claire once again met Lord Bertram in the parlour, closing the door behind herself before finding her voice.

"I am afraid I cannot marry you."

He tucked his chin. "Of course you can."

"Theoretically I could, but I don't want to. The truth is, I have suffered enough misery at your hands. I do not love you, and I know you don't love me. I am sorry you are in debt, but that is not of my doing. I have no doubt, were you to inherit, you would spend all of my great-aunt's money in short order and quickly regret marrying me. And I would regret it even sooner."

He stared at her, angry furrows raking his brow.

She pressed on, "I know I have made mistakes in the past, yet I deserve better than a loveless marriage."

"You are rejecting me?" he asked in disbelief.

"I am."

"Because of that Hammond fellow, am I right? Perhaps I shall have to tell him of our past . . . affiliation."

"Do what you must. He already knows."

That seemed to take the wind from his sails. He sighed and swore under his breath.

More gently, she said, "I take no pleasure in disappointing you. But there are other women who would suit your purposes far better. Miss Craven, for one. Now, if you will excuse me, there is somewhere I need to go."

As soon as she was able—after she had given Mrs. Ballard instructions and looked over the mending Mary had begun and praised her progress—Claire put on her blue spencer, a bonnet, and gloves and left the house by the outside stairs.

Lord Bertram's valet came out the front door at about the same time and paused to speak to her. "We'll be leaving today, miss. I'm on my way to the livery to have the coach-and-four readied."

She nodded. "Thank you for letting me know."

Claire wondered if Lord Bertram would leave payment for his stay. She did not know but was not about to ask the indebted man for money. She had more important things on her mind.

33

I love thee to the depth and breadth and height
My soul can reach.
—Elizabeth Barrett Browning,
"How Do I Love Thee?"

Leaving Broadbridge's, Claire walked up the street feeling free, whole, and full of life and hope.

She crossed the River Sid at the bridge and began the steep walk up Salcombe Hill. She was not certain if William had come this way or gone west to climb Peak Hill, but she could not sit still awaiting his return.

When she reached the first viewpoint, she paused, breathing hard and gazing into the distance, toward the deep blue horizon and the grey waves below.

She heard something and turned. There came William, descending from the summit at a brisk pace, leg muscles pressing against close-fitting breeches, arms pumping, and handsome features tense with concern or perhaps even anger. When he saw her, no welcoming smile softened his face.

"I hoped I might find you here," she said.

His long strides narrowed the divide between them, but a few yards from her, he stopped.

"I was on my way back," he said. "To tell you not to marry the man. I was a fool to tarry. The past does not matter. I may not have been a perfect husband to Vanita, but I will be a far better husband to you than that man could ever be. Tell me I am not too late. Have you already given Bertram an answer?"

"I have."

His body stilled, only his Adam's apple rose and fell.

"I said no," she hurried to clarify. "I don't love him, and marrying him would not redeem our past mistakes. He was preparing to depart as I left the house."

William released a long breath and walked closer. "What a blind fool he was to have a gem like you in his grasp and trample it beneath his feet."

He took her hand, and only then did she notice his other hand was empty. "Where is your stick?"

"Left it. Knew I might be tempted to thrash Bertram with it. In fact, if I hurry, I might yet do so."

Claire shook her head. "He is not worth the effort. Let him go. If you and Mamma can forgive me, then maybe I can believe God has forgiven me. Perhaps even forgive myself."

"My dear Claire, you are already forgiven. Don't you know I am in love with you?"

"Even now you've learned who I really am?"

He took her other hand as well. "Do you mean now that I know you are a kind, gentle, warmhearted woman who loves my daughter and treats me with far more consideration than I deserve?"

"William . . ."

Voice rumbling low, he said, "How you undo me when you call me by my given name. . . ."

"I have been afraid to hope. I was not sure you could ever care for another woman as you did Vanita."

"If you had asked me a few months ago, I might have agreed. I never thought I would love anyone, body and soul, as I do you. But I do. I love you, my dear, beautiful Claire."

"And I love you."

He loosed one hand to trace a finger along her cheek. "How I long to kiss you. . . ."

"Then please do."

He framed her face with his hand and lowered his head, his face nearing hers. Her eyes fluttered closed as his lips touched hers in a warm, sweet kiss.

Then he wrapped his arms around her and kissed her again more firmly.

Oh, heavenly . . . She melted against him.

She had been kissed before. Lord Bertram's drunken kisses. This was something else entirely. Something wonderful.

William released her and sank to his knees before her, right there on the damp turf of Salcombe Hill.

He pressed his hands to her waist and looked up at her. "Will you marry me, Claire Summers? Be my better half forever? For I shall be satisfied with nothing less than endless nights and months and years with you."

Her spirits soared. "Are you in earnest?"

"I would not stain the knees of my best trousers for just anyone." His lips tipped into a teasing smile.

Happiness bubbled through her. "Then, yes, I will marry you, William. With all my heart!"

She bent down and kissed that beloved, crooked smile right off his face.

As they gathered for luncheon that day, William told Mira the news.

"Well, my dear pumpkin seed. I have asked Miss Claire to marry me, and she has agreed. What do you say to that?"

The girl gasped. "Will she be my new mamma?"

"Would you like that?" he asked.

Claire hurried to say, "Your second mamma." She knelt and touched a gentle finger to the girl's chest. "You will always have your first mamma—your *amma*—in your heart and in your memories."

"And my painting."

"That's right."

Mira threw her arms around Claire's neck. Near her ear she whispered, "I prayed it would be you. I like Sonali, but I love you."

"And I love you too." Claire wrapped her arms around the little girl and held her close. Tears in her eyes, she looked up at William and saw his eyes were wet too.

A moment later the spell was broken when Mira pulled away and declared, "That means you can always oil my hair!"

William reached down and helped Claire to her feet.

"Now, *kaddu*, my marrying Miss Summers does not make her your personal attendant. You will have to share her attentions, affections, and time with me."

"Silly Papa. No one oils your hair."

"No, but perhaps I shall perform that service for my new wife, or demonstrate my affection in other ways. . . ."

Claire's neck heated at the thought.

He placed a gentle hand on the little girl's head. "So you won't have your new mamma all to yourself. Understand?"

Claire laughed. "Gracious. There's nothing to worry about in that regard. I have more than enough time and affection for you both."

William pressed Claire's hand and grinned at his daughter. "And so do I."

Sonali came in and they shared the news all over again.

She offered them sincere congratulations, saying, "I am most happy for you both." With a smile she added, "Although not in the least surprised."

They all gathered in Sea View's parlour: Mamma, Sarah, Emily, Viola, Georgiana, and Claire. Mr. Gwilt served them tea, wearing a toothy grin all the while. Sarah grinned as well as she looked around at these beloved women.

Her sister had been returned to them, completing their circle. Mamma had even hung Claire's sampler on the wall of her room along with Sarah's and Viola's.

For a moment Sarah closed her eyes in gratitude. *Thank you, God.*

As the women sipped tea, they shared memories of the past, teased one another fondly, laughed at each other's jokes, and made plans for the future. For a picnic later that summer. A special dinner for Georgie's seventeenth birthday. And to celebrate Christmas together.

Emily turned to Claire and said, "And in the meantime, you will start sitting with us in church, I hope?"

Claire smiled. "I would like that very much."

Mamma rose. "Excuse me."

A few moments later, she returned with the plate Sarah had broken last year. The porcelain plate rimmed in gold had been painted with a vivid image of three girls in Chinese robes, clustered close as a fourth read to them. Papa had given it to their mother long ago.

Claire stared at it, perplexed. "I remember this plate. What happened to it?"

"I dropped it," Sarah admitted. She did not mention she'd dropped it when her twin sisters burst into the room, arguing over an old bonnet of Claire's. Some things were best forgotten. "I doubted the shattered pieces could ever be put back together, but Mamma had it repaired by a skilled craftsman."

The broken pieces had been fused with thin lines of gold. It was forever altered, yet back in one piece.

"I have been thinking about this plate," Mamma said, running a gentle finger over the cracks. "Once broken, now restored, and still beautiful. Like us."

Sarah took one of Mamma's hands and one of Claire's. Around the circle, the others grasped hands as well. Not a dry eye remained.

Over a lump in her throat, Sarah said, "Beautiful indeed."

Once the engagement was announced, Mamma decided Claire should move into Sea View until after the wedding. For appearance's sake, for propriety, and to help the new lovers avoid temptation.

Considering the passionate kisses she and William had already shared, Claire could not fault her mother's logic.

"You can still go there during the day to help around the place and then come here at night. All right?"

"Very well, Mamma," Claire agreed. It was time to honor her mother after disappointing her before.

William agreed too, although with less enthusiasm. "If I were your parent, I would not trust me either, but I shall miss you."

She gave a little laugh and touched his cheek. "I shall be here every day. Well, almost every day. Mamma wants to take me shopping for wedding clothes."

"As she should. And though you will miss me terribly . . ."

"I shall."

". . . I know you will enjoy living with your family again after all this time. It shall be a balm to your bruised heart."

"You are right." She reached up and kissed him. He wrapped both arms around her and kissed her back, a kiss that quickly deepened.

He lifted his head and gently put her away from him. "And this is why your mother is right and you should spend your nights at Sea View. Not that having you here during the days won't be temptation enough." With one of his wry grins, he lifted her hand and kissed it.

Before leaving Broadbridge's, Claire talked to Mary, reassuring her that despite moving to Sea View, Claire was not abandoning her and would still see her often.

That evening, when Claire arrived at Sea View with her case and valise, Mr. Gwilt took them from her and hung up her cloak.

Mamma welcomed her with a warm embrace. Sarah, Emily, and Georgiana then embraced her in turns, while her brother-in-law James made do with a bow and friendly word of greeting.

Mamma said, "Now that the Cravens have gone, we have several vacant rooms. You may have your pick."

"Actually, what I'd like best is to share with Sarah, like we used to do as girls. If Sarah would not mind?"

Sarah smiled softly. "I would like nothing better."

Later that night, they cleaned their teeth, changed into nightdresses, and climbed into bed.

"Like old times," Claire said. "Oh, this brings back memories. All those heart-to-heart talks before sleep. Sometimes drifting off midsentence!"

Sarah nodded and rolled to her side, head propped on her hand. "When we opened the guest house, we all had to double up. Except for Georgie, who chose a room in the attic. I shared with Emily until she married. Sometimes I would look over in the half-light of dawn and think she was you. Your profiles are rather alike. How I missed you."

"I missed you too, but I'm thankful for this time together before I marry."

"I am too."

34

Broadbridge's Boarding-house in the
Market place no longer exists.
—Edmund Butcher,
The Beauties of Sidmouth Displayed

A few days later, Viola and her husband hosted a dinner party in honor of Claire's engagement to William, and Armaan's to Sonali.

It was a joyous night for Claire, celebrating with William and Mira, her mother and sisters, and new friends Armaan and Sonali.

There were toasts to family—original families, family lost, and family found. There was laughter and good food, thanks to Mrs. Besley's help in the kitchen.

At one point, Claire found herself standing beside Armaan while the others listened and laughed over some tale of Georgiana's.

He said to her, "This is good, yes? You shall have William, who needs you. And I shall have Sonali, who needs me more than she admits."

He grinned and the two shared a fond look.

Claire said, "William counts you as a brother, you know. And since I am to be his wife, you shall be brother to me as well. I am grateful I shall keep you in my life."

"I also am grateful. And sincerely wish you happy."

"I wish the same for you."

"Thank you, my sister. My *didi*. Who would have guessed when I lost Vanita I would gain so much?"

William came over and wrapped an arm around Claire's waist, heedless of the gathered company. "And what are you two talking about?"

She smiled. "Oh, only how happy we all shall be."

The next morning, when Claire arrived at Broadbridge's for the day, Mr. Filonov and Mr. Hammond were waiting for her in the morning room. The Russian artist was about to leave, and Claire was sad to see the kind, talented man depart.

"A humble gift before I go." Mr. Filonov presented them with a wrapped parcel. "In honor of your betrothal."

From the size and shape of the parcel it was easy to guess the gift was a painting. But when Claire pulled back the paper, what she saw took her breath away.

It was the painting he'd begun during their beach outing. She recognized the shore, the sea, the distant sails. And now in its final form, three figures completed the scene: A man and woman swinging a small child between them.

Claire's eyes filled. "Oh, Mr. Filonov. I love this."

"So do I. Thank you." William clapped the man's shoulder, and Claire noticed his eyes were bright with tears as well.

Later that day, Claire found William in his private study and asked, "Will you take me somewhere, my love?"

"It would be my pleasure. Where shall it be? Paris? St. Petersburg? Vienna?"

Claire shook her head. "Nothing so far as that. May Hill, Gloucestershire. I want to visit my father's grave."

"Ah. I understand. I would like to take Mira to see her mother's grave when she's older, but I fear it is too far. I will gladly take you to visit your father's."

When Claire mentioned the plan to her family, Georgiana begged to go along, eager to see their former home and neighborhood for old times' sake. Mamma, too, asked if she might accompany them.

None of the family had visited May Hill since the move to Sidmouth more than a year and a half before. And Claire had never seen Papa's grave. The visit was long overdue. Claire felt she needed to go there, to say her piece, and hopefully, to find peace.

Mamma confided she felt much the same. "And if you think I'm letting you travel without a chaperone, you are very much mistaken, young lady. Not until you're married. I am determined to make up for my previous neglect!"

Leaving Armaan and Sonali to watch over Mira and the boarding house—with help from the capable Fran—Claire, William, Mamma, and Georgiana left Sidmouth in a hired post chaise.

The journey was too long to undertake in a single day, so they made stops along the way for fresh horses and postilions, refreshment, and sleep.

During dinner at one of the inns, Georgiana could hardly keep her eyes open, so she and Mamma decided to retire early. After they had gone up, Claire and William lingered at the candlelit table. They talked about wedding plans, and Mira, and their shared joy over the engagement of Sonali and Armaan.

"Where would you like to go on our wedding trip?" he asked.

"I don't know. Will we be able to get away again? Leaving the boarding house for a relatively short trip like this is one thing, but we can't expect the others to manage things indefinitely."

"I've had a thought about that. I have not said anything to Armaan, because I wanted to talk it over with you first. What would you say to selling the place to him and Sonali? He told me he'd been thinking about his future even before he met her. He does not want to live with the Huttons forever. He wants to make his own way in the world, have something of his own."

"I know, but I thought you wanted to live there, to raise Mira as Vanita wished?"

"Vanita wanted her daughter to experience the English seaside her father had waxed lyrical about. She said nothing about a hostelry. I have realized I am not really cut out to be a boarding-house proprietor. I bought it as an investment, a source of additional income, but with the work the Foreign Office is now sending my way, I don't think it's necessary. I might even publish an account of my travels as other diplomats before me have done. But if you want to keep the place, if you enjoy managing it, then I won't mention it to Armaan."

Claire considered. "I have found it interesting, meeting people from different places. But the work itself? I don't have my heart set on it."

"And what do you have your heart set on, my love?"

Wings of excitement fluttered in her stomach and a smile tickled the corners of her mouth. "I think you know. My heart is fervently set on becoming your wife and Mira's stepmamma."

"And would you welcome more children, should God bless us with some?"

"With open arms and much thanksgiving."

He squeezed her hand. "And so would I."

A few minutes later, he led her upstairs to the door of the room she was to share with her mother and sister.

"I am going to kiss you good-night now." He stepped nearer, his masculine scent enveloping her.

Claire breathed in deep, wanting to press close.

He gave her one of his wry grins, and then those quirked lips touched hers in a light kiss, leaving her wanting more.

He wrapped an arm around her and drew her against him, raising his head to press kisses to her cheek, her forehead, the tip of her nose.

"And kiss you good morning, good afternoon, and good life to come."

She giggled until his mouth descended on hers once more, kissing her more deeply. She slid a hand to the back of his neck, drawing him closer yet.

The door creaked open, and Mamma appeared in her dressing gown. "That's enough, you two."

"One more minute, Mamma."

"Very well. I shall be watching the clock." There was a smile in her voice, and Claire knew her mother wished to make sure she felt cared for. That this trip, with nights spent in an inn with a man, would not be nights she regretted.

Mamma added, "I trust you will treat my daughter with propriety, Mr. Hammond."

"Of course. I would not have it any other way."

"She is a lady, after all. A respectable female."

"As I am well aware."

"Good."

Mamma closed the door, and Claire fell into more giggles, muffling them against his broad chest. "Though sadly not quite the respectable female you advertised for."

He remained serious, slipped a gentle finger under her chin, and lifted her gaze to his. "You, my dear, far exceeded anything I could have wished for, just as you are."

"Oh my . . ." She leaned on tiptoes and kissed him again.

Instead of pressing his advantage, he pulled her into his arms in a tight embrace. The sweetest, most satisfying embrace of her life. "I love you, Claire," he murmured near her ear.

Claire shut her eyes tight to relish the moment. "And I love you."

The next day they reached the parish church of All Saints. It held only a small graveyard, but her father, being prominent in the parish, had been laid to rest there.

Claire could hardly believe she was really here, walking among the headstones, chest tombs, and Celtic crosses adorning the sleepy, shady graveyard of her childhood church.

Memories played at the edges of her mind. Leaving the church as a family after a service, Sarah holding little Georgiana's hand, Viola and Emily giggling together, Claire taking her father's arm as they walked down the path, him smiling down at her. *"And how is the prettiest girl in the county?"*

A later memory, of finding Sarah there, crying over the loss of her Peter, lamenting his burial at sea that meant no gravestone, no lasting memorial.

And finally, the last time she was here—attending an evensong service during that ill-fated house party. Although there had been nothing godly in the way Lord Bertram had looked at her . . .

That memory she quickly cast from her mind.

Near the gate, Georgiana talked to a former neighbor girl and petted a stray cat, while Claire walked on, reading epitaphs, until she found it.

Here Lies
Harold Summers
Beloved Husband and Father
1763–1818
May he rest in peace.

Pain pierced her. Silently, she spoke to him. *Oh, Papa. I am so sorry. . . . I never meant to break your heart. I thought only of my heart. I thought I was in love. I was wrong . . . then. Please forgive me. I suppose it's too late for that now. Oh, God, will you forgive me, if he cannot?*

A gentle breeze rose, making the summer leaves dance. On its breath, Claire imagined she heard a soft voice say, "*You are forgiven, my daughter.*"

And the voice sounded a lot like her own father's.

Tears rushed to her eyes even as her heart lightened with relief and gratitude.

William and Mamma gathered around her. He took one of her hands, Mamma the other.

Mamma whispered, "Harold, my dear. I am sorry, but I cannot shun our daughter any longer. I choose to believe you would not want me to, now that you are with God. I hope you understand. We shall have a lot to talk about when I join you one day."

Claire pressed her hand, and together they took their leave.

A few days after their return to Broadbridge's, Claire joined William in his study. She looked at the maps on the walls while William sat at the desk nearby, going through the post, reading one letter with particular interest.

"I've received the reply from London I hoped for. It took all my powers of persuasion—not to mention a promise to continue my deciphering work—but the foreign secretary dispatched one of his men to East India House and procured news of our surgeon's assistant, Liam MacBain. They confirmed he is on the crew list of the *Clyde* and promise to make every effort to have him sent back on the next available ship."

"That is excellent news!"

"It is still a long journey, with many uncertainties. Even with good winds, it is unlikely he could arrive in England before the babe is born. Still, it is something. And in the meantime, Mary shall have a home with us."

"Oh, William, I am so grateful. As Mary will be when she hears."

She leaned down to kiss his cheek, but he slipped his arms around her and pulled her onto his lap.

She squealed in faux protest and laced her hands behind his neck. "Thank you, my love. You are quite wonderful."

"You can say that again, oh, a dozen times. I do so like hearing it. It gives me pleasure to please you."

He held her close and gave her a warm, lingering kiss.

At the door, someone cleared his throat.

William reluctantly lifted his head. "Ah, Armaan. Wretched timing as always, killjoy."

Claire scrambled from William's lap, face scalding. "Not at all. Just in time, I'd say."

Not the least embarrassed, William asked, "Well, what do you say to our proposal? Are you and Sonali interested in taking on Broadbridge's?"

Armaan nodded. "Most interested. Some guests may not respond kindly to us, we know. This is not London, after all. Even so, we are ready for the challenge. In time, we may also wish to change the name. I must ask, though—are you sure you can bear to part with the place?"

"With the place, yes. With you and Sonali, no. We are not yet certain where we will live long-term but shall likely stay at Sea View until we decide."

"As you wish. However, Sonali and I have talked it over, and you are welcome to stay and help us here until we *all* work out what we are doing."

"A generous offer." William rose and shook his hand. "Just promise we will remain on good terms once you learn how much work you've let yourself in for."

Armaan grinned. "I promise."

35

At the day and time appointed for Solemnization of Matrimony, the Persons to be married shall come into the body of the Church with their Friends and Neighbours.
—The Book of Common Prayer

When Armaan had left them to find Mira and Sonali, William turned back to Claire. "I nearly forgot. There is a letter for you as well. From a law office in Edinburgh."

"Really? I thought I had heard the last from them, unless it is to inform me which charity will ultimately benefit from Aunt Mercer's estate." She opened the letter and read, finding inside unexpectedly familiar handwriting—Agnes Mercer's.

Dear Claire,

I must say, I am surprised and impressed. If you are reading this it is because you have decided not to marry Lord Bertram. I daresay he will not be happy with that decision, but you may well be happier for it! Marrying him might have improved your social standing and reputation—or served to stir up all the old rumors again. Who knows?

As he did not fulfill the terms I set forth, he shall not inherit a farthing from me. I told him, should he fail, that my property would go to a favorite charity. And that it will.

One of my favorite charities is you.

Now, before you get too excited, I am bequeathing an endowment to the church and parish poor fund, so you don't get it all, but I am also leaving you, Claire Summers, my house in Edinburgh, where you served me with such long-suffering patience beyond anything I deserved. You will also receive the funds to maintain it with a small staff. You may live here or opt to sell the place outright. That is your choice.

You may wonder why I did not leave it to you in the first place instead of involving Lord Bertram. After looking into his financial dealings, and realizing how much he needed money, I feared if he learned you were an heiress, he might charm you into marrying him without revealing his true motive. So I decided to give you two options. If you still cared for the man despite his faults, or if marrying him was the only way to reconcile with your mother, then you could do so and benefit from the inheritance as his wife. Or, if you chose to refuse him, you would have a place to live and the means to keep body and soul together should your mother stand by her husband's command not to shelter you.

I believe you made a wise choice.

I know I was not as kind to you as I should have been. I hope you will forgive me and believe me when I say I grew quite fond of you. I sincerely hope you can put the past behind you and live a full, satisfying life of love and service.

Yours sincerely,
Agnes Mercer

"Good heavens . . ." Claire breathed.

William watched her in mounting concern. "What is it?"

"It is astounding—that's what it is."

"Good news or bad?"

"Good, I think. Unless . . . You were planning to marry a penniless woman. How would you feel about marrying an heiress?"

A short while later, Claire went to find Mary and explained what Mr. Hammond had learned about her intended, and the efforts made on her behalf to have him sent back on the next available ship.

"Oh, miss! I'm that thankful!"

"It is a long journey," Claire cautioned her. "And Mr. Hammond says Mr. MacBain is unlikely to reach England before the child is born. However, if all goes well, he could arrive soon after."

"And may I stay on? Till then?"

"Armaan and Sonali will probably manage the boarding house in future, and I cannot speak for them. But Mr. Hammond has promised you shall have a home, either here or wherever we live after we wed. So rest assured. He is a man of his word and incredibly understanding." Claire gratefully counted herself as another recipient of his compassion.

"Aye," Mary agreed. "How blessed we are to be loved by such men."

That night, when they retired to their shared room, Claire asked Sarah, "What would you say to going to Edinburgh with us after the wedding? I seem to have inherited a property there and would like your opinion on whether I should keep it or sell."

"Edinburgh?"

"Aunt Mercer left me her house."

"You're joking."

"I am as surprised as you are."

"Surely you'd prefer to travel alone with Mr. Hammond after you wed?"

"Not at all. I'd love to have more time with you too. And favorite sisters often travel with the bride."

"I don't know. It's a long way. I don't think I could leave Sea View for that long."

"Oh, I'm sure between Mamma, Emily, Georgie, and the extremely efficient Mr. Gwilt, things at Sea View will go on perfectly well for a fortnight or two."

"I suppose it's possible. I could consider it."

Claire nodded. "Good. And remember, if you went with us, we might visit that most generous friend of yours. Mr. Henshall? I could thank him personally for returning my necklace. And you could renew your acquaintance with the gentleman, who, according to Emily, is quite handsome and admires you a great deal."

"Emily romanticizes everything."

"Perhaps. But even I can see that dreamy look in your eyes whenever his name comes up in conversation."

"I could not just . . . call on him. It would be too forward."

"We would not be going simply to call on him. We are going to look at the house. And while we are there, it would only be polite to visit an acquaintance, especially one who performed such kind offices for our family."

"Now you sound like Emily. Very well, I shall think about it."

"You do that, Sarah. And while you're thinking, I will begin making plans."

On an early September morning, Claire rose from bed, stomach fluttering with anticipation as she prepared for her wedding. As in days of old, she and Sarah helped each other dress.

As she laced Claire's long stays, Sarah said, "You're trembling. Are you nervous?"

"A little, yes, although mostly eager."

Sarah gave her shoulders a reassuring squeeze. "It is going to be a lovely day. Relish it."

With her assistance, Claire donned an elegant new gown of ivory satin, which their mother had engaged a modiste to make for her. Mamma had also had a pretty new gown made for Sarah, who would serve as Claire's bridesmaid.

Soon after they finished dressing, Fran arrived to curl and arrange Claire's hair, as well as Sarah's, Mamma's, Emily's, and Georgiana's.

As Claire sat at the dressing table, Fran met her gaze in the mirror and asked, "Do you recall the first time I dressed your hair? For the Huntley ball?"

"I remember."

"I knew then you would be a most beautiful bride one day, and I was right."

They smiled at each other's reflections, then Claire rose to make way for Sarah. When all were ready, they went downstairs together.

Major Hutton sent his carriage to collect Claire, her bridesmaid, and her mother, while the others would walk to the church. It was a fine, temperate day for a stroll, and a perfect day for a wedding. Claire decided to take Sarah's advice and relish every moment.

When the carriage arrived at St. Giles and St. Nicholas a few minutes later, there was Mira waiting for them in a sweet ivory gown similar to Claire's, a wreath of flowers in her dark hair. Her father stood beside her, handsome in a dark blue frock coat, fine waistcoat, and snowy cravat. Armaan and Sonali stood just behind them and seemed to have eyes only for each other.

William stepped to the carriage to help the ladies alight, keeping hold of Claire's hand. His gaze, full of warmth and wonder, was a delight to behold and filled Claire with love and gratitude anew that this man would soon be her husband.

The party from Sea View and Westmount arrived on foot: Emily and James, Viola and Major Hutton, and a much younger man he introduced as his brother, Colin. Georgiana and Mr. Hornbeam brought up the rear.

Georgiana's hair—so recently and carefully curled and pinned by Fran—was already falling loose into her eyes, and her skirt bore grass stains.

"Georgie!" Mamma called. "What on earth happened?"

"Oh, nothing. Chips ran off with Mr. Hornbeam's walking stick, so I chased after him and wrestled it away."

"Of course you did." Sarah slowly shook her head, a tolerant grin on her lips.

"Well," Claire said, "you all look beautiful to me."

"And to me," William echoed, squeezing her hand. "Now, shall we go inside and get married?"

Together they entered the nave, and Claire was surprised by how many people were in attendance. There was Mrs. Ballard, Mary, Fran and her husband, Mrs. Denby, a few women she had met at church, and many others she did not recognize—a testimony to the affection the townspeople held for her family.

Claire walked to the front of the church and stood with William before the altar, Sarah on her other side as attendant, while Armaan stood near William.

The vicar began with the familiar words, "Dearly beloved, we are gathered together here in the sight of God, and in the face of this congregation, to join together this man and this woman in holy matrimony. . . ."

As the service continued, Claire felt a sense of unreality. For more than two years, she had all but given up hope of a happy life and a loving marriage. But now? *Oh God, I thank you*. She pulled herself back to the present and concentrated as the vows were read from the Book of Common Prayer.

When his turn came, William looked at her, green eyes warm with affection, and replied without hesitation, "I will."

The vicar next charged her, and Claire responded with a quiet yet resolute, "I will."

The pledges and prayers were read. The rings blessed and exchanged, William opting to wear one too, as some men did.

Then the vicar led the congregation in another prayer before pronouncing them "man and wife together, in the name of the Father, and of the Son, and of the Holy Ghost. Amen."

Gratitude washed over her. This *was* real. William was her husband and she his wife. God had given her such a great gift. How good He was.

Together they knelt and the vicar prayed a final blessing over them. Claire felt blessed indeed. She was now Mrs. Hammond!

When the prayer ended, William helped her rise, and they followed the vicar and parish clerk into the vestry for the writing of the marriage lines into the parish register, which was witnessed by Sarah and Armaan. As Sarah straightened from signing her name, she met Claire's gaze and the two sisters shared joyful, tremulous smiles.

During the wedding, Sarah had experienced a whole spice box of emotions: cinnamon sweetness seasoned with salty tears and the bitter tang of thyme. Would a man ever vow to comfort her, honor, and keep her? To have and to hold? To love and to cherish?

She was truly happy for Claire. Yet her heart ached. She too longed to be held. Loved. Cherished.

After the ceremony, Sarah hurried home, determined to vanquish the unsavory emotions with her usual tonic of hard work and serving others.

They were hosting the wedding breakfast at Sea View, which Mrs. Besley, Jessie, Lowen, and Mr. Gwilt had been busily preparing and setting out in the dining room. There were hot rolls, fresh butter, ham and eggs, boiled tongue, and braised fish. Cider, tea, and hot drinking chocolate awaited at one end of the table, and the bride cake crowned the center.

Sarah herself had made the cake for the occasion, taking extra time and care since the cake was for a favorite sister on her very special day. She'd followed the bride cake recipe she'd found in *The Experienced English Housekeeper*. It was a rich fruit-and-nut cake with layers of both almond and sugar icing. Sarah thought it looked rather well and hoped it tasted good too.

With William and Claire not being well-known in Sidmouth, the crowd was perhaps smaller than at Viola's and Emily's weddings, but the mood felt just as jovial. Sarah was heartened to see friends and neighbors gather to honor this sister they barely knew for the sake of the Summers and Hutton families they did know.

Dear Mrs. Denby was there, chatting with Mr. Hornbeam and Miss Reed, who would soon become his wife. Major Hutton, Viola, Armaan, and Sonali sat nearby, talking with Mamma. The major's younger brother, Colin, had come to town to congratulate Armaan and Sonali and had remained for the wedding. He sat teasing Georgie and Mira in equal turns.

Guests carried plates of food from the dining room to the parlour or drawing room and spilled out onto the veranda.

Mr. Gwilt fluttered about as usual, refilling cups and clearing plates with a smile. Sarah assisted him, cutting cake and handing it around, watching and listening with quiet satisfaction as guests exclaimed over how delicious it was.

She was also pleased to see Fran, Mrs. Ballard, and the housemaid Mary chatting together like old friends and enjoying the rare pleasure of sitting at their leisure and being waited on for a change. Maybe someday Sarah would learn to enjoy leisure as well. And perhaps, just perhaps, she would accept Claire's invitation to travel with them to Scotland.

Claire looked around Sea View with a sense of wonder. All of these people were here to celebrate with her, some because they were acquainted with her mother or sisters, yes, but still they had come. She no longer felt like a pariah, no longer felt shunned.

While she stood talking and laughing with James and Emily, William came along and grabbed her hand, pulling her into the quiet hall. There, he wrapped his strong arms around her and stole a kiss, away from the prying eyes of the wedding guests. Or so they thought.

From out of nowhere, Mira squeezed herself between them, pleading, "I want a kiss too!"

They separated and leaned down to oblige her with pecks to her cheeks.

Then Georgie appeared and took the girl's hand. "Shall we play a game of spillikins, Mira?"

"Yes, please!" And the two girls retreated happily into the parlour.

When they had gone, William wrapped his arms around Claire once more, grinning down at her. "I like all your sisters, of course, but at the moment, Georgiana is my favorite." He leaned down and kissed Claire again.

Happiness bubbled through her, heart and soul. God had

renewed her life and given her more than she could have asked for or imagined. Not only had she been restored to her family, but now she and William were about to start a family of their own. Claire reached up and held his beloved face in her hands as she kissed him back, filled with thanksgiving and hope for the future.

Author's Note

Thank you for returning with me to the lovely seaside town of Sidmouth on the south coast of England for book three of the ON DEVONSHIRE SHORES series. I hope you enjoyed it. For the rest of the story, please read *A Sea View Christmas*, which releases in September 2025.

A few notes:

If you were surprised by the condemnation Claire encounters in the novel, please remember that a woman's virtue and reputation were of utmost importance at the time and impacted not only her own future but that of her family. The gist of Mrs. Harding's admonition to Mrs. Summers to "throw off your unworthy child from your affection forever" was inspired by a letter Mr. Collins sends to "condole" with the Bennets after Lydia runs off with Wickham in Jane Austen's *Pride and Prejudice*.

William Hammond and his deciphering project are fictional but inspired by actual happenings. In 1823, eight years after the Napoleonic Wars, George Scovell (who is now credited with breaking the Great Paris Cipher) was asked to reexamine many intercepted French dispatches and to make recommendations about the use of ciphers in the British Army. (For more information, read *The Man Who Broke Napoleon's Codes* by Mark Urban.) Also, if you were curious, Mr. Hammond's various endearments for his daughter (*kaddu*, pumpion, etc.) all mean "pumpkin," which my father called me.

The cobbler Mr. Taylor, Mr. Wallis, Sir Thomas Acland, Lady Kennaway, the Countess Lieven, and Miss Marriott are historical figures, but they appear in the novel in fictionalized form. The penwork box or "casket" that contained Miss Marriott's shells is now a rare intact conchology collection valued at over forty thousand dollars. (You can view it online.) It is signed and dated the same year as this novel: *Eliza Marriott, 9th October 1820, Temple Cottage, Sidmouth, Devonshire.*

Along with the sources mentioned in the chapter epigraphs, other books that helped inspire and inform this novel include *Women of the Raj* by Margaret MacMillan, *Henrietta Liston's Travels: The Turkish Journals 1812–1820*, and *The Travels of Dean Mahomet*, considered to be the first English-language book by an Indian writer. Dean Mahomet was a former captain in the British East India Company's Bengal Army who later converted to Christianity. He was also the founder of the Hindoostane Coffee House, opened in London in 1810, thought to be the first Indian restaurant in the British Isles. His description of elephants inspired Armaan's drawing.

I hope it is clear that while I attempted to reflect a variety of historical attitudes toward people from India, I don't condone or agree with any derogatory comments.

Despite my best attempts at research, I am human and bound to make mistakes, so I am doubly thankful for sensitivity reader and friend Sonia Isaiah, who reviewed the culture and languages of India details in the manuscript for me. Any errors are mine and unintentional.

I am also deeply grateful to Nigel Hyman, prolific author, Sidmouth resident, and amazing tour guide, who reviewed the manuscript for me as well.

As always, I appreciate the helpful input I received from first reader Cari Weber, as well as Anna Shay, authors Michelle Griep and Erica Vetsch, and my agent, Wendy Lawton. Warm gratitude also goes to my editors, Karen Schurrer, Rochelle Gloege, and Hannah Ahlfield, as well as my entire team at Bethany House Publishers.

Finally, thank you again for reading my books. I appreciate each and every one of you! For more information about me and my other novels, please follow me on Facebook or Instagram, and sign up for my email list via my website, JulieKlassen.com.

Discussion Questions

1. Mr. Hammond refers to his daughter by various endearments (*kaddu*, pumpion, etc.) that all translate to "pumpkin." Did you have a childhood nickname? Or do you use any special endearments for your loved ones?
2. Claire responds to an advertisement (based on a historical newspaper ad) that read: *Wanted as partner in a genteel boarding house, a respectable female who could advance from £50 to £100. . . .* Would you have been brave enough (or foolish enough, depending on your viewpoint) to respond to such an ad? Why or why not?
3. Claire's past mistake elicits different responses from different characters (understanding, regret, gossip, censure). How did you feel about the condemnation Claire faces? Was it difficult to keep in mind how attitudes toward (and the importance of) a woman's virtue have changed over the last two hundred years? Also, did you recognize any nods to Jane Austen's

Pride and Prejudice (e.g., Mrs. Harding telling Mrs. Summers to "throw off your unworthy child from your affection forever" is reminiscent of the letter Mr. Collins sends to the Bennets after Lydia runs off with Wickham)?

4. In the novel, characters also react differently (some positively, some negatively) to those with origins, languages, and styles of dress different from their own. Do we see similar variations in how people treat those from other cultures today?
5. Did you find Mr. Hammond's former profession interesting? Did you understand his reasons for not talking about his past?
6. Mr. Hammond speaks a few different languages. Do you speak more than one language as well? Which languages have you studied, or would you like to study, and why?
7. Did you have a favorite chapter quote (epigraph), or did you learn anything new about this time period by reading the book?
8. Were you surprised by any of Aunt Mercer's actions? Did you warm toward her at all by the end of the book?
8. Sonali, too, starts out as a prickly character. Did you come to understand her or feel any sympathy for her by the end?
10. Sarah's story continues into the final book in the series, *A Sea View Christmas*. Are you looking forward to reading more about her and her romantic interest? Any predictions for the series' conclusion and Sarah's happily-ever-after?

Turn the page
for a sneak peak of

A Sea View Christmas

An
ON DEVONSHIRE SHORES
Novella

BY
JULIE KLASSEN

Return to Sidmouth one last time.
Coming September 2025!

1

Often, the bride's sister or closest female friend
accompanied the couple [on their wedding trip].
—Maria Grace, *Courtship and Marriage in Jane Austen's World*

October 1820

Miss Sarah Summers sat on her neatly made bed, a treasure in each hand. In her left, she held a letter from the man she'd been betrothed to before his death at sea more than three years before.

In her right palm lay a dried thistle—stalk, spiny bulb, and purple flower crown—the symbol of Scotland. It had been given to her by a Scotsman who, despite her efforts to forget him, still owned a large part of her thoughts . . . and, if she were honest with herself, her heart.

Callum Henshall and his stepdaughter had been their very first guests at Sea View the previous year and all the Summerses had liked them. Mr. Henshall had expressed interest in Sarah during his stay but Sarah had discouraged him. Now she regretted that.

Sarah carefully tucked both the letter and the thistle into the chest at the foot of her bed for safekeeping. For the impending trip, she was taking only a small leather trunk, one bandbox, and her reticule.

Was she really about to leave Sidmouth for an extended absence? Her pulse beat hard at the thought. Since moving to Sea View two years before, Sarah had never left for more than a few hours at a time. What was she doing? How could she just leave the guest house and Mamma? Leave their guests, their staff, and her responsibilities? Might there still be time to retract her agreement and change her plans? Sadly, no.

A knock sounded on the bedchamber door and her youngest sister, Georgiana, entered. At seventeen, Georgie was the picture of blossoming womanhood, although Sarah still saw glimpses of the rough-and-tumble tomboy she had been.

"All packed?" Georgie asked.

"Nearly."

"I wish I were going with you."

"I thought you loved it here?"

"I do. Yet I long to see more of the world. I've only ever been to Sidmouth and May Hill."

"You're young. You shall have other opportunities. For now, I need you to help with things here while I'm gone."

"I know." Georgie sighed. "You will pass along my warmest greetings to Effie, I trust?"

"Of course. If we manage to see them, that is."

"Why should you not? Mr. Henshall will probably convince you to remain in Scotland, and then there go our plans for a jolly Christmas here."

"That is unlikely to happen."

Georgiana studied her. "Still no reply?"

Sarah shook her head. "Besides, you know William and Claire don't want to leave Mira for too long. We plan to return in time for Stir-Up Sunday."

"I'm counting on it."

"Don't worry. I shan't forget my promise. I know the last few years have not been ideal but we shall have a far more festive Christmas this year, you'll see."

Again Georgie sighed. "I hope so."

Sarah regarded her usually cheerful sister with concern. "Are you unwell, my dear? You seem . . . well, sad."

"No, not sad. Restless, more like. But I am glad you are going to Scotland. It's time you had an adventure. Besides, he's not a bad fellow—you could do worse."

"Why, thank you," Sarah dryly replied. "Remember, we are primarily going to Scotland to look over the house Claire inherited. Seeing Mr. Henshall is only a secondary consideration."

Her sister snorted. "Right."

Sarah thought it best to change the subject. "By the way, Claire told me you have offered to spend time with Mira while she and William are away. That is kind of you."

Georgie shrugged off the praise. "Armaan and Sonali will be busy in the boarding house, and a girl that age needs to play out of doors."

"You certainly did. Still do."

Her sister nodded. "I'll also visit the Sidmouth school as usual to play with the pupils there. When I am not needed here, of course."

"Excellent." Sarah rose and embraced her. "And keeping busy like that, the time will pass quickly, you'll see."

She said it as much to reassure herself as Georgiana.

The family, except for James, who was away at Killerton, gathered to bid them farewell. Emily took Sarah's arm and led her out of the house. She leaned close and confided, "It's your turn, Sarah. I just know it. And I hope Mr. Henshall kisses more than your hand this time!" She grinned and squeezed her arm. "Oh, and if you should happen to meet Sir Walter Scott, don't forget to tell him your sister is a great admirer of his work."

William Hammond stood at the open door of the yellow

post chaise and handed Sarah inside to join Claire. Several others encircled the waiting vehicle: Viola and Jack arm in arm, Mrs. Denby in her wheeled chair beside them. Sonali and Armaan, little Mira in her uncle's arms. Mamma waving her handkerchief. Georgie holding the town stray, Chips, by the scruff, to keep him from nipping at the horses. And finally Mr. Gwilt, who was small in stature, stepped to the open window. He raised himself to his tiptoes and reassured her one last time, "Please don't worry, Miss Sarah. We shall take good care of Sea View while you're gone."

Would they?

After one last kiss to his daughter's cheek, William climbed in and closed the door. He took Claire's hand and leaned forward to address them both. "Are you ready, you two?"

"Ready," Claire agreed.

Sarah managed a wooden nod.

A few moments later, the hired post chaise rattled away from Sidmouth, beginning the long journey north. The chaise's snug interior had only one forward-facing bench, and she felt Claire's shoulder press into hers at every turning.

Sarah shifted on the padded seat, agitation gnawing at her, urging her to demand the vehicle stop and let her down. The cord that bound her to Sea View, to Mamma and her other sisters, stretched tighter and tighter, pulling at her ribs, until it seemed about to snap in two and tear out her heart as well.

She became aware of Claire's worried gaze on her profile. Felt her sister squeeze her hand. Sarah had no wish to dampen Claire's pleasure on this, her wedding trip. She turned to her and mustered a smile.

Claire and William had remained in Sidmouth for a few weeks after their nuptials before departing on this trip. They had delayed because they'd wanted to be on hand to witness the quiet wedding of Mira's uncle Armaan and Sonali Patel. And because they'd wanted to support the couple as they took over the management of the boarding house and help them until they had things well in hand. The two had also offered to care for Mira during their absence.

Did Mamma, Georgie, Emily, and Mr. Gwilt have things at Sea View well in hand? Would they manage without her? She hoped she'd remembered to show them everything that needed to be done: the menus, the orders and payments to butcher, greengrocer, coal merchant, and others. Had she left anything off her many lists? What if something went wrong? Would they be able to deal with any demanding guests that arrived?

Sarah reminded herself that she truly wanted to go to Scotland—or at least, to see a certain handsome Scotsman—but perhaps she should have refused. Let her sister and new husband travel alone together.

Both Claire and William had assured Sarah she was welcome to accompany them. A bride's sister or close friend often traveled with a new-wed couple. Husband and wife would, of course, have their own room at inns along the way, but the sisters could help each other dress and enjoy each other's company and conversation during the long hours on the road.

On Claire's other side, William lifted his wife's hand and kissed her knuckles.

Sarah pretended not to notice.

Instead she gazed out at the passing countryside through the front window. She looked past the two mounted postilions, who rode the left-hand horse of each pair pulling the chaise. Their boots and coats were already splattered with mud, and they had not yet crossed the Devonshire border. Sarah felt sorry for whoever had to do their laundry. At the thought, her stomach twisted. Had she remembered to detail the laundry lists?

Sarah forced herself to breathe slowly and deeply, and admonished herself not to worry.

While they traveled, they had to pause every few hours to change horses and often postilions as well. It would be a long journey, and they planned to break it up with several stops along the way.

They visited Bath, the picturesque ruins of Tintern Abbey, and the spa town of Cheltenham. Now and again, Sarah witnessed a sweet caress or stolen kiss between her two traveling companions and looked away, feigning interest in the view and feeling like a gooseberry.

As the distance between them and Sea View lengthened, Sarah slowly began to relax and enjoy herself. They'd come too far to turn back now.

Continuing north, they spent a few days admiring the scenery of the Lake District. Sarah joined William and Claire for meals, sightseeing, and shopping, but she insisted the two spend time alone together as well. She happily remained at the inn while they hired a boat for a romantic excursion on Windermere Lake. She recalled her own excursion in a small boat more than a year ago now, sailing along the coast with Callum Henshall, the sea breeze ruffling his hair, his warm gaze lingering on her face. . . . Would he look at her that way again? She certainly hoped so.

Every night, the new-wed couple retired to one room, and Sarah to another. Observing the tenderness between the two and Claire's glow of contentment, Sarah felt a pang. She was genuinely happy her sister had found true love, yet she increasingly longed for a love of her own.

They did not stop in Carlisle—a place of bitter memories. A few years before, Claire had been abandoned there by a lord who'd convinced her to elope with him and then changed his mind before they'd even reached Gretna Green.

Instead, they continued on toward Edinburgh. Their Great-Aunt Mercer had stunned them all by leaving Claire her house. Claire was eager to show it to both Sarah and William and gain their opinions on whether to keep the place or sell it. She had written to their aunt's solicitor to inform him of their upcoming visit. The man wrote back to assure them of a gracious welcome, explaining that Agnes Mercer's elderly butler had stayed on to oversee the property while it was unoccupied and would be there to open the house for them and provide a set of keys.

While they were in Scotland, they also hoped to see Mr. Henshall and Effie, who lived not far from Edinburgh. That prospect made Sarah both hopeful and extremely nervous.

She had protested that it would be too forward to pay a call uninvited, but Claire had assured her there was nothing untoward about it. They were traveling a long way to look at the house. While they were there, it would be only polite to visit an acquaintance, especially one who'd performed such kind offices for their family. Mr. Henshall had paid a call at Aunt Mercer's on their behalf to learn how Claire fared, and later redeemed Claire's necklace from a pawn dealer.

At her urging, Sarah had written once more to Mr. Henshall, letting him know of their upcoming trip.

She had received no reply.

And his silence only added to her unease.

Her sisters had tried to encourage her, saying Sarah's letter may have been lost in the post. Or his reply had been delayed for some reason. Of course he would be happy to see her again.

Sarah hoped they were right. Otherwise, how mortifying the reunion might be.

Reaching the outskirts of Edinburgh at last, Sarah craned her neck to take it all in. Claire pointed out the Palace of Holyroodhouse and, upon entering the city, the Edinburgh Castle high on its rocky hill.

As they continued on, winding through the Old Town and into the New, the tightly packed shops, sooty-grey buildings, and smokestacks soon gave way to rows of elegant, terraced houses of lighter sandstone, church spires, and tree-lined squares.

Finally they reached Aunt Mercer's home in just such a row of tall, connected houses. They alighted with stiff limbs and eagerness. Mr. Hammond helped unload their baggage and dismissed the postillions with an extra gratuity for delivering them safely. The men would take the chaise and horses to a local livery.

The door opened and an elderly man dressed in black appeared.

Claire beamed at him. "Mr. Campbell! How good to see you again. And how glad I was to learn you still live here. Allow me to introduce my sister Sarah and my husband, Mr. Hammond."

"Welcome, one and all. And pleased I was to learn who the new owner was to be! Your aunt did not breathe a word. A woman of surprises, was she not?"

"Indeed she was."

The former cook, maids, and footman had acquired new situations elsewhere, but Campbell had engaged two new housemaids and a kitchen maid to serve them during their visit, despite Claire's offer to take their meals at a nearby inn.

Campbell's own sister, who had been in service for many years like her brother, came out of retirement to serve as cook.

He said, "I hope you approve of the arrangements, Miss—er, Mrs. Hammond?"

"Wholeheartedly. Thank you so much."

Claire insisted Sarah waste no time in sending a message to Mr. Henshall, who lived near the town of Kirkcaldy, north of Edinburgh.

"Just to let him know we've arrived safely and would be pleased to receive him here or to meet somewhere at his convenience."

Sarah wrote a brief note in a shaky hand, and Campbell dispatched a messenger to deliver it.

Then the three settled in to explore Edinburgh while they waited.

Sarah accompanied William and Claire when they set off for the Old Town to visit the Palace of Holyroodhouse, her sister pointing out the pawn dealer as they passed.

The Edinburgh Castle had opened to visitors only that May. Before that it had been a military fortress and hospital, and had also housed prisoners of war.

They purchased their tickets from the stationers on Bank Street for one shilling each and toured the Crown Room to see the Scottish regalia. The rest of the castle remained off-limits. Sarah wished Mr. Henshall was there to help explain the significance of the various items on display.

Over the next few days, the three also strolled through the leafy squares of New Town, the air growing chilly in the autumn evenings, perused shops, and sampled Scottish cuisine.

But all the while Sarah was waiting and worrying. Why did Mr. Henshall not visit? Or at least send a reply? Had something happened to him or Effie?

In the meantime, William wrote to an old friend of his and soon they were invited to dinner at the home of Sir Robert and Henrietta Liston, who lived a few miles west of Edinburgh. William and the Listons had served together in Constantinople, where Sir Robert had recently retired as ambassador.

Sarah dressed with care, as did her sister, both of them somewhat intimidated by the prospect of dining with a former ambassador and his wife.

But upon arrival, their hosts quickly made them comfortable. The Listons were charming and warm with easy, unaffected manners. They entertained them with tales of the customs and mishaps they'd experienced in the Ottoman Empire and other far-flung places they had resided during their long diplomatic career.

The evening passed very pleasantly. And again, Sarah could

not help think how much Mr. Henshall's company would have added to their enjoyment. Or at least, to hers.

All too soon the time they'd allotted to Edinburgh began to draw to a close and there was still no sign of Callum Henshall.

"We can't return to Sidmouth without at least trying to see him," Claire insisted. "You have his direction from his letters. Let us go and pay a call. At least then you will learn why he hasn't responded, and you will not continue assuming the worst. And you need not fear you are putting yourself forward in an unladylike manner. I will say *I* insisted."

William grinned. "And I shall happily share the blame."

Sarah relented. "Oh, very well. Just to put my mind at ease."

Had Mr. Henshall given up on Sarah and begun courting someone else? Was that why he had not replied nor come to see them? She hoped the truth would not prove to be worse than she imagined.

They set out for Kirkcaldy early the next day, taking the new steam-powered *Broad Ferry* from the north of Edinburgh across the Firth of Forth and to the Dysart Harbour. From there, they hired a driver with an old landau and even older horses to take them the rest of the way. Since the day was fine, they lowered the folding hood to enjoy the views.

About a mile from the harbor, the driver pointed out the ruins of the rough-stone Ravenscraig Castle, and recognition flashed through Sarah. She recalled a long-ago dinner around the Sea View dining table, and Mr. Henshall's sea-green eyes, alight with nostalgia, as he enthralled them with tales of his childhood, describing the abandoned castles near his home and a time he and a few other lads "stormed Ravenscraig and laid siege to it with our wooden swords . . ." A land agent had set his dogs on them and they'd had to hide in a shepherd's hut until the beasts gave up the chase, lured away by haggis.

Even now, Sarah smiled at the memory. His handsome face, good humor, and rich, accented voice were still clear in her mind.

The driver hailed a delivery wagon and asked for directions to Whinstone Hall. Leaving the town of Kirkcaldy behind, they followed a wooded track until they reached a rambling, two-story house of dark stone, its front door and windows framed in lighter sandstone. Sarah saw stables, a few other outbuildings, and fields dotted with grazing sheep beyond. The front lawns were neatly trimmed but the shrubs were in need of pruning and the flower gardens grew in weedy disarray.

After helping the ladies alight, William led the way to the front door and knocked.

As they waited, Sarah's heart beat painfully hard and she twisted her gloved hands together. A friendly cat approached and rubbed against Sarah's ankles, seeking attention, but Sarah was too distracted to oblige. Would Mr. Henshall be there? How would he react to seeing her on his doorstep? Pleasure or discomfort?

A few moments later, a housemaid welcomed them inside and showed them into a nearby parlour. She said, "The master is away, but the lady of the house will be with ye shortly."

The lady of the house?

Did the maid refer to Effie, or . . . ?

Sarah's stomach sank. Had Mr. Henshall married someone else without telling them? Perhaps a Scottish woman who shared his homeland, his way of life? And if so, could she truly blame him?

Note: Final text may vary.

Julie Klassen loves all things Jane—*Jane Eyre* and Jane Austen. Her books have sold over 1.5 million copies, and she is a three-time recipient of the Christy Award for Historical Romance. *The Secret of Pembrooke Park* was honored with the Minnesota Book Award for Genre Fiction. Julie has also won the Midwest Book Award and Christian Retailing's BEST Award, and has been a finalist in the RITA and Carol Awards. A graduate of the University of Illinois, Julie worked in publishing for sixteen years and now writes full-time. Julie and her husband have two sons and live in a suburb of St. Paul, Minnesota. For more information, you can follow her on Facebook or visit JulieKlassen.com.

You Are Invited!

Join like-minded fans in the **Inspirational Regency Readers** group on Facebook.

From book news from popular Regency authors like Kristi Ann Hunter, Michelle Griep, Erica Vetsch, Julie Klassen, and many others, to games and giveaways, to discussions of favorite Regency reads and adaptations new and old, to places we long to travel, you will find plenty of fun and friendship within this growing community.

Free and easy to join, simply search for "Inspirational Regency Readers" on Facebook.

We look forward to seeing you there!

Sign Up for Julie's Newsletter

Keep up to date with Julie's latest news on book releases and events by signing up for her email list at the link below.

JulieKlassen.com

FOLLOW JULIE ON SOCIAL MEDIA

Author Julie Klassen

@Julie.K.Klassen

@Julie_Klassen

More from Julie Klassen

When their father's death leaves them impoverished, the Summers sisters open their home to guests to provide for their ailing mother. But instead of the elderly invalids they expect, they find themselves hosting eligible gentlemen. Sarah must confront her growing attraction to a mysterious widower, and Viola learns to heal her deeply hidden scars.

The Sisters of Sea View
On Devonshire Shores #1

When the Duke and Duchess of Kent rent a nearby house for the winter, the Summers sisters are called upon to host three of the royal couple's male staff in their seaside cottage—but soon they realize they've invited mysterious secrets into their home. With the arrival of their new guests, the sisters face surprising romance and unexpected danger.

A Winter by the Sea
On Devonshire Shores #2

Laura Callaway daily walks the windswept Cornwall coast, known for many shipwrecks but few survivors. And when a man with curious wounds and an odd accent is washed ashore, she cares for him while the mystery surrounding him grows. Can their budding attraction survive, and can he be returned to his rightful home when danger pursues them from every side?

A Castaway in Cornwall